STREAMING THE SEXTILLION

STREAMING THE SEXTILLION

1,000,000,000,000,000,000,000

FORTAIN C. BRADLEY

ISBN: 978-1-969865-62-6 Paperback
ISBN: 978-1-969865-63-3 Ebook

Rev. date: 12/09/2025

CHAPTER 1

I n a very distant quadrant of the universe a celestial conveyance of immense size was speeding its way to a destination known only to the One who had sent it. The vessel's exterior was iridescent in appearance which shimmered against the blackness of the great space and it was aerodynamically smooth with a huge round bow tapering to narrow stern ending in a point. Inside the ship were three unusual passengers on a mission that they were only given details a little at a time. The leader of the trio was an entity named "Melody". She was vibrant with joy and her eyes were big fluorescent windows which changed depending on her thoughts or the music she was channeling or singing. Her hair resembled live waving musical staffs which were auto populated with musical notes either at rest or in creative musical display. Next to her was "Harmony" whose head was multi-faced of three basic voices "tenor, base, and baritone" but he could increase to as many voices as he felt were needed to complete any harmonic combination. He was tall and athletic and had a beautiful resonant speaking voice but when he sang the galaxies danced. Sitting next to him was the third entity "Rhythm" who was covered from head to toe in colorful percussion instruments: a hat of cymbals, kalimba fingers, mid-section drums, xylophone arms, rainstick legs, and castanet toes. He was always animated with clanging, banging, thumping, twinkling, tinkling, pinging, vibrating and pounding. Rhythm was reclining in a cabin chair pulling on a straw drawing up a frosty fizzy blue drink while his castanet like toes clicked a random beat. Finishing his drink Rhythm impatiently asked loudly, "Do we even know where we're going?!" Melody turned in response to the question replying, "No, not until the Creator sends that information to CC3 who will notify us. So stop angsting and go back to your snacks."

CC3 which was short for "Celestial Conveyance 3". CC3 was not just a vehicle but a living thing spoken into existence by the Creator specific to this assignment. CC3 responded to Melody's reprimand of Rhythm and chimed in "The Creator" will be dispatching new directives shortly." Rhythm spoke up again "CC3 how fast are we traveling anyway?" CC3 answered, "We are traveling at light exponentia 5." Rhythm shot back "What's light exponentia 5?" "Mr. Rhythm it means that I'm traveling 5 times the speed of light until further notice from the Creator to either increase or decrease the speed", CC3 politely answered. All of a sudden CC3's announcement chime sounded and it voiced "The Creator" has sent the new directives for this mission to the attention of "Miss Melody". Melody's eyes went full gleam as CC3 telepathically transferred the directive to her and she then updated her companions, "We are being sent to a quadrant that the Creator wants to seed with a musical galaxy that can keep back the "Sessilum" a congealed virulent and aggressive darkness. A package holding the "galaxy seed" has been transmitted to CC3 and we will be given the instructions on when and where to plant the galaxy." Harmony started to hum in three part harmony acknowledging that they had a clearer picture of their assignment and their assignment was nearing completion. They pondered why they were given this assignment but they were reminded that the Creator was very concerned with another galaxy in a distant part of the universe so they took heart to be used to enforce Light in their eventual destination.

CC3 and it's three passengers continued to travel for an undetermined period of time before the large ship slowed but did not stop moving. At the slower speed Melody was able to hear and record the music of nearby planetary systems. When she did this her large eyes glowed and the staffs on her head showed the music she was hearing and her strong soprano voice trilled transmitting to Harmony who would expand the music through his voices and Rhythm intuitively joined with his vibrant percussions. They made music for a long time to CC3's delight who documented every note in the ship's database. After the ship passed through an anomaly it identified as the "Song Way" which was an extremely bright lengthy clustering of stars before it stopped and advised its passengers they had reached the coordinates given by the Creator. CC3 advised that they would be encased in an environ bubble and beamed outside the ship with a "galaxy seed". The trio would then sing a blessing to the "galaxy seed", "You are the new, the young, the strong, the undeterred, the undaunted, the refined, the faithful ones who know the light and its songs. The Creator who is true is watching over you and smiling in your triumph. So flourish, create, flinging your voices as swords against your enemies and their sluggish dullness. Your victory is pure and your "Song Way" brothers will make sure!" Melody opened the small white box and something like dust spilled out and began to whirl around with lightning and thunder noises; at this point their assignment was complete. The galaxy was in formation but it would be several centuries to its completion. CC3 beamed the trio back inside the ship and set a course to the planet "Astral Keep" the music capital of the Central galaxies. The three entities were beyond happy they had completed their assignment for the Creator and now they could go back to tutoring and giving concerts to the inhabitants of "Astral Keep" and CC3 could return to the Creator's shipping dock until needed again.

CHAPTER 2

Millenia past before the little galaxy "Symphonea" had formed. It was a reverse conical shaped with the widest end below and the tapered smaller end on top. On the smaller end was a planetary system of eight planets elliptically orbiting a medium blue white star and each dedicated to music. Each planet generated a sound which acted as a protective barrier from the chaos of the surrounding the "Staticsphere" of the untuned aggressive "Sessilum". Once every galactic rotation each planet sent out harmonic diplomats trained to vocalize through planet amplifiers located at the polar caps. First bass, then tenor, then contralto, then baritone, then alto, then first soprano and second soprano. These warrior singer musicians harmonized for one hour renewing and strengthening the barrier for another 100 year rotation.

One of the planets in the system, the smallest "Jazzo" had developed the purest, skilled and powerful singers and musicians who lead the fight to keep their planetary system free from their enemies the "Sessilum" who were musicless aggressors to light and life. From space Jazzo was purple with turquoise water covering two thirds of the planet crashing onto pink sand beaches. Jazzoan's would rather sing than talk so their language was a combination of the two.

The Jazzoan were divided into two classes the "Eccleum" the highly educated industrial class who lived in the colorful cities of the planet's eight continents and the "Ziggabim" the tribal agrarian class who lived on the plains in jungles and remote forest lands of the eight continents. Although the classes were very distinct the Eccleum did not exercise any oppressions toward the Ziggabim because they had an unbound creative artistic energy which showed up in their simple lifestyle and spilled over into the general global culture.

Each continent on Jazzo had a governor and advisors but the overall planetary ruler "Tempo Maximus V" was descended from a prestigious line of "Light Song" warriors. King Tempo was an accomplished singer in all the planetary dialects and had a keen sense of fighting to win when it came to defending his planetary system. He also was a dedicated family man to his wife Octiva and their thirteen year old daughter Jazzalin.

Princess Jazzalin Arpeggia Maximus had found her voice in her thirteenth year, a high clear first soprano which was a wonder because she was tall and very thin when most soprano's were short and on the chubby side. Her mother Octiva herself a first soprano was very happy for her only child, calling her "my thin reed". For all of Jazzalin's vocal giftings, able to hold lengthy supernal high "C" notes, trilling notes up and down the scale mimicking her middle name "Arpeggia" with joyous abandon while dancing around. She found formal training laborious and would find every opportunity to sneak away to the "Scat-De-Dat" district. "The Scat", as it was known, was an ostentatious 10 mile stretch of flamboyantly painted pubs, restaurants, shops and cheap inns. Young as she was Jazzalin thought nothing about skipping her last voice tutorial at the Academy and joining her cousin and best friend Beabop Symbella Bamm Zynoplee, a sparkling alto, and running off to their favorite hangout "Voco Stellar". Voco Stellar looked like an explosion in a paint factory both inside and out, a dizzying swirl of neon pink, orange, green, and purple most likely visible from space. This pub allowed local musicians and singers to perform on their small stage to whoever happened to be present at the time. Inserting a disk of music into the audio system the two girls took the stage coordinating their voices swelling with emotional rushes of their innocence, youth, liberty, beauty of their love of their family, friends, and their homeland. The listening audience loved their singing and would hum along where they could but when the girls' harmonies crescendoed no lazy hum could follow. Unknown to the mischievous girls King Tempo had assigned a covert android guardsman to follow wherever Jazzalin went that was not within the accepted perimeters of her family life and her education. The guardsman who was disguised in Scat attire reported to her father that his daughter was truant and singing her heart out in a Scat district pub.

Jazzalin and Beabop realized they were running late to be at their respective homes. They made a quick end of their song and made a quick bow to the small clapping audience then bolted to the exit door. The sun was giving way to night and they knew their parents would be waiting with reprimands. They jumped into a "hover cab" to speed their way home. Beabop was dropped off first to her family's large showy residence where her mother was glaringly waiting in the driveway. Beabop yelled "bye" over her shoulder and ran past her mother into the house. The cab then continued up the hill to the "Royal Residence". As the vehicle curved around the circular driveway Jazzalin saw her maid Gingee nervously waiting. When Jazzalin exited the cab she immediately started talking "Your father is livid and he's waiting for you in the drawing room. You should know he knows why you're late. Run along now!" Jazzalin envisioned her father's stern face and his tall form rigid with anger. Once Jazzalin was inside the entry her father's voice boomed against the high domed ceilings "Jazzalin!!" As she entered the drawing room he proceeded, "You are aware that your education is not only important to our planet but to the entire planetary system. You must discipline yourself and stay away from the Scat district! Do you understand?!" She dropped her head and nodded and mumbled "Yes, father." "Come on our dinner is getting cold", the king said in a less angry tone. Jazzalin was happy he hadn't sent her to her room without dinner because she was starving. Upon entering the beautiful decorated dining room she skipped towards her mother's chair and pecked her cheek smilingly said "Evening Mommy!" "Evening dear", Octiva cheerfully replied. Continuing she said "Fortunately we didn't have to wait too long for you. We already blessed the table so we can start." Dinner was regular soup, salad, and entree with an ordinary dessert of mixed fruits and cream. Jazzalin inhaled her food and politely asked if she could be excused from "Evening Song". "Evening Song" was a ritual that all Jazzoan families observed, which was a gathering usually in a family room, parlor, balcony, or kitchen to sing out the day and welcome the night. Her father gave permission but sternly said this would not be a regular omission. Jazzalin thanked him, kissed both parents and ran out of the room but not before she heard her father's clear mellifluous baritone voice mingled with the steep sweet soprano of her mother as they sang "This day's end and now you friend come to us this way with shining stars and quiet hours til the sun brings back the day."

When Jazzalin got to her room she ran to balcony to call Beabop for an update. The call was received by Beabop's personal transmission screen and Jazzalin whispered "How'd you make out? Your mother looked set to kill." Beabop smiled into the screen and replied "I'm on punishment for a week. It would have been more but your mother called my mother and told her I was with you. You do know your parents have you watched?" Jazzalin shot back, "Yeah, but I have friends who can help me disappear if it's necessary. But why would I want to leave my family? Well, we'd better call it a day we have school tomorrow. Goodnight Bea." "Goodnight, Jazzalin. See you at school tomorrow", Beabop replied and disconnected their call.

Next, day at school the two girls met after their first class giving their "twinkle finger" greeting. Both were dressed in the traditional Academy black and white striped jackets, white pleated skirts, and black high top boots. They both grimaced that they still had two more classes and an afternoon mentor workshop so their meeting was in transit with no time for amusement. On the way to her workshop Jazzalin bumped head long into a tall young man she hadn't seen before at school. He was a head or more taller than she with an athlete's build, his hair was cut close on the sides with massive black curly waves on top. His eyes were green with gold flecks, almond shaped, and wonderfully rimmed with long thick lashes. Jazzalin also noticed in the collision that his mouth had a beautifully tapered top lip and full bottom lip which had formed a dazzling smile. Her mother had told her that very handsome men, referring to her husband the King, always had beautiful mothers. Thank the Creator for maternal genetic transference of good looks to their sons. Her mind finally cleared and she heard him apologizing, "I'm so sorry. Are you alright?" She blinked and cleared her throat replying, "Yes, I'm fine." He smiled again showing an army of even white teeth and said, "I'm Adagio Jammon Skyes." Jazzalin had heard of the Skyes family, that they were wealthy music producers for popular musicians and singers who for the most part were "Scat" district trash. She replied, "I'm Jazzalin Maximus, nice to meet you. Gotta run. I'm late to my workshop. Bye!" She ran past him with a quick glance back.

In her voice workshop she was somewhat distracted due to her crash-up with the cute guy in the hallway. She quickly regained her composure and followed her scales in harmony with the others in the class. She met Beabop after her workshop and relayed the crash-up episode with Adagio "Gorgeous" Skyes. Beabop's mother pulled her hover car to the pickup zone just when Jazzalin's event details were getting juicy but were cut short as her mother signaled her to get in the hover car "now!". "I'll call you!", Beabop blurted out just as her mother floored the accelerator of the vehicle and sped away to the skyway. Just seconds later Jazzalin's android chauffeur arrived to convey her to the Royal Residence. The girls' parents were being very watchful so the Scat district was off limits for a while.

When she arrived home there were a number of diplomatic conveyances parked in the driveway. Jazzalin's mother Octiva met her in the hallway to say she would send her dinner to her room because of an important meeting going on in the Formal Dining room. The Princess nodded in acknowledgement before pecking her mother's cheek and bounding upstairs to her room. In her room Jazzalin activated the concealed Viz scanner in the formal dining room. Turning up the volume to hear High Councilman Blenn Dyn say, "The Sessilum have breached the frontier. So far they have only accessed several large asteroids but their current course will be to planet "Audia Prime" reaching it in about two years' time. Our scientists have calculated an armada of our best vocal soldiers dispatched now can neutralize this attack and repair the spatial breach." Jazzalin was surprised at what she had just heard and wondered how the leaders would dispatch the armada without the general populous getting wind of it. Eavesdropping a little longer, Jazzalin heard the diplomats agree that King Maximus should lead the armada. Her father was certainly a good candidate but her mother wouldn't want him to accept this dangerous quest.

Once Jazzalin had asked her father why the "Sessilum" were so terrible. King Maximus responded without levity explaining, "Sessilum are an abysmal black vacuum of irrhythmic noise propelled by death itself. They are without harmony, tune or light, and are lifeless because of it." Naively Jazzalin responded, "So they just want to gobble us up and destroy our music?" The king leaned down close her and responded with great finality "Yes, and that's not going to happen. Ever!" In her history class she'd learned that eons ago the Sessilum had devoured the remote planet Shalla and its inhabitants. Shalla was on the farthest rotational path in their planetary system, its inhabitants were industrious and scientifically more advanced than other planets in the system. Their scientists developed ships equipped with "sonic pulse engines" which allowed them to take trips into the "void". Everytime their ships returned to Shalla parasitic void viruses were introduced into the atmosphere and eventually the infection began to eat away at the very substance of the planet and corrupting their ability to sing or play music. The other planets in the system sent drone messenger ships warning the Shalla citizens that their planet was in dangerous position of total destruction and to evacuate as soon as possible. Many of the Shallan citizens were able to transport to nearby planets but the more skeptical ones refused to leave. The other seven planets gathered their most brilliant musician-scientists who determined that Shalla would eventually implode creating a rift that would pull the entire planet to its destructive compressed absorption by the Sessilum. The scientists researched every probability and theorem until King Syncopy, Jazzo's king at the time, discovered the "Light Songs" of the planetary elders. These songs held such power that they could explode planets, extinguish stars, and create impenetrable barriers around any object it was directed to protect. The old king did used the Light Songs to erect the barrier around the seven remaining planets in the system before Shalla was swallowed up by the void becoming assimilated by the "Sessilum" an unrelenting compressed crystalline aggressor. Yes, Jazzalin was descended from a prestigious great lineage and because of that, great things were expected of her. As she was only 13 years old these noble ancestral facts did not impress her since she only wanted to sing and make music for fun not for intrigues and war.

Jazzalin finally called Beabop and gave her all the details of the smash up with "Adagio". Beabop advised, " He's a huge flirt and you're not in his league in age or society so you should put away any fantasy about him." Jazzalin responded, "You're just jealous because you didn't bump into him." "My tastes in boys are more orchestrated and sophisticated", Beabop said, feigning maturity. "You've never met anyone as "quizit" as "Adagio". Admit it!", Jazzalin giggled. "Well, maybe not but I'm not planning a wedding based on a happenstance meeting", Beabop giggled back. "You are too annoying. Got to go, my dinner's here. See you tomorrow. Bye!", Jazzalin said. "Bye. See you tomorrow!", Beabop replied and disconnected. The next day the girls met after classes in front of the Academy where their respective rides home were on time to prohibit any "Scat District" escapades. The girls gave each other their "twinkle finger" sign before hopping into separate hover cars. Both girls resigned themselves to a month of lockdown of parental hovering.

CHAPTER 3

Two weeks had passed to the day her father was to depart for "Audia Prime". King Tempo sat Jazzalin down in his study and sternly told her that he expected her to be on her best behavior in his absence. He continued emphasizing to her that he did not want to hear any reports of her going to the "Scat" pubs during school hours or any time for that matter. Jazzalin promised he could depend on her obedience while he was away. Jazzalin accompanied her parents in the royal hover conveyance to the Jazzo Military Garrison where the Royal lightspeed ships were kept. The King's entourage included his personal assistant and secretary, two personal commando guardsman, and his three master musicians who all boarded the ship while he said goodbye to Octiva and Jazzalin. He kissed his wife and explained specifically to her not to worry as this was a routine issue in spite of what she thought. The King turned his gaze on his daughter who stiffened expecting a stern tirade of parental dogma but instead he grabbed her and hugged her while soundly kissing her cheek saying "Be good, I love you and I'm watching you even five light years away." Jazzalin smiled her amber eyes wide and replied, "Yes Papa, I love you too! Be safe." Smiling, the King turned and boarded the huge silver lightspeed ship, its door slid closed, its powerful engines purred to start then keened as it effortlessly lifted slowly to accelerate and disappear in the sky.

When Jazzalin and her mother returned home their maid ran up to them holding out a bright orange envelope. Breathlessly the maid said, "The special postal droid delivered this just after you left to see the King's departure. It's for you Princess Jazzalin", giving the colorful envelope to her. Jazzalin recognized it was some type of invitation. Tearing open the envelope she pulled out a "techvite" with a built-in response transmitter. The brite plastic sheet lit up with the smiling face of Adagio who spoke "You're invited to my 17th birthday celebration next Santzday at my home address "81760 Ethereal Heights. Hope to see you there!" When the sheet dimmed two buttons appeared on the bottom, a "yellow" one to accept or a "red" one to decline. Jazzalin whirled around to her mother asking, "May I go mother?" Octiva looked at her daughter and smiled answering her, "Yes, go ahead and accept." Jazzalin squealed and jumped up as she pressed the yellow button while simultaneously thanking her mother with a peck on her cheek. She ran to the stairway on the way to her room to give Beabop the news but in mid step she heard her mother call out that dinner was in an hour. The Princess acknowledged with "Yes mother!" all the while dialing Beabop's communivox number. Once inside her beautifully appointed aquamarine and floral pink room with its large round aquarium of dotty fish and yellow sun guppies she stretched out on her window seat just as Beabop answered the call. She immediately blurted, "Bea!! I got an invitation to Adagio's birthday party next week! Can you believe it?!" Bea cleared her throat before responding, "Don't be so smug, I got one too. Your fantasy smashup crush obviously knows we are party partners." "Well, don't you be so grouchy since we're both going. I needed this since we're cut off from the Scat. We're going to have the best time," Jazzalin replied. They began to discuss clothes, accessory colors, shoes, hair styles until Jazzalin heard her mother's voice on the intercom calling her to dinner. They quickly agreed they had a week to brainstorm their party ensembles to ensure a "quizit" time partying in the "Ethers"!!!!

King Tempo sat back in his seat and began to review the incoming reports from Audia Prime about the breach. He closed his eyes and remembered his old history tutor had once told him of a speculation that 900 years ago the eighth planet "Shalla" was destroyed being pulled into the "Staticsphere" that a group of purist zealots called "The Shyneens" did not evacuate the planet as many others had. The Shyneens although being simple folk were master singers with total knowledge of the "Light Songs" and all their applications. The tutor advised that if any Shyneens were somehow alive in the Sessilum's spatial habitat their Light Song environment would create a safety zone abscess that eventually would cause an destructive atomizing of the Sessilum who existed there. His old tutor had dismissed the possibility saying,"It's only a theory." Now that the galaxy's existence was in peril he was open to any reason why 900 years later a real threat was knocking at their door demanding entrance. What if the Shyneens had survived and were possibly trying to escape? He had a week's traveling at quantum lightspeed to research this theory with the onboard planetary data bank.

Jazzalin and Beabop had decided on their party ensembles and to arrive thirty minutes late. Jazzalin decided to give Adagio a book application "Light Songs for Beginners" which he could install on all of his media. Beabop on the other hand determined she wasnot giving a gift since her presence at the rich boy's party was enough. The girls arrived at 8:30 to the brightly lit hilltop mansion. The communivox inside the royal hover car went active with Queen Octiva's voice, "Jazzalin, you're to be in the hover car on or before midnight. Do you hear me Jazzalin?" Jazzalin grimaced and replied, "Yes, mother, on or before midnight. We're here! Bye mommy!" Beabop yanked her arm and pulled her through the open door of the hover car yelling, "We're late, come on!" They ran up the steps to the grand entry stopping for a quick perusal of their appearance. Jazzalin's long dark purple hair had been braided with woven multi-colored ribbons down her back and tendrils around her oval face. She'd chosen to wear a puffy sleeved white blouse and a short ruffled multi-colored skirt matching the ribbons in her hair along with pink leggings and pink sequined boots. Beabop's hair was loose and straight with a full bangs across her forehead which she embellished with a glitzy costume jeweled tiara. She wore a blouse and a short skirt with leggings and boots similar in style to Jazzalin's except her outfit was all in variations of lavender and purple. They both agreed they looked ready to be at this upscale party and with that they stepped inside.

Once inside the mansion the girls were overwhelmed at the celebrity studded attendance, not to mention the beautifully decorated room dedicated to Adagio's birthday celebration. Their eyes were wide with excitement because the music playing was loud, rhythmic, and wonderful.

Without warning Adagio appeared in front of them. Jazzalin was stunned because he was even cuter dressed in tailored formal wear. All she could do was smile and blink her large amber eyes to focus that he was real and not a dream. He smilingly spoke "Jazzalin, Beabop so glad you both made it." Jazzalin replied, "Yes, we made it and here's a gift for you." He thanked her then escorted the girls past the dancing guests to a library which was filled with brightly wrapped birthday gifts. Jazzalin placed her small gift on a nearby table. Then Adagio turned to her asking her to dance and took her hand leading her onto the crowded dance floor. Beabop had already jumped on the dance floor with her arms waving in the air and her feet keeping time to the techno beat. She was enrapted. Jazzalin felt honored that the birthday boy was doing his due diligence by dancing with the King's daughter before joining any number of gushing ingenues, flirty debutantes, and wily female celebrities smiling at him around the room. She went "Princess" mode keeping herself grounded and enjoyed the obligatory attention.

After the music stopped Adagio excused himself from Jazzalin as his father beckoned him over the audio system to the small stage at the front of the ballroom. When he joined his father "Hamilton Skyes" on the stage the room quieted as he officially wished his son happy birthday and handed him an ignition keycard to the newest model compact hover car in neon blue which was shown on a vizo screen above the stage. This hover had all the apps and links for domestic airspace as well as interstellar travel. Father and son hugged and left the stage and the music immediately blasted again inviting a frenzy of dancing bodies. From across the room Jazzalin saw pop singer "Celestia Anomalee" dressed in a very fuchsia strapless decollete party dress with thigh high sequin boots walked up to Adagio and offered her acrylic nail hand for a dance. Seconds later the couple was gyrating to the music. Jazzalin thought they were beautifully paired, Celestia tan, tall, voluptuous, with a mass of black curls piled high on her head and Adagio olive complexioned, even taller, muscular, and very well groomed. When the music changed to a lilting dreamy ballad the space between the couple melded as they followed the melodic song around the floor in a slow rhythmic glide. Everyone watching, including Jazzalin, were very impressed by how well matched the couple was but she soon became bored with the reality that she was four years younger than Adagio and not nearly as pretty as the multitude of females he could choose from at his party. And anyway he was a commoner, although a very wealthy and quizit to look at commoner. Exasperated with her thoughts she went to the balcony to watch the multi-colored exploding skyworks display.

The Skyes mansion was the largest in the "Ethers" district and was built on a cliff overlooking the "Aquavast Sea". From the balcony she could see below the family's massive impressive yacht moored to their private pier. Yes, the Skyes family was over the top wealthy and not ashamed to show it. As she turned from the balcony to go back to the party she saw Adagio walking towards her offering her a glass of sparkling wine. She had had her first intoxicating beverage a year ago during her parents anniversary party and had shown remarkable stamina after two glasses of wine, which her parents advised was her limit. She took the glass he offered and thanked him. She took a sip of wine and said, "I want to thank you for inviting me to your party. Usually when people know who I am they're reluctant to socialize with me. Well, maybe not Beabop she has no boundaries." Smiling, Adagio responded, "My family is very cross-cultural on this planet, as well as throughout the planetary system. The music business crosses all barriers." He cleared his throat and for the first time and addressed her formally, "Princess I know King Tempo is enroute to Audia Prime regarding a spatial breach." Jazzalin's eyes widened as she replied, "Well, Mr. Skyes, that information is classified and confidential and I'm not at liberty to discuss it with the party host. You'll excuse me but I'll be leaving now." That being said she realized that the party invite was a ruse to get her to divulge state secrets. She thanked Adagio and used her communivox to notify the chauffeur to be in front in ten minutes. Adagio tried to explain that because of his family's access to some of the planet's cutting edge science his father has been aware of the breach for five years now. Since his father's business is sound he commissioned a group of scientists to study the Staticsphere breach and the information they had gathered may be of some interest to the King. Jazzalin was busily scanning the dance floor for Beabop and when she saw her began waving her to come on. She pulled her into a corner and whispered she could either leave with her now or stay and get a cab home. Beabop said it was only ten o'clock and she was not ready to leave yet. Adagio chimed in and said, "I'll make sure she gets home within her curfew." Beabop smiled big and told Jazzalin she would be fine and she could go ahead and leave. The girls twinkled fingered their goodbye. Jazzalin thanked Adagio for a fun evening and that he needn't patronize her under the guise of friendship in the future before jumping into the waiting hover car and slamming the door. In the days ahead Jazzalin was very careful to avoid any contact with Adagio during her time at the Academy, even curtailing socializing with Beabop as a failsafe.

King Tempo sent a vizo communique to Jazzalin when they landed on Audia Prime. She was so glad to see his face and hear his voice after two weeks, she was after all a consummate "daddy's girl". He had already spoken to Octiva who had only good things to report about their daughter. Being an intuitive father he realized that Jazzalin wasn't just being good by staying away from the Scat, skipping classes to go to the shopping district or to the "Vizix" to watch the latest fashion or pop music videos. She seemed less her vibrant self so he asked, "Is everything alright Jazzalin?" "Yes daddy. You said you expected me to on my best behavior and I have been." "Your mother said you were invited to a birthday party in the "Ethers. How was it?", he inquired. She engineered her brightest voice and chirped, "It was great! Celebrities everywhere, and Mr. Skyes the music mogul was there and presented the birthday boy with a factory fresh hovercraft." The King could tell she wasn't telling him everything but at least she wasn't giving her mother any problems, he would settle for that now. "I'm still holding you to your promise," he said. Jazzalin responded, "I know daddy." "I love you "Jazzy" with all my heart", her father said. "I love you back with all my heart", she replied. Then he sang, "To my dear little one. A sweet note I wrote that is music to my heart forevermore." Jazzalin was always reduced to tears when he sang to her. "Love you daddy," she choked before the planetary transmission ended.

At dinner she was unusually quiet so her mother initiated a conversation. "Jazzalin, a confidential envelope was delivered today for you from "Adagio Skyes. I forgot to give it to you earlier," she said. Jazzalin replied between bites of her food, "I'm sure it's not all that important." Her mother had the maid bring the envelope to her at the dinner table. After dinner in her room she opened the envelope and read, "Jazzalin, I want to apologize for approaching a topic that you felt was none of my business. I admit I was presumptuous on that issue but my invitation for your attendance at my party wasn't patronage. I hope you can see the difference and that I wanted be helpful although I came off as pushy. So here's another attempt to be helpful to enlighten you with information my father's contacts in the scientific community have gathered. The King and his advisors are not current on the "breach"' issue because it' has been encroaching at least five years or more. It seems that the breach isn't responsive to the traditional "light songs" our scientists directed at it because a more intense sound is emanating from inside the breach and bouncing back any attempts to close it. My father's scientists are confirming that a static breach is opening in an attempt to rid itself of an environ bubble of "light singers". Dr. Oto Graffix our planet's premier astrophysicist was funded by my father five years ago to set up an observation laboratory on a small atmospheric planetoid near the breach, about a light year away. From this location they have monitored the breach documenting the correlation of how the breach has responded to the recordings of traditional "light songs" directed at it. I have included Dr. Graffix's five years of scientific findings with this note. I hope your feelings towards me stemming from my overzealousness at the party won't keep you from getting this important information to your father." He signed simply "Adagio".

Jazzalin went to the desk in the corner of her room and activated her compu-tran. She took a wand and carefully began to scan the reports Adagio had sent her and she quickly entered the address of her father's computab. She prefaced the report with, "Daddy, a friend from school gave this to me because it may be useful with the breach issue in the Staticsphere. Love. Jazzy." She pressed the "send" key and waited to get confirmation the information was enroute to its destination before flinging herself on her bed. Her thoughts were convoluted and anxious. How did she get so messed up she asked herself. Not only alienating a new acquaintance but also distancing herself from her best true friend Beabop. She shook off the brain fog showered and dressed for bed. Once in bed she felt emotionally drained and fell fast asleep.

She hadn't had any free time with Beabop for almost two weeks and she did not want that to continue. She decided to call Beabop right away and her first words were, "I'm so sorry Bea. I've been a mess since the party." Beabop countered, "Yeah. What happened, did Adagio get fresh?" "No, but he was nosy", she said. She continued, "Bea, let's go to the "Vizix" and hangout at "Voco" for the afternoon like the well brought up young ladies we are!" Beabop replied, "Quizit! I'm in. I'll meet you in front of the "Vizix" in 45 minutes." Jazzalin answered, "I'll be there! Bea, thank you for staying friends with me even when I'm spazzing." "I have a low threshold for friends. Twinkle fingers! See you soon.", Beabop giggled her reply ending the call.

The girls met in front of the "Vizix" theater and hugged each other before buying admission to the latest installment of "Estelle Galaxy Princess". These action movies were almost identical to the ones before it but Jazzalin and Beabop never seemed to notice. They devoured candy, salty crunchy snacks, and icy effervescent drinks while intently staring wide-eyed at the actress speaking formulaic dialogue full of choptalk words like "quizit, spazztic, riffic, xurious" designed to entertain thirteen year olds and maybe older teens but causing adults to cringe. When the last scene of the movie came showing the heroine unraveling an obvious mystery, rescuing a diplomat, and saving the galaxy once again the girls cheered "quizit!".

Jazzalin had dismissed her driver when she arrived at the Vizix so she and Beabop could stealthily exit the theater through the side doors which would put them on the subtrans level where they would board the hovertrans to the Scat District to Vocostellar. Jazzalin was sure she had eluded her bodyguard but this android was programmed very well and had attached a small adhesive tracker to her shoulder inside the theater. The tracker would allow her to feel she was on her own but it would notify her driver to arrive at Vocostellar in an hour to take her and Beabop home.

At "Voco", a band was already on stage that the girls had not heard before. The music was eclectic pop jazz fusion. Jazzalin was dumbfounded when the bass guitarist turned around and it was Adagio. He played with effortless skill melding acoustic and electric cords blending with the sound of the keyboard, violin, drums, and flute played by the quintet. He smiled with recognition when he saw the girls seated at a nearby booth staring up at him on the stage. When the band crescendoed their final note Adagio made his way to their table. Smiling down he said, "Good afternoon Princess. Beabop." Clearing her throat Jazzalin replied, "Jazzalin is fine." And Beabop flippantly added, "Beabop is fine too." Jazzalin poked Beabop in her side frowning, communicating that her greeting was not funny and continued, "How's everything with you Adagio?", Jazzalin asked. "I'm fine. I didn't know you came to the Scat district," he replied. Not waiting for her to answer since he knew she most likely was not supposed to be there he continued, "I come here a lot to try out new music with my band "Mixit". Do you girls ever go up on stage?" Jazzalin wanted to be coy but decided she'd be better off telling the truth since he was obviously calling her out to see if she would back down. She was a princess and no brat rich boy was going to get the best of her. "Bea and I sometimes sing a duet of improvised strains from jazz, pop, or classical," she said with boldness. She nudged Bea who agreed, "Yeah, yeah we do." Adagio said, "That's great! We can start a harmony and you two can join in." Jazzalin asked, "Do you know "Purple Comet in the Evening Sky?"

Abruptly Jazzalin and Beabop stopped singing when the Voco commu tran screen powered on announcing a message from King Tempo. The king spoke, "I want to advise the people of planet Jazzo that I am currently on "Audia Prime" as part of a fact finding council regarding the "Staticsphere" eruptions. I will keep you all informed as we determine if this phenomenon presents any threat to our planetary system and galaxy and its inhabitants. I am always you king and servant." Adagio looked at Jazzalin who had grabbed her satchel and signaled Beabop that they were leaving now. Quickly Adagio caught up to Jazzalin at the door and said, "Don't worry your father and his advisors are the sharpest minds in the planetary system and they'll fix this situation if it turns out to need fixing." She smiled and replied, "I appreciate your encouragement." The expression on her face changed when she saw the royal hover car waiting at the curb in front of "Vocostellar". She managed to disguise her surprise to say, "I enjoyed the session today. Maybe some other time and place, til then, bye!" She and Beabop got into the hover car as the driver held its door open for them.

When she arrived home her mother's maid met her at the door and motioned her to the grand room. The grand room was always full of sunlight, let in through floor to ceiling windows. There were always huge flower arrangements from the palace gardens or hothouses placed around the large room. Her mother's grand keyboard and standing harp were also displayed there as well as an large aquarium populated by dotty aquotts, sun fan aquotts, and bright green and blue wigglums. This room exuded elegance and sophistication to everyone who entered it. Besides her own rooms this was her favorite in the royal residence. Her mother took her hands when she walked into the room and guided her as they sat down together on the teal and purple upholstered sofa. Octiva spoke, "Jazzalin, did you see the message the king made today?" Jazzalin nodded. Her mother continued, "He called me just after the speech saying he had received some information from you a few days ago. He's very impressed that the "Skyes" scientific friends have been keeping an eye on the breach for five years and he's reaching out to Dr. Graffix on the planetoid for additional insight on bringing this problem to an acceptable conclusion." Jazzalin started to explain about being at "Voco" but her mother interrupted, "You've done well in your intermediary sessions at the Academy so I'm going to have you tutored at home for your senior and final undergraduate courses." "But mother, all my friends are at the academy", Jazzalin countered. Her mother smiled and said, "It's been decided and it's final. Now, go wash up for dinner. We're having roasted poultry of some kind with veggies and emerald berry pie for dessert. Yum!" Her mother leaned towards her and kissed her cheek pushing back her thick hair at her temples whispering "My thin reed is rapidly becoming a woman and I intend to make sure you're the very best you can be. Now go!" She was relieved that her mother had not made any reference to her Scat district escapade but she was overwhelmed with what she had just been told.

In her room Jazzalin pondered the sudden change her life was taking on. Being tutored at home for her final academic year before becoming an apprentice to an ultra planetary diva. She knew there was no use in discussing this issue with her father because her mother's statement "it's been decided" indicated he was already a contributor to the final decision. The little girl in her wanted to give in to tears and pouting but the princess in her was not willing to fall apart at this new wrinkle in the fabric of her young life. She was too depressed to talk to Beabop now, maybe after dinner.

CHAPTER 4

The last week of the school year Jazzalin was preoccupied about the future but she managed to focus enough to do well on all her finals. To celebrate the successful end of the school year Jazzalin and Beabop took the public hovertrans to the local shopping hub headed to the "Luncheria" food court. They ordered their favorite fried foods accompanied with icy syrupy carbonated drinks. The girls sat down and began to devour their food but they both stopped mid-munch when they saw Adagio walking hand in hand with "Paisley Pulsar" a new "screech queen" out of the Scat district recently signed by the Skyes music label. The pair were unaware of being observed as they were caught up in some private conversation. Jazzalin thought, how could she come out in public like that wearing a transparent plasticine tunic over strategically placed body decals with knee high bright red boots. Beabop between snickering whispered, "My mom says her lady parts are her only talent and neither she or they can sing." The girls suppressed their laughter trying not to choke on their food. As if on cue Paisley laughed and tossed her bleached multi-colored hair back, then leaning towards Adagio she whispered something that made him laugh as well. Jazzalin signaled Beabop that they should leave before they were spotted by the fawning pair. Sliding down from the table close to the floor, the girls slipped out of a side exit of the food court and found their way to the shopping level to get some fashion ideas for their impending joyful summer vacations. All in all the day was idyllic with them being themselves with the "quizit" anticipation of summer vacation. Beabop was being shipped off to her grandmother's mansion in the Continental South region for the entire summer while Jazzalin would only get one month at the seashore with a governess and the rest of the summer being dedicated to vocal training to sustain her voice at 5.5 octaves as a first soprano of the Light Songs. Jazzalin turned to Beabop and said, "It seems there's a lot of things against us remaining friends but, I'll be contacting you every week you're away by commun tran or even bot mail. You are my best friend and nothing's going to change that. Oh, you have to come to my birthday party the last week of summer cycle!" "You know I wouldn't miss it, a chance to party with royalty!", Beabop snootily replied. The girls laughed and continued to window shop for a while before the royal hover car arrived to take them home.

On the day of Beabop's departure for the summer Jazzalin sent her a vocogram in which she sang, "Truer none can be than you are to me to me. May our friendship abound forever free, truest friend to me." She finished the message by saying, "Until we meet again, twinkle fingers. Enjoy your granny's giant house and her charge accounts!"

The next day Jazzalin's maid assisted her with packing for her seaside vacation. She was packing light because she intended to make day trips to the nearby beach city named "Blootown" for the trending summer fashions. Her mother Queen Ociiva accompanied her on the trip to their beach house on the Aquavast Sea which was an hour's flight from "Jazzopolis City". When they arrived at the beach house Jazzalin brightened as she realized she would have thirty days with an all too manipulable governess "Miss Quaver", miles of pink sand beaches, a speed boat, a nearby resort city with a shopping hub, and her best friend's communtran code. Her mind was already organizing summer scenarios to fill all thirty days. "Fun!!!", her spirit shouted.

The royal summer house was a beautifully designed structure of glass and metal with artful plant accents at the entry and on the lower and upper balconies. The gate voice activated security system responded to the Queen's voice and opened to allow their hovercraft entry. Once inside Jazzalin ran upstairs simultaneously speaking to her mother, "This place is "quizit"! I love it here!" Her mother replied, "Please use the correct word "exquisite" and remember you only have thirty days here so make the most of it. I would enjoy a day or two here but I have to be the available face to the people of Royal authority should it become necessary in your father's absence." The queen and the governess inspected the pantry and sundries as well the perimeter security system. Jazzalin ran downstairs and hugged her mother watching the Serva-droid bring her luggage inside. She half listened to her mother's instructions while gazing at the turquoise water lapping up to the pink sand shoreline. She daydreamed of ski-planing up the coast, laying out on floating deck reading or watching digi movies, and especially catching the day ferry to the Continental South to run wild with Beabop. Jazzalin knew Miss Quaver, her governess was romantically preoccupied with a new boyfriend and would spend the majority of the time cooing on her view-com and laughing in a high pitched way that only her boyfriend could appreciate so there wouldn't be any watchful scrutiny towards her on this vacation.

Her mother finalized her checklist with the Serva-droid confirming all was in order; she kissed Jazzalin's cheek advising she would be contacting her at least twice a week by view-com. Jazzalin responded in her best compliant daughter manner, "Yes mommy." The chauffeur opened the rear of the royal hover car waiting til the Queen was securely inside. She blew a kiss through the window to Jazzalin and the vehicle ascended and was gone. After waving goodbye to her mother she realized how tired the trip had made her. She told Miss Quaver she was going to her room to take a nap. Entering her room with its water blue and lavender walls and a flower filled balcony open to an ocean view she removed her travel clothes. Yawning she twirled on her toes and flopped backwards onto her bed and fell asleep instantly.

The next day Jazzalin woke early to go out to the anchored floating deck to swim and read glossy periodicals and watch digi videoes. She had sent a digicom message to the kitchen android to pack a lunch of beverages and snacks to carry in the speedboat she would use to get to the deck. She had chosen a bright yellow one piece swimsuit and wide brim sun hat and packed her towel, sun lotion, digi video player, and her commun-cat so she could call Beabop. She maneuvered the speedboat with skill to the deck remembering what her father had taught her last summer vacation. Securing the boat to the deck, she unloaded her gear arranging it for maximum ease of access. Completing this she removed her hat and poised herself on the edge of the deck and dove into the warm turquoise waters of the "Aquavast Sea". She was an inherent athlete and swam Frolicking like a sea creature. She swam for a long time before deciding to climb onto the deck to rest, snack, and enjoy digi music videos. After watching several music videos she fell into a drowsy mood and stretched out on a towel with her eyes half closed. So when she heard the "whirr" sound of engines she didn't know it was real so she ignored it. Suddenly she heard Beabop's voice yell, "Wake-up lazy!" Jazzalin jumped up to see a shiny blue hover car above her and Beabop being lowered by a metallic tether from it onto the deck. Jazzalin screamed, "Bea! How?!" Beabop pointed up and Jazzalin followed her finger to see Adagio at the controls of vehicle smiling down at her. Bea explained that her father "Razaf Magnus Bamm-Zynoplee" was a jazz artist on the Skyes label "Eclecteek" both vocal and instrumental for 10 years before his death. Jazzalin's eyes became wide as she realized Beabop was on the inside with Adagio. She smiled in spite of the realization and said, "Well, to what do I owe this unannounced visit?" Beabop grinned and replied, "We came to rescue you. We plan a day at the "fling fields", a picnic, and a sleepover at Granny's house since she's gone to "Vivensville Spa Space Station" for the week. And she just had a new audio system installed through the whole mansion and it's cosmic quizit!" Jazzalin knew she should decline but she needed some fun. She had studied hard to pass all her courses and had been obedient for her parents sake, so without hesitating gave a nodding "yes" to the plan. Jazzalin gathered her belongings from the deck tossing them into the speedboat. She instructed her friends to park on the pier of the beach house. She sped back to the pier and tied off the boat and entered the patio she yelling out, "Miss Quaver!!, where are you?!" The governess ran into the patio wearing a pink house robe and fuzzy slippers with her disheveled hair tied with a scarf. It was obvious she had just woke up. She bowed quickly and said, "Your highness." Jazzalin advised the governess that her best friend Beabop had come to take her for the day to the Continental South to her family mansion. Miss Quaver was relieved because she knew "Beabop" and her family. She smiled and she advised her charge it was fine for her to go with Beabop as long as she kept her commun-tran on for any necessary updates. Jazzalin advised, "If mother calls tell her I went to the Plaza for shopping and then to Bea's for the rest of the day and she can reach my commu-tran." Miss Quaver had her own plans for a quick jaunt down the coast to see her beloved. The two females understood the other's need for privacy and were in agreement for the other to have her own. Running past the governess she went to her room and changed into dark blue leggings, a bright orange hoodie shirt, and soft leather short boots. She also threw a few personals in her overnight bag knowing she could rely on Beabop for anything else she needed. Running downstairs Jazzalin waved goodbye to her unkempt governess and ran through the patio to the parked hover car on the pier. Adagio opened the door of his shiny blue vehicle and Jazzalin jumped in the backseat with her bag. Beabop turned around from the front seat and gave her twinkle finger greeting. Jazzalin's blood ran electric through her veins to be with friends on an adventure. Her mind shouted, "To the fling fields and beyond!"

CHAPTER 5

In the various regions of Jazzo there existed gravitational anomalies that were called "sky eaters" by the indigenous people the "Ziggabim", whose fat cattle called "bovas" were victimized by them. The pastel skinned people with wild purply or multi-pastel hair lived in the forests on the outer edge of these "sky eaters". They focused their lives on mining the amethyst stones used in their jewels, rituals and raising the huge bova cattle for themselves and for the citizens of Jazzo. These people never ventured to these fields in question because they were barren and rocky. The larger Jazzo population eventually named the anomalies "fling fields" because anything flung or thrown into these fields was caught away to disappear into the sky. As the Ziggabim's cattle wandered into these anomalies they would be caught up and carried away into the upper atmosphere, sometimes the cattle would be found miles away from the Ziggabim villages and sometimes the animals would disappear all together. The Ziggabim determined that someone was taking advantage of them and stealing their cattle so they stationed warriors in the trees of forests surrounding the dry rocky areas to catch the bandits but were totally surprised when they saw several of their cattle float upward and get carried into the upper atmosphere. Being creative in spite of their many primitive attributes they wove a large canopy platform of plant ropes which they attached to eight columns of tallest cut trees securely embedded in the ground with boulders layered on top for added strength located on the outer perimeter of the "sky eaters". The platforms were secured just above the height of a large bova so if they did wander into an anomaly the animal would only raise a few feet off the ground and the Ziggabim could easily use a hook rod or rope to pull them out of the no gravity field to safety. The Ziggabim were so pleased with their success in stopping their cattle from being spirited away by the "sky eaters" they began celebrating thanksgiving festivals where young men and women would tether themselves to the each of the eight pillars and fling themselves up into the gravityless air above the colorful platforms while their fellow tribes people would marvel and whisper prayers.

As Jazzo's continental south and west regions underwent progressive development by the industrious Eccleum, many Ziggabim tribes were assimilated into the current technical culture so that the "fling fields" were fenced off and trespassers were warned of the danger of being pulled into the upper atmosphere to their death. However, this warning only increased the curiosity of "the young" who not only trespassed but created their own rights of passage featuring the "fling fields". A dozen students from a local military school in a South Region Jazzoan city acquired a massive boulder from a nearby quarry and managed to somehow transport it to a fling field. The young men tied synthetic ropes around the boulder and around their waists then cutting the fence accessed the fling field two at a time while the others watched outside the fence. The two were immediately caught in the zero gravity of the fling field. But the boulder was not immune to the force of the non gravity field and began to be pulled through the opening in the fence and the two boys were oblivious to the danger of being drawn into space along with the boulder. The other boys in a panic launched themselves on top of the boulder for added weight and successfully pulled their two unsuspecting comrades to safety. They made a speedy retreat from the fling field leaving the rope covered boulder to float weightlessly in plain sight. The next day the public viewcom screen headlined ""Large rope covered boulder floating in midair in a nearby fling field." The story elaborated that this vandalism was most likely a "right of passage" stunt by cadets from a local military school but since there was no active surveillance equipment at the site nothing was captured to identify the vandals. The story went on to say that local authorities would be using heavy equipment to remove the boulder to prohibit it from endangering flying vehicles or perhaps even falling on citizens causing severe injuries or death. The city would also be placing aerial security drones on surveillance to hinder any future encroachments into the field.

The planetary government became interested in the fling field anomalies and funded a scientific investigation to reveal the characteristics of the fields. Their studies found that the fields were spacial wormholes and could be dangerous only if the proper precautions were not taken, like weighted stations in the ground outside the field's zero gravity. The scientists referenced the Ziggabim's rope platforms as an example of an acceptable safetynet to avoid getting spirited away by the fling fields. After the scientists completed their research a mega billionare purchased the fling field acreage and set a troupe of research and development architects and designers to create a profitable use of the fields. The billionaire's R&D team created an amusement park "Fling World" which was a series of patterned elevator columned stations drilled deep into the ground surrounding the numerous fling fields and filled with the strongest liquid stone. Each 25 floor column had multiple platforms usually four and fitted with waist harnesses or float chairs with "release" and "retraction" cable controls depending on the rider's preference. And as an added precaution each field was covered with a poly synthetic fabric canopy to prevent anyone from floating off into the void. Also each field had a theme such as "Star Fling", "Fantasy Fling", "Quizit Fling", "Royal Fling", "Planet Fling", "Zigga Fling", and "Sportz Fling" with decor and music associated with that theme. All the fling fields offered the same level of attention to safety except for "Sportz Fling" which was designed to draw the athletically inclined. Sportz Fling had only two access tiers much higher than the other fields requiring a breather since it accessed the upper atmosphere and only 4 waist tethers on each tier so only the physically fit and strong would take the "fling" higher and farther. The fields were test marketed to great popular applause and were soon opened to the public. The revenue from this venture flowed like water to increase the wealth of all investors involved and the billionaire was praised as a genius for turning a problem into profit. The "fling field" mania lasted three years before it began to fade as other technologies and fads took over the Jazzoan consumer vanity. But the fields were not completely forgotten by its fickle former customers as they were often rented for weddings, birthday parties, just because parties, various reunions, seasonal fairs, and music concerts. In the summer the fields were open to the public to fling to loud pop tunes while gorging on greasy, salty and sugary snacks. So today the planet's princess would join the thousands of Jazzoans enjoying the gravitational anomaly of being flung into the sky while being tethered to the earth, giving new meaning to "feet on the ground with your head in the clouds". Jazzalin, Beabop, and Adagio had a great time free floating on multiple fling fields but agreed they would bypass "Sportz Fling" as none of them felt up to physical stamina required to fling in the upper atmosphere and after 3 hours they were flung out and ready to leave. Climbing into Adagio's blue hovercraft they headed to Beabop's granny's mansion.

CHAPTER 6

Beabop's granny's mansion was sprawled over a large acreage with a ten bedroom main house, a seven bedroom guest house, a sportsman size swimming pool, a five acre flower garden, a two acre vegetable garden and an eight hover vehicle garage. Adagio pulled up to the garage entrance and Beabop spoke into the voice recognition scan causing the garage door to open. When Adagio parked his hovecar the group alighted and entered the house through the kitchen. Beabop lead the way into the library entertainment center all the while chattering about how granny's mansion had been reviewed by the Jazzoan Architectural Guild as the most unique residential structure in the South Region, and probably the entire planet for its use of stone both liquid and solid, metal, and glass to form curves, waves as well as straight walls and a floating balcony facing the Aquavast Sea. Jazzalin's jaw dropped when she saw the floor to ceiling shelves filled with vidbooks and rare ancient paper bound books. There was also a holographic globe of planet "Jazzo" in rotation which lit up a corner of the big room. On another wall were shelves of hundreds of digimusic disks of all kinds. The room was truly dedicated to entertain with an overhead theater sized vision screen, a state of the art audio acoustic system, lush potted plants, and a wall width aquarium filled with rare pink flitterby aquotts, polkadot lady aquotts, and yellow fairy aquotts. Jazzalin thought that Granny must be extremely wealthy to have so many rare aquotts when just one of them would be an average Jazzoan's month's pay. Beabop yelled, "Jazz, come on I want to show you your room!" Turning to Adagio she said, " Addie will be alright. Won't you?" Adagio smiled over his shoulder as he thumbed through Granny's exhaustive music collection. On the way upstairs Jazzalin asked, "When were you going to tell me that you knew Adagio before he came to the Academy?" Beabop replied, "Why do you care? He's too old for both of us and less royalty than me. But he's really dreamy, huh? His greeny gold eyes are amazing!" Jazzalin rolled her eyes at her friends fawning over Adagio's good looks but secretly agreed that he was handsome. On the second floor Beabop opened the door of a room which was beautifully decorated in shades of pink and accented with black. The room also had a balcony overlooking a garden of blooming perennials. Beabop preened as she bowed, waving Jazzalin to enter the pretty room. Jazzalin responded with a curtsy before letting out a loud "quizit!" upon seeing the room. Beabop pressed an intercom button to the kitchen to have the kitchen droid set up a snack tray and drinks in the library. Jazzalin turned on the vizicom on the wall and saw the news reporting the update from Audia Prime. The report said that envoys from all seven planets were currently in conference with renowned scientist Dr. Vektor Graffix who had been studying the breach encroaching their galactic territories. Jazzalin's mind became calm knowing that her father had used the data Adagio had sent her. Coming back to now she cleared her thoughts acknowledging that she was on holiday and was ready to eat, drink, and have fun with two of her favorite people.

Descending the staircase the girls heard the jazz fusion music of the Ziggabim electric stringist "Par Ming" who played keen fast notes that rifled off and mingled with tribal drums and harmonic chants. The music took them and they began to dance down the steps into the library where Adagio grabbed the hand of each girl in an effortless twirling jig that they continued til the song ended. A kitchen droid entered the room and placed a large tray of roasted poultry, salad, bread, fruit tarts, and chilled sparkling wine. The trio ate hungrily washing everything down with cold bubbly wine. Between bites Beabop suggested, "Let's go to "The Platform" for some fun! We can dress down and dance til we drop!" The Platform was an orbiting entertainment venue ship around Jazzo featuring the best ethereal experimental pop jazz fusion groups produced by the planet. Also the club offered its customers to dorn space gear secured by tether cords allowing them to free float in space. Weddings, school graduations, debutante parties and familial reunions and anniversaries were popular events on The Platform for a generous price. The girls looked at Adagio who smiled and gave an affirmative nod since they knew his father was the owner of The Platform. Jazzalin and Beabop let out screams as they ran upstairs to coordinate their quirkiest outfits which was less than ten minutes. Jazzalin chose a black leotard interrupted by a fluffy bright pink tulle skirt and sequin short boots of the same color. She smiled that her outfit mimicked the guest room's colorful decor. Her purple hair was gathered into a tail at the back of her head and tied with a jeweled band and a full bang adorned her oval face just above her eyebrows. Beabop on the other hand chose chartreuse leggings with a neon purple tunic and matching purple boots. Beabop's thick curly red hair was always ready to go so she just forked her fingers through it, smiled at her mirrored reflection and she was set. Adagio gave an appreciative whistle as they sauntered down the stairs. Beabop took time to enter security codes for Granny's mansion before joining Jazzalin and Adagio in the hovercar. Jazzoan technology had advanced to allow their atmospheric hover vehicles with fuel injection and engine enhancements to easily access the upper atmosphere and space to the many entertainment venues, shopping centers, businesses, and military outposts orbiting above the planet. Adagio adjusted his vehicle to accelerate to the upper atmosphere and the trio sped off to The Platform. In less than an hour they were entering the landing bay of "The Platform". They could already hear the music blasting through the speakers on the ceiling above their vehicle. The girls recognized the band performing as "A View From Space" playing a techno fusion ballad called "Love Is A Spiral Galaxy". The girls sang along, "Up and down, around, narrowing then expanding. Linear motions of your emotions. Ooooooooooooh! Love is a spiral galaxy for you and me!" Adagio signed with his finger to his lips that they should not be so loud since they were under age and he did not want his father to know about this escapade which could lead to his hover car being confiscated. He whispered, "This way", as he opened a door to a private banquet room overlooking the main floor for the general public. The girls began to dance to a throbbing techno instrumental a new band had just started, they waved to Adagio to join them. He went into his street dance mode swaying over to them acting as partner to both girls. They enjoyed the music with youthful abandonment. When the music stopped Adagio blurted, "We didn't sneak in here just to dance". He simultaneously pressed the door of a nearby storage cabinet which opened to reveal several colorful space suits with tether cords. Jazzalin's and Beabop's eyes got big and they both let out squeals of delight because they had no idea they would get to tether float on "The Platform". According to their color preferences Jazzalin claimed a pink space suit and Beabop grabbed a bright purple one. Adagio chose a more conservative silver suit and all three started to climb into the suits. Being the elder of the three, Adagio took precaution to make sure the girls were safely enclosed in their suits and their tether cords were securely connected. He ushered the girls to another door and pressed a control panel button which activated an automated voice to announce "Please secure your helmets as the cabin is being pressurized to allow the exterior doors to open. The time for your tether float is fifteen minutes at which time you will automatically be reeled back into the cabin. Have a fun float." Adagio took Jazzalin and Beabop by the hand walking to the cabin ledge and released them to float in space. The girls were giddy with excitement as they whirled giving their twinkle finger salute to each other. Using the suit's interlink speaker he had the girls look to their right where a young couple were getting married. The bride wore a white float suit with a bouquet of white flowers attached to her gloved hand and the groom wore a gray float suit with the word "groom" printed on the helmet. There were several pastel dressed bridesmaids and gray suited groomsmen in the happy party. They were obviously a well to do family since it was significantly expensive to space float off "The Platform" for one person let alone for a group of at least twenty. An official of some kind was presiding overall and when he finished the couple touched helmets as they would have to wait to take their first kiss as husband and wife inside the ship. The girls followed Adagio farther out from the ship so they looked down at the planet below. Jazzo was a beautiful planet Jazzalin thought and from this vantage point city lights twinkled like a jeweled tapestry, turquoise ocean's gleamed offset by stretches of pink sand shorelines, and bright green forests spread over vast areas intermingled with numerous mountain ranges. Their reverie was interrupted by the simultaneous tug on their tether lines and the automated voice announcing, "Your allotted float time has expired and you are being reeled back into your cabin. Please wait until the green light confirms cabin pressurization is complete before removing your helmets. Thank you for floating on "The Platform". The girls hurriedly removed the float suits as did Adagio and returned them to the storage closet. Jazzalin and Beabop turned to Adagio and tiptoed to place thankful kisses on each cheek for giving them an experience they might never have had otherwise. Beabop yawned unashamedly admitting, "I'm bushed and sleepy. Guys lets go home. Adagio you stay in the guest quarters above the garage since it's another thirty minutes to your house." Adagio replied, "Thank you for your generous offer but my family has a beachfront condo less than two miles from your granny's place." Beabop smiled replying, "I forgot you're obscenely wealthy and too well brought up to compromise the reputations of two underage girls." Adagio smiled at her sarcasm and bowed pointing them to the exit. Tired as she was Jazzalin managed to get to the hovercar and into the vehicle and fell fast asleep. She dreamed, imagining herself grownup and on her own with a sporty hover car and dating someone like Adagio. By the time they were descending just above Granny's mansion Jazzalin was sleep's captive and Adagio had to carry her inside where a service droid came to relieve him of the sleeping girl. Beabop thanked Adagio for being their chauffeur and escort and if he could bear them after the unsophisticated impression they made today they were free for any fun times tomorrow. Adagio advised that he had to get back home and wouldn't be able to see them for at least a week. Then the handsome young man hopped into his sleek hover car/ spaceship waved goodbye to Beabop and sped off.

Tired as she was, she managed to verify the mansion's security systems were activated. Granny had drilled her numerous times, "Bea show me the steps to activating the security system, because if you can't I'm not leaving you in my house for a month alone. I trust you because you are my grandchild but I won't tolerate ignorance and ineptness. You are an heiress of monumental status which is not tandem with scatterbrains. Do you understand? Now, show me quickly as I have things to do." The security system was not stellar quantum physics, all of two buttons and a light, but you would have thought so the way Granny carried on. She finally climbed the flight of stairs to the guest rooms corridor and entered Jazzalin's room. She shook her awake demanding "Wake up and take off your boots and brush your teeth! Jazzalin you're such a child." Jazzalin regained some composure and yawning replied "Well, I'm not trying to impress anyone, least of all you! Now, go away so I can go back to sleep." Beabop responded, "Suit yourself." Too tired to be confrontational Beabop staggered down the hall to the sanctuary of her chartreuse and purple accented room, put on her jammies, brushed her teeth, finally twirling on her toes fell onto her bed face down and was instantly asleep. Jazzalin did manage to remove her boots but would risk not brushing her teeth until morning. With a big silly smile on her face she reviewed the day: rescued by friends, fling field fair fun, and an off planet float in space. "Quizit day!", not at all a dull day, she thought and went back to sleep.

CHAPTER 7

Jazzalin woke to the bedside commu-cube "pinging" announcing that Queen Octiva was calling. Half awake Jazzalin pressed the answer key on the cube and said, "Good morning mother." The Queen responded, "Jazzalin, your governess said you did not come back to the beach house last night. Where were you young lady!" "Oh, mother! Ms.Quaver knew I was with Beabop and I spent the night at her granny's. I'm sorry I didn't call her with an update. Mother you can't expect me to languish my summer vacation alone with Ms. Quaver." Her mother responded, "I do expect you to be responsible, which means contacting the governess about deciding to stay over at Beabop's granny's house!" Feeling she was about to lose this battle meekly responded, "Mommy, I will be more responsible and check in with you everyday. Please let me stay at Bea's granny's house for the rest of my vacation." Queen Octiva relented not wanting to oppress her only child when her future would be somewhat different than she expected and replied, "Alright Jazzalin, but I require a call everyday. You understand Jazzalin?" Sensing victory Jazzalin brightened and replied, "Yes mother! Thank you. Love you. Does this call count for today's check in?" The Queen laughed and replied, "Yes, this call counts for today's check in. Enjoy your visit. Love you, goodbye." Jazzalin threw her arms wide and hugged herself and screamed "Quizit!!" Jumping out of bed she ran to Beabop's room. Beabop was still asleep. Finding a feathery decorated writing stylus on a bedside table, Jazzalin began to brush it back and forth, tickling her sleeping friend's nose. Beabop batted at the offending annoyance and muttered, "Jazzalin, I'm going to massacre you if you don't stop. Why are you awake so soon anyway?" Jazzalin whispered, "My mother gave me a wake up call and demanded a daily check in call but she also gave me permission to spend my summer vacation with you at granny's mansion. Bea, we're going to have mega fun!!!!!" The girls got into motion showering and brushing their teeth and tossing on house robes to run downstairs to the kitchen. Jazzalin programmed the kitchen droid to make her favorite fruit smoothie and a buttery muffin. Beabop heard Jazzalin's breakfast order and requested the same for herself while activating the commu-monitor screen. The screen lit up giving the latest news from the "Galactic Council" on Audia Prime. The newscaster advised the council meeting was a heated exchange as to using the traditional "Light Songs Harmonies" or warships to push back the aggressive Sessilum encroachment on their planetary system. Jazzalin felt a twinge of anxiety but recovered quickly knowing that her father was a wise leader, a "Light Song" proficient and a fearless visionary warrior to put their enemy to flight.

After breakfast the girls decided to spend the day outside lounging by the pool reading popular digi-magazines, drinking sugary carbonated drinks and consuming sweet and salty snack food while discussing which male teen actor was stellar cute or just basic cute. Jazzalin became tired of being inactive and dove into the warm blue water of the large pool and swam with ease to the other end. Propping her arms on the edge of pool Jazzalin called,"Beabop jump in, it's great!!!". Beabop lazily replied, "Swimming isn't an activity I enjoy. I like wearing cute swimwear and lounging poolside and when possible being appreciated by cute boys." Jazzalin laughed knowing Beabop was wonderfully superficial but likable at the same time. Beabop used the commu-screen remote to turn it on and select the popular music channel "Music Stream" and to her surprise "Adagio" was speaking into the transmitter commenting about his father's music company. Beabop screamed, "Jazzalin! Adagio's on the commu-screen, come see!" Jazzalin swam to where she see the screen without getting out of the pool and there he was "stellar cute" and speaking with ease and knowledge through the screen introducing new artists on the "Skyes Label". She thought how polished and grownup he was and that he would not be interested in a skinny 13 year old even a royal one like her. Crestfallen, Jazzalin turned away from the screen and resumed swimming laps down the pool. She finally got out of the pool going to lounge next to Beabop inquiring, "What's on the schedule for this evening?" Beabop replied,"'We could go to the "Shop Along

Plaza" for the food court and see a new Vizix action adventure, or just stay here and listen to Granny's excessive interstellar music collection. Oh, I could also give you a tour of the mansion. This place is massive." Jazzalin responded, "I'm not in the mood for the"Shop Along" crowds and noises and I still have to check in with mother. We're music students so lets do a deep dive into Granny's music collection after dinner." "I'm game. We can do the mansion tour tomorrow", Beabop agreed. A kitchen service droid came poolside requesting the food preferences for lunch and dinner from the girls, who rattled off their choices. The droid recorded the list of foods the girls had chosen from entrees to desserts and returned to the kitchen to prepare the list of yummy dishes.

After a poolside lunch the girls decided they had spent enough time outside and retired to the rooms to shower and change. Jazzalin took time to call her mother for the daily check in confirming that all was well with her. She thought the check in call was a small price to pay to have a "quizit" summer with her best friend. Beabop just finishing a shower saw her view-comm light up with her granny's smiling face calling her name, "Bea! Bea! Where are you?!" Beabop ran to the bedside table and turned the view-comm screen around so her grandmother could see her face and answered, "I'm here Granny. What's up?" Granny responded, "Don't use that vulgar language with me young lady. Now, I'm cutting my stay at the spa because I met the wife of the governor of the Eastern Region who begged me to participate in their "Summer Festivals", so I need to come home to coordinate an appropriate wardrobe for these events. Normally I would not have required payment but since my spa time was interrupted the governor's paying exponentially for my time and talent. Forgive me dear none of this is your concern. And how's your guest "the princess" doing?" Beabop replied, "Oh, Jazzalin's fine. She spent the day swimming while I relaxed poolside." Granny's face smiled on the screen as she responded, "I'm so glad you girls are having a practical summer not running wild at the "Shop Along" or at the "Scat-de-Dat" district. Yes, I know about your escapades. Love you sweeting and I'll see you tomorrow, bye now." Beabop smiled into the screen transmitting her image to Granny hoping it didnot betray her jitteriness at Granny's reference to the Scat district escapade when she said, "Love you too, bye Granny." Thank goodness it was going to be a short return so hers and Jazzalin's summer would not suffer from Granny's smothering.

CHAPTER 8

Audesse Lyrelle Bamm, Beabop's charismatic flamboyant grandmother, was Jazzoan aristocracy from birth. The Bamm family were cousins to the King going back several generations and also first level musicians in all music as well as the revered "Light Songs". Audesse was the youngest of the five Bamm children all of whom were educated and trained in all voices from high sopranos and tenors, medium altos and baritones, and low contraltos and basses. Unlike her brothers and sisters who went into music academia, all teaching and tutoring in the planet's most prestigious conservatories, Audesse chose a career as a stage performer and recording artist. Her exceptional voice was her fortune making her a stellar singing celebrity on Jazzo and even to other planets in their Spiral galaxy. She was not only renowned for her voice but for her beautiful face and form. Endowed with a statuesque figure, glowing soft lavender complexion, flashing hazel eyes, a ready friendly smile, and a thick mane of bright pink hair she was much sought after by Jazzo's most eligible bachelors. With all of the anatomical gifts, her voice and looks and social advantages, royal ties and wealth, she was surprisingly modest and level headed only going into "silly female" mode on occasion when it would achieve a desired result. In the early stage of her career she was always cast as an ingenue but as she matured she was always the leading lady, heroine, or primary love interest. Her voice remained a favorite for any female starring role at "Theatre Muzeek", and her music discs were always on the top ten sellers planetwide. Even when she retired from the stage she still sang at private gatherings and community and social events. She loved all the glamor, notoriety, and publicity but her private life was very guarded. She even employed a personal security team accompanying her from her penthouse apartment in "The Ethers" to whatever venue she was performing, or party or social event she was attending and back again. So any interested suitor would have to clear an obstacle course to get close to her as she did not allow chance meetings. In her prime as a performer she caught the eye of an off worlder "Xanaaz Zynoplee" from Xantreya, a planet in a galaxy five lightyears away. Xanaaz was a multi currency trillionaire on Jazzo to generate business interest in a portal technology that would make lengthy space travel expedient and affordable. He had seen Audesse's one woman show on the commu-viewer and was enrapt so that he sent a memo to his android administrative assistant to complete a "bio-file" on her within the hour. When the dutiful android sent the bio-file to Xanaaz's commu-viewer along with a compilation of the singer's personal information and music playlist in alphabetical order the smitten man activated the sound system and Audesse's beautiful voice filled his hotel suite. His breath caught and his eyelids slid closed as he listened to her sing about springtime on Jazzo. She sang from her heart with a voice that transcended anyone he had ever heard and captured his usual hyperactive attention with its sonic beauty. From her bio-file he knew she would be a challenge but he was all about not succumbing to challenges. His deep bronze complexion covering a tall athletic frame, chiseled jawline just below a full lipped mouth housing radiant white teeth, intense amber eyes, and fashionably trimmed jet black hair were weapons he used on women on his planet and throughout the galaxy, even his business associates were not immune to his good looks driven by a lucid charisma. He first attended her evening performance at Theatre Muzeek's production of "Songs of Life Atop A Spiral". She was dazzling in a decollete black and white silk gown with a lengthy pearl necklace adorning her long neck and a huge neon red flower at her waist. She was accompanied by a large orchestra of obviously Jazzo's most proficient musicians and choral singers. He had one of the android ushers take a "tech note" to her dressing room introducing himself and inquiring if she would consider a meeting as he was an avid fan. The "tech note" required a verbal reply and he was not surprised by her response which was, "Mr. Zynoplee, I appreciate your enthused affinity for my singing but I don't meet with my fans no matter how wealthy and well known they are. Yes, I'm aware that you are the techno business whiz visiting our planet. I'm glad that you find my singing a point of interest in your otherwise busy schedule on Jazzo. Enjoy your stay here. Goodnight." He smiled to himself, but was undaunted by her response. Returning to his hotel suite he activated his android admin assistant giving it a list of tasks to initiate the next day: to buy out the evening shows at the Theatre Muzeek for an entire week, find a local floral distributor of pink and blue pom-pom flowers, contact his off world gems and geodes mines, and notify his home planet office that his time on Jazzo would be somewhat longer than he originally anticipated. For the next week Xanaaz attended the evening performance at the Theatre Muzeek in formal attire sitting front row center, while the other 1,499 seats were occupied with large bouquets of Audesse's favorite blue and pink pom-pom flowers. She complained to the theater management who advised since the house was bought out for the week and she had a contract to perform unless deathly ill. Being a disciplined performer she determined she could endure one week of one excessive fan. He always stood to his feet and loudly applauded at the very end of the concert. She refused to do curtain calls even when he yelled encore only to enter her dressing room that was crowded with floral arrangements of her favorite flowers which she happily distributed to the orchestra members and choral singers. The following week the concierge in her building called Audesse's android maid advising that an armored hover vehicle was delivering a large container addressed to Miss Bamm. Since Audesse had gone out with friends the android accepted the container taking it up to the penthouse on the floor lift. When Audesse returned the android handed her an envelope containing a chip key. She inserted the key into the slot that opened the container, when opened revealed a treasure trove of precious jewels made of gems of various cuts, faceting, designs and colors. There were even chunky crystal geodes for the living room table or curio case display. She was totally overwhelmed and then she saw the name printed inside the container's lid "Zynoplee Mines". There was no contact information so she had no way to return the millions of credits in jewels he had sent her. Minutes later an advertiser hovercraft printed out the contact info in the sky for her to call Xanaaz. When he answered on the commu-viewer screen his handsome face was smiling when he said, "Miss Bamm, so good of you to call me. I venture that you received the package I sent you. Please don't be offended. I just wanted you to see that I would seriously like to see you socially." Audesse managed to smile back, reminding him that if she did accept an invitation from him it wouldn't mean anything and that she couldn't accept the gift he'd sent. He responded that on his planet Xantreya once a gift had been given it couldn't be returned. Letting out a sigh she finally advised that next week her run at the Theater Muzeek was over and he should contact her with possible outings she might be inclined to accept. He was clearly happy with her response and advised his administrative assistant to send the info to her commu-viewer within the hour and smilingly bade her goodnight, until next week. And so it began: their first meeting was a dinner date at a restaurant in the East Region known as one of the best on the planet, followed by dancing on The Platform, a weekend beach house party with some of Jazzo's most prestigious, influential and beautiful people in attendance, and trips off planet in his state of the art "format ship" traveling at exponentials of light speed that thrilled and frightened her. Xanaaz knew that she was courageous but he also knew he was a techno extremist as some of his colleagues whispered about him so when he took her hand on one of their off planet jaunts and said, "Don't be frightened; I would never risk your life. You are precious to me songbird." Audesse recalled this was the point he won her heart but she did not let him know right away. She studied him and was impressed that he had such knowledge of her career and of music in general. Their courtship lasted for a year until finally on a picnic on a remote island in the Aquavast Sea he presented her with a massive pink diamond solitaire set in platinum. Audesse's eyes widened as he asked the question, "Will you marry me?" Leaning towards him she pressed her lips to his and whispered, "Yes." Their engagement was media wildfire but the enchanted couple were above and beyond being harrassed by it, and kept a sure pace to solidify their relationship leaving no strings untied. Their wedding was a grand affair with members from the bride's and groom's immediate families present, captains of business, industry, and science assembled, and the colorful eclectic Jazzoan music and other creative artisans who floated in like a spectral shower, and even young King Tempo and his betrothed Princess Octiva attended. Audesse was resplendent in a pale pink silk organza gown with her hair brushed into a bun accentuated with

jeweled pins, a string of showy pink pearls adorned her neck, and she held a bouquet of lilies and pom-pom flowers, while the groom wore a tailored light gray formal suit with a small white lily in the buttonhole of his lapel. They were such a gorgeous couple they seemed to radiate a glow as they walked down the aisle as "man and wife". The newlyweds had a year-long honeymoon visiting the most beautiful landmarks on the planet and even off-planet locations, while their new house was being constructed in the South Region. Their new home was on the coast of the Aquavast Sea surrounded by trees and a large garden designed to showcase all of Audesse's favorite flowers and plants. They moved into their huge mansion three months before the birth of their son "Razaf Maximus Zynoplee". Due to immigration laws the baby's last name had to be the mother's "Bamm" for Jazzoan citizenship to apply. So little Razaf had two birth certificates, one from Jazzo his last name as "Bamm" and another from his father's planet Xantreya showing last name "Zynoplee".

The couple doted on the child who thrived, growing chubby and happy natured daily. One day little "Razzie" as his mother called him, made sounds that seemed musical to her ear. Audesse immediately told her husband that they should enroll him in the music academy when he became of age. Xanaaz responded, "Darling, on Xantreya children can start music training as young as six months of age. I'm surprised Jazzo does not have a "First Song Academy". The theory is that young children still remember the music they heard and sang in eternity before being born to whatever planet their parents live on. So you may want to look into it as a project." Audesse being a new mother did not want to divide her time with her son with a project that would take her attention away from him. She did record the "First Song" info in her journal and flagged the date as "Razzie's" first musical event. Unfortunately, the couple was unable to have other children but their son was their complete joy.

As Razaf grew he was increasingly interested in his father's numerous scientific and technical endeavors but he also kept a place for music in his focus because he loved it and his mother wouldn't allow him to forget that he was part "Jazzoan" which meant music could not be ignored. He studied music at "The Jazzoan Music Academy" focusing on voice, keyboarding, and song writing. By his seventeenth birthday he had a jazz fusion quintet, and a contract with the "Skye Music Label" obligating the young man for at least one album per year and three live concerts as well. When he had any free time he would sign into a tutoring droid his father kept updated with data so his son could stay current with the latest scientific and technical developments on Jazzo and off planet. Using the droid he could test his knowledge on the information he was being exposed to and even generate 3D images of Zynoplee laboratories or sites where new and innovative science and technology were being applied since he didn't have time to actually visit them. He was a handsome youngman with his father's bronze complexion, black hair and height but he had his mother's bright hazel eyes and smile. And like his father he was extremely attractive to the female gender of which he had many friends and acquaintances. He was happy as a single man; he was very wealthy, very well educated, and well socially connected. Then at the South Region Summer Jazzo Music Festival he met "Chantelle Cylk Tunz" and everything changed. She was backup singer in a North Region band with a multiple ranged voice from soprano to alto, with a virtuoso scat style, and she was beautiful. Her deep tan complexion covered her voluptuous tall frame, voluminous shiny auburn hair was fashionably styled on her head, her oval face was set with purple eyes fringed by long lashes, a mouth that belonged in a lip color advertisement, and she was articulate and friendly. When he first introduced himself she acknowledged that she knew the leader of "Frequency Five" quintet and the son of Jazzo's wealthiest entrepreneur. She was not at all overwhelmed like most of the young women he met, although she kept referring to him as Mr. Zynoplee until he stopped her. By the end of the festival he felt secure enough to invite her on a date, which she readily accepted. On the first date he took her to the new off planet venue launched by Skyes Music "The Platform" for dinner and dancing. He learned that she grew up in a working class family in a small North Region town. Her parents ran a small "Sing-Along Cafe" which is where she got exposure to scatting and other singing styles. She could have been insulting him for all he knew because he was totally fixated on her expressive purple eyes and her lips that were covered in an orange pink color. When he took her home she thanked him for a lovely evening and quickly placed a kiss on his cheek. He acted just as quick to capture her mouth with his in a lingering kiss. He raised his glazed eyes to hers admitting, "I've wanted to do that all night. I hope you're not offended. Chantelle, would you let me know when I can see you again?" She smiled and said, "I'm going home tomorrow but you can reach me there. Here's my commu-viewer address. I'll wait to hear from you. Goodnight." "You will, goodnight." he replied. He waited until she entered the hotel her band was staying for the festival then hopped in his hover car and drove home.

In the days that followed he was going to the North Region so often his mother noticed and finally asked who the girl was that had captured his attention that he would make a two hour trip three or four times a week. He did not want to reveal anything about Chantelle but his mother was so intuitive, he knew she was a romantic at heart; he also knew that his father had programmed a state of the art camouflage surveillance android designated for protection and gathering non familial information and his mother most llkely already knew, so he told her everything. At twenty-three he felt that Chantelle was the one woman for him and that he wanted to marry her. His parents trusted his judgement and emotional maturity as they had observed his infatuations with "band groupies", "scheming debutantes", "would be singers", and obvious "fortune hunters", but his involvement with Chantelle was different. When she finally came to meet them for a weekend house party his parents were impressed by her style and beauty. She wore a summer dress of pink and black print and complimentary strappy sandals, with her hair was loose and bouncy on her shoulders. She was socially fluent, smilingly navigating through Razaf's family and friends with ease. To his parents her love for their son was apparent in the way she looked at him, touched his hand, and the way she spoke his name. He had asked his father if there was anything like a "purple diamond". Mr. Zynoplee said he only knew the semi precious purple stone "amethyst" but that he'd check with his gemologist and get back to him. The next day his father sent him a commu-viewer message confirming diamonds did come in purple and that his off planet mines had numerous samples he could choose from. He also gave him the name of his jeweler who could make the ring. Razaf laughed to himself because his parents were way ahead of him. It took a week for the diamonds to transport from Zynoplee Mines off planet to Jazzo. He took the diamonds to the family jeweler who helped him chose a ten carat square cut deep purple diamond to be surrounded by paler violet diamonds set in platinum. It took three days for the jeweler to execute the design Razaf had chosen and even he was impressed with the beauty of the large purple diamond surrounded by it's lesser violet sisters. He thought, "Some girl's going to be really happy when she gets this." Razaf showed the finished engagement ring to his mother who gasped at the beautiful symbol of love and kissed her son's cheek giving him her blessing. Enlisting his mother's social secretary and events planner he anonymously rented Chantelle's parent's "Sing Along Cafe" for the surprise engagement party on a weekend. He requested purple decorations and cut flowers and there would be catered food and drinks including a large cake decorated in purple frosting that said "Always My Love". He made a dinner date with Chantelle on the day of the party as a misdirection from the surprise. She had dressed in a stylish evening dress and heels which only heightened her natural beauty. Razaf was to start driving them to a restaurant and then pretend he'd forgotten his computab in the men's room at her parent's cafe so he would have to return and get it. Razah requested she come inside with him because she might need to get her parents to let them into the cafe. Chantelle observed nonchalantly walking towards the cafe entrance, "Seems to be a lot of hovers parked on the street for this time of day." Walking ahead of her Razaf was able to open the door without resistance. Standing aside he let her enter first and when they both cleared the threshold the lights came on to reveal a room full of smiling family and friends. Razaf took the hand of a shocked Chantelle simultaneously "shushing" the happy crowd. He took a small plush box from his pocket and pushing open the lid to reveal the purple diamond ring and said, "Chantelle, love of my life, will you mary me?" With tears streaming from her purple eyes she chokingly said, "Yes." Then regaining her voice she said strongly, "Yes!" Razaf slid the opulent engagement ring on her ring finger, while placing a warm kiss on her lips. A burst of cheers and applause rose up in the festively decorated cafe. Chantelle's parents came forward to hug her and admire the gorgeous ring solidifying love and fidelity, as they initially had doubts thinking the rich young man was toying with her. Also coming up to congratulate the young couple were Razaf's mother and father; Mr. and Mrs. Zynoplee had made the trip north to support their son on this special occasion. Razaf hugged them both and they in turn hugged their son and their soon to be daughter-in-law. Music filled the room and Razaf pulled Chantelle on the floor to dance. She placed her hand on his shoulder and the large diamond flashed a purple light on the walls and ceiling of the cafe creating an ambience of true love that everyone observing felt. After the engagement party the couple determined that three months would be sufficient time to plan and organize their wedding, especially since Razaf's mother put her expert event planner at their disposal who could work wonders for any occasion as she had for their engagement party.

The Zynoplee wedding was the social event of the season. It was held in the chapel adjacent to the Jazzoan Royal Palace which was made available because of recognition of familial ties no matter how distant. Chantelle was beautiful but even more so on her wedding day. The bride wore a designer satiny floating lavender gown which perfectly accented her svelte body. On her head she wore a wreath of showy purple flowers around her auburn hair and she carried a bouquet of purple flowers: a melange of lilies, anemones and ranunculus all tied with purple silk cords. Razaf wore a tailored gray suit much like his father wore when he married his mother. The groom was stellar handsome and many of the young women attending the wedding could not resist staring at him while being a little envious of his bride. His parents sat on the front row of the chapel. Audesse was regal wearing a flamboyant wide brimmed hat adorned with large silk flowers and a bright pink silk dress while her husband was more subdued and elegantly attired in a tailored black suit. They had aged very little and could have easily been mistaken for the bride and groom if they weren't already married.

As was the custom the newlyweds took a year to honeymoon. Razaf's parents gave them access to their private island house in the Midland Ocean. The house had an ocean view from any of its twenty rooms, a garden of fragrant indigenous blooming flowers, a small wharf which moored a yacht named "Xannie's Joy", and there was a pool should they choose not to go down to the pink sand beach. Also his mother's impeccable staff had been dispatched ahead to prepare the house with everything they would need in the way of food, drink and toiletries. Being Xanaaz Zynoplee's son and daughter-in-law also meant that a very covert highly effective security system was present to make sure the couple had no unwanted intrusion to their nuptial bliss. When they got settled in, Chantelle called Audesse to thank her for everything. Audesse advised her that there was no need to thank her and that their North Region house would be ready for them when they returned. However, their honeymoon was cut short six months due to an invitation to attend King Tempo's and Princess Octiva's wedding. They were happy to return for such a happy occasion which also ushered them to move into their new house gifted to them by Razaf's parents. They were beginning life as a genuine Jazzoan married couple. By the end of the year Chantelle announced that she was pregnant with their first child. Audesse and Xanaaz were overjoyed to learn they were grandparents and sent a list of the North Region's prominent prenatal medical contacts to the young parents to be. About the same time King Tempo and Queen Octiva announced they also were expecting Chantelle's pregnancy was textbook with oppressive morning sickness during the first trimester, food cravings for tart fruit desserts and fried foods, and infamous mood swings. Audesse insisted on a well known mid-wife among those in the know called "Materna Humm" who had assisted in delivering some of Jazzo's most prominent citizens and because she did not trust the maternity wards of the public health centers. And so little "Beabop Symbella Bamm-Zynoplee" was born in late spring to much familial fanfare. She weighed seven pounds, had a rosy complexion and reddish fuzz covering her round head, her eyes were either gray or green it was hard to tell, and when she cried her lungs were described as singer quality like her grandmother. Her parents were happy but exhausted due to the fifteen hour labor Chantelle endured causing an emotional drain on Razaf, who felt the "star" mid-wife had not done enough to expedite the birthing process. The midwife was the picture of calm assuring him, "She's fine, the baby is getting into position. Don't worry, just a little longer." You would have thought she referring to an athlete prepping for a sporting event. Audesse and Xanaaz had come to give their nervous son their much needed support. Audesse described her own maternal experience to her blushing son, "I nearly crippled your father's right hand during the ten hours it took to push you into the world. It was no easy feat but well worth the effort." Kissing her son's cheek she praised him for being a good son, a loving husband and new father. Audesse remained with the new parents in the North Region for another week but Xanaaz returned to their home in the South Region to coordinate several business issues and pending projects that only he could complete. Having his own android piloted high speed hovercraft gave him freedom to bypass the commercial hover transportation and he would be home in less than an hour.

Upon arriving at his South Region mansion Xanaaz Zynoplee exercised his patriarchal authority by updating his will to include the newest family member "Beabop Symbella Bamm-Zynoplee". He notified his legal counsel on Jazzo and sent express space courier to Xantreya to update his home planet's records as well. He had also advised his son Razaf to create a will for his new family because it was the smart and responsible thing to do. Xanaaz's other business priority was the finalization and testing of his latest project the "format ship" to revolutionize interstellar travel. The fusion powered "format ship" was designed to format up five stages based on the distance that was being traveled; the farther away the higher the format. With each "format " the ship's flexible hull would make structural changes to accommodate the speed chosen; formats one through four were triangular variations reaching light exponentia eight or eight times the speed of light, while at format five the ship's hull would morph to a rounded bow with a narrow pointed stern reaching speeds light exponentia nine to fifteen or nine to fifteen times faster than light. The ship also provided "bio chambers" for the passengers to ensure their bodily safety at the such extreme speeds. Xanaaz had been testing the prototypes using android pilots making trips between Jazzo and Xantreya a five lightyear distance and these test runs were proven successful. The next step would be a man piloted test flight and since the ship was his own technical design he felt he was best suited to manually pilot his ship. To give his son a change of pace after a nine month period of husbandly duties he would invite Razaf to accompany him when everything was in place for the trip. Currently the ship could only carry three passengers and a pilot and "bio chambers" for each but as soon as the "Jazzo Astronautics and Science Board" reviewed and approved the ship for safety Zynoplee Research and Development would design a larger passenger capacity for the "format ship".

Six months had passed before Xanaaz was able to schedule the manually piloted format ship flight that did not conflict with his or

Razaf's prior obligations. Razaf left his wife and baby daughter at his parent's home since he and his father would be launching their flight from a South Region airbase. A local news station did a human interest story highlighting that South Regions most prominent resident, businessman, and scientist was flying his newest aeronautical creation the "format ship". The craft had just cleared the Jazzo Aeronautics safety review and Mr. Zynoplee and his son would be taking the ship out on its first man piloted maiden voyage. Actually 2 ships would be making the trip, the second ship piloted by the android who had made the original test flights as a precaution should there be any malfunctions. Since the trip was on a strict timetable the scientist and inventor would not give an interview; Mr. Zynoplee and son simply boarded the ship getting clearance from the aeronautic control tower. The two shiny silver ships vertically ascended and quickly accelerated out of sight.

Xanaaz set the coordinates to travel to Xantreya his home planet. He chose format four which was light exponentia eight, which is eight times the speed of light and had the onboard navigation computer to hold this course until they arrived within the Xantreya atmospheric boundary. About one hour into the trip the ship seemed to stop cold but the ship's instruments showed they were still moving. Xanaaz quickly contacted the secondary ship to have it's android pilot to power down, to proceed no further and run diagnostics to show what was causing the ship to stall. The android scanned the spatial coordinates of the primary ship and advised Xanaaz the Sessilum encroachment seemed to be advancing beyond their usual habitat territory and were enveloping his ship preventing any forward movement. Xanaaz remembered he chose not to include the "Light Songs" library in the ship's database which would have been a useful weapon now. He tried for several hours without success to break the hold that was restraining the ship and finally decided to send a coded message to his wife and a general message to his legal and business associates on Jazzo. Razaf also sent a similar coded message to his wife and infant daughter. These messages were transmitted to the secondary ship's database along with all the navigational and technical readings Xanaaz collected from the Sessilum attack on his ship. He continued to transmit scientific data to the secondary ship until the attack on his ship cut off communication to contact the secondary ship. The android had been instructed to remain where it was until Xanaaz's ship went silent and then to return to Jazzo but not to the airbase. Xanaaz had built into the cliffside of his South Region house a three level garage with a 2nd floor "research and development lab", and a 3rd floor "airship hangar". Audesse only knew about the garage level for parking their many hover vehicles as he had not let her know about the 2nd or 3rd floors, only he and ten tech androids had access. The android pilot would relay the primary format ship's information to Xanaaz's legal and scientific staff and coded personal messages to Audesse and Chantelle before accessing the secret aircraft hangar to let all concerned believe both ships had been lost. Following Xanaaz's instructions to use the ship's stealth mode when entering Jazzo's atmosphere and using the transmitted door access code the android seamlessly guided the returning "Format ship" into the hangar, parking it in a corner of the large space to cover it with a tarp. Having completed his tasks the android went to its charge port, powered down until it would be needed again.

Within a few hours the South Region news was broadcasting that "the Xanaaz Zynoplee's maiden voyage in his "Format ship" ran into technical difficulties causing loss of both ships. The story flashed across thousands of Jazzo commu-screens, "The Tragic Format Ships Disappearance." The news also advised "Neither Mrs. Zynoplee or her daughter-in-law were available for any comments." The coded message was sent to Audesse's private commu-cube flashing personal and private, she tearfully listened to her husband's last words to her, "Audesse, my love these grimmy Sessilum are moving outside their known habitat and they've grabbed my ship. I didn't document any of "Light Song" info as I did not feel the need for it on my ship. I've tried to get loose without any success, so beloved it looks like I won't be returning to you. I've sent my legal counsel notice that all my assets are to be transferred over to you. Don't miss me songbird, I'll always be with you in spirit. Our son has sent you his own message to follow mine. Love you now and through eternity. I am forever your loving husband, Xannie." He then quickly included, "Oh and kiss little "Beeky" for me. Love you both!" Xanaaz had never liked "Beabop" for his granddaughter's first name and had insisted on calling her "Beeky" which was a Xantreyan endearment. Audesse went into shock which rendered her speechless and motionless. She sat with tears flowing nonstop down her face.

Chantelle however cried in loud uncontrollable sobs. Baby Beabop's nurse was the only somewhat coherent adult in the large house. Using her employee access for "family emergency contacts" she reached out to Audesse's sisters in the North Region who advised they were already enroute to her home. A shroud of heaviness had enveloped the beautiful house. Audesse's sisters were very attentive to their baby sister and stayed by her side until she came out of the stupor transitioning to inconsolably weep. Her sisters decided to have a South Region doctor they knew examine her. Their doctor friend said she would be glad to come to the mansion to help the stricken lady in her time of need. The doctor gave Audesse a calming sedative and ordered a local chemist to fill a prescription and deliver it as soon as possible to the mansion. The doctor also gave the same treatment to the equally devastated Chantelle. It took a week to get all the tragic details in painful order so that a service could be arranged in memoriam of husband and father Xanaaz Zynoplee and son, husband and father Razaf Bamm-Zynoplee. Unfortunately, the widows of the deceased were still too overwhelmed and sensitive to attend the services so King Tempo gave the eulogy via commu-viewer transmission from the Royal Chapel to honor the two great men who had met with such a tragic end.

It would be several months before Audesse's heart and mind began to recover from heaviness and sadness so that she no longer needed medication or a medical attendant. Chantelle and little Beabop were still resident at the mansion for as long as it took the young widow to be on her own. Audesse finally felt strong enough to go through Xanaaz's personal belongings to determine what to donate to Jazzoan charities or keep. She finally got to a box labeled "Razzie's". She almost succumbed to melancholy but she steeled herself opening the box; her eyes were drawn to her son's baby book. She opened the colorful book and flipped through the pages and stopped at an entry documented "Razzie's Musical Event". She read, "Razzie at seven months exhibited some musical talent. He gurgled out a musical note while playing with a toy. His father told me about "First Song Academies" on Xantreya where babies at six months start musical training. He said that babies remember the songs they sang in eternity before being born. He also suggested I start a Jazzo First Song Academy. Good idea but not now, Razzie is too young and and I'm a new mother." With tears running down her cheeks she called her business coordinator to put an outline together to initiate and realize a Jazzo "First Song Academy". Money was no object, she was a trillionaire and within the week she had a chosen location, architectural drawings and a list of child music education specialists. She also had an interplanetary courier sent to Xantreya requesting any information and suggestions on successfully running a "First Song Academy". It was this project that bought her back to life, it was her rescue. In a year's time the academy was finished; the campus included seven buildings of classrooms, auditoriums, recording, and audio-visual studies. There was also student and faculty housing, a food court, guest friendly gardens, and numerous playgrounds. In the main garden Audesse commissioned a large statue of Xanaaz and Razaf located in the middle of an alley of pom-pom flower bushes which were her favorite flowers. The academy was marketed to the Jazzoan public for children as young as 6 months and Lady Bamm-Zynoplee gave her poignant testimonial about her son "Razzie" being her inspiration broadcast on numerous media. The parents of Jazzo responded in droves contacting the newly opened academy to have their little darlings audition for admittance to the First Song Academy. The auditions were held monthly in the sunny Xanaaz Zynoplee Auditorium facing a glimmering view of the Aquavast Sea. Mothers and fathers with their noisy chubby progeny were provided a small sound amplifier camouflaged in a toy and they would coax the child to sing their pre-birth songs. Mostly the babies would just gurgle or scream, only once in a while a little one sang a melodic "momma, momma, ma, ma" or "aah, aah, aah, aaaah!". None of the young children were disqualified as music teachers were available to give lessons and mentor the "not so talented" for a small fee which was setup as a savings account to be reimbursed whenever the student graduated or chose another non-musical career. For those who exhibited some talent even to the smallest degree these were scholarshipped to study at the "First Song Academy" through age seventeen. Audesse built her life around the academy dedicating the scholarship in the name of her son "Razaf Magnus Zynoplee's First Song Academy Musical Scholarship". She was restored and became vibrant with joy regaining her love of singing. She accepted singing engagements for public and civic occasions as well as weddings, reunions, or anniversaries for family and friends.

Now when she thought of her husband and son it was as if they were present, alive in the moment helping her to make Jazzo's young become proficient and prolific singers and musicians.

CHAPTER 9

After five years Chantelle felt strong enough to be on her own and move back to the North Region with Beabop. Due to popular demand Audesse had begun a North Region First Song Academy which allowed Beabop to continue her studies that were started with South Region First Song Academy. Chantelle also requested Audesse's expertise in decorating her new North Region house. Audesse was glad to lend her sense of style to the house her two favorite people would be occupying; she was happy on so many levels since her life had drastically changed.

When the North Region "First Song Academy" was completed six year old Beabop was enrolled in the singers program and met her current best friend. Jazzalin, Princess but just best friend of Beabop. The girls now stood in Lady Zynoplee's beautifully appointed entryway to welcome her home for a short visit to her grand mansion. Both girls heard the hovercraft driver open the passenger door for "granny" and her strong musical voice as the security system's voice recognition opened the front door for her to enter. Lady Zynoplee smiled as Beabop bolted to hug her screaming, "Granny! You're home!" Still smiling she replied, "Yes, I'm home lovey. Now let me see if you're the young lady I expect you to be." Beabop did an elaborate twirl on tiptoes while granny nodded approvingly. Lady Zynoplee was tall, slim, larger than life woman who didn't look like any "granny" Jazzalin had ever seen. Granny turned her gaze to Jazzalin and said, "Jazzalin come and give me a hug. I don't stand on formality in my house "Princess". You're not exempted from my affections." She held out her arms as Jazzalin shyly walked into the embrace of the land graceful, no lumpy bumpy grandmother body, she could have been a fashion model. She wore a summer green floral print dress which only emphasized this point. Her healthy lavender complexion was flawless; her bright pink hair framing her oval face was shoulder length with a casual upward flip at the ends. She even wore strappy sandals which were being worn by girls years younger than she. Audesse began giving instructions to the housekeeping droids to take her bags upstairs and to run her a bath, then turning to the girls she said, "How about we go out for dinner tonight? I can take you to "Lift A Pinky". What do you say?" Both girls knew "Lift A Pinky" was a trendy restaurant that only the well to do could afford and they knew "Granny" definitely could afford it. They gave a smiling "yes" in response to her inquiry. Actually, Lady Zynoplee was a silent partner of the owner of "Lift A Pinky" Victor Keys. Victor had been a fellow singer when Audesse performed at the "Theatre Muzeek" who had an ongoing complaint that his wife Tsaung was the worst cook on Jazzo. Audesse challenged him to find a solution to his complaint. He responded that he had but he was going bankrupt taking his family out to restaurants for breakfast, lunch, and dinner. After Audesse married and left the "Theatre Muzeek" she remembered her suggestion to Victor and contacted him with a proposal to help him open a restaurant with the best chefs making food every Jazzoan knew and loved and in an ambience that would entice and capture their culinary imaginations. Patrons would be able to reserve tables on one of three floors but the first floor would be restricted to families with young children and a food take out options for those who wanted to picnic in the surrounding landscaped gardens. He salivated with joy and was so excited about the venture he said, "My wife won't need to lift a pinky at any more attempts at cooking. Yes, and that's the name for the restaurant "Lift A Pinky"." Audesse advised she would put up the startup capital and wouldn't require payback, but after the restaurant started to show profit she would receive three percent of that profit and she would always have an assigned table on the restaurant's 3rd floor overlooking the planned flower garden. "Lift A Pinky" took two years from conception to completion and Audesse had fond memories of Xanaaz escorting her for the restaurant's grand opening and how romantic it had been. The restaurant was an instant success drawing customers from all over the South Region and gaining popularity planetwide causing "Lift A Pinky" to become a global corporation.

Victor and his wife Tsaung had both gained considerable weight being restaurateurs but they were never happier. Tonight Audesse would take the girls there and as she had not been there since Xanaaz's death.

Dinner at "Lift A Pinky" proved to be the second bright spot in the day for the threesome, Audesse's homecoming being the first one. From the time they entered the welcoming building the staff was on alert by the owner Mr. Keys to provide Lady Zynoplee and party with optimum courtesy and customer service. The hostess greeted Audesse by leaving her entry post to personally escort her and the girls to the floor lift and advised that her waiter would be at her table waiting to take their orders. Reaching the third floor they saw their table was ready with a vase full of blue and pink pom-pom flowers in the center and three place settings around. Jazzalin felt like she and Beabop could have been Audesse's daughters because she was so noticeably young and attractive. She had chosen to wear a flouncy white dotted on black background dress with a large silk black flower in her hair, she was stunning but totally unaffected by the admiring glances of the other diners there. Once seated Audesse ordered her favorite grilled poultry, chopped summer vegetables in cream sauce with noodles and buttery rolls. She each had a carafe of house wine which she allowed the girls to have a half glass. The girls were not so provincial in their selection both choosing Bova patties grilled served on buns topped with special sauce and a salad with carb fries on the side. They also had an icy "Blue Fling" carbonated drink which was served in special glasses mimicking fling fields. The orders for the three were substantially large and unable to be eaten in one setting so there would be leftover bags and they ordered desserts to go. When they returned to the mansion Audesse strongly advised the girls, "You two go straight to bed, now. I'm leaving early tomorrow morning and I want you to see me off." Normally the girls would grumble but they were both too full and too tired to engage in any confrontations. They all took the floor lift upstairs, the girls to the second floor guest rooms while Audesse continued to the third floor suite she once shared with her late husband. Inside her beautifully decorated room with gradient shades of pink, orange, and blue adorning the walls and filled with eclectic sumptuous furnishings she undressed and put on her robe, then going to her huge walk-in closet she began to search for suitable ensembles for the East Region

Summer Festival and for business meetings as well. She chose a color palette of pastels: turquoise, lavender, orange, yellow, and green for the festival and two dark business suits for any more somber social meetings there. Her android maid packed her selections in a roomy travel case and left her room. How she loved her life now that she had the "First Song Academies" and a singing career, though limited, was active on her terms. She always said "goodnight" out loud to Xanaaz and Razaf before she fell asleep every night, seeing them smiling back at her in her mind's eye.

In the morning Audesse used the guest room comm-links to wake the girls who were accustomed to getting up much later than she was. With their eyes still puffy and barely open Beabop and Jazzalin made their way downstairs to the kitchen where the kitchen android had laid out a breakfast of purple tea, muffins, toasted cheese sandwiches, and the take home "epi-fruit tart" from "Lift a Pinky" the night before. The smell of food energized the girls to wake up as they immediately started to ingest the simple breakfast. Between bites Beabop said, "Good morning Granny. Thanks for waking me up so I wouldn't want to miss saying goodbye." Audesse responded by placing a kiss on her granddaughter's forehead and proceeded to pour herself a cup of tea advising, "Now, I'm singing in concert tomorrow and I want you two to watch the commu-transmission. Also I'm going to be speaking with the region elders and social leaders about starting an East Region "First Song Academy". It seems the "First Song Academy" has made a favorable impression there, so I'll be away for as long as it takes to finalize the project. It seems there will soon be First Song Academies in all eight regions. What a prospect!" Jazzalin who had not spoken cleared her throat and said, "Lady Zynoplee I feel you are the most progressive woman on Jazzo and it's my honor to know you." Lady Zynoplee replied, "Thank you Jazzalin. I feel you are just as progressive young princess. Your future will reveal this to you. Now let's finish breakfast as I'm on a tight schedule and I want to depart on time."

At the front entrance of the mansion Audesse hugged her granddaughter and her best friend bidding them goodbye before entering the luxurious hovercraft to travel to East Region. She made sure to tell them that she had programmed a driver/ pilot android to be available for any trips they wanted to take to the many nearby shopping hubs, summer festivals, as well as daytime concerts in the area. She also admonished them not to annoy Adagio since he is too old for them and he's not their chaperone. Both girls stared at her with wide eyes unable to reply and thinking what did she know. The driver started the hovercraft engines and Audesse spoke loudly from the passenger compartment, "Goodbye dearies. I'll call you when I arrive. Enjoy your summer! Love you both." With that the rear window closed as the silver streamline hovercraft rose upward and was soon out of sight. Returning to their rooms the both got dressed before meeting in the library to discuss their plans for the day. Being a little melancholy over Audesse's quick visit and departure the girls decided that only shopping would be the remedy to raise their spirits. Beabop's wrist holotrans began to "ping" an incoming message and generating the smiling face of Adagio who said, "Hi, Bea! What are you two up to today?" "Well, Granny told us not to socialize with you because you're too old and not a proper chaperone," Beabop said, smirking. Adagio replied, "You know our friend the Princess is under constant surveillance." "Yeah, she's got issues", Bea giggled. Continuing she said, "We're going to the "Shop-Along Center"., Granny programmed a driver android for us to use. Tomorrow there's the "Oonee Berry" Festival and we'll have to plan something after that. What do you have in mind?" Adagio replied, "Well, I'm busy with family business today and tomorrow but midweek mother is throwing a cook-out at our beach house. It's not really a cook-out because mother hired a chef from "Lift A Pinky"and they are catering everything, a divine yum-fest. So it's really a catered picnic party with live music. I'm inviting you two to come. Will that be acceptable since you said I'm off limits?" Beabop responded, "Adagio, Granny's gone for another two weeks so it's no problem to accept your gracious invite for both of us. Thanks for the invitation. Got to run! Jazzalin's already in the hover and screaming for me to come on. Send your address and directions to your beach house to my holotrans mail. I'm activating the security system and I need to focus. Talk to you later!" Adagio laughed and replied, "I'll send the directions for the "cook-out". Be sure to dress casual and bring your swimsuits. Bye!"

The girls spent the day in the "Shop Along" shopping hub going from every seventh floor teen specific shop. Both girls had unlimited credit vouchers which they were very adept at using so much so that they needed two store droids to assist them to the hovercraft with their purchases. Once back at Granny's the girls tried everything on and congratulated themselves on being true fashion geniuses. The next day the girls attended the local village's "Oonee-berry" festival. They wore silly yellow and purple hats of the farmers, joined the dancing in the streets to cacophonous farmland jazz all the while gorging on oonee-berry candies, cookies and tarts, and washing it down with the yummy bubbly non-fermented oonee-berry cordials. When they got home both girls were too tired and nauseous from the oonee-berry festival and it's fare so they showered and went right to bed. The next day the girls woke up early to get ready for Adagio's cook-out. Jazzalin chose a fluorescent orange halter dress and matching sandals and gathered her thick purple mane in a top knot accented with a silky scarf. She packed a yellow swimsuit for the beach. Beabop chose a red and white summer dress and red slip-on shoes and she packed a playful abstract print one piece swimsuit. Adagio had transmitted his beach house address to Beabop's holotran receiver which she uploaded to the navigation system of the hovercraft Granny had assigned her. The compliant android confirmed, "Coordinates received and ready to execute Miss Beabop." Beabop replied, "Good, but we're not ready yet. Give us ten minutes." True to her word Beabop and Jazzalin hopped into the hovercraft within the promised ten minute window. The android maneuvered the vehicle skyward and sped off to Adagio's coastal summer house. When they were near the house they could see multiple shiny chauffeured hovercrafts parked on the long curved driveway of the beautiful blue building. Smaller sporty hovercrafts were tethered to the roof tether stations of the large house hanging in the air like colorful inflated toys. A joyous spirit pulsed from the house to their hover car and both girls squealed in anticipation of "mega stellar" fun in store for them. Adagio had included parking instructions with his directions which the android flawlessly executed into the family garage parking next to his sharp bright blue hovercraft. Adagio suddenly appeared to open the passenger door for the girls who scrambled out with youthful exuberance. Beabop exclaimed, "Adagio, this place is quizit!!! Is the whole village here?" "No, just a few friends and family", he replied. Turning to Jazzalin he made an elaborate bow and said, "Princess, so glad to see you graced us with your presence."

Jazzalin rolled her eyes and said, "Stop being sarcastic and get us to the party!" A big smile formed across his handsome face as he led the way to the rear garden with its covered courtyard, bright colored tents were scattered over the spacious lawn, and a small stage for entertainment. The girls recognized the music in the air was by "Holo-Sonic" and were duly impressed. The members of this jazz group were graduates of their academy "The North Region First Song Academy" and had created the "holo instrument" technology which allowed them to play any instrument holographically. The four musicians could generate an entire orchestra or just a quartet holographically. Today the jazz group was an eclectic jazz fusion quartet playing energizing and heady sounds.

As the three stepped into courtyard they saw a tall slender woman with pale lavender complexion and a stylish mane of multi pastel hair. She wore a flowy fabric dress that mimicked wings as she went from guest to guest like a large "flitterfly". Adagio piped up, "Mother! Here are some friends I want you to meet." The woman turned towards Adagio and party to reveal her beautiful face. The girls had seen her in all kinds of fashion media since they were little girls, "Sylphine Spectra Ooma" was a fashion icon. She was a Ziggabim wild child raised on deserts of the South Region riding sinewy long necked "eqqs" and herding their fat "bova" cattle with her father and brothers. She was discovered when a naturalist photographer used her image in an article about Ziggabim families and their customs. She was an unrelenting beauty archetype: lithe, voluptuous, with large lavender eyes, full lips, amazing complexion, with bright pink hair. Within a few weeks of the publication of the article one of Jazzo's largest fashion and cosmetic conglomerates had signed her to a contract. Her face embellished advert signs, commercial media as well as influencing fashion and make-up and the toy industry through a look alike doll. She eventually met, was successfully wooed by and married to Hamilton Skyes to become "Slyphine Spectra Ooma-Skyes". The girls now knew where Adagio got his awesome good looks. With a musical sounding voice she chimed back to her son, "Darling, you know I want to meet all your friends especially the special ones." "Mother, may I introduce "Princess Jazzalin" and "Miss Beabop Bamm-Zynoplee." The beautiful woman actually curtsied to Jazzalin and said very formally, "So nice to meet you "Princess" as I missed you when you attended "Daggee's" birthday party at our Ethers house, but I did meet Miss Beabop at the Ether's party. So glad you both could join us again for fun and festivities today. There's all kinds of food and drink and if you feel like swimming there's a tramm station to take you down to the beach. Let the house droid take your bags to the storage area for safe keeping. Now, girls do have maximum enjoyment as your hostess it's my job to see that you do." Jazzalin was overwhelmed at the warmth the beautiful woman had directed to her and Beabop and could only reply, "Thank you, you are most kind." When his mother was out of earshot Jazzalin growled at Adagio, "Why didn't you tell me your mother was famous?" He replied, "She's my mother and I forget that she was a fashion icon before marrying my father. Come on let's see what food we can grab and take to the beach with us." The threesome perused all of the colorful food tents and selected goodies they could easily transport to the beach for an impromptu picnic. They remembered to retrieve their swimsuits before heading for the cliff tram to start their fun and maybe some minimal relaxing. Just before the trio reached the tram a service droid approached the and announced, "Mr. Adagio, Your father is calling to speak to you privately in his office commu-viewer." Turning to the girls he said apologetically, "Sorry, hopefully it's not too demanding an issue. Dad's grooming me for so much family business lately. I'll catch up to you as soon as I'm done." Jazzalin responded, "Don't stress yourself. We know all about getting groomed for the family business ordeal. Don't we Beabop?" Nodding her head "yes" as she chewed a mouthful of battered fried meat on-a-stick, rapidly taking another bite. As Adagio turned back to the rear entrance of the house the girls took seats on the cliff tram which made its way to the beach below. The beach was equipped with little dressing rooms which allowed Jazzalin and Beabop to change into their swimwear in minutes and make a run to blue-green waters of the "Aquavast Sea". After several minutes of wild screaming cavorting they took time to dive into the picnic food they had bought from the backyard buffet while enjoying the music of "Holo-Sonic" due to the Skyes amazing sound system. Thirty minutes had past when Adagio joined them on the beach by which time they had devoured the majority of the picnic food. Adagio advised them he would have a service droid bring down more goodies. The service droid did bring a large platter of assorted sandwiches, sweets and a crowd of female Adagio enthusiasts wearing pretty much just their smiles. Realizing that this was no longer a silly teenager environment Jazzalin and Beabop gathered their things and took the tram back up to the house. Mrs. Skyes met them as they stepped off the tram and offered to give them a tour of the beach mansion. She showed them the large entertainment room and library, then a beautiful atrium and art gallery, as well as, a state of the art kitchen which was occupied by the "Lift A Pinky" staff continuously turning out scrumptious food for her guests. The girls were very impressed by the attention this fashion icon and billionaire's wife was showing them. Suddenly her attention was captured by a service droid and she apologized to them that she would need to handle "this" whatever "this" was. The girls graciously thanked her and they returned to the patio to listen to the great music and get a second helping of the "quizit" food provided by their hostess. After another hour they realized they had maxed out their party spirit and wanted to go home. Adagio was still being cooed over by a flock summer beach beauties as he should be since he was in his prime at eighteen years old, physically gorgeous, and heir to a billionaire fortune and with all of this favor he was amazingly kind and pleasant. It could be said "his mother raised him right". The two girls found Granny's hovercraft in the garage. Beabop gave verbal commands to the android chauffeur that they would be returning to Granny's. Just as they got to the garage Adagio showed up breathless his hair and torso still wet from the beach. In tandem the girls thanked him for the inviting them and assured him it was everything and more than they expected, both tiptoeing to give him a peck on the cheek. Their hovercraft passenger door swung open and they hopped inside waving and chorusing "Bye Adagio. You throw a great party even in the daytime!!!" He smiled and waved back as their hovercraft exited the garage and followed it's coordinates back to the Granny Zynoplee's mansion. As the hovercraft entered Granny's garage the android driver spoke, "Miss Beabop and Princess Jazzalin, a service android at Lady Skyes bought a box to the vehicle just before you decided to leave the party. It's here in the front seat and there's commu-note attached." Commu-notes were inexpensive verbal attachments that were scannable to any physical surface making handwritten notes obsolete on Jazzo. The note would blink the designated party or parties name(s) until the designated party or parties identified themselves to get the message. Beabop chimed up loud enough to trigger the note, "This is Beabop, give me the note please." The automated note voice responded, "Thank you Miss Beabop." The note then took on the voice of its sender Lady Sylphine Skyes, "Hi, girls Lady Skyes here. So sorry I was too distracted to say goodbye but I was alerted by my personal assistant that you were going to the garage so I had the kitchen staff pack up an assortment of goodies for you to take home. Again so glad you came today and I hope to see you both socially again in the future. Enjoy and goodnight!" By this time both girls were out of the hover and opening the front door on the passenger side to see the sizeable pink pastry box with a "Lift A Pinky" logo printed on the top. Without any decorum they both lifted the top and with a surprised intake of breath they marveled at the collection of confections inside. There were fruit tarts, cookies, bars, iced rolls of all kinds and even small savory pies, it would take them at least the rest of the week to finish this feast. The box was actually too heavy for them to carry inside. Beabop summoned the kitchen droid to carry the box into the kitchen. The girls agreed to call Lady Skyes to thank her for her eclectic largesse in the goodies she'd sent home with them. All in all the day had been a success and even though Adagio wasnot a relative he was as much a "big brother" to them both and they were happy to be included in his social circle. They decided to shower and dress for bed then maybe watch the news about the meetings on Audia Prime since it was a reality that involved their entire planetary system. Their good intentions fizzled out as they both fell asleep within minutes of getting into their beds and turning on the "current events" stream which the auto monitor turned off in each girls' room after recognizing they were fast asleep.

CHAPTER 10

On Audia Prime the Planetary Elders Council headed by King Tempo were all assembled in the High Council Chamber to brainstorm the current threat of the Sessilum encroachment. The Sessilum had recently sent a transmission of staticy cryptic noise which a planetary interpreter had laboriously deciphered as their attempt to communicate with the Council. With help from the onsite technicians the interpreter modified the translation system enabling it to decipher, "You Symphonea virulent vermin we are notifying you we will not succumb to the weapon you have infiltrated into our habitat. We demand you cease your weapon from causing light quakes with aftershocks and tremors. We will destroy it just as we did to the projectile launched into our habitat thirteen years ago. We crushed it, we obliterated it! You will remove your weapon immediately or we will unleash lethal destruction on your entire planetary system!" The message stopped and only a fading sibilant growl remained. Everyone in the Council chamber was astounded by the hateful message. King Tempo remembered that 13 years ago Xanaaz Zynoplee's "format ships" had disappeared while enroute to his home planet and now he knew the Sessilum were responsible. The King addressed the other Council members, "Fellow Councilmen, our enemy is accusing us of having infiltrated some kind of weapon into their habitat, which is entirely untrue. We need to find out what this weapon is the enemy says we have infiltrated into their territory and we need to compose a reply to the Sessilum that can uncover the identity of our unknown ally without escalating this already festering situation." Turning his gaze to the planetary interpreter team the King continued, "Interpreters please initiate this transmission on the Sessilum frequencies in reply to their statement. In response to your recent transmission accusing the "Symphonean Planetary Alliance" of infiltrating a weapon into your habitat, we absolutely refute any aggressive actions of any kind against your habitat. We have no knowledge of the weapon you are referring to, although the incident of thirteen years ago was a Jazzoan citizen in transit to planet "Xantreya" when he was aggressed upon by your habitat." The nervous linguistic experts clutched their translator tablets adjusting them from the general Symponean languages to the scratchy static frequencies used by the Sessilum as speech. Confirming the King's reply between the interpreters the message was sent to their adversary. Within a few minutes a noisy Sessilum transmission accessed the commu-trans in the Council Chamber saying, "You vermin somehow were able to get the weapon past us. The weapon is causing light quakes and rhythmic temors all throughout our habitat. We demand that you remove your weapon from our habitat immediately or we will unleash lethal destruction on your entire planetary system. We demand you remove "Lilitine and Luling" now!!!" The transmission came to an abrupt snarling stop.

The Symphonea Planetary council members were thoroughly baffled by the Sessilum using feminine proper names "Lilitine and Luling" for the weapon. King Tempo cleared his throat and volunteered a theory to the council that could possibly shed some light on the "weapon", "Fellow councilmen, my esteemed professor and mentor "Dr. Lew Syd" related that centuries ago when our sister planet "Shalla" was pulled into the Sessilim habitat there was a group of "light song" zealots residing on the planet. These zealots were either unable to get off the planet or refused to leave the planet for some reason. But the zealots excelled in the "light songs" in heart and spirit which allowed them to create a safety zone which the Sessilim aggressive assimilation couldn't penetrate. "Lilitine and Luling" sounds like names of zealots, probably the last two survivors. We need to see if we can get the Sessilim to let us speak with this weapon, our unexpected "ally"." Turning to the group of interpreters King Tempo dismissed them all except the senior interpreter and said, "Interpreter we need you to compose an inquiry to the Sessilim requesting the coordinates of the "weapon" so that we can best remove it from their habitat. What an interesting development to find we have someone in the enemies camp that's giving them grief and hardship. Hurry now and show me the message before sending it." The interpreter left the council chamber for several minutes, then returned with the composed inquiry and showed it to King Tempo who read it out loud to the council members, "We are requesting the coordinates of this weapon so we can most effectively remove it from your habitat. Please provide this information to facilitate a speedy extrication of the weapon from your habitat. Your immediate response is requested." The King returned the senior interpreter's translation screen, nodding his approval to send the message to the Sessilim. The interpreter keyed the message into the translation system which transmitted it out into the darkness of the Sessilim habitat. Within minutes an incoming transmission providing astral coordinates was received by their navigation computer which mapped the location and contact frequencies of the "weapon". The onsite scientific team set about sending out transmissions per the coordinates received requesting a response to the Symphonea Planetary Alliance offering ready assistance to help them leave the Sessilim habitat. The message was sent multiple times over a period of an hour. Then finally voices speaking in unison came through the council chamber transmitter, "We are responding to your message. We are Lilitine and Luling daughters of Shalla zealots pulled into this hostile environment centuries ago. We are receptive of any assistance from the Symphonea Planetary Alliance to exit this oppressive place." King Tempo responded, "I am King Tempo leader of the Symphonea Planetary Alliance and we want to thank you for responding to our message. Please bare with me but I must inquire how is it possible that you are alive in the Sessilim habitat when no one ever drawn into their habitat has survived?" Again in unison the voices answered,,"King Tempo our parents were a part of a light song community who lived in a mountainous region of "Eversong". So peacefully remote were they that they did not realize that Shalla had succumb to the disaster of being drawn into the Sessilum dark assimilation until on their annual trek to the nearest city Chantillon for supplies. It was then their light guardians revealed the scorched terrain of the city beyond the barrier, and would not allow them to go further informing them that their small village was the only remaining one on what used to be their planet. Their light guardians ventured out to the dead areas of the planet and were able to gather enough information about the enemy

Sessilim advising that as long as our light songs were sung daily we would be safe from assimilation indefinitely. Our parents "Lilta" and "Joen" were still very young when this tragedy took place and had not come into full induction of the light songs and their use as weapons against darkness. The seven village elders began to mentor all the villagers into the escalated knowledge of the light songs. After all the villagers were proficient both adults and children the seven elders were translated to Astral Keep. Eventually our parents realized they were light compatible, their thoughts and inclinations identical, so they became betrothed and shortly married. Individually they were outstanding light singers surpassing the elders who had taught them but as a couple they were apexual. They regulated seasons within our village, caused crops to grow, kept water flowing, as well as prolonging the lives of themselves and the other villagers. As high masters of the "light songs" they created an environment through their daily singing of the light songs which allowed us to live within the light's security and provision. Our mother became pregnant within the light shelter and with nine months of daily infusion of our parent's faithful light song litanies we were anointed and imprinted with light knowledge while in the womb. Mother said we were born with our eyes open and full of light. By our first birthday we were humming along with our parents when they sang the light songs. As we grew older the light songs words and music were intuitive, and we joyously sang them everyday. The Light Guardian became our teacher and mentor meeting all of our learning needs giving special insights into the words and music of the traditional light songs. We were even taught how to create our own new light infused songs. Over time many villagers became laxed in singing the light songs causing entire families to vanish from the light shelter. The Light Guardian explained that the disappearing villagers had succumbed to resentment feeling they should not have to sing the light songs anymore which made them susceptible to Sessilim monitoring frequencies which pulled them into their habitat. The village's population decreased until only our family and our farmland remained within the shelter. For a very long time our parents remained healthy and alive with us until our thirteenth birthday they came to us and said, "Daughters our souls are being called to "Astral Keep" by the Creator as you are to continue here with the Light Guardian to complete your education in use of the light songs." They imparted the light song mantle equally between us and as we joined together singing a medley of light songs they were translated, their dear bodies becoming light and caught away from us. The Light Guardian comforted us as we were sad to see our parents leave us. We continued to be tutored by the Light which often take our form to allow us to relate in the absence of our parents. The Light taught us that it tolerated no darkness of the irrhythmic greedy Sessilim who have slithered beyond their borders to threaten planetary systems, stars, and even galaxies. We were assured by our mentor that at the appointed time the Sessilum would be destroyed out of existence. We are kept young inside the light shelter but we are no longer children and the Light Guard has told us that the appointed time for us to leave this limited hateful environment was fast approaching. We were deeply saddened when the brutish Sessilum caught and killed the travelers thirteen years ago. The Light could not console us as we watched the Sessilim snarl and taunt the travelers until their lives were snuffed out. King Tempo the Light Guard captured a memory from the traveler's mind, which disclosed that there was a second format ship which the brute Sessilum darkness did not catch which was safely returned to planet Jazzo. If you could have that ship come within the outer boundary of these coordinates the Light Guard will transport us on board so we can go to "Astral Keep". The Light Guard will not allow the Sessilum to harm us and will annihilate them after we have successfully vacated this place. In the meantime we sing so that we are surrounded with songs of deliverance. We await your reply." The twin zealots' transmission ended.

King Tempo jumped to his feet and advised the other Council Members that he needed to speak with someone from his home office on Jazzo. As he walked to his private suite the wheels in his mind had flashed the name Hamilton Skyes who would have the access to locate the missing "format ship" the twins had enlightened him had safely returned to Jazzo. The King thought to himself that Hamilton Skyes had already been helpful by providing a scientific report about the Sessilum encroachment and his sphere of influence would most likely know where the format ship was hidden. Once inside his elegantly furnished private quarters King Tempo sat down at his desk and activated the planetary commun-tran entering Hamilton Skyes private code requesting him to contact him as soon as possible on a matter of the highest urgency. In his North Region top floor office Hamilton Skyes was finishing up a business meeting with a new client when his android administrative assistant notified him that an urgent planetary communique from King Tempo was holding in his office. The busy mogul acknowledged that he would take the call as soon as possible. Entering his office Hamilton activated the vizi-com screen allowing the planetary call to connect and show King Tempo's stern tired face. The King greeted the other man, "Good morning Mr. Skyes." Without waiting for any response the King continued, " I'm contacting you about a highly urgent issue compounding the current Sessilum threat. We have been informed that Mr Zynoplee's second "format ship" which accompanied him 13 years ago returned safely to Jazzo. The Planetary Alliance is requesting your assistance because of your sphere of influence and diverse social contacts to locate the missing ship. We need the ship to be found as it is needed in this tense issue with the Sessilum." Hamilton left his desk to walk to the wall of windows of his seventy fifth floor office to gaze out on the buzzing hovercraft traffic of the city at both eye and surface levels as he reviewed the King's description of him which was a veiled insult because what the King really meant was "you associate with the scum of our planet", but he was not who he was by responding to veiled insults. He was very enthusiastic that the King was seeking his influence and counsel regarding the Sessilum aggression. He smiled to himself because his priority was personal and his family came first so whatever the King wanted would have a royal price. He listened closely as the King continued, "As I said we have it on good authority the second format ship returned to Jazzo safely and is integral in a rescue mission. I believe the ship most likely returned to a secret hangar somewhere on the Zynoplee estate but I can't send legal authorities to search Lady Zynoplee's estate as that would cause a political and social scandal on top of everything else. No, this has to be an inside job. If you educate your son with just the essential importance of locating the ship and with his open door relationship with Lady Zynoplee's granddaughter he could leisurely scan the property and see if the ship is there. There is a time constraint as Lady Zynoplee is due to return to her home in another ten days. We would like this to be unknown to her. What do you say?" The King finally gave Hamilton leave to speak, "Your Majesty, thank you for considering me and my family instrumental in this high planetary drama. Your Majesty for the requested service which involves my son "Adagio", I require it documented that Princess Jazzalin is betrothed to my son in marriage on her seventeenth birthday. The betrothal would need to be in writing bearing the royal seal and signet. No action to locate the ship will proceed until the document is transmitted to my viz-com for recording in my "e-data" file pending printing it. These are my terms to expedite your request." Both men were silent. King Tempo wanted to argue but there was too much at stake for him to posture as an overprotective father. The betrothal was three years away, maybe his son might fall in love with one of their contracted screech queens and Jazzalin would not be obligated. Jazzalin was a free spirit and he knew she would not accept an arranged marriage, there would be resentment, anger, and emotional alienation. King Tempo finally spoke, "This is a high price but there's too much at stake to delay the search for the ship. I reluctantly concede to your terms. I'll have the document generated within the hour and sent to you along with contact directions to submit your findings to my private viz-com. Mr Skyes, I trust you will keep your word. Oh, and you cannot divulge this to your wife, at least not until this thing comes to an end." Hamilton said, "Your Majesty, I am a man of my word and when I get the betrothal document I will start the search for Zynoplee's format ship. I am humbled to be considered to carry out this task for the Symphonea Planetary Council and for our planet Jazzo. So I don't want to delay the search getting started. I'll remain in my office until your transmission comes through. I thank you for the opportunity to serve the our planetary system." King Tempo let out a deep breath and answered, "You've shown yourself to be a resourceful Jazzo citizen and in this hour I am honored to know you and I will remember how you've been accessible with useful information. I'm going to end this call now so we can begin to finish this drama." The King's call disconnected and Hamilton Skyes smiled again that he had navigated the conversation with the King without it getting into a battle of wills. It was obvious with the ease King Tempo had acquiesced regarding betrothing his daughter this issue was beyond personalities. He could not tell Sylphine about the betrothal just yet, but he could wait. She was a royal watcher. Since she was raised in the Ziggabim wilderness she had come to respect the structure of Jazzoan royalty and she admired Princess Jazzalin often referring to her as "darling girl". She would go supernova to know that in three years Jazzalin would be her daughter-in-law. His wife had always wanted to have access to the "royal's" world, now she did. He notified his admin assistant to locate his son. The admin advised him Adagio was at their beach house. He would call him as soon as the King fulfilled the agreement which would make his son a member of the royal family.

CHAPTER 11

Jazzalin woke from her sleep, stretching out a yawn as she realized it was 9:30 morning time and she had overslept. Hopping out of bed she grabbed her robe and ran down the hall to Beabop's room. She faced her friend who stood in front of her smiling. Jazzalin took her hand and pulled her to her brightly colored bathroom which adjoined her bedroom. Jazzalin commanded, "Wash up! I'll run downstairs and have the droid get breakfast going. We can dive into the box of goodies Adagio's mother gave us with big cups of purple tea. And we can plan out our day." Running downstairs, Jazzlin advised the waiting kitchen droid to lay out the pastries in the "Lift A Pinky" pink box and to make a big pot of purple tea. Music began to fill the air as Beabop had activated the house's excellent sound system playing the jazz fusion by "Cosmic Waunda Group". Jazzalin knew the music and her first soprano voice caught the melody and effortlessly followed it while dancing around the kitchen before running back upstairs to get herself groomed and dressed. Both girls came downstairs to find their breakfast arrayed on the kitchen table. As always they ate with healthy appetites with a steady stream of girlish chatter. They plotted out their schedule for Jazzalin's last three days of summer vacation. Today they would take a day trip in Granny's hover car to local museums as well as visiting a nearby Ziggabim village to shop for their handmade jewelry and souvenirs. The next day they would spend the day at the "Shop-Along" Center to see the latest summer Vizix feature and most of all they would enjoy being thirteen year old friends who have common interests and tastes, but there was a melancholy air about them because their summertime together was ending soon. On their last day together they decided to listen to Granny's mega music collection, and sadly get Jazzalin packed up for home. Queen Octiva sent Jazzalin a reminder to her commutran that the royal hovercraft would arrive at 10:00 morningtime on Firstday to convey her home. Tears formed in Jazzalin's eyes as she realized her going home would change her life, home schooling. No daily fun and music with her best friend Beabop. It was too much to think about, so she started to sing, "My heart is soaring above it all and nothing can break its climb. Little flit fly, fly, fly in the blue, blue open sky. Creator see me here so far but so near and make me strong as I fly along in the blessed atmosphere!" Finishing her made up song on a high note she felt better able to face her last vacation day.

As arranged on Firstday at 10 morningtime the royal hovercraft was parked in front of the Zynoplee mansion's front entrance. Dressed conservatively Jazzalin was ready and waiting in the large foyer with Beabop standing by her side. The girls hugged and confirmed that they would see each other next week for her birthday party. The service droid took Jazzalin's luggage along with multiple shopping bags and put them into the utility compartment of the hovercraft. Holding hands the girls walked to the shiny silver vehicle and said goodbye again. Jazzalin climbed into the plush passenger seat while the driver droid closed the door. Jazzalin waved to Beabop from the window as the hovercraft lifted into the blue sky and in seconds was speeding back to the North Region and to the royal residence. She slumped back into the plush cushioned back seat and closed her eyes to nap for the one hour flight time it would take to get to the North Region and home. Her summer had developed into a bright memory she would imprint on her memory forever. She would always love Beabop for rescuing her from the royal beach house and taking her to Granny's South Region mansion and the daily fun they had there. It had been quizit.

Jazzalin was roused by a bell tone and the android's voice saying, "Princess Jazzalin we will be descending to the royal residence momentarily, please fasten your seat belt. Welcome home." The hovercraft made a soft landing into the circular driveway of the royal palace. The droid opened the passenger door for Jazzalin and she dashed out to run inside and there in the doorway was her mother Queen Octiva. The Queen embraced her and kissed her forehead and whispered, "Welcome home darling. I see you got some sun and maybe put on a few well needed pounds. How was your trip?" Jazzalin braced herself so she would not cry and said, "Mommy, glad to be home and it was a quizit vacation. I slept the whole way here and I'm famished. Can the maid bring some lunch?" The Queen took Jazzalin's hand all the while giving instructions to the maid to bring in the prepared lunch into her office which was a small pink and lavender salon adjacent to the family drawing room. The two walked into the dainty room which reflected the Queen's aesthetic of a cloistered high ranking female, soft furnishings, vases of hothouse flowers wafting their perfume and a museum of her loved ones and paintings displayed on the walls. The maid using a serving trolley brought in a large tray of assorted sandwiches and pastries, sliced fruits and vegetables with dips, a small pink frosted layer cake, and a frosty pitcher of punch. Jazzalin took a plate and started to pile on her favorite sandwiches and fried chips along with a large glass of punch, she had skipped breakfast at Granny's being too hyper about coming home. Her mother took a plate of cut fruit and a smaller glass of the punch and she looked at daughter and said, "Jazzalin I want your input on the arrangements for your birthday party. My event planner suggested a "pink and purple" color scheme, a multi tier cake decorated with musical instruments or other objects of your choice, large sauce and sausage pies, a self service drink fountain for carbonated drinks, cookies and sweet bars, frozen fruit cream, and take home goody bags. What do you think?" Still munching a bite of sandwich she mumbled out, "It sounds great so far but I'd like to choose the music. And Mommy I'd like to invite Adagio Skyes and his mother Lady Sylphine. He's a little older but he has been very nice to me on more than one occasion and his mother is quizit." Her mother smiled and said, "I'll send the invitation express. So finish your lunch and you can run upstairs and take a nap." Jazzalin nodded while continuing to fill her mouth with chips, sandwich, fruit and sips of punch thru a straw. Coming from behind her desk Queen Octiva kissed her hungry offspring's cheek and left to check on something in another part of the palace. Jazzalin finished lunch with a healthy slice of the sweet pinkberry cake before proceeding upstairs to her bedroom carrying a plate of fruit. Inside her room she ran and dove into the soft familiarity of her bed with it's happy floral print covers and large fluffy pillows. She found her commu-tran and entered Beabop's number which signaled only once and Beabop answered, "Hi, so you made it home safely?" Jazzalin shot back, "I 'm royalty what did you expect. How are you fairing being alone in Granny's massive house? I mean, aren't you a little scared?" Beabop answered, "Jazzalin, this house is a fortress. When you left I set security on optimum mode so I'm safe big time. Did you get all weepy and sentimental when you saw your mother?" Jazzalin answered, "No I did not! I was the epitome of refined young femininity until I sat down to lunch and ate like a field laborer." Both girls laughed. Recovering Jazzalin said, "Mommy's trying to involve me in party planning and I couldn't care less but I did have her invite Adagio and his famous mother." "Good call Princess. Got to go Granny's pinging on her private commu-tran to check up on me. I miss you already but I'll be the first party guest on Fiffsday. Love and twinkle fingers salute. Bye now!", and Beabop disconnected the call. Jazzalin was able to squeeze in, "Bye Bea!" before the connection went silent. She decided a nap would be nice after all, and undressed and slipped into a nightshirt, peeled back the covers and slid into the clean smoothness that was fresh bed linens. She was asleep almost immediately. Tomorrow she would plan out her party details as much as concerned her, and go over to "Voco-Stellar" for some improvisational singing. She thought she was not at all like her mother who had lived with her parents Count and Countess Rondo all life before an arranged marriage to her father. Queen Octiva had gone from one male dominated cloistered environment to another. She never went out for anything because everything came to her; society, merchandise, media, art and entertainment. She had never lived on her own, ran wild in the streets, floated in the upper atmosphere or worn unconventional clothing; all of which her daughter had done by her fourteenth birthday. Although she loved her mother dearly she was her antithesis, except for singing. With these thoughts she smiled into her pillow and drifted deeper into sleep.

The week was a blur of activities all leading up to Jazzalin's party on Fiffsday afternoon. Jazzalin had chosen to wear a multi floral colored tulle crinoline skirt with a silky purple-pink blouse with long sleeves and jeweled button closures and a pair of yellow-green leggings with the same colored short heeled shoes with purple-pink bows on the toes. Her mother had insisted her hairstylist do her hair which resulted in lavender streaks throughout her hair; the sides brushed flat, a full bang, and a blunt cut to just above her shoulders. To top off her new "do" her mother supplied a small crown.decorated with floral carved amethysts accented with green garnet leaves set in platinum. Continuing the color scheme was a matching pair of dangly amethyst and green garnet earrings. Her nails had been done in acrylics alternating purple and green polish. Her mother was determined she look like a princess for this party and not the "athletic ruffian" her mother described her appearance most of the time. The Queen's hair stylist was also a make-up artist and applied a modest amount of make-up to Jazzalin's eyes, cheeks and mouth. After all of the prep Jazzalin looked in the full length mirror and the image looking back was a pretty well dressed young lady who happened to be a princess. When she descended the stairs her party guests were starting to arrive. Her mother walked to meet her with an approving look in her eyes and said, "Jazzalin, you look really beautiful or as you would put it, you look "quizit"." Taking her daughter's hand the Queen led her to the main palace drawing room which had been transformed into a fantasy of flowers, pink and purple streamers, colorful floating air globes and android servers dressed to match the color scheme guarding a glass cache housing colorful party take home bags. There was a long table of food that guests could self serve and another long table where gifts could be placed. This was a rare occasion that Queen Octiva was not wearing a dress but she chose to wear a tailored dark pink pearlized silk pant suit. This was the most casual Jazzalin had ever seen her, and it was refreshing. Throwing her arms around her mother, Jazzalin fervently said, "Mommy this is so "quizit"! It's so so girly without being repulsive. Thank you for making it happen." Suddenly from the hallway she heard Beabop's familiar voice saying, "Happy Birthday Princess!" Jazzalin ran into the hallway with a big smile on her face to stand full stop in front of her best friend who like herself was elegantly attired. Jazzalin gained her composure and said, "Bea, so good to see after five days apart. Love your outfit. What color is it?" Beabop retorted, "It's an extreme turquoise with glass beading on the jacket. Granny sent it to me from a shop in the East Region. It's a great accent to my complexion." Beabop did an exaggerated spin in her matching short beaded boots while making expressive arm gestures. Her usual curly red hair had been straightened ending past her shoulders with a dramatic side part and bangs and adorned with a crystal flower pin accent. The girls giggled and hugged before going into the party staged drawing room. Jazzalin had compiled a disc of her favorite music artists both vocal and instrumental which was creating a light airy atmosphere for the party. Just as Jazzalin and Beabop entered the drawing the doorman droid announced, "Lady Sylphine Ooma-Skyes and her son Adagio Skyes." Minutes later the girls saw Adagio walking next to his beautiful mother carrying a huge multi-colored box topped with a gaudy purple bow. Smiling Adagio approached Jazzalin and said, "Happy birthday Princess. Where can I deposit your gift?" Jazzalin thought he's so quizit and no wonder his mother was beautiful. Smiling back at her guest she directed him to the gift table. She made a point of greeting Lady Sylphine and introducing her to her mother. The exotic Lady Sylphine made an elegant curtsy and greeted Queen Octiva saying, "Good Afternoon your Majesty and thank you for inviting my son and I to participate in the celebration of your daughter's fourteenth birthday." Queen Octiva smiled and responded, "Lady Sylphine so happy you could attend. Jazzalin told me how you were so kind to her at a recent event at your summer home. Is this the first time you've had occasion to visit the royal palace?" Lady Sylphine answered, "Yes, but I hope this won't be the last time. I must say your event planner has done an excellent job creating a festive environment for the party." "Thank you Lady Sylphine. It would be my pleasure to show you around the palace's public areas and gardens. Oh, I am a fan from your fashion career days. Let's go this way." Gesturing to Lady Sylphine to accompany her, Queen Octiva started to give the beautiful guest a tour of the palace. Party guests were flowing in now and the main drawing room was full of people dancing, eating, and generally socializing. Planet Adagio as usual had accumulated an admiring group of female satellites all vying for his attention. He seemed oblivious to this attention since he was aware that he was young, wealthy, and had been blessed with amazing good looks. Being the good friends they were, Jazzalin and Beabop decided to rescue him even if he did not want to be rescued. The girls confronted him by dancing their way in front of him making it obvious they wanted him to join them. The other guests looked on at the exhibition of female boldness but since it was the Princess and her best friend they knew to mind their business, it was a party after all. The threesome danced together right up to the sound of a bell announcing the presentation of the birthday cake. It took two service droids to bring in the huge five layer cake alternating purple and pink frosting, topped with a sculpted candy figurine of Jazzalin holding a banner with "14" on it. When the cake was safely placed on its table Queen Octiva requested everyone's attention and signaled Jazzalin to join her. Queen Octiva began to sing in her beautiful soprano voice, "You were born today, what a happy day. I can't say it any other way except happy, happy birthday. Happy happy birthday to you!" Jazzalin hugged mother with tears in her eyes as the party guests started to sing "Happy, happy birthday to you. Happy, happy birthday to you!!" The Queen presented Jazzalin with a huge jeweled handled knife and assisted her to ceremoniously cut the first slice of cake, the rest of the cake cutting would be done by a caterer. The room was filled with electric joy and it was everything a party for a fourteen year old Princess should be. Jazzalin did think it would have been even better if her father had been able to attend but he was a king and he would not shrink from being king even though he loved her. Then Adagio approached her requesting to dance with her to a slow instrumental that was filling the air. She wanted to refuse but her mind whispered, "Don't be a coward. It's just an obligatory gesture." He was a good dancer and thankfully the music transitioned into a faster upbeat tune so they parted and danced separately to Jazzalin's relief. Adagio bowed and thanked Jazzalin for the dance after the music stopped. She was flattered by this attention but her reply was, "Adagio stop being so formal, we're friends." The party continued until well after sundown when the Jazzoan gentry knew to thank the Queen for the excellent social gathering, food and entertainment and to return to their own homes. Beabop had left early because her Granny wanted her inside the mansion before dark. Jazzalin was sad to see her leave knowing she would be home schooled this term and she and Beabop would not have the luxury of their daily romps at the Academy, "Voco-stellar", and any number of the places they frequented. After her last guest had departed Jazzalin started to excavate the large pile of gifts that were deposited on the gift table. She opened Beabop's first and found a purple beaded jacket just like the turquoise one Bea had worn today. She tried on the pretty jacket which fit her slim body perfectly. This made her melancholy so that she didn't want to open any more gifts just now. Summoning a service droid she had the gifts taken to her room to be opened later.

Jazzalin assembled a plate of party snacks which included a healthy slice of birthday cake as well as a tumbler of punch to take to her room. Leaving the drawing room enroute to her room she passed her mother's office in time to overhear her mother say, "Tempo, how could you! This won't be good." Her father's voice replied, "It couldn't be helped. This was the only way I could ensure the Sessilum issue would go in our favor." Since her office door was not completely closed Jazzalin lingered to hear more. Queen Octiva's voice saddened, "But to betroth Jazzalin in marriage when she turns seventeen seems drastic. I don't think she should know right away especially since she's homeschooling her last term before graduating the Academy." Her father responded, "We have three years. A lot can happen in three years." Jazzalin was dumbfounded that she had been used as a bargaining chip in a planetary dispute. She did not wait to hear anymore and calmed herself enough to pass her mother's door unseen. Making it to the stairs she ran the rest of the way to her room, slamming the door behind her. She was willing to comply with homeschooling but she was not willing to be bartered in marriage to a stranger. Really, she thought "what a surprise", and on her birthday! Her mind was firing any number of ideas as to what her response should be to the arranged marriage revelation. She remembered a gag gift from Beabop, an "Undercover Princess Kit" from a year ago. The kit included an untraceable wrist holo-tran with a power neutralizer, dark glasses, and dark gray hooded jacket and matching slacks. Who would have guessed that this silly gift she and Beabop had laughed about would help formulate an escape plan. She would wait until the service droids powered down at midnight so they wouldn't see her and she could use the power neutralizer to open the gate from the palace driveway to make her way to the public hovercraft going to the South Region. She whispered to herself, "Beabop here I come." She would use her hard currency she kept in her jewelry box not her traceable credit plate. She counted one hundred Jazzoan dollars putting fifty of them readily in a zipper pocket of her of jacket, hiding the rest in her small travel case. She dressed in the grey jacket & slacks and got into bed and waited. Her mother looked in on her and said, "Goodnight Jazzalin. I love you. Sleep well. We'll go out together tomorrow for some shopping. Alright?" "That'll be fine Mommy. I love you. Goodnight and thank you for today", Jazzalin said. Queen Octiva replied, "You are so welcome. Sleep well my love." Quietly her mother closed the door and so the adventure began.

CHAPTER 12

The time monitor on the side table of her room flashed midnight. Jazzalin quietly slid out of bed and put on her soft leather sport shoes, gathered her travel case and stealthily left her bedroom going downstairs exiting the palace. With the power neutralizer she disarmed the gate security system and was able to slip out to the public streets. She ran to the end of the block turning to a busy city street that would take her to the public hovercraft station. Purchasing a ticket to the South Region Jazzalin boarded the hovercraft. She breathed a sigh of relief and closed her eyes for the two hours it would take to reach the South Region. Sleep enveloped her so she had to shaken awake by the hovercraft attendant when they landed in the South Region hovercraft station. Gathering her things she exited the hovercraft and went to the local transport hovers to get to Granny's mansion. She had the driver let her out a few yards away from the gate of the Zynoplee estate. Using the wrist holo-tran she called Beabop who did not answer until the second call. In a sleepy voice she answered, "Granny. Anything wrong?" Jazzalin replied, "It's me not Granny and yes something's wrong! I've run away and I'm in front of your house. Let me in!" Beabop wide awake now responded, "Sure! Give me a minute to shut off the security system." Choking back tears Jazzalin said, "Hurry." "Alright. Just another set of numbers to enter and the gate should be opening now.", Beabop replied. In a few minutes a tired bedraggled Jazzalin entered the front door of the mansion and flung herself into Beabop's arms weeping. As friends neither of them had ever experienced anything that was cause for the kind of emotional meltdown Jazzalin was having. Beabop lead her still crying friend into the library and sat her in a comfortable chair and waited until her crying subsided before asking, "Jazzalin, what's wrong?" The question started her crying again before she whispered out, "Oh, Bea my father betrothed me to some unknown stranger on my seventeenth birthday so he could get some help in defeating the Sessilum. I heard him and mommy talking after the party. It's not enough they want me to homeschool for my last school term but this was the last straw." Handing Jazzalin a tissue Beabop said, "You know the royal guard will be hot on your trail in a few hours. Your mother will contact me first to find out where you are. What do you plan to do?" Jazzalin gave depressed sigh, "Oh Bea I don't know. All I know is I can't go back right now. I used the untraceable holo-tran from the gag gift "Undercover Princess Kit" you gave last year. You must be a seer." "Naaah! I was just joking around. Let's get you to bed. I think you should stay in my room tonight. You can sleep on the pull out bed of my couch. Come on. Let me reactivate the security system. Come on let's go upstairs." The girls made their way upstairs and got ready for bed. Once they got settled Jazzalin was able to say, "Thank you Bea for this. You're a true friend. I love you." "I know, now go to sleep. Oh, Adagio is coming over tomorrow so you'll have to hide somewhere." Beabop said as she slipped back into sleep. Already fast asleep Jazzalin did not hear the Adagio update as all the birthday activities and her flight to the South Region had physically taken its toll. At seven o'clock in the morning Beabop's bedside commu-tran pinged louder than usual. Pressing the answer option she heard the soft feminine voice of Queen Octiva, "Good morning Beabop this Queen Octiva. Is Jazzalin there by any chance?" Taking a deep breathe Beabop replied, "No your Majesty. Is she missing?" The Queen's voice wavered with emotion in response, "It seems she's run away. If she shows up at your house please have her call me so we can get things sorted out. Thank you Beabop, goodbye." Wide awake now Beabop jumped out of bed and went over to where Jazzalin slept and shook her awake. Yawning Jazzalin moaned, "Stop, I'm awake." Angrily Beabop said,"You better be awake, your mother just called and she sounded really sad. I'm going to get you set up in one of Granny's chauffeur hovercrafts. They have a lot of passenger space. Come on grab your stuff. I'll get some snacks to tide you over until Adagio leaves." "What do you mean til Adagio leaves?", Jazzalin asked. "I told you last night he's coming over to tour the mansion and grounds. You must have been asleep. Well no matter, you have to stay out of sight until he leaves. I'll rush him along as much as I can. Stay here while I get the food ready and I'll ring my comm-tran to signal you to come downstairs. Okay?", Beabop explained. Running downstairs Beabop opened the "preservatory chamber" and pulled out fruit, bread, an icy bottled juice and healthy carbo squares. Shoving the food into a plastic bag and dialed the commu-tran to signal Jazzalin to come downstairs. Jazzalin came downstairs still wearing the nightshirt she had borrowed from Beabop and carrying a blanket and pillow to make her hideaway comfortable. Beabop handed her the bag of food and led her to the huge garage where over a dozen hovercraft of all sizes were kept. Beabop went to a dark gray classic chauffeur hovercraft with shaded privacy windows. Opening the door she motioned for Jazzalin to get in the rear passenger compartment. The hover was immaculately clean with a bright blue velvety upholstered interior which reminded Jazzalin of the chauffeured hovercrafts used by the royal family, her family. She carefully climbed into the passenger compartment arranging the blanket and pillow to maximize her comfort while hiding out. She also shoved the bag of food into a small perservatory chamber built into the wall of the vehicle. Beabop advised, "Now finish your sleep and stay quiet and I'll come for you as soon as Adagio leaves. Oh, and think about what you intend to do next. I don't want to go to prison for harboring a runaway royal." Jazzalin stuck out her tongue at her and Beabop slammed the hover's door in return. Running back upstairs and back to her rumply bed. Adagio was not expected for another three hours so she set the alarm on her commu-tran to time a two hour nap.

Beabop grudgingly woke up when the commu-tran pinged multiple times that her naptime had expired. She went to her bathroom, took a quick shower, and completed her hygiene regimen before she went to her walk-in closet and chose a suitable outfit to entertain her best male friend. Promptly at eleven o'clock Adagio's sporty blue hovercraft set down in the driveway of the mansion. Beabop ran to the front door as soon as she heard the engines of his hover idle to land. She watched as his tall body unfolded to leave the hovercraft and ran out to greet him with a hug. Smiling down at her he said, "Hi brat. How's the quizit life?" Smiling back at him with a gleam in her eyes as she thought about Jazzalin hiding in Granny's hovercraft she said, "Hi, yourself! The quizit life is exponentially high. Can I offer you lunch before we go on the tour?" "Yes, I'll have lunch. What's on the menu?" "The kitchen droid is broiling bova patties with salad topping on a bun, carbo fries, fruit ice and yummy birthday cake from Jazzalin's party." "Sounds great," he said. "Come inside and let me get everything setup. You can pull your hovercraft into the garage if you want," Beabop said. "Thanks, I'll put it in the back with the chauffeur hovers. Where are you setting up lunch?", Adagio inquired, "The atrium next to the kitchen will do. Go park your hover and come back and everything will be on the table," said Beabop. Adagio made quick work of about how Queen Octiva had befriended his mother. Beabop smiled knowing the birthday girl parking his hovercraft then joined Beabop in the atrium. "Beabop this is great. Your kitchen droid is a great cook," Adagio said while taking a bite out of the bova sandwich he had to hold with two hands. The two friends talked about Jazzalin's party and all of the fun it had been. Adagio spoke was sleeping in the garage. Finishing their lunch the couple set out to tour Granny's extensive property starting with the outside recreational area, pool and guest house. They walked through the expansive gardens filled with all of Granny's favorite flowers and shrubs which led to the garage. Adagio said, "Bea lets check out your Granny's hovercraft collection." Beabop replied, "Sure, but I'm not really interested in hovers." They went inside together and immediately Adagio started to name the make and model of the rare and expensive hovercrafts kept safely in the garage. When he walked to the "one where Jazzalin was sleeping Beabop kicked over a tool box and yelled out, "Ouch!!!" as a distraction. Adagio spun around to face her and said, "Are you alright?" Beabop said, "Yes, I'm fine," nervously. Adagio looked toward a shelving unit which was obscuring a door, he walked around the hovercraft asking, "Beabop what's behind that door?" "How would I know? I never come in the garage. And I don't usually socialize in the garage since it's dim and smells of exhaust fumes", she replied. Effortlessly Adagio pushed the shelving unit away far enough to better access the door. "Bea, this is a lift access not a closet door. See there are floor indicator buttons", he said pointing to tarnished metal strip housing two buttons marked "two" and "three". Jazzalin had woke up due the noise of Adagio's discovery and using her blanket as camouflage she quietly observed Adagio and Bea enter the floor lift and saw the second floor button light up. She quickly changed into her gray jacket and slacks so at an opportunity she could sneak onto the floor lift to locate a better hiding place. Adagio was adrenalin charged when the door to the lift opened to the second floor and with a grasp said,"Wow!!!!! This is a full research and development lab. Bea your Grandfather was a very progressive man to have his type of lab in his home. It has everything a scientist would need to plot out theories and prototypes! Let's see what's on the third floor." Beabop replied, "No thanks. I'm going back upstairs. This is your adventure and I'm tired of gagging on chemical fumes." As she headed for the floor lift she yelled over her shoulder, "Don't stay down here too long or my desire to be your tour guide will expire." Not really listening to her Adagio replied, "Yeah. I'll be quick." Beabop took the floor lift back up to the garage and ran over to the hovercraft where Jazzalin was hiding. Tapping on the glass window she whispered "Stay put, he's nearly done and I'll come and get you when he leaves." Staying behind in the lab Adagio raffled through blueprints strewn on a draft table which were of the "format ship" Xaanaz Zynoplee built. Feeling an urgency he went to the floor lift and pressed the third floor button and when the door slid open he was stunned to see Mr. Zynoplee's "format ship" parked in the middle of a huge hangar. The large ship was sleek gleaming silver in the afternoon sunlight shining through shaded glass of the hangar door. Walking towards the beautiful craft he was hyperventilating at the reality that this ship was a key to defeating a dreaded enemy. While he was caught up in admiring the ship he heard a voice say, "Are you Mr. Zynoplee's technician?" Startled, Adagio quickly turned to see a pilot droid standing behind him. He responded, "No, I'm a friend of the Zynoplee family. Is the ship still flight worthy?" "Yes, the ship is in optimum condition for space travel. Are you seeking to use the ship for a mission?", the android inquired. Adagio responded, "I need to speak with my father first. Wait here and I'll be right back." Going over to a corner of the hangar he took out his commu-tran and called his father's private access and his father answered, "Yes son. Any news on the ship?" Adagio excitedly replied, "Dad, you were right Mr. Zynoplee built a R&D lab and a huge hangar beneath his top floor hovercraft garage and the ship is housed here. According to the pilot droid the ship is travel ready. What's the next step?" In reply Hamilton said, "Hold on, I have to notify King Tempo." Activating his second access on his commu-tran he called King Tempo. King Tempo answered and Hamilton Skyes relayed the good news about finding the "format ship" on the Zynoplee estate and it being travel ready. King Tempo advised that the ship should be dispatched as soon as possible to Audia Prime. Disconnecting his connection with the King and going back to Adagio's call to advise, "Son the King wants the ship to go to Audia Prime as soon as possible. Are you able to pilot it?" "I don't have to because there's a pilot droid but I can accompany it on the trip," Adagio said. Father and son agreed to speak again once he landed on Audia Prime before saying goodbye. Adagio returned to the pilot droid and asked, "Does the ship have sufficient fuel to travel to Audia Prime?" The droid advised, "There's enough fuel for several trips to Audia Prime and beyond. Mr. Zynoplee kept a box of extra fuel cells in the supply cabinet." Adagio advised the droid to bring the box of fuel cells to the ship and put them on board. He then went back up to the garage level and found Beabop in the mansion's huge library listening to popular screech artists band "Laser Point". Adagio smiled at her revelry and said, "Bea, I think I've toured your mansion enough today and I'm going to depart for home. Thanks for the lunch and the pleasure of the your "quizit" company." "You are welcomed, anytime", Beabop replied. She started to get up to follow him back to the garage but Adagio advised, "You don't have to come with me I can find my way out. It's been fun, til next time." "Bye!", they said in unison. Jazzalin had seen Adagio get out of the floor lift and go into the mansion giving her a chance to get out of the hovercraft hideaway. She decided to take a look at the two floors beneath the garage since it was new to her as well. When the door opened on the second floor she saw it was a laboratory of some kind and she chose to remain in the lift and go to the third floor instead. When the door to the lift opened onto the third floor she saw the beautiful silver ship parked in the middle of the huge hangar. Her breath caught in her throat and she walked to the ship in a trance but a quick glance she saw the pilot droid so she crouched low to evade being seen. She saw the door to the ship was open and she scrambled inside and made her way to the rear of the ship where a utility closet was open providing a perfect hiding place. She thought she was going to stay here until Adagio left the mansion. Back on the garage floor Adagio opened the door to his hovercraft and activated the auto-drive option and entered his apartment address. Using his hover remote he started the hover's engines and guided it out of the garage and sent it skyward to the landing pad outside his thirteenth floor apartment. Making sure he wasn't seen he went to the floor lift and took it back to the third floor hangar. The pilot android greeted Adagio advising, "I have put the fuel cells on board, sir." Adagio said a reflex "thank you" before realizing he was speaking to an android. Adagio asked the droid "How many passengers can the ship accommodate?" The droid answered, "Four passengers and two pilots, six total." Adagio and the droid got into the two pilot seats facing an impressive dashboard of lights, buttons, and dials. Adagio then advised the pilot droid to set a course into the "navigational system" for Audia Prime. The droid activated the onboard remote that opened the huge hangar door and then the ship's engines came online with a high pitched whine. Jazzalin had not expected to be a stowaway on a spaceship but she was one now. When the droid had shoved the box of fuel cells into the utility closet she was barely able to conceal her presence. She thought that she should reveal her presence but she decided against it. Since she had heard Adagio's voice she felt she would be safe while they were in transit and once they landed she would notify her parents that she was off world but safe. She wondered why Adagio was piloting this huge ship with a droid copilot and where they were going. The ship lifted to glide effortlessly out of the hangar and pointing its nose skyward to the upper atmosphere and into space. The utility closet was very uncomfortable but Jazzalin was determined not to give herself away. Once the ship had achieved planetary space the engines were not so loud although they seemed to be traveling even faster. Jazzalin primed her ears to hear any information that would enlighten her about their destination but the two pilots were very quiet The ship did have a second level which had a lavatory and bunks for sleeping. Adagio spoke to the droid loud enough for Jazzalin to hear, "What's our estimated time of arrival on Audia Prime?" The droid replied, "Three hours. With the coordinates in the navigation drive the ship knows the way." With that update Jazzalin decided she could not spend three hours folded in the utility closet. She made a noise when she stood up in the closet loud enough to prompt Adagio to ask, "Who's there?!" "It's me, Jazzalin", she said meekly. "Jazzalin! How did you get on the ship and why are you on the ship?" Adagio asked. "I can ask you the same questions", she fired back. "I ran away from home last night and Bea took me in. I was hiding in one of Granny's hovercrafts when you found the floor lift. So I did a little exploring but I didn't know the ship was going on a trip. I had planned to wait til you went home and go upstairs to figure out my next move. This is a bit extreme but I'm too far away so the royal guards can't take me back", she said solemnly. "Why did you run away?", he asked. Tears formed in her eyes and she said "I can't talk about it." Hugging her, Adagio said, "It's that bad. Well I won't push the issue, but we're on the way to Audia Prime where your father is presiding over the Planetary Council. He will probably be very upset that you're there and not at home on Jazzo." "I'm sure he'll be furious but I'm too happy to show him that I am not chattel!", she said angrily. Adagio knew he was in the dark about the inner workings of the royal family and felt it was best he didn't pry into the matter. Changing the subject Adagio said, "I was going to the loft to rest for the three hours it takes to get to Audia Prime. There are four loungers if you want to relax but if you're hungry there aren't any snacks unfortunately." "I would like to relax and Bea gave me a bag of snacks to tide me over til you were gone which I had the presence of mind to bring with me," said Jazzalin. She pulled the plastic bag from her travel case which contained the fruit, bread, carbo squares and juice. Beabop did not have any domestic skills as she had not bothered to wrap the various snack items to keep them separate but had merely thrown them into the plastic bag. Jazzalin smiled when she thought of her friend and what she must be thinking when she can't find her in the mansion. Offering her snacks to Adagio, Jazzalin asked, "Is it possible to call Beabop to let her know where I am so she won't worry?" "Let me ask the droid", Adagio replied. Going down to the main cabin Adagio asked the pilot droid if the ship's communication system had enough range to make a commu-tran call to Jazzo. The droid advised yes the ship would be able to send a call to Jazzo but it would need to be now as they would be out of range within fifteen minutes.

Adagio advised the droid to transmit frequencies of Beabop's wrist holo-tran and he was delighted to hear her answer after several minutes. Excitedly he said, "Beabop, Jazzalin and I are on your Granfather's format ship enroute to Audia Prime. Jazzalin had me call you so you wouldn't be worried when you couldn't find her in your Granny's hovercraft." "You two should be arrested. I've been out of my mind looking for her. Put her on the speaker", Beabop commanded. When Jazzalin spoke through the ship's commu-tran Beabop started to cry and Jazzalin said "Oh Bea, don't cry. I'm fine. I'm sorry I left without you knowing I'd gone. I went to the third floor of the garage and hid in your grandfather's spaceship and Adagio and a droid confiscated it to go to Audia Prime. I'm an accidental stowaway." Beabop began to laugh and said, "This is the weirdest birthday adventure ever. What are you going to say when you see your father?" "I'll figure that out when the time comes. This is all kinds of exciting, especially within twenty-four hours of my birthday. Beabop, the ship is getting out of range so I'll call you from Audia Prime. Love you," Jazzalin said as the communication died. She turned to look at Adagio and said, "Thank you." "You're welcome", Adagio replied. The two snacked on the meager food Beabop had provided and shared the fruit juice in plastic cups from the ship's stark pantry. Jazzalin chose a lounger facing a window and stretched out her slim body. She watched as the distant stars and galaxies whizzed by. She turned to ask Adagio something and saw he was asleep and decided not to disturb him. Her thoughts were anxious about seeing her father but she calmed herself because this whole thing was based on a decision her father had made. Her eyes slowly closed as she rested on a speeding vessel through the great space. She began to dream of two figures clothed in gleaming white robes with beautiful lavender eyes. They spoke in unison to her, "Thank you for coming to help us. Don't fret, this will be a blessing." The vision woke her and she heard the droid announce, "There's an incoming call for Mr. Skyes." Jazzalin reached over and shook Adagio commanding, "Wake-up! You have an incoming call." He opened his eyes and gathered himself pushing his body up to go to the pilot console and take the call. "This is King Tempo calling to speak with Adagio Skyes! Please respond!", King Tempo spoke loudly. Adagio attached the headset activating it providing a state of privacy silencing the overhead speaker. Jazzalin got anxious that Adagio might tell her father she was on the ship and she did not want him to know so she sprinted to the main section of the ship flailing her arms to get Adagio's attention. Adagio turned to see her mouthing, "Please don't tell him I'm here." Still speaking to King

Tempo he nodded his head that he would comply with her request. Adagio took off the headset and switched to the console speaker and they both heard King Tempo say, "I need you to be clear on this issue. The Sessilum in retaliation have released some kind of virus here on Audia Prime and it would not be wise to have you land here. We are all in hazard wear and masks. You should proceed to the Sessilum frontier and the Shalla zealots will be beamed onboard the ship and then you're to take them to "Astral Keep". I will have my navigation technician transmit the coordinates to your ship's navigation system. I want to impress upon you the importance that these directions be carried out precisely so that the Sessilum habitat can be eradicated as soon as your ship is out of range. I want to thank you young man for all you have done and what you are yet to do. You and your family are to be commended and rewarded for your service. Godspeed." The important message ended abruptly. She looked at Adagio and was in awe that her father had given him such an important assignment and she was somewhat happy that she would witness the rescue of the two figures she had seen in her vision. "Adagio I'm sorry that I'm an added burden to your responsibilities. I will try not to be a problem and if I can assist with the smooth administration of the assignment I'm at your service. How far away is the Sessilum frontier?", she asked. Adagio asked the pilot android who advised the Sessilum frontier would add five hours to the travel time. Jazzalin felt this was the best birthday present she could have ever received from anyone. She took a breath and resolved to be brave and to see the adventure to its end.

Inside the protected bubble where the twin zealots and their guardian were present, the Sessilum habitat around it was experiencing violent rippling lightquakes and light storms. King Tempo had his communication team send a message to the previous coordinates they had used initially to contact the "weapon" that was causing the Sessilum immense grief. The message advised the twins that the format ship had been found and it was enroute to the Sessilum frontier and their Light Guardian should be on alert to translate them to the ship. Lilitine and Luling were refreshed in their spirits to know their departure from the Sessilum habitat was imminent, and they began to sing the Light songs with effortless energy as they waited to be extracted to go to Astral Keep. The zealots responded by thanking the King for his expeditious location of the format ship. They also advised him to repel the Sessilum biological warfare by singing the light songs from the polar tower on Audia Prime. King Tempo notified his fellow council members to meet at the polar tower with their Light Song notes. Within minutes the polar tower was filled with planetary voices of the Symphonea planetary system. They began to sing, "We sing the light that is victorious and glorious, that darkness shall not reign over us. We sing the light that wins the fight and routes darkness away, we sing the light! We are full of might, we sing the light and we win the fight in glorious light!" After the last note was sent through the polar amplifier a huge vaporous cloud was drawn away from Audia Prime into the void and it was replaced with a protective sonic barrier to encase the entire planetary system. The King and the other light singers sent up a loud cheer that the Light Songs were still a potent weapon against darkness. The group of victorious singers returned into their conference chamber where each one contacted their planets to let them know that the crisis had been abated and there was only one more event before they could call it complete. There was an atmosphere of freedom that had not been among them for many weeks. Hopeful, the King decided that all the preemptive steps to rescue the twin zealots were in play and he would not return to Jazzo until he was notified they were safely on Astral Keep. On the tail of that issue there was to make sure Adagio, his tentative son-in-law, and the format ship would arrive safely back in Lady Zynoplee's garage hangar. He felt there was nothing else that would put demands on him like the Sessilum encroachment but he did not know his daughter the Princess of Jazzo was onboard the format ship speeding enroute to the Sessilum frontier.

CHAPTER 13

On Jazzo Beabop began to feel guilty that Jazzalin had become a stowaway and was now lightyears away from home leaving her poor mother extremely worried. To absolve her guilty conscience she determined to call Queen Octiva and tell her the truth. Queen Octiva had not slept at all the night before hoping the royal guards would find Jazzalin and return her to the palace so she would not have to tell the King about it. Sitting in her office she laid her head on her arms and prayed that her daughter would come home safely. When her commu-tran pinged she jumped and pressed the connect key and immediately said, "Queen Octiva speaking." Beabop answered, "Your Majesty this is Beabop. Ma'am, I want to apologize for lying about Jazzalin's whereabouts. She ran away because she overheard you and the King talking about betrothing her to someone and she lost it and concocted her plan of escape. She came to Granny's house all distraught and weepy and I couldn't turn her away. She was safe in the garage hidden in a chauffeured hovercraft but she became curious and went down to Grandpa Zynoplee's lab and she thought she would hide on his spaceship, which King Tempo had commissioned Adagio to find and bring it to Audia Prime. Jazzalin was hidden onboard and became an accidental stowaway. If she were still on Jazzo I would have insisted she call you but since she's lightyears away, I didn't feel you should suffer not knowing where she is." Through tears Queen Octiva replied, "Thank you Beabop for being my daughter's loyal friend. Thank you for the empathy you've shown to both Jazzalin and me." The Queen thought of the irony of the whole drama since Jazzalin was aboard the spaceship with the person her father had betrothed her to. She breathed a sigh of relief knowing where Jazzalin was physically but she was still concerned since it was lightyears off planet. The Queen determined that she would not tell the King any of this since his decision had initiated their daughter's emotional response in the first place. Beabop ventured to ask, "Your Majesty are you alright?" Graciously the Queen responded, "Oh, Beabop I'm fine and I am so glad that you care about Jazzalin's well being to help when she needed it. I need to go now and coordinate some things, but again I thank you for all you have done, it won't be forgotten. Goodbye now." Feeling relieved Beabop said, "Goodbye your Majesty." The Queen sent a message to the captain of the royal guards and told him to cancel the search for the Princess as she was safe with a trusted family friend. The Queen notified her staff she would be indisposed for the rest of the day and to refer all issues to her secretary. She took the floor lift as she was too tired to climb the stairs to her bedroom where she intended to get some much needed rest.

The Sessilum habitat was raging in angry slamming, splintering its black elements into jagged shards pounding at the barrier that housed the "weapon". Thunderous yells and screams also buffeted the light bubble without effect. Lilitine and Luling remained calm and sang the litany of Light songs to ensure their safety until they were removed to travel to Astral Keep. Their Light Guardian was now manifested as a armor clad warrior with intense light radiating from its eyes and periodically saying, "Blessed ones your transport is very near here. The shiny ship is speeding its way to your rescue and I have sent out the call to the brethren to start their journey to eradicate the Sessilum infection out of existence. The message has been sent to a distant part of the universe accessible by only special star beings, beautiful in the form but formidable in battle. They are called the "Sextillion" as they are innumerable and they are traveling at the speed of light exponentia infinity to get to their brother's aid, singing as they proceed:

> God of our fathers whose almighty hand
> leads forth in beauty all our starry band,
>
> Of shining worlds in splendor through the skies,
> Our grateful songs before Thy throne arise.

Thy love divine hath led us in the past,
In this free space by Thee our lot is cast;

Be Thou our ruler, guardian, guide and stay,
Thy Word our law, Thy paths our chosen way.
From war's alarms, from deadly pestilence,
Be Thy strong arm our ever sure defense;
Thy true religion in our hearts increase,

Thy bounteous goodness nourish us in peace.
Refresh Thy people on their toilsome way,
Lead us from night to never-ending day;

Fill all our lives with love and grace divine,
And glory, laud, and praise be ever Thine."

Inside the format ship Jazzalin and Adagio spoke about the pending rescue that they were only another hour away from. Neither had ever been any farther than the upper atmosphere of Jazzo; now according to the pilot android they were eleven lightyears away from their home planet and another hour away from their destination. Jazzalin became suspicious of Adagio being involved in the rescue of the twin zealots in the Sessilum territory. She wanted to know details but she held her peace because her own presence on the ship was veiled in a family secret. The thought of her father knowing she was in intergalactic space and not on Jazzo caused her to shutter. She set herself to remain composed and cooperative to see the mission successfully carried out. From the pilot console came the announcement, "We are approaching the Sessilum frontier coordinates. The ship will decrease speed to the access point. Please fasten your seat belts."

Adagio had already joined the pilot android at the dashboard while Jazzalin took a passenger seat and secured her seat belt. When the ship came to a full stop the trio could see the convulsions of the Sessilum habitat against the blackness of space. Adagio keyed in the communication coordinates and waited for a response. After a few minutes a voice came through the speaker, "This is the Light Guardian assigned to the twin zealots light singers "Lilitine and Luling" that you are to transport to Astral Keep. I must advise you once they are onboard the ship to make haste from these coordinates as the Sessilum habitat will be under eradication within seconds of your departure. I am transporting my charges to your ship now." With that announcement a bright light appeared inside the ship forming and materializing into the two zealots "Lilitine and Luling". At the moment of their complete boarding the ship's pilot android set the format ship on a high format speed to put them several lightyears from the Sessilum frontier. Even at their considerable distance from the Sessilum habitat there was a visible flash of fiery light and sound waves that crossed lightyears showing all the territory the Sessilum had occupied and stolen over centuries. The Sextillion brethren were a wall of light purifying every nano measure that had previously been occupied by the evil Sessilum. The twins looked at the brilliant lights that had been a dark hostile place; they could only smile that they were finally free. Jazzalin was in awe of the twins' radiant tan complexions, shiny lavender eyes, and shoulder length fluorescent purple hair. They were pretty in a fresh faced way and wore gleaming white tunics over matching leggings and no shoes. They were a little taller than Jazzalin but not as tall as Adagio. Adagio ventured to speak to them, "I'm Adagio Skyes and I want to welcome you onboard and we'll be taking you to "Astral Keep". Unfortunately, we don't have any food onboard but traveling at our current speed we should arrive at "Astral Keep" in an hour." In unison the twins responded, "We know who you are and we are able to survive without physical food for an hour. Thank you for your expeditious location of the format ship and bravely traveling the distance to rescue us from the Sessilum infection." Turning their twin gazes to Jazzalin they said, "Princess Jazzalin so nice to meet you. We know what you know but we know what you do not know. Since you do not want to return to Jazzo when we get to Astral Keep we would like to have you as a cultural consultant since we have lived in isolation for all our lives until now and we would appreciate a person of your caliber to educate us on the current dress, music, dance, and an overall feminine point of view. You do not have to answer right now but do think about it." Jazzalin looked back at them in amazement and said, "I'm flattered that you would like to enlist me as a social consultant. Which one of you is "Lilitine" and which one is "Luling?" All three laughed out loud as they fell into easy girl talk. The twins had never seen a young human male and asked Jazzalin if all males looked like Adagio. Jazzalin advised them they should wait until they were on Astral Keep to form an opinion. Jazzalin accessed the ship's commu-data files and showed the twins how to search for topics of interest to them. They immediately caught on and began to speed through the data files absorbing what they wanted and rejecting the rest. "Princess, we would like to get shoes because since our youth we have not worn them and the Light Guardian said we did not need them", they said in unison. Smiling at their enthusiasm for one of her best topics "shoes" Jazzalin replied, "Ladies it would be my pleasure to take you shoe shopping on Astral Keep." The hour travel time seemed to fly until they arrived within the upper atmosphere of "Astral Keep" and had to provide ship identification from King Tempo to access the planet. "Astral Keep" was a large planet in orbit around its even larger sun which in a single planet system, the system was sometimes called "The Lovers" because of this. Astral Keep also had two moons which regulated its seasons, ocean tides, atmosphere and had become an off-planet transmittal stations for interplanetary communications. The large planet had three levels: the first level was the planet itself where the humans lived their everyday lives, the second level was where the transcendent ones lived who had mastered living in the thin atmosphere above the planet in a domed platformed city, and the third level was where the human spirits lived occupying their spatial territories from all over the universe. The twins could choose to live on the first level or on the second level with their parents who had been translated there centuries ago but since they wanted to have Jazzalin as their consultant and friend they chose the planet's first level. The ground control gave the pilot android the landing coordinates and within a short time the format ship landed safely on "Astral Keep". When the door to the ship opened the twins walked down the stairs and were met by the "Astral Keep" Chancellor. The smiling dignitary welcomed the brave zealots and gave them an envelope containing keys to an estate, a hover vehicle, an unlimited line of credit donated to them for their service in destroying the Sessilum menace. The twins were gifted with huge bouquets of the planet's most beautiful flowers and physically carried by service droids to the Chancellors open hover vehicle for a parade through Astraline City. The local media broadcasted their arrival planet wide also highlighting the bravery of the pilot "Adagio Skyes" of Jazzo and passenger "Princess Jazzalin" also of Jazzo.

In the heat of the moment Jazzalin forgot that she should keep a low profile and when her father saw the news about the twins' arrival on Astral Keep, she was done. It was too late to hide. Jazzalin joined Adagio in a second hovercraft that followed the Chancellor's hover through the streets of Astraline City to great crowds singing, "See the brave ones who mastered the darkness and drove it away. Welcome, welcome, welcome to stay. You who sent the darkness away!" The parade ended at the Astraline City Center where a lavish lunch had been prepared for the twins and company and as many Astraline citizens that could be served. The twins ate and drank their fill but soon realized they were physically overwhelmed with all of the activities. The atmosphere was potent with elation but the twins were exhausted and managed to communicate that they really would like to go to the house that was gifted to them for some much needed rest. The Chancellor had the twins and company secreted out of the City Center to a waiting hovercraft that took them to a suburban area where a large white house surrounded by gardens and fountains waited to be occupied. The twins were overwhelmed by the sight of it letting out a grasp in unison, "Aaaaaaaaay!!!! So beautiful!" Jazzalin was equally impressed as the twin's main house was visibly larger than the Jazzo royal palace. The twins ran up to the front door of the large house and inserted the key which opened the double door and walked into the entryway to be greeted by a maid service droid who advised the twins it would give them a tour of the house now or at another time if they were too tired. The twins opted to take a bath and sleep, and tour the house tomorrow. The droid led them to the floor lift which took them to the second floor and the rooms, one for each of them. They were giddy with the extravagant accommodations that they could not have imagined would ever be theirs. Baths were drawn for them by additional service droids who were on standby for back scrubbing if requested. Jazzalin was led to a large suite with soft blue walls and green accents. She knew she would not be going back to Jazzo when Adagio and the droid returned the format ship to Lady Zynoplee's garage hangar and she would be very happy to have this room as her home for as long as she needed it to be. She made her way to a large bathroom with a separate shower and bathtub. She opted for a bath and she was too tired to stand up for a shower. Her bathtub looked out on a courtyard garden full of blooming flowers. She made quick work of her bath otherwise she would fall asleep in the warm soapy water. Her thoughts kept going to her father and the pending call from him. She told her mind to stop showing that scenario as she was going to sleep, and she did. Adagio was led to a beautiful room and he was able to take a hot shower and have the service droid take his dirty clothes to be cleaned. All of a sudden his wrist holo-tran pinged showing the face of King Tempo. He thought, "Not now." He answered the call, "Good evening your Majesty. How are you?" King Tempo replied, "I'm happy and relieved and I want to congratulate you on successfully transporting the twin zealots to Astral Keep. I have to ask, how did Jazzalin happen to be on board the format ship with you, the zealots, and the droid?" "Well, your Majesty it seems she ran away from home and was first hiding at Lady Zynoplee's mansion and somehow she thought the format ship was a better place to hide. I didn't know she was onboard the ship until we were in interplanetary space and she came out of the utility closet. I tried to get her to tell me why she had run away but she wouldn't tell me. You know how she is", Adagio explained. "Yes, I know", The King replied. He wanted to get more details and he would need to speak to his wife for the information he wanted. "I figured that Jazzalin was the initiator of her presence off world. Anyway, when will you be returning to Jazzo?", the King asked. "Well, the pilot android and ship are getting a tune up with the Astral Keep techs and I could use a full day to rest. I would say, day after tomorrow. The format ship makes fast work of the distance," said Adagio. "I would imagine Jazzalin is already asleep?", the King asked, "Yes sir, she and the twins made a straight line to bed after the celebration and I'd really like to turn in as well. Goodnight your Majesty," Adagio said curtly, disconnecting from the call. The King thought the young man was rude to just disconnect the call but then he had performed a task that even some seasoned specialists couldn't have executed with such precision. His next step was to call his wife and then call Jazzalin in the morning. It seemed that neither Adagio or Jazzalin had a clue they had been betrothed as a result of the Sessilum crisis. Even with the Sessilum menace gone he was still tying up loose ends. Standing in his suite in the Planetary Council building on Audia Prime looking out into the night sky he could see the light from the ongoing erasing and purification of the space the Sessilum had occupied for centuries. The Sextillion brethren would not stop their work until every molecule and particle was evaporated and no more before they returned to their far away galaxy. He smiled to himself that his daughter had been able to witness this phenomena from a much closer vantage point than he and she had met the zealot twins, and participated in their victory celebration on Astral Keep. She was Jazzo's royal representative even though she had usurped his authority by being on the format ship in the first place. He would go to bed now and try to sleep as he still had a few wrinkles to smooth out in the morning.

CHAPTER 14

The next morning when Jazzalin woke up to be greeted with the smiling faces of the twins standing by her bed and they spoke in unison, "Good morning Princess. We wanted to get the day started with you. The service droid said breakfast is ready when we are." Jazzalin gathered herself enough to reply, "Good morning Lilitine. Good morning, Luling. Ladies if you give me a minute to wash up I'll be right with you." "We'll be here and we can all go down together. Adagio is still sleeping and we did not wake him. Also we want to start an itinerary of your consulting and tutelage after breakfast," they announced. Coming from the bathroom Jazzalin took a robe from the nearby closet and put it on. She smiled at her students and said, "Come on, let's go downstairs." The trio were energetic as they made their way to a kitchen with a large table full of food and multiple pitchers of juices and teas. They took their seats at the table and began to choose from the many breakfast items. The twins chose the thick sour cream topped with fat red and blue berries and toasted sweetened grains and large cups of purple tea, while Jazzalin had a hard boiled poultry egg and thick slice of toasted bread topped it with a fruit jam and a cup of purple tea as well. Between bites the girls talked about how beautiful their house was and that they wanted to tour the grounds as it seemed to be a very large area. They also activated the kitchen commu-file to search for shopping options through the "E-stores" or at local stores in Astraline City. They decided to try both options not wanting to limit their shopping choices. As they were still enjoying breakfast when a service droid came to the table addressing Jazzalin that she had an incoming call from her father. Putting on a brave face Jazzalin she excused herself to follow the droid to the library to a commu-tran.

Putting on the headset she hit the connect key and said, "Good morning father." The King cleared his voice before replying, "Good morning. You don't have to be formal with me bundle. Jazzalin I need to know why you ran away from home. Your mother would not give me any information and told me to speak to you. Tell me what happened." Jazzalin replied, "Daddy, I overheard you tell mommy that you betrothed me in marriage on my seventeenth birthday in order to resolve the Sessilum crisis. I could not believe you were attaching my future as a solution to the Sessilum territorial aggression. I was offended and I couldn't stay in the palace anymore so I ran away. Beabop was kind enough to take me in. She hid me in a hovercraft in the garage when Adagio came over to tour Lady Zynoplee's mansion. They found the floor lift and went down to the floors below the garage. When they came upstairs I took the floor lift to the third floor and I hid in the spaceship having no clue that it was going to be sent on a rescue mission. So now I'm here on Astral Keep as the cultural consultant to the twin zealots so I'll be staying here indefinitely." "I see now, and I understand. You are my daughter and as much as I want to demand your return to Jazzo, I want you to have this experience as Jazzo's representative to those precious twin zealots who have adopted you in a fashion. I only ask that you stay in touch with your mother and I on a regular basis and I would advise you to contact Beabop as well. What's your response." Through her tears she said, "Daddy, thank you for not making this possible for me. I had visions of you commissioning the royal guards to drag me back to Jazzo. I'm on my best behavior as Jazzo's representative to the zealots on Astral Keep. Be assured I'll be calling you, mommy and Beabop regularly. Thank you." In response the King said, "Bundle, I don't have any jurisdiction on Astral Keep and it would take over a year for our spaceships to get there and back. We're going to diplomatically ask Lady Zynoplee's to use the format ship to develop a fleet of the commercial format ships which will make it possible to travel thirteen lightyears within hours not years. Again, in spite of everything I am thankful for how things have developed. I'm walking to the ship to go home since the threat has been destroyed. Thank God. I love you Jazzalin and belated happy birthday!" In a joyous voice Jazzalin replied, "I love you too daddy and thank you for the birthday wish. Tell Mommy not to worry about me. Love you both!" The call disconnected and Jazzalin used the sleeve of her robe to wipe away the tears from her eyes before going back into the kitchen to join the twins. The twins were still enjoying breakfast and they both looked up at her and asked, "He's going to let you stay?" "Yes! My father was very understanding and he was kind to me. So I'm going to finish my breakfast and we can start making our itinerary," Jazzalin said. Before the trio completed their meal Adagio appeared into the kitchen and greeted them, "Morning ladies." The girls returned the greeting, "Morning Adagio." He looked at the table of food and grabbed a plate and loaded it with as much as the plate would hold and took a seat next to Jazzalin. Turning to Jazzalin he asked, " Has your father called you today?" She answered, "Yes, I spoke with him minutes ago. We worked it out and he's not sending the royal guards to drag me home. So it's fine for me to be on Astral Keep. It's so freeing to know I'm not under parental condemnation. Lilitine, Luling, and I will be planning our social itinerary." Adagio thought, thank God. He smiled with relief and said, "That's good to hear. I'm going to the Astral Keep airport to see if the format ship is alright for my return to Jazzo tomorrow. You ladies can accompany me if you like." They all said no thanks to his invitation. With admiring gazes the three females watched as he devoured his breakfast and washing it down with a large tumbler of fruit juice. The twins giggled among themselves knowing he was Jazzalin's betrothed and she was oblivious. With their advanced spiritual insight they saw them as their future selves as a happy couple fully realizing their musical careers. They enjoyed knowing they would be involved in their ongoing love story for the next three years. Excusing themselves the girls went upstairs to dress for the day. Jazzalin looked in the large closet in the room she occupied and found it was empty except for the robe she was wearing. She ran downstairs to catch Adagio before he left for the airport. She said, "Adagio, I changed my mind I need to go to the Astraline City Shopping Hub which is on your way to the airport. I only have my ugly jacket and slacks which leave a lot to be desired fashion wise." Looking up she saw the twins coming to say they wanted to go to the city to go shopping for clothes and shoes. Adagio bounded upstairs and got dressed and came back downstairs to find his entourage waiting in the drawing room to go with him. The chauffeur droid had bought the hovercraft to the front driveway. They all climbed into the rear passenger seats and were on their way to the city. When they reached the city the girls were dropped off at the entrance of the shopping hub while Adagio proceeded to the airport. The trio took the floor lift to women's apparel and shoes level. The twins wore big smiles on their faces as they marveled at all the colorful shops, stalls and kiosks selling everything imaginable. They were oblivious to the stares of other shoppers watching them as they made their shoeless path from shop to shop. Since shoes were a priority for the twins the trio chose a store named Shoozee's". The twins were entranced by all the styles they could choose from. Jazzalin advised them that they should invest in a good pair of walking shoes for the shopping spree today and everything else would be whatever met their fancy. Wearing shoes for the first time created a sensory elevation the twins had never experienced. To have one's toes and heels encased in the cushiony interiors of fabric covered flats or animal and synthetic leather of various heel heights in a myriad of colors adorned with buttons, buckles, laces, jewels, and bows but their feminine spirits embraced wearing shoes with joy. Walking, running and dancing would be next level mobility for them. The shoe salesperson was very helpful as she would be getting a big commission for three females buying a significant number of shoes. After the shoes were purchased the trio went to several women's clothing stores and purchased many colorful outfits both casual and dressy. Before leaving the women's shops the twins had changed into one of their new outfits and were wearing cute walking shoes. They also purchased toiletries such as floral perfumes, oils and lotions. They also went to a nearby hair salon for shampoos and haircuts. The cosmetologist was aware of who the twins were and felt honored to service them. They left the shop with bouncy purple hair. Jazzalin had also followed suit changing into a blue shirt and skirt set which went well with her shampoo and new haircut. The threesome even took time to have lunch in a massive food court in the shopping hub. The twins had never had the flat savory pie with toppings nor the carbonated drinks that everyone was enjoying around them. After their first bite of the pie they were in love. They vowed they would have this treat repeatedly in the future. Jazzalin decided she wanted a sandwich and chips and her favorite blue carbonated drink. They were totally caught up in their shopping adventure and hadn't noticed how late it was. They quickly finished their meal and called a local hover transport to take them back to the twins' estate. When the hovercraft dropped them off in front of the mansion it took two service droids to assist them with the packages they had somehow managed to get home. They made sure the packages went to the correct bedroom but they all met in the hallway modeling their outfits for each other. It had been a successful shopping spree providing at least a dozen pairs of shoes for each twin and fifteen similar outfits. Jazzalin had a little less of a haul, only seven pairs of shoes including boots and a dozen new outfits. She felt this was a good start to develop a trendy wardrobe as the closet in her room was huge. The girls ran downstairs when Adagio came back, all of them telling him about their time at the shopping hub and flipping their hair to show that it was freshly shampooed and clipped. He was overwhelmed that he had to put his hands to stop the deluge of attention from the trio. Adagio announced he would be returning to Jazzo in the morning. The girls agreed to go with him to the airport to say goodbye in the morning. Since lunch was huge they all decided to skip dinner and go to bed early. Abandoned by his three housemates, Adagio was left to forage dinner for himself, which he ably had a service droid prepare and bring to his room. He would get to bed and be ready to return to Jazzo in the morning.

The next morning the twins, Jazzalin, and Adagio were chauffeured to Astral Keep airport. There on the landing strip was the beautiful silver format ship glinting in the morning sun. The entry hatch was open and the pilot android stood waiting for Adagio to board the ship. The girls followed Adagio to the ship and each one hugged him before he climbed the steps to enter the ship that would take him back to Jazzo. "Adagio, please tell Beabop to call me when she gets a chance. I'll also contact her on the commu-data stream. And thank you again for everything. Goodbye and Godspeed." Adagio responded, "I'll tell Bea to call you. It's been fun getting to meet you "Lilitine and Luling". Goodbye until we all meet again." Waving goodbye he entered the sleek ship and the gangplank was drawn up and the entry sealed. The trio watched as the ship rose effortlessly upward and in a flash jettisoned out of sight. Jazzalin spoke first, "Well, let's get home and have breakfast and get ready for the day." The twins replied, "Princess, we want to look into traveling to the platform city to visit our parents there." "Sure, I'll be happy to research that for you but I need some food first," Jazzalin said. The twins nodded their compliance and they climbed into the hovercraft and were chauffeured back to their estate. During their breakfast Jazzalin accessed the coimmu-data file for travel to the Astral Keep Platform City. She asked the twins their family last name and was advised it was "Vizun". She found the address for "Joen and Lilta Vizun" at "3 Victorie Lane/ Platform City". The data file showed they only needed to go to the Ascension Station located in Astraline City and buy a roundtrip day pass as well as a breath helmet since the atmosphere on the Platform City was rarefied. The twins were elated and they finished their food and ran upstairs to coordinate an outfit and shoes for the trip. Jazzalin also got ready for the outing to Platform City to meet the twins parents and see the place where they lived. In thirty minutes the girls were dressed and ready to go. They were chauffeured to the Ascension Station and purchased three day passes and breath helmets and boarded the public hovercraft to travel the thirty minute distance to the Platform City. The twins wearing bright red outfits and coordinating black short boots were visibly excited at the prospect of visiting their parents who had been separated from them for many centuries. When the hovercraft landed at the Platform City Station they took a local hover transport to the address "3 Victorie Lane". The residence was a large lot with lush green gardens surrounding the large bright yellow house. The girls were very impressed by the beautiful building and they approached the door and pressed a doorbell. After a few minutes a service droid opened the door and the twins in unison said, "We are Lilitine and Luling and we've come to see our parents." The droid stepped aside while saying, "They have been expecting you. Do come in." The interior of the house was just as impressive as the exterior. They entered into a green entryway which led to a lavender living room furnished with various shades of green upholstered chairs, couches, tufted stools, draperies and a vase of riotous shades of purple flowers. Suddenly from the hallway they heard footsteps and their parents calling out, "Lilitine!, Luling!" The twins in response called out, 'Mommy! Daddy!" There was an emotional collision between parents and children with much hugging and kissing. After several minutes of the love festival the twins remembered that Jazzalin was standing there and the said, "Mommy, daddy this is

Princess Jazzalin of Jazzo who is our consultant on Astral Keep. She was involved in our rescue from the Sessilum habitat." Still wrapped in each others arms their father said, "Princess we're so happy to meet you and thank you for helping with orientating our daughters to their new life on Astral Keep." In her most grownup voice Jazzalin said, "Thank you Mr. Vizun, it's my pleasure to be of service to your brave daughters who were a hidden weapon against the Sessilum which resulted in their ongoing destruction." "We welcome you to our home today and you are welcome here anytime while you are still on Astral Keep", Mr. Vizun said with a smiling face. Mrs. Vizun interjected, "And we would love to teach you the Light songs while you are living here on Astral Keep, but right now I have prepared a delightful lunch for us all. Follow me to the rear garden courtyard. Lunch is buffet style so take a plate and help yourselves." Five happy people set around a table and talked while enjoying luscious food, although the girls had to navigate eating under their breath helmets but it didn't seem to matter. After the meal was finished the twins and their parents performed a series of Light Songs to celebrate the defeat of their enemies. Their voices were blending, full, clear, and melodic ranging from soprano, alto, tenor and base. Each song documented their pre-Sessilum days on planet Shalla, their quarantined time in the protective environ on the Sessilum habitat, and their survival through the aggressive pressures awaiting their rescue. Jazzalin even hummed the melodies as she did not know the words but she was anxious in anticipation to study the Light Songs and become proficient in all aspects of their music for enjoyment or as weaponry. Their communion of kindred spirits was cut short as their return to the planet before their passes expired. Mr. and Mrs. Vizun accompanied their daughters and Jazzalin to the Descent Center for their return trip to Astral Keep. They arrived just in time for the last hovercraft to the planet. The twins said a sad goodbye to their parents promising to call them regularly as well as visit as soon as they were fully settled into their estate. The three were silent on their trip home and when they got inside the twins located the internal audio system. They wanted to inundate themselves in sound but did not know what music would serve that purpose so they looked to Jazzalin. Jazzalin, being a music student, came to the rescue and chose a cross section of classical Jazzoan jazz, off world planetary eclectic jazz, Ziggibim jazz fusion, and some of the few lucid smooth "Screech" singers. She put the volume on medium which was plenty loud enough to fill the entire house. They gathered in the library sitting in comfortable chairs and drank in the music, sometimes humming along and sometimes dancing in place or skipping around the room. After two hours of continued listening they all went to their rooms but allowed the music to play on in their rooms. Jazzalin fell asleep just as the Ziggibim jazz fusion group "Amethyst Fractals" a quartet composed of a flutist, a harprist, a drummer, and a keyboard started to play. Their music was so transcendent and transporting that even if she wasn't bone tired she would have relaxed totally from listening to it. Her mind went to thoughts of Adagio and whether he got home safe. She made a mental note to call Beabop first thing in the morning for an update.

CHAPTER 15

An hour from entering the Jazzoan upper atmosphere Adagio called his father to let him know that he was close to returning the ship and completing the mission. Reporting in Adagio said, "Hi, dad. I'm about an hour from entering the upper atmosphere and returning the format ship to Lady Zynoplee's garage hangar. Everything went smoothly except that Princess Jazzalin stowed away on board and got to witness the Sessilum eradication and a free trip to Astral Keep. It must have been some big family squabble but she wouldn't give me any details. So how's everything with you?" Hamilton Skyes inhaled after learning that Jazzalin was no longer on Jazzo and he would have to remind the King of their agreement. Most likely she had gotten wind of the betrothal and reacted by running away. Thankfully the two parties involved in the betrothal were still in the dark. He composed himself enough to answer his son, "Hi, son. Good to hear everything went as planned except for the royal stowaway. Son, we want to prevent any interaction with Lady Zynoplee so returning the ship should be quiet and flawless. When it's done I can send my hovercraft to take you home. I'm sure you're tired from the long trip, and we can discuss the trip later." "Alright dad. Another thing dad, this ship is a miracle of engineering someone on Jazzo should create a fleet of them. It took only fifteen hours to cross intergalactic space from Astral Keep back to Jazzo which with old technology would take over a year of travel time. Well, I'll see you soon. Goodbye", Adagio said. Mr. Skyes smiled to himself that he and his son were very much alike in seeing an opportunity. He saw great days ahead for the Skyes family.

Onboard the format ship the pilot android announced to it's co-pilot Adagio, "We are accessing the Jazzoan atmosphere enroute to the storage hangar on the Zynoplee estate. Please fasten your seat belt." Since the pilot android had provided a flawless flight both to and from deep space locations Adagio felt he deserved to be thanked so he replied, "Thank you pilot android," while fastening his seat belt. The ship floated in front of the cliffside hangar door as the android activated the dashboard remote and the door slid open to allow the ship entry. Once inside the hangar the ship's engines keened, went silent and allowing the cabin door to open. Adagio was elated at being on solid ground again. The pilot android walked over its charger station and powered down. Adagio felt a little sad that the android was not equipped with more interactive programming with humans to say a simple "goodbye". Adagio went to the floor lift and used his wrist holo-tran to call Beabop so that she would not be terrified to suddenly see him in her Granny's mansion. But unknown to the young man a covert security scanner was recording his presence in the hangar and had recorded his first visit there, and this information had been sent to the owner of the property. Beabop was lounging in the library listening to music and feeling a little melancholy since her best friend was lightyears away and was not going to return to Jazzo for a long time. Suddenly her comm-tran pinged and Adagio's face appeared to her surprise he said, "Beabop I'm back returning your Grandfather's ship. Can I come inside while I wait for my dad to send his hovercraft to take me home." She screamed, "Adagio! You sneaky person you! Some tour of Granny's place, you were looking for the spaceship the whole time. I should make you wait outside for your ride and set a service droid to "protect mode" and have it break your head. Come through the garage door through the kitchen it'll be open by the time you come up the lift. You culprit! I can't wait to see you!" When he opened the garage door to the kitchen he was met with Beabop's body launched at him, her arms wrapping around his neck causing him to respond, "Whoa, Beabop!!! Sorry I deceived you but it was a life or death situation", Adagio said breathlessly. Peeling her arms from around his neck and placing her in front of him as he continued to explain, "The king actually asked my dad to have me check your Granny's mansion to see if the ship had returned here after your Grandfather had been captured by the Sessilum. King Tempo had been contacted by the last two Shalla zealots living in a protective bubble on the Sessilum habitat. These zealots had read your grandfather's mind while he was still alive which showed that he sent the second format ship back to Jazzo and most likely to his house. So because I was sneaky enough to find the format ship the twin zealots were rescued and the Sextillion Brethren unleashed to destroy the Sessilum. And I was able to get the ship back in the hangar before Lady Zynoplee came home. Again I apologize for pretending to want to tour the mansion with an ulterior motive to find the ship." Looking up at him she said, "I forgive you since you saved our planetary system from being gobbled up by the nasty Sessilum but I am very upset that my cousin and best friend is way too far away to visit or have fun with." "Yeah, there's that. Jazzalin's presence was a complete surprise to me but she and her father worked it out so her stay on Astral Keep has his blessing," he said. "Can I get something to drink? Space travel is very draining", he said smiling at her. She took his hand and pulled him into the kitchen and opened the door of the preservatory and let him choose from the large selection of juices, waters, and carbonated drinks. Adagio chose a large mixed juice as well as a vitamin water which he drank both within seconds. He had called his father's office so the hovercraft had been sent to the Zynoplee estate and was pinging his wrist holo-tran that his ride home was waiting. Adagio thanked Beabop with a smack on her cheek before telling her, "Jazzalin said you should expect a call from her either today or tomorrow. I'll send you the commu-tran access code she gave me when I get home. I'm really beat so after I've gotten some sleep I'll send you the info. Bea, you're the best. Thank you for everything," he said while climbing into his chauffeured hovercraft with "Skyes" logo on the door.

King Tempo had arrived home a day before Adagio's return. He had the arduous task of explaining to his wife why Jazzalin was not with him. Queen Octiva listened as he explained that she had overheard about the betrothal and now resulting in her being on Astral Keep as a consultant to the twin zealots for possibly the next three years. This was old news to the queen but she knew that Mr. Skyes would make sure that the betrothal was upheld or it would be an embarrassment to the royal family. She was secretly proud of her daughter's determination to not be a victim of circumstance even though in the end she might be. At least she had a clear sense of self that would not let her settle for something that was unacceptable to her point of view. She was growing up fast and she would be alright and a lot of things could change in three years. She smiled that her only child had traveled lightyears to another galaxy and become a consultant to the heroes who initiated the enemy's destruction. Yes, she was proud of her little girl who had just turned fourteen three days ago.

Without delay Hamiltion Skyes called King Tempo the same day the format ship was returned to the Zynoplee estate. With as much formality as he could muster he said, "Your Majesty my son and the format ship are back on Jazzo, however, I've been advised that Princess Jazzalin is currently on Astral Keep for an undetermined period of time. I'm just calling to remind you that the betrothal is still in place in spite of her being on Astral Keep." King Tempo was dreading this call and he stabilized his emotions before replying to Hamiltion Skyes saying, "I have been expecting your call. First, I want to congratulate you on the flawless location of the format ship and the execution of the rescue of the zealots carried out by your son. My daughter overheard my conversation with her mother about the betrothal. She ran away to her best friend Beabop who is Lady Zynoplee's granddaughter and unfortunately decided the format ship was a good hiding place and when she was discovered onboard the ship they were at the Sessilum frontier and there was no turning back. She's been asked to be a consultant to the twin zealots on current cultural trends and she's going to remain on Astral Keep for the time being. I will make sure that on reaching her seventeenth birthday that she is on Jazzo to fulfill the betrothal.Anything else on your mind?", the King asked. Hamilton replied, "Yes, my son mentioned that the format ship should be mass produced since it makes interplanetary travel faster. Since I don't have any influence with Lady Zynoplee to get access to the technology it would be advantageous on many levels for you to ask her to allow a science team to study Mr. Zynoplee's designs. It would create a whole new avenue for commercial travel to nearby planets as well as other galaxies in record time." The King knew Hamilton Skyes was trying to get his control on the format ship technology and he responded, "I'll be speaking with Lady Zynoplee in time on this issue. It will be entirely her decision whether or not she releases the format ship designs and plans to anyone." The King was being very implicit that he and Lady Zynoplee were determining the future of Jazzoan space travel, not Hamilton Skyes. "Well, your Majesty we all rely on your discretion on this issue as well as the marriage of my son to your daughter, and on that note I'll say goodnight", Hamilton Skyes said and unceremoniously disconnected the call sending a message that he would make trouble if the betrothal did not end in marriage between Jazzalin and Adagio. The call to Lady Zynoplee could wait especially since she was still visiting the Eastern Region of Jazzo raising funds to build a "First Song Academy" there.

For the last week Lady Zynoplee had been receiving security spikes in her commu-tran. One incident showed the front gate opened at three in the morning and Jazzalin coming inside, a second incident showing access to two floors below her garage, which she didn't even know existed. A third incident showing the outer door of the third floor open allowing a ship to land inside and an android and Adagio to disembark. She was too busy to drop everything and run home since Beabop seemed to be handling everything without losing control. Lady Zynoplee would spend one more day in the East Region before returning to her home to get a clear picture of the strange activities in parts of the mansion she didnot know about until recently. She expected that others were involved in this breach of her property and possessions. She made her daily calls to Beabop, "Good morning darling." "Good morning Granny", Beabop replied. "I just want to tell you I'll be coming home tomorrow. Please have the kitchen droid make a tray of those small sandwiches I like as well as a berries with sponge cake. I can't wait to see you and sleep in my own bed. Well love, I'll see you tomorrow. Til then love you!" Lady Zynoplee disconnected the call. "Goodbye Granny", Beabop answered and then jumped out of bed and went to the droid instruction panel and input "whole house clean". She was glad Granny was coming home and she wanted her to see that she had not turned the house into a junk pile of neglect. Hopefully Granny had not heard anything about the Princess Jazzalin drama, the hidden lab and spaceship hangar. There was another week of summer left and she wondered what else could happen to top the last week's events. She could only wait and see.

King Tempo had assigned his best guardsman to keep Lady Zynoplee under surveillance and to inform him the minute she returned home. He wanted to make sure Hamiltion Skyes did not get to her before he had a chance to approach her about the format ship. The chauffeured hovercraft set down in the driveway of the Zynoplee mansion and Lady Zynoplee gracefully alighted and proceeded to walk to the front door which flew open allowing a energetic Beabop to throw her arms around her waist in a hug declaring, "Granny so glad you're home!" Hugging her back Lady Zynoplee smiled down at her granddaughter and replied, "So glad to be home darling. Now, let me get inside so I can start enjoying my very own domicile. Did you and Jazzalin have a good time being on your own?" "Yes we did and last week she had her fourteenth birthday party which was quizit", Beabop reported evading the fact that her friend was now five lightyears away and also betrothed in marriage on her seventeenth birthday. Once inside her home Lady Zynoplee took a brief walk through the living room, library, atrium and the kitchen before taking the floor lift to her third floor suite. She advised the service droid to bring up the sandwiches, fruit tray, cake, and a pot of purple tea. She advised Beabop to give her thirty minutes to shower and to join her for lunch in her room. The two had lunch together and since Granny expressed that she was tired from her trip so Beabop intuitively kissed her on the forehead before going downstairs to enjoy the library's music collection and to possibly receive a call from Jazzalin. After an hour of listening to a playlist of old and new music her wrist holo-tran pinged to show a unclear image of Jazzalin which said, "Hi Beabop, it's me Jazzalin. Please answer because this call may disconnect due to the long distance." Beabop activated the connect key on her holo-tran answering, "Oh, Jazzalin I'm so glad you called. Adagio just got back two days ago and Granny just came home today. I'm happy about you putting some distance between your problems, a whole five lightyears of distance. How's everything with you?" The faint image smiled and replied, "Beabop everything is great. When I spoke with my father he was surprisingly understanding so for the time being I'm going to remain on Astral Keep as the zealots' cultural consultant. I just wanted you to know how much I appreciated your help. My transmission is fading. Love you, I'll call back soon. Bye now." "Love you back. Call when you can. Be happy. Bye til our next call," Beabop replied. Jazzalin's image disappeared and Beabop felt better knowing that her friend was not under parental condemnation and that she was happy. Feeling a weight lift from her Beabop went to her room to get ready for bed. Before closing her eyes she thought how quizit it must have been to travel lightyears to another galaxy. She wondered if Granny would allow the format ship to be flown again.

The next day Lady Zynoplee felt more rested than she had in a while since she had been raising funds for the East Region First Song Academy for most of the summer. She was successful in getting all the funds needed to get the East Region First Academy constructed. She could breathe a sigh of relief knowing all of her efforts had been fruitful to the desired end of educating the youth of Jazzo in music of all kinds. Yes, she was refreshed with this knowledge and she set her day to relax in her beautiful home with the company of her granddaughter. Her thoughts were curtailed when her commu-tran pinged an incoming call from King Tempo. Connecting the call she heard King Tempo speak, "Good day Lady Zynoplee. Hope you are well today." She replied, "Good day King Tempo. I am well today and I have been expecting your call. How can I help you?" The King decided to come to the point, "Lady Zynoplee, I want to preface this conversation with an apology. When we were in the height of the Sessilum aggression we discovered two surviving Shalla zealots living in the enemy's habitat. These zealots informed us that your late husband's second format ship had not been destroyed thirteen years ago and had safely returned to Jazzo. They requested that this ship be located to effect a rescue from the Sessilum habitat and take them to Astral Keep. The Planetary Council determined since the ship did not return to the Jazzo Astronautics hangar that it must be somewhere on the Zynoplee's estate. So I contacted Mr. Skyes to see if he could assist with this issue, and he was instrumental in assisting with locating the ship. Mr. Skyes used his son Adagio's social relationship with your granddaughter to be the leverage to access your estate to successfully locate the format ship two floors beneath your garage. The second floor was a research and development lab and the third floor housed the format ship. Our enemy was escalating their aggression towards the Symphonea planetary system and we were under a time constraint. We verified that the ship was flight worthy and we authorized the format ship to be flown to extract the zealots just before the Sessilum habitat was destroyed. Adagio accompanied the pilot android as an ambassador to the zealots once they were onboard the ship. Because of the format ship we were successful in rescuing the zealots and getting them to Astral Keep as well as returning the format ship to your garage hangar. I am asking your forgiveness for the way this all happened but since the Sessilum are destroyed and the zealots were saved we hope you'll be lenient." "Well, your Majesty, what can I say to having my home entered under a false pretext and having personal property taken without my consent. I understand the urgency that led to these events but I don't have to like them", Lady Zynoplee replied. Continuing she said, "My very expensive security system notified me about three outstanding security breaches that all occurred last weekend. I have recorded images of your daughter accessing my home at a very early hour, another image showing Adagio finding the elevator to the two floors below the garage, and the image of the format ship being taken from the hangar. There's also another image showing the return of the ship to the hangar two days ago. So I was aware of things happening without my consent." King Tempo saw that his diplomacy had to go to the next level when he said,"Yes, my daughter sought out her best friend in a personal emergency and I am so thankful that she was able to depend on Beabop being there for her. But setting that aside as an unrelated issue to my call. Lady Zynoplee, I want to ask if you would consider allowing the Jazzo Astronautics science team to access your husband's research and development plans for the format ship so that it can be possibly duplicated as a commercial conveyance for faster deep space travel?" "Your Majesty, the issue of your daughter's running away from home is very much related to this issue since she was recorded getting inside the ship going out but not recorded getting out when the ship returned. Is it safe to say that Jazzalin is still on Astral Keep?", Lady Zynoplee knowingly asked. Using his cousin's first name the King said, "Audesse, let's not fight. My daughter ran away and accidently was onboard the format ship and she went to Astral Keep as the zealots cultural consultant. She has my permission to remain there for a time. But back to the format ship issue. Would you please allow our Astronautics team to access the plans for the format ship?" Lady Zynoplee took a deep breath before she said, "I will allow them access to Xanaaz's plans for the ship if Adagio is given a royal title and if he heads the corporation that forms to produce the commercial format ships. For myself I want to receive ten percent of profits generated by all aspects of the commercial production and utilization. I want the corporate name to be Zynoplee Astronautics. Also I want free passage for myself and my family to any destination. I'll have my solicitor draw up the initial plans after you give Adagio his title." King Tempo felt her demands were acceptable and he responded, "Thank you Audesse. I'll contact Adagio and let him know that he's to be titled the "Duke of Northling" and given the Northling Estate near the Aquavast Sea. We'll have the ceremony at the palace and you and Beabop can attend." "You're welcome. You would not want your daughter's future husband to be a commoner?", Lady Zynoplee said. "How did you know?", the King asked. "I know Hamilton Skyes. He would not have volunteered the services of his son without getting something in return. Fortunately for Jazzalin her betrothed is very handsome and very astute. I'm sure she'll get over her resentment by her seventeenth or eighteenth birthday. We'll discuss this further if necessary to get all of the details ironed out. I'll be looking for my invitation to the investiture ceremony. Is that agreeable for you cousin?", Lady Zynoplee casually replied. King Tempo said, "That's agreeable to me, cousin. You'll be getting your invitation soon. Thank you for everything. Goodbye for now." The two powerful personalities disconnected from the call, each feeling satisfied with the outcome. Lady Zynoplee called her office and spoke to her secretary to have an appointment setup with her legal counsel and then went to her balcony facing the ocean while enjoying her cup of purple tea. The King set about to contact Adagio with the news about the title ceremony and getting his staff in motion to make the arrangements for the ceremony.

CHAPTER 16

Hamilton Skyes ran into his wife's studio holding an invitation to Adagio Skyes' investiture ceremony as "Duke of Northling" scheduled in two weeks at the royal palace. He held the royal invitation in the air as he approach his wife yelling, "Sylphine, Adagio is going to be invested as a Duke because he was involved in the Sessilum conflict. Get out your silks and satins we're going to the palace!" In response to his announcement his wife screamed and ran up to him snatching the invitation from his hand and read it. "Hamiltion, did you know about this?" she asked. "No I'm totally surprised by this," he replied. "Let's call our son," she said as she ran to the commu-tran in her studio. When they called Adagio they got his "leave a message" option. Somewhat deflated but their spirits still ran high even if Adagio was not immediately available to share their joy. Hamilton had the kitchen droid bring a chilled bottle of sparkling wine for a toast to the pending wonderful event in their family. Hamiltion was very elated that King Tempo would recompense his son this way and he was very pleased that all the events leading to his son being so honored had gone well. His son invested as a Duke what an honor. It was something above anything he could imagine endowing on his one and only son but in spite of that he was happy for Adagio. When Adagio got home his commu-tran auto activation notified him that his parents had called. He listened to his father congratulating him while his mother screamed teary endearments from the background. A day before he had received a call from King Tempo's personal secretary advising him of the investiture and to expect the notification by courier within forty-eight hours. He was overwhelmed by this honor since he had only been a passenger onboard the format ship. If anyone should be honored it should be the pilot android but not being a living being it was disqualified. He was glad he had a week and a half to prepare for the ceremony because he still was recovering from the Sessilum, Astral Keep adventure. He wondered how Princess Jazzalin was faring since she had braved the intergalactic trip as well as her father's scrutiny. For someone so young she had shown herself to be level headed. He wished her well but his plate was quite full lately without any extra concerns. He would have to make an appointment with a tailor to be fitted for a formal jacket and trousers required for the ceremony, but that could wait. He was going to shower and go straight to bed. Life is funny he thought to himself as he showered that he would be royalty in a few days based on a ride in a ship built by a dead genius off worlder.

Lady Zynoplee opened the large engraved envelope displaying the royal seal. Inside she found the invitation to the investiture of Adagio Skyes to the Duke of Northling to be held at the Royal Palace. She smiled to herself thinking how fast King Tempo had arranged Adagio's change of social status. She was looking forward to the occasion when Jazzo's highest and best would be rubbing shoulders for an afternoon of greeting people you have not seen for a long time, eating finger foods, and sipping a variety of the King's best wines and spirits. She would take Beabop to her local dressmaker because she would not be embarrassed with her wearing a micro skirt and knee boots at the palace. Her own wardrobe was sufficient so that she need not buy anything new, she need only decide what would be best for the occasion. She wondered what Adagio's flamboyant mother would wear, one could only imagine.

On the day of Adagio's investiture the King and Queen were in their full regalia wearing jeweled crowns, satin sashes and capes. They were an impressive couple. They had determined to say Jazzalin was ill and not able to attend today's ceremony, which among the royals was code for "her absence is none of your business". The ceremony was taking place in the grand throne room. All of the guests had assembled at least fifteen minutes early in the throne room because to be late meant no admittance. At the exact time the herald announced, "Their Royal Majesties King Tempo and Queen Octiva". The couple walked majestically towards their seats on the throne while all the guests bowed in honor. Once they were seated the herald then announced, "Today we are here to present an investiture to "Adagio Jammon Skyes" for services rendered to the Crown to end the Sessilum threat. Please come forward Mr. Skyes". Adagio was exceptionally handsome today. His six foot plus frame was dressed in a beautifully fitted bright blue formal suit. His hair was beautifully cut and styled. As Adagio came forward all the women in the room look approvingly at him and the men gave him credit for being a good representative of their sex. Adagio stopped at the steps leading to the thrones and bowed on one knee and in turn King Tempo stood and approached him. The herald then handed King Tempo an ornate jeweled livery collar which he placed over the kneeling Adagio's head to have it rest on his broad shoulders. The King then said, "I now appoint you Adagio Jammon Skyes as Duke of Northling and endow you with the Northling Estates attached to the title. Stand now Adagio Jammon Skyes "Duke of Northling". The herald then announced, " I present to you all the "Duke of Northling!" A loud applause rose up from the courtiers as he walked the aisle receiving pats on the back from the men and the women did quick curtsies addressing him as "your grace". Among the ladies were the strikingly attractive Lady Zynoplee and her formally dressed granddaughter Beabop both curtseying to honor him. Finally, his parents approached him. His beautiful mother was dressed like a queen herself in a soft yellow dress and a billowing yellow hat with tears in her eyes pressed her cheek to his and said, "I'm so proud of you. I love you very much Daggie." He hugged her gently and whispered back, "I love you very much also mother." Hamilton Skyes cut a striking figure in a pale gray formal suit with bright purple handkerchief in the lapel pocket as he grabbed his son and hugged him he said, "You make me proud your grace." Adagio replied, "Thank you dad." They all came to attention as the herald stuck his staff to indicate the King and Queen were exiting the throne room allowing the courtiers to file out after them. The court servants directed the courtiers to a massive banquet room where a beautiful buffet lunch had been prepared for this occasion. King Tempo came to the new Duke of Northling and offered his hand as a sign of admiration and respect to the young man who had been instrumental in the Sessilum defeat. After shaking hands the King said, "This is just the beginning. You have an exceptional future Adagio." "Adagio replied, "Thank you Your Majesty." A servant with a tray of sparkling wine offered the two men to take a glass. Queen Octiva joined them directing a comment to

Adagio, "Congratulations, so happy for you Adagio. Are you ready to decorate Northling Estate?" "No, Your Majesty. I'm sure my mother will be happy to help me with that task. If you'll both excuse me I have an errand to complete," he said bowing as he left the banquet area. Adagio found a quiet corner in a nearby hallway and activated his holo-tran to call the Interplanetary Transmission Center to make a connection to Astral Keep. He was successful in reaching the twin zealots commutran and requested to speak to Jazzalin. Jazzalin connected to the call answering, "Hi Adagio is there a reason for your call?" "Yes, there is a reason for the call. I'm here at the Palace and I think you should speak to your mother since you haven't done so since going to Astral Keep," he said. Continuing he said, "I'm going to have her take over this call and I hope you will be respectful and not disconnect the call." "Oh Adagio I'll be happy to speak to mother. I have been so busy with the twins and just haven't had a chance to call her. Please put her on the call I'll hold", she said. Returning to the banquet Adagio approach Queen Octiva who happened to be at the buffet table. In a low voice he whispered to her, "Excuse me Your Majesty. I was able to get a call through to Astral Keep and I have Jazzalin on hold to speak with you. Is there a private place I can transfer this call to you?" The Queen's eyes grew big at the prospect of speaking with her estranged daughter and replied, "Adagio, my office is just down the hallway. You can transfer the call there. Follow me. Thank you for getting this call through to me." Opening the door to her office the Queen activated her commutran and Adagio seamlessly transferred the call to the call. As he was leaving the Queen's office he heard her say, "Jazzalin, it's mommy. So good to hear from you darling." On that note Adagio returned to the banquet room and started to graze the buffet. He felt very satisfied in his first action as Duke of Northling in joining an estranged mother and daughter together. The ceremony and buffet lasted until late afternoon before most of the guests retired to their personal abodes. The Skyes family left together in the afterglow of the ceremony, the following camaraderie they experienced during the investiture ceremony, and the following banquet. Sylphine Skyes had finally accessed the realm of the royals she idolized. She was now the mother of a Duke who would not be expected to marry a commoner, not if she could help it. She would start to research the eligible female royals on Jazzo and organize social events designed to get them together. Her busy life had taken a new turn as mother of the Duke she would be his interior decorator, landscape architect, social director and if necessary matchmaker. Her maternal senses instincts were on high alert for any and all advantages to benefit her son the Duke of Northling whether people, places or things. She was in her element and unstoppable.

After speaking with her mother Jazzalin felt that she had settled into a peace she had not had since the day she stumbled upon being betrothed in marriage. She made sure her mother was at ease with her being only fourteen and living with the zealot twins on Astral Keep. The call had taken a load off of her shoulders and she had promised to call her mother once a week. Today she and the twins would be going through the Lightsong Litany that was song while being on the Sessilum habitat. Lilitine and Luling sang in alternating voices sometimes trilling, harmonizing and sometimes singing solo. Jazzalin was a very willing student and her first soprano voice was up to the challenge. The sang for several hours before they took a break for lunch, and to discuss what would be the best way for them to proceed in teaching Jazzalin the Lightsong Litany. The twins had a low threshold for studying so after lunch they refused to go back to tutoring Jazzalin and opted to search the datafiles for popular music artists and the interplanetary social scene. They were addicted to the glitz and gossip of their favorite topic in the datafiles. Jazzalin was not a fan of this datafile topic so she took a book to read in the flower filled garden. She had no sooner found a comfortable spot under a cloud tree when she heard the twins screaming, "Jazzalin, come here! You need to see this!" Springing to her feet she ran back into the house and ran into the library where the twins were watching a royal file from a day ago. What they were watching was Adagio's investiture as Duke of Northling. He cut a handsome picture in the tailored dark blue suit and his chiseled good looks. The twins were swooning remarking, "Jazzalin, isn't he pretty?!" He's so tall and well made." They looked at her for a comment but she was not up to being diplomatic as her relationship with Adagio was prickly if not cold and she said, "He's alright." She wondered why he had not mentioned anything about his investiture when he called her a day ago. Oh well, she wasn't too concerned about his new social status but she was sure his mother would enjoy it. The twins continued to "oooooh!" and "aaaaah!" over Adagio which she could not stomach anymore so she gladly returned to her book. She realized the twins were in many ways very naive and immature with no buffers to their emotions or opinions. It would be interesting to see how they navigated their personal lives when it came to men.

King Tempo called his cousin Lady Zynoplee two days following Adagio's investiture to follow through with their agreement. Lady Zynoplee advised, "Your Majesty you are very timely with getting this enterprise underway." King Tempo replied, "The sooner we get started the sooner I'll be able to travel to Astral Keep to see Jazzalin and the twin zealots." "I'll have my secretary send the papers to the Palace by private courier as soon as I review them with my legal counsel," Lady Zynoplee said. "Thank you Audesse for expediting this issue to make it a reality for all of Jazzo and the planetary system at large," King Tempo replied. "You are welcomed cousin. Just make sure the Astronautics team knows they will only have access to the garage area and for only four hours total per day for one month to get the tech information for their project and Adagio is to be heading all of this activity," she said. "I'll stay in touch to make sure we're on target with everything. Goodbye for now," said the King. Within two days the legalities were finalized that set things in motion for the format ship venture. Adagio was contacted by King Tempo to enlist him in the format ship venture to head its initiation through to corporate development and product completion. He thought to himself that he was an eighteen year old and not used to a very regimented work ethic now being asked to head a technical project for the development of a commercial fleet of format ships for fast space travel. He would no longer be able to attend the many parties the Jazzo popular music folk invited him to attend. He would need to hire an administrative and clerical staff to keep records and schedule meetings and appointments. It seemed that his participation in helping defeat the Sessilum had launched him into adulthood a few years sooner than he had anticipated. He did not want to complain to his father because he would side with his premature adulthood. His mother would provide him a sympathetic ear if things got too overwhelming and he was sure things would. The next day a courier arrived to deliver the contracts related to the project for his signature. He was glad his mother had insisted he have an office in his apartment so that he could scan documents, make copies and file records. He did not want to read the documents so he scanned the contracts and had the legal program decipher the legalese for him. After being assured he would not be bound in any way by taking the lead in the project he signed the contracts and arranged for the courier to return them to the Zynoplee Corporate Office. Next he had to meet with the Jazzo Astronautics scientists and technicians to coordinate their involvement in the project. He was somewhat excited to see how everything would come together for all concerned. On another note he had to make time to go to his duchy and evaluate what needed to be done to make the main house suitable for him to live there. He would obviously take his mother's advice and enlist her artistic sensibilities to give it style without being too ornate or garish. He let out a breath as he realized all that was on his plate but somehow he would manage.

The following week found Adagio and ten Jazzo Aeronautic scientists and technicians standing in the driveway of the Zynoplee estate. A service droid was stationed at the garage door and greeted them and allowed them to enter the large garage. Leading the way Adagio went directly to the floor lift at the rear of the garage and pressed the button to open the door. Fortunately the lift was large enough that eleven of them fit inside the compartment. The door opened on the second floor and it was as Adagio remembered it, a large research and development laboratory with all manner of drawing boards showing graphs, tables piled with paperwork, and a large green board full of calculations. The scientists and techs split into teams and began to examine all the data that was displayed there, documenting everything in digital pictures which were uploaded to their datafiles. It took them an hour to gather and compile all the information in the R&D lab then they proceeded to the third floor. When the third floor door opened the Astronautics team were in awe of the shiny format ship sitting in the middle of the large hangar like a large silver bird. Adagio was just as impressed by the ship even though he had been a passenger onboard the wonderful craft. Their activity in the hangar activated the pilot droid who stepped free of its charger station and asked, "Are you seeking to take the ship out?" They all turned to see the pilot droid and Adagio answered, "No, we're here to look at the ship and get some idea of how it's built and how it works. Do you remember me from the trip to Astral Keep two weeks ago?" "Yes, Mr. Adagio, my memory file documents that transport. May I assist you with something today?" "Yes, we would like to examine the ship's interior and any input you can provide would be appreciated," Adagio replied. "I am able to assist you with that request. I will activate the hatch now," the droid said while the ship's hatch slid open. Adagio asked, "Droid, did Mr. Zynoplee give you a name?" "Yes, Professor Zynoplee called me "Droid #2"", the droid replied. "Then we'll call you "Droid #2" as well", Adagio said. The scientists and techs entered the ship and were surprised at its dimensions being large enough for a six foot man to stand up without hitting his head and also how well laid out the seating was on the first level and the smaller upper level. The head Aeronautic scientist advised Adagio that they needed to move the ship and the droid to their laboratory to better determine system calibrations, interfaces and parameters; the equipment for these measurements would be too cumbersome to transport to the Zynoplee estate. Adagio assured the scientist that he would get permission to have the ship and Droid#2 moved to the Astronautics lab as soon as possible. He did not feel at ease going directly to Lady Zynoplee so he used his new status as Duke of Northling to call King Tempo to provide leverage with Lady Zynoplee. The King was very willing to relay the request for the transport of the ship and it's pilot droid to the Jazzo Astronautics Lab. As a result of the request Adagio received a call from Lady Zynoplee's administrative assistant inviting him and the Astronautics team to lunch the next day. The next day when Adagio and the Astronautics team showed up to the Zynoplee estate a service droid directed them to the rear courtyard. Lady Zynoplee was there and greeted them, "Duke of Northling and Astronautics team, I welcome you to my home. Please make yourselves comfortable. You'll find snacks and finger foods on the tables along with various pitchers of beverages. Lunch will be grilled bova patties with salad toppings and your choice of sauces and dressings and a variety of desserts. Again please relax and enjoy." Turning to Adagio she said, "Duke of Northling, may I speak with you for a moment?" Adagio said, "Yes, Lady Zynoplee." She led him a little ways away from the Astronautics team who had begun to dive into the snack foods that were bountifully displayed on the tables. She addressed him, "Adagio, I want to let you know you needn't feel intimidated by me as I am completely in agreement with this project and whatever needs to happen to make it a success. As far as taking the ship and droid to the Astronautics Lab you have my permission, I only ask that after the successful production of commercial format ships that my late husband's original ship be returned to its hangar on my estate. In future you can contact my office and my administrative assistant will notify me and I'll get back to you as soon as possible. Are we in sync?" He was so glad she was making this easy for him and he replied, "Lady Zynoplee, thank you for taking a weight off my shoulders. I was not at all looking forward to asking you to move the ship and droid but you have made it painless. I do appreciate you making yourself accessible for any future issues that might arise. We'll take care with the original ship and return it when we're done. Also thank you for lunch." "You are welcomed. Now let's see where Beabop's got to. She is really missing Jazzalin these days, so we need to get the ship done so she can travel to Astral Keep to visit her until she's ready to come home", Lady Zynoplee said wistfully. "I want to get back to the food before my colleagues devour everything in sight," Adagio said with renewed vigor. The two made their way back to the lunch area to find everyone actively enjoying the grilled bova patties with carbo fries and desserts. By this time Beabop had joined the crowd and ran to her grandmother when she came into view. "Granny, thanks for making this yummy lunch for everyone", she said grazing her cheek with a kiss. Lady Zynoplee replied, "I don't make lunch dear, I plan lunch or order lunch." Turning to Adagio Beabop said, "Hi your dukeship. How's everything in Northling?" Adagio replied, "Well brat, I'm fine and I haven't been to Northling yet, but soon I'll have time to survey my dukedom." After lunch was finished it was decided that Adagio and the Astronautics Team would arrange for the format ship and Droid#2 to be transferred to the Jazzo Astronautics Lab the next day. Lady Zynoplee waved goodbye from her doorway to the Adagio and his colleagues as the hovercrafts lifted skyward. She was glad that she had cleared the air with Adagio so that he didn't see her as an adversary but a partner in the format ship venture. She thought Xanaaz would approve of Adagio as he reminded her of their son Razaf.

The next day only Adagio came for the ship since he had experience with Droid #2 on a previous trip. When he entered the third floor hangar

Droid #2 approached him and said, "Good morning Mr. Adagio. Are you here to take the ship out?" Adagio replied, "Yes, Droid #2 we're going to the Jazzo Astronautics Lab. It was the place your first flight originated. You should have that location in your memory." Droid #2 took a second to review his memory files before answering, "I do show that location in my memory files. I can input the flight pattern into the ship's navigation system." "Then we can get onboard and be on our way to the Astronautics Lab", Adagio said as he watched the ship's hatch slide open allowing access. Once they were onboard the Droid#2 activated the hangar door to open while the ship's engines keened lifting into the air then proceeding outside the hangar and climbing skyward to go to the Jazzo Astronautics Lab which would only take minutes for the speedy ship to reach. Within minutes the ship was in sight of the Jazzo Astronautics landing strip. Adagio had already notified the Astronautics head scientist of their approach so that the ship could be guided into the huge hangar for the evaluation and research needed to produce successful copies. The head scientist advised Adagio they would need at least a week to gather their initial data to begin working on a model. Adagio advised that from this point everything was in the scientist's and his team's hands but that he was there to help with any administrative non-scientific issues that might arise. Since Adagio, Duke of Northling had not seen his new endowment of Northling he was using this time to travel to the Jazzo North Region to acquaint himself with the property. It was an hour's trip in his sporty hovercraft to the south shore of the North region, and he had asked his mother to meet him there so that they could map out a plan to refurbish and renovate if it was necessary. When he was approaching the Northling Estate he saw his mother's chauffeured hovercraft already parked in front of the large main house. From the vantage point of several feet in the air it looked very neglected and rundown. He knew his mother would be undaunted by this project; she was a decorating dynamo with seemingly unlimited contacts and resources to accomplish her desired eclectic harmonious visionary end. He set his hovercraft next his mother's hovercraft. They greeted each other with a hug and proceeded to the entrance. Adagio keyed in the entry code for the door which allowed him to turn the handle letting them walk into a large entryway. Lady Sylphine made a disapproving sound, "Eeeeeooooh!!

This place needs a lot of work." Taking out her digital recorder she began to take pictures of the rooms and making verbal notes of what her ideas were for each room. Adagio was overwhelmed with how large the place was and what time and energy it would take to make it basically presentable before it could be a designer showplace. He heard his mother say, "Daggie, we need to clear out a couple of rooms and set up camp here in order to expedite this project. I'll have my admin assistant come out to help me. Don't worry son, I'll have this place gorgeous in thirty days." Adagio was not really listening to her as he went to the rear of the house to the doorway leading to a courtyard and an empty swimming pool. The courtyard stretched the entire rear of the house but it needed a considerable amount of work as did the pool. Going beyond the courtyard there was what used to be a garden and an orchard. He did have a love for gardening so he would look forward to reclaiming the landscape around the house to a pleasant green space. He could envision garden parties and picnics in the gardens he would create. He went back inside to join his mother as she moved speedily from one room to another with her digi recorder scanning all of the rooms which were being uploaded to her design program in her studio with virtual details. Adagio found the utility room which housed three service droids standing in their charging stations. He activated them and deployed them to assist with basic cleaning of floors, windows and vacuuming the carpets in the front rooms. They remained another hour in their preliminary survey of the Northling main house and determined to return to their North Region Ether house and start their plan of attack to gather all the contributing artisans and artists to transform the Northling main house into an eclectic liveable space.

It took Lady Sylphine one week to compile her arsenal of construction and decorating professionals to descend upon the Northling house. As she promised Adagio in one month the interior of the house had been transformed and within the budget that the estate had allotted for restoration. Adagio had also gotten into the spirit of creativity which resulted in landscaped stately front gardens and casual rear gardens, and he had the orchard trimmed and treated with fertilizers to ensure productive growth. He also built a large greenhouse so that his favorite plants could be propagated out of season. He was very happy that the restoration was turning out to be successful but with his mother in charge it couldn't be anything less, she was already planning an open house party. Indeed, Lady Sylphine had started to research every eligible female royal on Jazzo to include on the guest list. She was not leaving anything to chance; she would make sure Adagio had exposure to as many possible royal liaisons for a hopeful marriage and grandchildren. Her plan was to give a party once a month until something congealed with one of the royal girls. She knew Adagio was very particular when it came to girls. He had only had one real girlfriend who was seeing someone else while dating him and he decided she was not the one for him. Since then he had become reserved about girls only going to big parties and social events with them and never seeing them again. He got a nickname of "one date" Skyes. Because he was young, handsome, and wealthy he got away with any number of eccentricities. In spite of this his mother adored him and would always see him as her bright blameless Daggie.

It had been over a month since Adagio had any contact with the Astronautic's scientists or Lady Zynoplee which meant things must be going well. Nonetheless he called the Astronautics head scientist just to keep tabs on their progress. The head scientist advised that they had done a thorough and detailed systems and mechanical evaluation of the ship and droid which would allow them to go into production as soon as funds and materials were in place. That information was just what he needed to hear. He hurried to call his partner Lady Zynoplee and give her the good news. Their venture was on the brink of an explosive future and he was in the very middle of it all and he was not yet twenty years old. He could not wait to get the production of the commercial format ships underway. Now if he could only steer clear of his mother's strategic matchmaking he'd have it made. She was meddlesome like a flitterfly that didn't get the message even after being shooed away but she was an exceptional mother in all the ways that counted.

On the day of the house warming Adagio had spent the day in the orchard installing six new fruit trees which allowed him to evade the event planner and her staff of decorators and caterers. He had seen the guest list and was very impressed that his mother had managed to gather a healthy number of royal female singles, about thirty of them. There were the regular royals King Tempo and Queen Octiva, Lady Zynoplee and Beabop, Beabop's mother, the Astronautics team, his father and mother and a number of Jazzoan aristocracy. He came into the house within an hour before the festivities and took a shower in his newly decorated blue and white master suite. He would wear the same suit he wore for the investiture since it was brand new and only worn once before. His mother had surpassed herself with her decorating skill in completing a total interior makeover of a forty room mansion in record time and tonight it shined like a star with all of the extra touches for the party and the massive floral arrangements. The guests began to arrive on time and were greeted by his mother's administrative assistant to show them into the Northling house, home of the new Duke of Northling. Adagio was very impressive as he stood greeting his guests and welcoming them to the beautifully restored main house. His mother had made sure the finest audio system had been installed and now it played light airy jazz fusion setting the ambience for the evening. Everyone was impressed by the bright tasteful decor that flowed from the front door throughout the entire mansion. He allowed himself to be spread thin as he sought to dance with each of the very eager fawning royal singles but he remained aloof and polite. Finally he got to dance with his mother and was able to thank her for all she had done to make this event possible. "Mother everyone is impressed with the house, most of all me", he said, twirling her around the dance floor. Continuing he inquired, "But did you need to invite the entire unmarried royal girl troupe?" Lady Sylphine smiled at him, "Darling you know my plan is to get you married to a wonderful girl of spirit, beauty and royalty. You're my prime point of interest now and even after you're married. I'll always be there for you as will your father." "Where is your father?", she asked. Adagio located him talking to King Tempo while sipping sparkling wine. "There he is talking to King Tempo. They seem to be very intense about something", the Duke observed. "It's like watching two male bovas butting heads. They are very similar, your father and King Tempo. You know this party will be posted on the interplanetary social files? Your friends on Astral Keep will see it." His green flecked eyes widened as he looked down at her. She smiled at him and said, "Your father told me everything about how you helped the twin zealots escape the Sessilum habitat. I'm so proud of you, Your Grace." He placed a kiss on her forehead and continued to dance with her for the rest for the classic jazz vocal then thread her arm through his and escorted her to the elegantly decorated courtyard lit with hanging lanterns where a sumptuous array of food was spread across long tables. The party continued close to midnight but the King and Queen and their closest couriters had left long before. The last to go were the odd royal singles looking winsome and lonely and had to be actually told that the house was being closed to get them to leave. His parents were invited to stay the night in any of the nineteen guest rooms which they gladly accepted. Yes, his housewarming/ open house had been a thorough success establishing him in both Jazzo and Northling societies. The service droids made quick work of clearing the party leftovers. Adagio carried a plate of party food and a cold bottle of sparkling wine to his room to cap off the day before going to bed.

The aftermath of his social obligations as Duke of Northling he was called upon to head the formation of the corporate entity that would start production of the commercial format ships. In a meeting at Zynoplee Corporate Offices which included Lady Zynoplee and King Tempo's personal secretary as the King was not expected to attend ordinary business meetings. Lady Zynoplee opened the meeting, "Gentlemen we're here today to finalize the corporate agreements allowing production to begin on the commercial format ships. The head Astronautics scientist has advised that they begin the first ship in their hangar but that a factory will need to be built for mass production at some point. My research team is looking for a large enough land area to build the factory. Duke we are appointing you to lead the project to completion as Chief Executive. You'll have a salary commensurate with your position of five hundred thousand Jazzoan credits to start, subject to an annual raise. The paperwork before you Duke is for your signature to be scanned and filed. If you need time to review them with your legal counsel you're welcomed to do so." Adagio responded, "Lady Zynoplee I trust that you have my best interest at heart but just for my own sake I'll have my solicitor review the paperwork before I sign it and send it to you by courier." "You are your father's son but it's your prerogative. Then if there are no further concerns this meeting is adjourned", Lady Zynoplee said as she stood and left the room. Adagio reflected how much he had come to like Lady Zynoplee for her no nonsense attitude but she was a visionary which was refreshing.

Jazzalin and the twin zealots were taking a much deserved break following a lengthy lightsong session by diving into this week's planetary social datafiles. Opening a file for planet Jazzo there was a vizo journal titled "The Duke's Housewarming". The animated commentator said, "This is a glorious night the Duke has chosen to show off his newly restored Northling main house. King Tempo and Queen Octiva are attending as well as many of their courtiers. Oh, there's Lady Zynoplee and her granddaughter Beabop Zynoplee, as well as several young ladies of the aristocracy: there's "Bagatelle Farely, Cappella Wattalin, and Cadence Knotes to name a few. They are all beautifully presented from head to toe. The young Duke may have difficulty choosing a favorite with so many lovely possibilities. This is the highlight of the summer season. Let's go inside and have a look around." Lilitine and Luling were completely enrapt as they watched the screen. Jazzalin was glad to see her father and mother were getting out of the palace, if only for a housewarming party. Again the twins sighed in unison when Adagio's face came on the screen, "Aaaaaaaaaah!!!! Isn't he stellar beautiful. Inside and out!" Jazzalin was irritated with their fawning naivety and responded, "You two are so superficial. You have no experience with boys and when you do they'll probably take advantage of you. Just wait and see." "Oh, Jazzalin stop being such a stringent old grouch. Your future's being directed and you still are not aware of where it's leading," they said in unison. "Oh be quiet, and would you please stop talking in unison, it's weird", Jazzalin snapped back. "Our thoughts are aligned so that we speak in unison. When the time comes for us to speak separately we will. In the meantime you should practice tolerance as we do towards you", they said in unison. "I'll try", Jazzalin said and continued to watch the broadcast from five lightyears away. She was in awe of the design and style of Adagio's restored house. His mother, Lady Sylphine had a talented eye for combining color, accents and furnishings which was evident in the Northling main house renovation. Adagio must really enjoy living in such an eclectic environment. When she returned to Jazzo she would make a point of visiting him there. As annoying as the twins could be sometimes she was glad for their company and their unbound spirits energized her to do her best and to try things that she had never thought about. She and the twins had gone swimming without suits in the purple waters of a river on their estate.

It was a super warm day and they had hiked through their woods when they came upon the river and the twins reacted without any hesitation, and were undressed and in the river in a flash. Normally she would have resisted but they were having such fun she followed suit and they spent a good hour splashing and swooshing like fish in the cool river water. Another occasion they went to a local village festival and got up on the platform and sang a melody of popular songs that they had recently learned from Jazzalin. They pulled her onto the platform with them demanding her to sing harmony. Their unplanned concert was met with exhilarated applause. The twins lived in a perpetual free state without any apprehensions, no wonder they were able to withstand the Sessilum, they were beyond capture or bondage. She did not regret staying on Astral Keep with them. They were the sisters she never had, they were family, especially since she was too far from her Jazzo surrogate sister Beabop. Her life away from Jazzo was necessary; she knew she would return there someday but not right now.

CHAPTER 17

The Jazzo Astronautics head scientist was very confident that his team was in tune with the design and construct of the format ship project. In their large hangar they began to build the first commercial format ship. For the pilot and droid they had the best Jazzoan robotics specialist to interface with Droid #2 who basically educated on his interior systems creating a diagram of how to build its duplicates as well as upgrading them. The whole project was never rushed because it had to be done right the first time. The Zynoplee Corporation had managed to obtain a sizable property to build the factory for mass production of the commercial format ships in the South Region. The factory was laid out by the Astronautics scientist to maximize production and it would take a year to complete. The young Duke was proving to be a great ally as he signed off on everything and did not pretend to be scientifically astute but he did want to see the progress on the initial ship periodically. He also indicated he wanted to participate in the product testing as a passenger on the original format ship he would be sensitive to any glitches in performance in the duplicate. The scientists were very careful to follow Mr. Zynoplee's notes and designs and the pilot droid was equipped with a wealth of technical data that it was very willing to supply when needed. This project was shaping up to be a productive venture for all concerned. The scientist was going to his business broker to have him purchase several shares in the new format ship as it would be very profitable when it finally became public knowledge.

On Jazzalin's weekly call to her mother she ventured to say that they had seen the report on Adagio's housewarming party. "Mommy, we saw the report on Adagio's housewarming party. You and daddy looked really great! I was glad to see you both getting out, Adagio's mother is really talented. She designed the interior to appear contemporary posh without it being overdone," she said cheerfully. "Well, I'm glad you're keeping up with the news here on Jazzo. Adagio has also been assigned the "commercial format ship" project to have one in operation in a year or so. It will make it possible for me and your father to come to Astral Keep to visit you and the twin zealots", the Queen said wistfully. Jazzalin replied, "Mommy that would be so quizit. Do come when you can, You'll love Astral Keep! And the twins are the best people if not a little eclectic, but you'll love them." The conversation continued for another several minutes until the lengthy distance of the call started to cause static and choppiness making them bid the other goodbye. The Queen was always sad after these calls but she was glad that Jazzalin was safe and more than that she was not angry at her or the King anymore. Her heart was hopeful for the completion of the format ship as she would make sure she would have passage on it.

Jazzalin called Beabop next and it was always an energy transfer between these Jazzoan kindred spirits talking with five plus lightyears between them. Beabop lamented of how dull the Academy would be this year without Jazzalin and that she really admired her bravery for stowing away to Astral Keep. She also gave detailed report on how Lady Sylphine was giving the duke sponored luncheons inviting a bevy of single royal females. "Jazzalin, I really feel sorry for Adagio the way his mother is forcing him to choose one of the royal golddiggers. Some of them are pretty enough but they don't have the "quizit" gene. They can't sing in all the genres or dance with "smazz". If they weren't born on Jazzo they could be mistaken as Sessilum," Beabop said and they both laughed. "Beabop, do you think your Granny will allow you to come to Astral Keep when the commercial format ship is completed?", Jazzalin asked. "Jazzalin, I'll ask her as soon I get a chance. I'm sure she'll agree especially since your mother will be a passenger on the ship's maiden voyage to Astral Keep." "Oh, I can't wait for you to meet the twins you'll love them. Well, I have to go now we're going to a public concert. We'll talk again soon. Love you Bea. Goodbye for now", said Jazzalin ending the call. After she said goodbye to Jazzalin Beabop ran to her grandmother's bedroom suite yelling, "Granny where are you?!" "I'm on the balcony and don't yell, I'm not deaf. What's the urgency?"

Lady Zynoplee said. Catching her breath Beabop said, "Granny I just spoke to Jazzalin and I want to be listed for the maiden trip on the new commercial format ship. I know your corporation owns the project so please put my name on the list." "Darling they are still building the ship but I'll see what I can do. I hope the phone call is being paid for by your Astral Keep friends", Lady Zynoplee replied. "Granny, the twin zealots were endowed financially by an entire planetary system in gratitude for their service in eradicating the Sessilum. They are even wealthier than you Granny and I know you are very wealthy. Yes they can afford to pay for the calls Jazzalin makes to me", Beabop said proudly. "Don't be smart with me. I doubt that they are wealthier than me. I was having a snack on the balcony, come and join me," Lady Zynoplee offered. "Thanks Granny, I think I will. Do you have any of the small fruit pies I like?", Beabop inquired. "Yes, I do and an entire plate of small sandwiches and citrus punch to wash it all down. We can enjoy the view of the Aquavast as it's very scenic this time of day" Lady Zynoplee said invitingly. The two sat down at a glass top table and continued to converse as they enjoyed the late afternoon snack together. Munching on a fruit pie Beabop asked, "Granny how did you not know about Grandpa Zynoplee's lab and space ship hangar?" "Well, your grandfather was a very brilliant man. He could juggle multiple interests at a time and he was selective about what he thought would be good for me to know. He knew I had no interests in his scientific technical pursuits so he did not feel I needed to know about his building a lab and a hangar to store his format ship into the design of our house. One day you and I will have to tour the two floors together", Lady Zynoplee said. "Let me know Granny so that I won't be preoccupied with anything to distract my full attention from the tour", Beabop said with veiled sarcasm chewing another bite of pie. The two enjoyed each other's company until Lady Zynoplee's secretary interrupted her for an important matter from the corporate office. Beabop went back to her room to possibly call her mother to see if she was at all interested in her returning to the North Region to live with her when the school year started in a week. She hoped not. She wanted to live on campus at the Academy and go to the South Region on the weekends with Granny, Adagio had recently taken to staying at his South Region apartment to avoid the numerous spur of the moment gatherings his mother generated inviting giggly fawning female royal singles. He had to ask her emphatically to cease and desist the event planning as it was becoming tiresome and obnoxious. Lady Sylphine had managed not to cry but she had been hurt that her efforts to expedite a royal engagement had been rejected by him as interference. "Mother, as much as I know you have my best interests at heart, I do not want anymore instant parties under some pretentious social obligation related to my being a duke. I can choose my own significant other when I'm good and ready and I'm not ready yet!", Adagio said firmly. "Daggie, forgive me. I got carried away after decorating your house. I just wanted to fill it with intimacy for you but I will back off and leave you to create your own intimacy. Don't forbid me to visit you sometimes with prior notice", Lady Sylphine said, leaning to kiss her protesting son's cheek. "I forgive you mother and I'm going to be staying in the South Region to be closer to the format ship project and to make sure the new factory is up to code", Adagio informed his mother. She would bide her time until things were settled with the format ship venture and he would need her social skills to help him with a celebratory success gathering which she would gladly provide.

The prototype commercial format ship was finished in a year while the factory was still in progress of being built to build duplicates. There were many technical tests for the ship and the pilot droid. Finally the first commercial format ship was ready for its maiden flight. Everyone involved from Zynoplee corporate executives and the lowliest technician were in high spirits for the ship to dispatch to Astral Keep. The Astral Keep Astronautics Department had been notified of the departure time and their expected arrival time. The passenger list was only fifteen passengers which included Queen Octiva, Adagio Skyes, Beabop Zynoplee, the Aeronautic head scientist and eleven of his technicians would travel the fifteen hours in the exceptionally fast format ship. On arrival on Astral Keep they would have two whole days there before returning to Jazzo. Adagio had taken up the task of educating Queen Octiva and Beabop on how to secure the seat belts in the ship as well as where to access the restrooms on the upper level of the ship. The Queen and Beabop were also advised to wear recreational clothing with either short boots or canvas shoes; no glamor on this trip. They would be leaving the week of Jazzalin's fifteenth birthday and the Queen was bringing a significant trove of gifts for Jazzalin. Fortunately, the ship's design included onboard baggage storage which would accommodate the Queen's generosity. The maiden voyage for the format ship was not a media event since the entire project had been within strictest confidence. On the day of departure all the passengers had to arrive before sunrise for boarding. Once all fifteen passengers and the pilot droid were boarded the Astronautics control tower started the countdown to ascent. The pilot droid began to countdown in tandem with the tower while activating the engines. The ship lifted from the ground and ascended slowly at first then accelerated into the upper Jazzoan atmosphere then into space. The pilot droid began to inform the passengers about the speed of the format ship, the planets, and star routes they would be passing as they traveled to Astral Keep. About seven hours into the flight Queen Octiva asked Adagio about the frequent light flashes which were lighting up a vast area of space. Adagio was just as ignorant as the Queen and directed an inquiry to the head Astronautics scientist to identify the lights. The head scientist answered, "The lights you are seeing are the Sextillion Brethren purifying the space contaminated by the Sessilum." The Queen replied, "It's been over a year since the conflict was resolved. Why haven't they returned to their galaxy?" The scientist answered, "The Sextillion will remain as long as there's the smallest trace of Sessilum matter remaining to be erased. They could remain in this area indefinitely, they also will reconstruct the affected area and place several of their brethren to light up the space. These living stars are eclectic with their own ways and means." The scientist's answer seemed to satisfy the Queen's curiosity as she relaxed in her seat and thought about seeing her daughter after one year of being apart. She was anxious to see how much Jazzalin had changed after being away from her and her father.

Lilitine and Luling were very intrigued that within a year Jazzalin's betrothed had managed to get a commercial format ship built and was returning to Astral Keep accompanied by her mother and a school friend. They had planned to have a party for her fifteenth birthday which would be extra special now since loved ones from Jazzo would be arriving in several hours. The twins had never had parties in their lives and had to research the concept in the datafiles to know how to plan one. They had enlisted a local event planner to help them with the details so their first attempt at a social gathering would not be tragic. Their plans included eccentric party decorations, a huge colorful cake confection, mountains of savory and salty foods and snacks, a fountain of juices and drinks, fresh fruits and frozen dairy desserts. It was very fortunate that the twin's estate was exceptionally large to accommodate their pending interplanetary guests. The day of the arrival of their guests the twins had locked the access to the large dining room so the event planner and service droids could decorate it and arrange tables used for food placement. Since Jazzalin always ate in the kitchen it was not difficult to keep the party preparations secret. The twins were in high spirits as they felt energized to be able to grace their consultant, instructor and friend with a celebration of her fifteenth year of life. The three of them were counting the hours until the speedy format ship would arrive on Astral Keep and they would be in the company of dear family and friends if only for two days.

CHAPTER 18

Jazzalin was tense with anticipation to see her mother, Beabop, and even Adagio. She hoped that her mother did not expect her to return to Jazzo because she was not at all ready or willing to return there, but her father would insist she return to Jazzo. Lilitine and Luling would double up in one room so Queen Octiva could have their spare room. Jazzalin and Beabop would share her room while Adagio would have the same room he had on his first visit to Astral Keep. The Astronautics scientist and his technicians would be housed in the spacious separate guest house on the property. All of the people descending on the twin's estate reminded her of times on Jazzo when the palace was full of visiting guests and everyone was on their best behavior. She could only hope good behavior would be on target especially with the twins who could be blunt and obnoxious when they had a mind to be. The next few days would prove to be a mix of sentiment, fun, camaraderie and love. The twins canceled their social tutoring today with her, as they, like her, were too excited to focus on learning while waiting for guests to arrive.

The pilot droid announced to the fifteen passengers that they were thirty minutes away from entering the Astral Keep upper atmosphere and to please fasten their seatbelts as the ship's deceleration could be dangerous to anyone standing. Beabop and Queen Octiva were staring out of the ship's windows and were breathless when they got their first glimpse of Astral Keep. From their vantage point it was plain to see that Astral Keep dwarfed Jazzo several times but it's green and purple topography was similar to that of Jazzo. The lights of the cities however were more vast than on Jazzo covering entire continents. Then there floating considerably above the planet was the domed platform city which was well outside the atmosphere of Astral Keep. The droid announced that the ship was in descent to the Astraline City Astronautics Space port. With programmed technical skill the pilot droid landed the first commercial format ship crossing over five light years in fifteen hours. When the ship's hatch was opened the Astral Keep's Astronautics commander approached Adagio and the Jazzoan Astronautic's head scientist congratulating them on the ship's technology that had allowed them to make the non-stop trip within hours when standard technology would take over one year to arrive with refueling. They had arrived in late afternoon and the blue sky above was tinged with shades of orange, pink and purple painting the way for evening. Adagio excused himself briefly to call the twin's estate to inform them that he, Queen Octiva, and Beabop had arrived and would be there soon. For the Jazzoan Aeronautic head scientist and his techs this trip was strictly in name of science, so he refused invitation to stay at the twin's estate and opted to accept the offer of the Astral Keep's Astronautics commander to use the barracks of the city's guardsmen who were all on furlough for the summer. The Jazzoan techs helped unload the Queen's many packages and luggage from the ship and loaded them into an Astral Keep military hovercraft. Before departing to the twin's estate Adagio confirmed that he could be reached by the scientist if there should be any emergency. Using his position as Duke of Northling he commanded the scientist and the technicians to attend the party tomorrow for Princess Jazzalin. They boarded the hovercraft and proceeded through Astraline City to a residential area of large houses. The hovercraft turned into a driveway leading to an exceptionally beautiful large house. As soon as the hovercraft stopped in front of the entrance the door flew open and Jazzalin ran out. Not waiting for the usual formal vehicle door opening Queen Octiva opened the door herself and jumped out to throw her arms around her daughter crying, "Jazzalin, Jazzalin. Thank heaven you're alright. It was a year ago that I saw you on your fourteenth birthday. Let me look at you!" "Mommy, I'm so glad you came! Where's Bea?", Jazzalin said. "Here I am. You owe me again for making me travel over five light years to see you", Beabop said while hugging her best friend. From inside the twins said in unison, "Come inside and greet each other in comfort." Adagio spoke, "Yes, let's get inside.

Lilitine and Luling how are you both?" The guests and their family and friends made their way inside to a beautifully decorated hallway adjacent to a large living room full of colorful furnishings, plants and art. The reunion and introductions continued in the living room. "Mommy, I want you to meet the excellent twin zealots heroes of the Sessilum conflict Mistresses Lilitine and Luling. Lilitine and Luling please meet my mother "Queen Octiva of Jazzo", Jazzalin introduced. The twins curtsied before Queen Octiva and in unison said, "It is an honor to meet Your Majesty. Welcome to our home and thank you for allowing Princess Jazzalin to be our social consultant. We are hoping your visit will be pleasant and we are at your disposal to provide anything you may need." Queen Octiva replied, "Thank you ladies for welcoming me into your lovely home and for your kindness to my daughter. You both are most welcome to visit my home anytime you want to make the trip." Jazzalin turns to Adagio and says, " Adagio, thanks for getting Lady Zynoplee to build a commercial format ship so my mother could visit me. I saw your investiture to Duke of Northling on the interplanetary datafiles. It was very impressive and you were very deserving of the honor." Smiling, she shyly hugged him. "Come on Mommy and you too Beabop. I'll show you to the rooms we have for you. I'm sure you want to rest and get your bearings. Let me know if either of you want to have dinner in your rooms," Jazzalin said while escorting them upstairs. The service droids had taken their luggage upstairs already. "Adagio you have the same room you had when you were here before and we'll have a service droid bring your dinner to your room. We're having a roast of some kind and a rich veggie casserole and fresh bread rolls. There's also dessert that the twins made from summer berries, cake and whipped cream. We're so excited you all are here!" After making sure her mother was settled in her room she went to her room where Beabop was waiting. "Jazzalin, you came out on top in spite of everything. You're over five lightyears away from Jazzo living with planetary heroes in a mansion. It's amazing how things turned out for you. You know it's exactly a year tomorrow that you left Jazzo", Beabop said while sitting in the middle of Jazzalin's large bed. Jazzaliin responded, "Well, I was motivated and providence was on my side. So here we both are, my dear friend and I wouldn't have it any other way. Let's get you settled and call for dinner. The twins will have already had their dinner sent up. They are very punctual about meals." The friends continued to chat as Beabop got ready to shower and Jazzalin ordered dinner for them to be sent up in thirty minutes. She left her room to run next door to make sure Queen Octiva was alright and to speak to her about something. Jazzalin tapped on the door and quietly entered the room to find Queen Octiva had finished her bath and was brushing her thick dark hair while sitting on a small pink couch. Acknowledging her the Queen said, "Jazzalin come in. This is a really beautiful house your friends were gifted. Is there something bothering you?" "No. Mommy I just wanted to apologize to you in person for any stress you experienced because I ran away. I was so overwhelmed with what I heard I just reacted and then I accidently stowed away on the format ship and ended up here. Mommy I am still not ready to go back to Jazzo. The twins depend on me to help them acclimate to this new lifestyle. I help them and they are teaching me the Lightsong Litanies. We have a reciprocal relationship which benefits the three of us. I hope I'm not being obstinate because that's not what I want to be", Jazzalin said tentatively. Queen Octiva smiled and replied, "Jazzalin, I came to visit you not to command you to return to Jazzo. I am so proud of the courage you had to be moved to influence your destiny by setting out on this adventure. When I was your age I would never have had courage enough to do anything like you've done. Your bravery has made me brave too. I would never have traveled over five lightyears unless it was to see you. So your actions may have been impulsive but have resulted in your mother being a passenger on the first commercial format ship which successfully traveled to Astral Keep to see her exceptional daughter. You'll come home when you're ready. I'm happy you're here. Now, give me a hug and call for my dinner." While hugging her mother she whispered, "Mommy you're the best, and I love you." Returning to her room she found that Beabop had already finished her shower and gotten into bed and was fast asleep. She was a victim of flight lag after not sleeping during the long flight from Jazzo. Jazzalin joined her mother again and they had dinner together in her bedroom. When the service droid removed their dinner trays Queen Octiva yawned and Jazzalin realized she should let her mother get some rest. Kissing her forehead Jazzalin said, "Goodnight Mommy. We'll talk more tomorrow. Love you." "Love you too", Queen Octiva replied as she snuggled into the fluffy covers of the bed. As soon as Jazzalin had gone into her bedroom Lilitine and Luling stealthily tapped on Queen's bedroom door. "Come in", she said sleepily. The twins came into the room to advise her that for Jazzalin's birthday tomorrow it would be an all day celebration starting with breakfast and ending in a full on party in the afternoon going into evening. The Queen thanked them for informing her so the birthday presents she bought with her could be distributed to Jazzalin throughout the day. Having completed their task they quickly said goodnight and thanked Queen Octiva for participating with their plan.

The next morning the twins woke up before sunrise and had the service droid start breakfast and decorate the kitchen with floating globes,streamers and a banner that said "Happy 15th Birthday Jazzalin!!!" Jazzalin and their guests did not wake up until around nine o'clock. The twins prompted the kitchen droid to make tea, to bake the breakfast bread, and to put out the clotted dairy and fruit. When Jazzalin walked into the kitchen followed by her mother, Beabop, and Adagio the twins broke into a harmonic song, "Happy birthday to you as happily we celebrate you, happy birthday, happy birthday dear Jazzalin to you!!!!" Jazzalin was encircled by her mother, Beabop and the twins in a group hug. Adagio stood apart until the twins pulled him into their circle. After several minutes Jazzalin said, "Thank you for remembering my birthday today. I was not really expecting anything. I appreciate all of you so much. Now, I'm starving and I smell fresh baked bread and there's a teapot steaming. Let's eat!" They all took a seat at the kitchen table as the service droid placed the food and tea on the table. They leisurely ate at the same time chatted about various topics. Finally Jazzalin asked, "Adagio since your commercial format ship has proved successful when will you put them into production?" Adagio finished his bite of bread before replying, "I have to meet with Lady Zynoplee and the board when I get back to Jazzo. Also the factory for production of format ships is several months from completion. At this time everything is pending." "Jazzalin stop being such a smarty we came here to visit you and to celebrate your birthday. Let's go upstairs and see what I brought you five lightyears away", said Beabop saucily. Taking Jazzalin by the hand Beabop lead her back upstairs to the bedroom.

Inside the bedroom Beabop opened her luggage case and took out a beautiful multicolored silk jacket with matching slacks and a pair of silk covered flats. The outfit was Jazzalin's size and complimented her tan complexion. "Beabop, it's quizit!!!! You always had quirky taste in clothes but a great eye for fashion", Jazzalin said as she hugged Beabop. "You know it. I have a quizit sense of what looks good on me and I got the same outfit for me in another color. We can wear them to your party later today", Beabop said. "Nobody's said anything about a party today", Jazzalin said. "Jazzalin you are so dense. Those weird twins are up to something and it's a party. Your mother has brought a load of presents with her for you. There's a party happening today", Beabop said knowingly. Jazzalin laughed out loud at her friend danced on tip toes into the bathroom to take a shower and get ready for the forecasted party.

Queen Octiva joined the twins to set the stage for Jazzalin's unsuspected party. The Queen was expert at party planning and was quite impressed with the way the twins had set up the decorations in the dining room. A large side table was prepped for food and there was a beverage station. Also hundreds of colorful floating globes were aloft, with a tangle of streamers and happy birthday banners that created a joyful atmosphere. She gave her approval to the twins that she did not need to contribute anything more to what had already been done. She excused herself to go upstairs to get ready for the birthday party for Jazzalin which would be very different from last year's party, especially where location was concerned. Queen Octiva also took time to make a call to her husband the King. When he answered she said, "Tempo it's me. I'm sorry I did not call you last night but I was distracted by seeing our daughter again. We arrived safe and sound. The ship is amazing and I hope you have invested in it. But back to Jazzalin, she's so grown up for her fifteen years. We're having her fifteenth birthday party today and I'll have her call later." "Well, I'm happy you arrived safely and that you're happy to find Jazzalin in good health and spirits. I look forward to Jazzalin's call. Let's make this call short because it's very expensive. I'll say goodbye now. I love you", said King Tempo. "Goodbye Tempo. I love you too", the Queen replied. Around three o'clock in the afternoon a loud cymbal crash came from downstairs bringing everyone out of their rooms to see what was happening. The twins were dressed in bright pink party dresses with floral garlands around their heads standing in the hallway with a service droid holding a pair of cymbals above its head. In unison the twins said, "We are inviting all residents and guests to celebrate the fifteenth birthday of Princess Jazzalin Apreggia Maximus of Jazzo, to be held in the main dining room today. Please dress accordingly, recreational wear is not acceptable. There will be food, music, and dancing. Festivities will start when all are present." Jazzalin and Beabop hurried to their room to put on the matching new outfits, as did Adagio go into his room to change into his party clothes. The Queen had already dressed for the occasion and used this time to have a service droid to bring down the many gifts she had bought for Jazzalin. In less than thirty minutes Jazzalin, Beabop, and Adagio entered the main dining room which had been transformed into a colorful celebration space complete with hundreds of small twinkle lights to illuminate it all. The twins had become experts at programming the music system and had compiled a number of bright and lively tunes both vocal and instrumental to accompany their activities. Queen Octiva approached Jazzalin and said, "Darling, this is all for you, enjoy it." Pointing to a stack of beautifully wrapped packages she continued, "I took Beabop with me on a shopping spree at the Shop-Along Center and we got a little carried away. You won't have to shop for a while, we got everything from clothes to shoes." Jazzalin hugged her mother and said, "Mommy thank you. I know it's been a difficult issue this past year but I'm so glad you were able to give me the space I need right now." With big smiles on their faces the twins said in unison, "Do you like it Jazzalin? We never had parties when we were in the Sessilum habitat but we researched the data files and got some advice from your mother about the lighting. Say that you like it!" Jazzalin embraced them both at once and replied, "You both are so dear to me. I couldn't be more pleased that you wanted to give me a party and for your first try it's "quizit"!!!!" There was a knock at the front door and the service droid answered and announced that the Jazzo Astronautics scientist and technicians had arrived. The group of noisy guests came into the party and were introduced to Queen Octiva and Princess Jazzalin. The twins had also invited the neighbors from next door and their several daughters so there would not be too much of an uneven amount of either gender. After several minutes Adagio approached Jazzalin and said, "Jazzalin, I'm so glad things worked out for you because last year this time we were flying in a confiscated format ship and you were a stow away. I just want you to know that you're missed by everyone on Jazzo. Here, I want to give you this for your birthday." He handed her a small wrapped square package. Wide eyed Jazzalin looked at him while taking the present from him she said, "Thank you Adagio, you didn't have to. I know I've been a pain to my family and friends this past year but thank you for being understanding. I appreciate you calling me during your investiture to remind me I hadn't called mother since arriving on Astral Keep. She was so relieved and it opened a door for me to call her often. I'll open this later and thanks again." Tip toeing she kissed his cheek and turned to go deposit yet another present on the table that was already full of them. The minute she left Adagio the twins made a direct line to him, one on either side of him, smiling while gazing up at him. Being used to this kind of adoration he took it in stride and spoke to them like they were drunken children. They pulled him to a clear place on the dance floor and the three of them danced to an upbeat instrumental. Beabop said to Jazzalin, "Your twins have no shame but at least they know how to dance. Did you teach them?" "No, they watch the weekly music shows on the datafiles. They have adhesive memories, anything they see sticks and if they want to they can duplicate it. They do have a weakness in the man department. I hope they meet the right type because they are great girls, somewhat strange but great. I think I'll rescue Adagio before they drown him in drool." Jazzalin waited until another song was playing before going up to the threesome and unceremoniously grabbing Adagio's hand saying to the crestfallen twins, "Birthday girl privileges. Come on Adagio, let's dance." Adagio smiled and said, "Thank you Princess for the rescue." "You're welcome. The twins are still smoothing out certain social wrinkles like "gang dancing". You happen to be a favorite topic of theirs since they first saw you on the ship last year." The party was in full momentum when Queen Octiva called for everyone's attention in order to sing "happy birthday" to Jazzalin and to have her cut the enormous pink and purple cake. Jazzalin was in tears with the sheer joy of being in the midst of so much affection and was caught off guard when Adagio kissed her full on the mouth. It was a brief kiss but a kiss nonetheless. She quickly regained her composure and asked her mother to help her call Jazzo to speak to King Tempo. The two left the dining room and went upstairs to the Queen's room. The Queen input the contact code for King Tempo's private commu-tran. There was a brief wait because of the vast distance to complete the call. Finally King Tempo answered, "King Tempo speaking. Jazzalin is that you?" "Yes papa it's me. I'm here with mommy. I wish you could have come too." The King answered, "One of the monarchy has to be present "on planet" at all times so we both couldn't be away from Jazzo. Well, happy birthday to you bundle!" Responding she said, "Thank you papa. The twins threw a party for me, but I think they got some help from mommy. I'll send you a vidi of the party. How are you these days?", "I'm fine, busy keeping the planet in tune. So how are you and your betrothed getting along?" Jazzalin took in a sharp breath before asking, "What do you mean?" Apologetically her father responded, "Oh my, I've spoken out of turn, you didn't know. Is your mother still in the room?" "No, she left to give me privacy but what did you mean about getting along with my betrothed?" "Jazzalin, Adagio is the person you are betrothed to. His father insisted on the betrothal to enlist Adagio's help to find the format ship on the Zynoplee estate without a socio-political uproar. The situation was at an urgent level with the Sessilum threatening to destroy the planetary system, I had no choice. I thought your mother or the twins had told you by now." "Does Adagio know?" she asked. The King said, "I don't know because he's never approached me to inquire about it and I told his father he shouldn't say anything about it until the Sessilum aggression had been handled. It's been a year, so maybe he knows. Has he said anything to you about it?" "No he hasn't. I'm totally overwhelmed about this. Here I am over five lightyears away from Jazzo and I'm still trapped by the same issue I ran away from a year ago on my fourteenth birthday. It's funny how things remain the same wherever you are", Jazzalin said her voice trailing off into a whisper. Sensing his daughter's anxiety the King responded, "Don't be upset Jazzalin. You still have two years until this betrothal has to be finalized, and by then Adagio could become involved with someone else and insist the betrothal be dissolved. I'm sorry I was unable to keep this information from you. Your mother is the one who has discretion and you take after her in that regard. I was never good at keeping secrets. But if worse comes to worse, Adagio is not a bad choice he's sought after by the most eligible single females on Jazzo. Bundle, don't let this ruin your party celebration. You're a Maximus and that means you don't crumble over every little disappointment. I want you to be the Princess of Jazzo that you are and don't let your mother know I told you anything. Understand?" "Yes, papa, I understand", Jazzalin said. "I'm going to say goodbye since this call is on my bill and it's super expensive. I love you bundle and this whole thing will work out fine for all of us, you'll see. Goodbye Jazzalin, all my love", King Tempo said. "Goodbye papa", Jazzalin said before the connection died. She looked at her reflection in the bathroom mirror to see if the news about the betrothal had visibly scarred her. She felt scarred but it was internal and she was going to do her best to hide it. Going downstairs back to the party she saw the twins had found two very handsome technicians who seemed to reciprocate their enthusiastic attentions. Beabop met her as soon as she walked into the room and said, "Did your father demand you come home? You look a little frayed at the ends. Come on let's get you some liquid refreshment." Grabbing her by the hand Beabop pulled Jazzalin to the drinks counter and requested two glasses of pink sparkling wine. Jazzalin took a large gulp of the cold drink and said, "I'm betrothed to Adagio. Did you know that?" "Yes, my Granny told me just before I left on this trip to Astral Keep but I was sworn to silence and not to say anything about it to you or anyone else. So your father spilled the secret to you?", Beabop said while sipping her drink. "Yes, my father let it slip out while we were talking. How can I get through the rest of this party knowing what I know?", Jazzalin said anxiously. "You'll just stay near me and we'll avoid any contact with your betrothed for the rest of the party and you can run upstairs as soon as the guests start to leave", Beabop said resolutely. Queen Octiva walked over to them and asked, "How did your call go with your father Jazzalin?" "It went really well. You know papa's to the point. Happy birthday and let's not over do the call time", she replied. "Well I'm a little tired so please excuse me, I'm going to get ready for bed. I'm sure you and the twins are able to handle the activities from here. Happy birthday again love. Goodnight Jazzalin and you too Beabop", the Queen said and left the dining room to go upstairs. The two friends saw the ever popular Adagio was surrounded by the neighbor girls who recognized him as Duke of Northling of Jazzo. He was being his long suffering self and one of the braver girls asked him for a dance which he graciously obliged. He seemed to enjoy his dance with the pretty Astral Keep maiden and she was covered in blushes that he was actually speaking to her with interest and she even curtsied to him at the end of the dance. Jazzalin turned her attention to the pile of birthday gifts and began to open them and was amazed at her mother's taste but then she realized that Beabop had been the fashion consultant so she would not look like a Ziggabim ruralite. Beabop stood close by to help Jazzalin with the bounty of gifts being stacked into a basket for the service droid to take to her room. At ten o'clock the twins got everyone's attention by tapping a spoon against a glass announcing, "We want to thank you all for attending the celebration of Princess Jazzalin of Jazzo's fifteenth birthday, unfortunately we have to bid you good evening but we send you home with a gift as a token of our gratitude and because we had too much birthday cake left. You can take a gift bag from the table in the entry hall." They beckoned Jazzalin to stand and to speak to her guests, "Yes, thank you all for joining in my birthday celebration today and please know how much I appreciate your presence here as well as your gifts given and I graciously bid good evening to you all." A burst of applause went up and a chorus of "Happy Birthday Princess Jazzalin!!!!", from all of her guests as they proceeded to leave. "Jazzalin, this has been the best day for us and it wasn't even our party!", the twins said with big smiles on their faces. "It was a joy! I can't thank you enough but I don't want a repeat of your event planning for my sixteenth birthday. Alright?", Jazzalin said. Lilitine and Luling smiled sweetly and replied, "It's a year away and so much is still up in the air for you. But we will honor your request for now but just for now." "Ladies, let's not get serious as we're all a little tired. Let's all get some sleep and discuss weighty issues in the morning. Alright?", Adagio said diplomatically. "Thank you Adagio, you're right. Come on Beabop I may want to open a few more gifts before I go to bed. Goodnight Lilitine and Luling and Adagio. Sleep well. See you all in the morning", Jazzalin said as she and Beabop proceeded upstairs. Once inside her room Jazzalin went to the basket of gifts that had been taken to her room and searched for the box Adagio had given her. She found the beautifully wrapped box and tore off the wrapping and found a pink geode box. She lifted the lid of the box and saw a pair of hoop earrings encrusted in pink diamonds. She turned to Beabop holding the pretty jewelry up and said, "Bea, look what Adagio gave me. Do you feel this is a little much? What do you think?" "Oh Jazzalin, at least it wasn't a ring. If I were you I'd wear them in the morning with my most casual slacks and tunic so that he sees that you are not overwhelmed that he gave you diamond earrings. And please don't be a droopy face around him and your mother tomorrow. I'm beat and my counseling services are closed for today", Beabop said then yawned. "Oh, stop being so mature!", Jazzalin said as she threw a pillow at her friend who had evasively scrambled under the bed covers. The large house was quiet as its residents and guests had retired from a current of festive energy and joy. The service droids were actively going about their programming to clear away the party decorations and clean up all the crumbs and spills generated by the party guests.

The next day everyone woke up late except the twins and Adagio. Adagio came downstairs around 8 morning time and he greeted the twins, "Good morning ladies. I didn't expect to see anyone up this early except me. I have to run over to the Astronautics airfield on a business issue. So if anyone asks, tell them I'll be out until the afternoon", he said as he poured himself a cup of purple tea. The twins were so in awe of him, so cleanly groomed and dressed that all they could say in unison was, "Yes, we'll be sure to let everyone know you are out on business until the afternoon." Finishing his tea he smiled at them and energetically went to the front door leaving the house for the waiting Astral Keep military hovercraft. The twins followed him to the front entrance and watched him as he was chauffeured off in the topless hovercraft. They thought how could Jazzalin not like him when he was very masculine, kind, and intelligent. The twins had lessened their fixation on Adagio because they had made a connection with two brothers who were with the Jazzoan scientist's technicians whose names were Metre and Mezzur Bynary. The handsome brothers had given the twins their Jazzoan contact information so that when they returned to Jazzo they could stay in touch with them. They were beside themselves as to when they should call their new found liaisons and what they should talk about since their social experience with males was limited. They would have Jazzalin give them some pointers although her behavior towards Adagio made them skeptical that she would be a reliable source on the subject. Just then Jazzalin, Beabop and Queen Octiva descended the stairway, gave them a brief greeting, and passed them enroute to the kitchen. Jazzalin gave a menu to the kitchen droid which consisted of fluffy breakfast cakes and fruit syrups, clotted dairy with fresh berries and toasted grain toppings, scrambled bird eggs and lots of strong purple tea with citrus. The droid assembled the food in minutes and brought it to the kitchen table where the three hungry females sat waiting. "Everything looks yummy. I'm having some of everything", the Queen said while serving up her plate with scrambled eggs, breakfast cakes drowned in syrup, a big bowl of clotted dairy and berries and pouring a big cup of purple tea. Jazzalin had never seen her mother eat so much, especially in the morning when she usually only drank a small cup of purple tea with citrus. Today she was eating like a farm worker. She must have perceived Jazzalin's thinking and smiled, "I didn't eat much of the party food yesterday. It was good but I wasn't hungry for party sandwiches and pastries but this is so fresh and well cooked I can't resist it." "Oh, mommy I'm so glad you like the food. Please enjoy it, don't have any worries about criticism from anyone", Jazzalin said to crush any embarrassment her mother might feel about enjoying her breakfast bounty. Both Jazzalin and Beabop followed suit by enjoying a healthy assortment of the breakfast fare until all their plates were empty and they were very sated. Afterwards they found the twins in their study intently sifting through the social threads for the news of celebrities and fashion trends. They both looked up and said, "Good morning. If you're wondering, Adagio went to the airfield on a business matter and he'll return later this afternoon. In the meantime Jazzalin will be your gracious hostess. Oh and lunch is anytime you want it just speak to the kitchen droid and it will prepare whatever you want. Oh Jazzalin, you might want to show your mother the flower garden you were so instrumental in designing with your Majesty's favorite flowers. This is our research time and we make full advantage of it. You ladies can join us if you like, but suit yourselves." Jazzalin gave them an annoyed look as she replied, "Yes, mommy let me show the garden we planted with all the Jazzoan flowers you taught me about. We had to order them, it took weeks to get them from garden societies on Astral Keep. Come on it's through the atrium past the patio." Taking her mother's hand she lead her and Beabop outside into the warm daylight. Queen Octiva commented, "What lovely earrings your wearing today Jazzalin. They are very beautiful, pink diamonds on platinum I think. Where did you get them?" "Oh they were a birthday gift from Adagio. Something I can wear everyday", Jazzalin responded nonchalantly. "Jazzalin, I know jewelry, and those earrings are very expensive and I'd advise you to be careful about wearing them casually everyday", the Queen said sternly. "Mommy I'm not a careless person and I still have the first gold hoop earrings you and papa gave me when I was five", Jazzalin said somewhat irritated. Her mother squeezed her hand and said, "I know you are a responsible person but again those are really expensive earrings and it would be a pity to lose them when you're busy during a shopping spree or planting your garden. Come on take me to your Jazzo garden on Astral Keep. The weather is very plant friendly it seems." "Yes you just have to put a seed or seedling in the soil and it starts to grow. Here through this gate. We have a garden droid we call it "Planter One" because it's the first model of its kind for home use. Normally they are used in commercial nurseries but when the twins were gifted this house they included "Planter One" to help them with gardening since they were from an agricultural background. The twins are not at all interested in agriculture now but Planter One was very helpful in putting this garden together and keeping it healthy" Jazzalin said while leading her mother and friend through a maze of hedged garden rooms. "Planter One, where are you?", she yelled. Out of nowhere a tall droid appeared dressed in drab work overalls and a cloth cap. "Good morning Miss Jazzalin. How are you today?", said the droid with human inflections. "I'm fine. Planter this is my mother Queen Octiva and my best friend from planet Jazzo, Beabop and I'd like you to show them the garden you helped to create and maintain of Jazzoan native plants", Jazzalin said to the tall droid. "My pleasure Miss Jazzalin. This way your Majesty and Beabop, I just finished watering the Jazzo garden. It is a favorite of mine because it has a large variety of plants that aren't native to Astral Keep and require a different regimen to keep them growing. Here we are ladies, the Jazzo garden", said Planter One. "Oh Jazzalin this is glorious!", Queen Octiva gushed. Jazzalin smiled at her mother's enthusiasm to seeing the Jazzo garden which was in full bloom. There's blue "Rain lilies", yellow "Trilla flowers", multi-colored "Gee-gee" flowers, pink "Sun Spray" lilies, blue

"Cyrstalline flowers", pastel "Pom-pom brushes", black purple flowering "Spirrel vines", orange "Scatta flowers" red and white "Star lilies", and white "Omne flowers" which were all happily displayed in dedicated flower beds on this warm mid summer's day. Planter One was actively providing information to Queen Octiva who was an avid gardener herself. Jazzalin and Beabop found a bench under a small Cloud tree as they hadn't had time to catch on the latest news on Jazzo. "Beabop so how was the Academy this past school year?", Jazzalin asked. "Well, I told Granny I would try to continue going to the Academy but that it would be difficult with you gone. She took it to mean I would do poorly and she spoke to mother to allow me to live with her for the school year and she would have a tutor assigned to continue my education. Since my mother is all about dating and finding a new husband she saw her opportunity and said yes to Granny's offer. So I got a really lucid, and single tutor "Mr. Reed Aubade". He is so quizit. Both his parents sing with the Jazzo Classical and Jazz Music Guild. His knowledge of music history and current music technique is so on point. I've learned more in the last school year than all the time I've spent at the Academy. I have his picture on my wrist commu-tran, let me bring it up on the screen'" Beabop said while scrolling through data until she located her instructor's image. Holding the her wrist up to Jazzalin's line of vision Beabop cooed, "Isn't he dreamy?" Jazzalin saw the angular features of Mr Aubade's handsome face with intelligent blue-green eyes, a wide full mouth, and a thick head of dark blue hair. "Yes, he's quizit but somewhat old for you", Jazzalin replied. "I'm not going to marry him I'm just his admirer for the time he tutors me. He's so clueless because I'm very good at concealing my feelings. Anyway he's dating some Theatre Muzeek five octave soprano starlet so he's safe from my seductive wiles", Beabop said snidely. Jazzalin laughed and nudged her with her elbow for being an aware and unaffected young female and for being her best friend. Queen Octiva rejoined the girls with Planter One following her saying, "Jazzalin Planter One is a wealth of information on gardening and has given me invaluable tips on making my garden at home as beautiful as yours here on Astral Keep. Planter says it's able to send me a data stream to my commu-tran on Jazzo." Jazzalin happily replied, "Yes, it's connected to the Astral Keep Horticultural data stream and that gives it access to multiple planets regarding gardening information. I'm so glad you found Planter One informative and helpful. It's getting late and I'm hungry again. Let's get some lunch." Going back into the house they found the twins already in the kitchen inputting their requests for lunch into kitchen droid. They both turned to the trio and smiled advising, "We're getting lunch prepared, it'll be a few minutes more. We ordered a grilled poultry and mixed greens salad, fresh baked grain rolls, a berry tart, and an assortment of beverages depending on your preference." "That sounds wonderful ladies", Queen Octiva said. The girls went to the guest restroom to wash up and as they were going back to the kitchen the front door opened and Adagio entered. "Good afternoon everybody", he said. "I had an early meeting with the Astral Keep Astronautics Board and we managed to get done sooner than expected. It looks like I got back just in time for lunch", he said following the Jazzalin, Queen Octiva, and Beabop back into the kitchen. "Your timing is great. Is everything alright with the format ship project?", Jazzalin asked. "Everything's fine, the format ship is prepped and ready for the return trip to Jazzo bright and early tomorrow morning. I'm carrying back some very good news for Lady Zynoplee which is too techy and confidential so I can't talk about it with you but I'm really excited about it", he said brightly. The kitchen droid had set the table with a huge bowl of the grilled poultry and mixed greens salad and a basket of whole grain rolls and the berry tart was just coming out of the oven. They all set down and enjoyed the light but filling lunch together in an atmosphere of friendly communion. Queen Octiva ever practical advised, "I think I'm going to get my things packed so I don't leave anything I'll miss other than you Jazzalin." "Oh, mommy you make me feel guilty. I'll come up and help you pack. Beabop come join us", Jazzalin said sadly.

The three excused themselves and went upstairs to pack for the return strip to Jazzo. After the Queen had packed her travel case and laid out her casual outfit for the trip she told Jazzalin she and Beabop should go enjoy the reminder of their time doing something other and keeping her company. The girls went downstairs and joined Lilitine and Luling who was back in their study but since Adagio was present he had their attention not the planetary datafiles. As Jazzalin and Beabop joined them and Adagio spoke, "The twins were just telling me that they are in contact with the Sextillion Brethren. Isn't that amazing?"

"Really? They were supposed to have returned to their galaxy after destroying the Sessilum. You mean their still in our galaxy?", Jazzalin asked. "Yes, they are still here and they say they will leave a battalion of their brethren to occupy the space that the Sessilum had once infested. They feel that their presence will be a memorial to the numerous lives that the Sessilum decimated and every one hundred years their battalion will rotate back to their galaxy. They will sing and bring light for all who live in the neighboring planetary systems and safety for all who travel throughout the galaxy", the twins said in unison. "How do they contact you?", Jazzalin asked. "Our Light Guard who protected us on the Sessilum Habitat is one of the Sextillion and will always be in union with us", the twins replied. "This is all very interesting but I'm a bit drained and since we have to be ready to leave at six o'clock in the morning from the Astral Keep Astronautics airfield, I'm going to get some sleep. Goodnight ladies. It's been a joy being back in your home again", Adagio said as he rose and headed for his room. "We love you being in our home. You are welcome here anytime", the twins replied cheerfully. "I guess I'd better follow Adagio to go to bed since I have the same schedule tomorrow. Lilitine and Luling it's been such a pleasure meeting you and you must come to Jazzo to visit me sometime", Beabop said as she awkwardly hugged the twins. "Come on Jazzalin let's go up and get me packed for tomorrow's trip home", Beabop said pulling her friend to her feet steering her towards the stairway. Jazzalin helped Beabop get her travel case packed and her travel clothes laid out. They got into bed and Jazzalin said, "Bea, please come back next year when you get summer vacation. We'll stay in touch but you have to come back for the summer.

Don't be mad with me for not wanting to go back yet, I just can't yet." "Don't be silly. I know you're still sensitive about things and I will definitely come back for summer vacation. Let's go to sleep since I have to be ready to go before sunrise and we're getting chauffeured by the local military and they won't hesitate to leave us if we're not ready", Beabop said as her eyes slid closed. "You're quizit Bea!" Jazzalin said before turning into her pillow to sleep.

The visitors from Jazzo were up and ready by six o'clock to meet the Astral Keep Astronautics military hover shuttle. The twins had programmed the kitchen droid to prepare a take along breakfast and food for travel consisting of lots of sandwiches, salty chips, cookies, fruit, and cartons of juices. It was a sizable box of edibles but with the twelve other passengers sharing it would be finished long before they reached planet Jazzo. The twins opted not to go to the airfield with Jazzalin and the others since she would be returning to their estate. The twins said their goodbyes to the Queen, Adagio and Beabop from their driveway. The drab colored shuttle climbed upward for the thirty minute trip to the airfield. During the ride there Jazzalin snuggled close to her mother as if to absorb her presence. "Mommy, when Adagio finalizes the format ship industry and they are in production you could visit more often", Jazzalin half whispered. "The Queen readily replied, "The same applies to you dear, but I know you are sticking to your resolve to be away from Jazzo for the next two years. You know I'll be returning at least one or two times so don't you fret about it." The shuttle soon descended to the Astral Keep Astronautics airfield and the four passengers got out. The head Jazzo Astronautics scientist and his eleven technicians were waiting so they all could board the commercial format ship's return to its maiden voyage point of origin, Jazzo. Jazzalin was teary eyed as she said goodbye to her mother the Queen and to her best friend Beabop vowing to call them within seventeen hours since the trip was a mere fifteen hours. Awkwardly she also said goodbye to Adagio advising, "You'll probably be here a lot for business issues so I'll say goodbye for now." "Yes, the success of this technology is going to create a lot of business for both Jazzo and Astral Keep and I'm kind of the middleman. So goodbye for now", Adagio said. Per regulations Jazzalin had to wait in the Astroport as everyone boarded the shiny format ship and the hatch slid closed. To the minute of eight o'clock the ship's engines hummed then keened lifting it upwards to momentarily hover before disappearing upward and out of sight. Jazzalin was glad she had a tissue because her eyes were a watery fountain of tears. She finally got control when the droid shuttle driver asked, "Miss are you ready to return to your residence?" "Yes, thank you. I'm ready", she said sadly. When she arrived back at the twins estate she ran to her room and fell on her bed to finish crying. Being as intuitive as they were, the twins did not disturb her but after an hour they checked her room to find she had fallen asleep. They decided to make her favorite things for dinner and dessert and to make sure she did not miss her seventeen hour window to call the Queen and Beabop. They were very happy that their mother and father were less than an hour away in Platform City and maybe they should schedule a day trip this week to see them. What a busy day this was turning into and it wasn't even midday.

158

CHAPTER 19

Onboard the format ship the box of travel rations had been opened and after the Queen and Beabop made their selections the thirteen male passengers swiftly made short work of the remaining sandwiches and snacks. Thinking to himself Adagio thought he would make onboard food a point of research since fifteen or more hours of paid travel time should include sustenance of some kind. He made a mental note to pursue the topic with the Zynoplee Corp study group. The Astral Keep Astronautics Board wanted to proceed with building their own format ship factory but would take receipt of three format ships from Jazzo's factory, and meanwhile building their own format ship factory in partnership with Zynoplee Corp. Leaning back in his seat and closed his eyes and he wondered why Jazzalin was so aloof and standoffish towards him. He knew she could be haughty but she was actually cold. She was definitely in that mean teen stage. Well, she was still growing up and she wasn't an issue for him but he felt sorry for her parents. He had other things on his mind since he was currently dating the Theatre Muzeek's five octave soprano star Levitee Chymes. He saw her smokey hazel colored eyes and her full smiling mouth and her pale blue complexion and bright green hair continually. She was an ethereal creature and she let him know she liked him and that her schedule was always flexible where he was concerned. He had sent her a commutran message from Astral Keep to let her know he was returning to Jazzo and if they could meet tomorrow. She had enthusiastically said yes and invited him to her apartment for dinner. She was the apex in his personal life and he intended to see that their relationship advanced on all levels. Between conferring with the Jazzo scientist periodically Adagio's mind was caught in a visual of Levitee's beautiful face, and her lithe graceful figure as she danced and sang in the most recent musical at the Theatre Muzeek. He smiled at the way her beautiful voice made the hair on his neck stand on end.

After a seamless flight the voice of the pilot droid announced that the format ship was on approach to the Jazzo Aeronautics airfield. The passengers had been silent the majority of the trip either reading from the onboard datafile library or reviewing scientific data generated from the format ship's internal systems now began to stir fastening seat belts in preparation of landing. The format ship began to receive landing instructions which the pilot droid flawlessly executed, setting down in the designated area away from the public travel zone. The ship's door opened and Queen Octiva exited the ship first followed by Beabop and Adagio and the Jazzo Astronautics scientist and his technicians. The official royal hovercraft was waiting for the Queen. She took a minute to hug Beabop and Adagio before entering the chauffeured hover and speeding to the palace. Adagio offered to give Beabop a ride to her Granny's before going to his South Region apartment. Enroute to Granny's, Adagio asked, "Bea is something going on with Jazzalin and her parents? She was really tense and remote on Astral Keep." "Yes, she's still dealing with that runaway business from last year and her parents want her to come back to Jazzo but she's not ready yet. It's a waiting game and she can be really stubborn", Beabop replied. "Well she's with the best possible people, the twins. They are true and strong so she's safe with them. I hope they can help her to be less skittish in the future." "I feel that way too and they have the Sextillion Brethren hovering nearby so she's safe alright. For the skittish part I'll see what I can do", Beabop agreed. He waited until Beabop entered Granny's house before guiding his sporty blue hovercraft upwards to his apartment. He still felt that there was a big piece of information he was missing about Jazzalin but she was just a friend not an intimate. He did want her to get her life back on track but he was going to get home and call someone who was on the fast track to his heart and her name was Levitee. First he would check in with Zynoplee Corporate Office and transmit the Astral Keep contractual information so that the interplanetary legal necessities could be reviewed and finalized. His commu-tran began to ping an incoming call from his mother. He smiled at her unfailing connection to him as he answered, "Hi mother.

Yes, I'm back. I'm just parking my hover. Can I call you later? Love you too." He felt great being back on Jazzo.

True to her promise, Jazzalin called her mother within two hours after the fifteen hour landing. Queen Octiva comforted her daughter that she had arrived safely home on Jazzo. Jazzalin then called Beabop who answered, "Jazz, you kept your promise." "I told you I would call you two hours after you landed on Jazzo. I won't be long winded, you probably have travel lag. I just want to keep in touch like we said before you left Astral Keep", Jazzalin said. "I need to let you know you officially creeped out Adagio. He said he felt you were cold and skittish. So next time you see him you may want to be less frozen and nervous around him. The way he talked about you it sounded like he thought you should be medicated. Just a word to the wise", Beabop said straightforwardly. "Well it's not like I'm going to be around him everyday, at least not yet. Give me a break! My father had just revealed that a friend was betrothed to me. I'm going to stay on Astral Keep until the very last minute that I have to fulfill my part of this archaic agreement. Anyway the betrothal has nothing to do with our friendship, does it?" Jazzalin inquired. "You know it doesn't. I just wish it just didn't have the impact on you that its had. Anyway, I'm drained and I'll talk to you later when I'm well rested", Beabop said. "Alright I'll let you go and get some rest. I'll call you next weekend. Til then, goodbye Bea!" "Goodbye Jazzalin. Talk to you soon", Bea replied. Each girl was aware that they were friends first and their relationship shouldn't be influenced by outside events. Although over five lightyears were between them, their friendship spanned the distance and was sure.

Adagio met with Lady Zynoplee and the corporate committee to review the Astral Keep proposal for development of the format ship industry on their planet. Lady Zynoplee was very pleased with what Adagio had accomplished on the two days he had to meet with the Astral Keep Astronautical Board of Directors. Based on the successful outcome of the interface of both parties she proposed that Adagio Skyes be made Chief Operations Officer twenty-five percent of shares of the company's stocks. Adagio heard Lady Zynoplee's voice as if from far away. He would be able to choose his own staff and the entire thirteenth floor would be his office space. He had always thought he would be in the Jazzo music industry but now his interests were being divided between two polar opposites, science and art. In some ways science could be art and music had some scientific elements in it. He would find a way to balance the two. The next several months saw the completion of the Jazzo Astronautics Format Ship Factory and the initiation of production of the Astral Keep order of three commercial ships.

WIth his professional life in full force Adagio directed his every free moment to Levitee. He was most often seen seated front row center at her Friday night show. He had standing reservations for them at the Lift A Pinky third floor window section which they always made thirty minutes before closing. When Adagio opened his Northling house for the season Levitee was always on his arm dressed in the most eclectic style and wearing one or more of the jewels he had given her. When they danced together it was fluid grace in motion as they anticipated rhythm, beat, and timing. She was always polite and gracious to his mother but Lady Slyphine did not have a warm place in her heart for this enigmatic Ziggabim daughter. Her son was totally enrapt by Levitee and would refuse any negative comments about her, so he would have to find out on his own. From the point of view of the general public it seemed the Duke of Northling had found his Duchess. The Astral Keep three format ships were finally finished by the Jazzo factory and ready for delivery, as their factory would not be completed until the summer of the next year. Adagio along with seven Jazzo Astronautic technicians would make delivery to the planet over five lightyears away. Beabop was getting a ride to visit Jazzalin for summer vacation. This trip would be a week long as he had to review the status of work that was being done on their format ship factory and report back to the Jazzo Board of Directors. He was thankful that the twins had offered him to stay at their estate while he was on Astral Keep. The seven techs would have access to the Astral Keeps Military Barracks. The four format ships left Jazzo's airspace and the pilot droids set coordinates for the fifteen hour trip to Astral Keep. Beabop was very quiet during the trip as she didn't want to discuss anything that would put Jazzalin in a bad light. She was aware that he had a lot on his plate with the format ship business and his personal life being occupied by the exotic singer actress Levitee Chymes. He did not know what his father and King Tempo had arranged for him and Jazzalin. There would soon be an explosive revelation that could create a familial rift that could not be repaired. By being quiet Beabop assured herself she would not be the one who blabbed anything to her friend and surrogate big brother. The format ship was truly a wonder, making a trip across multiple lightyears in less than a day and technically undaunted. The pilot droids announced their approach to Astral Keep airspace and quickly descended to their Astronautics airfield. Because this trip marked the beginning of a huge business venture between two planets and also for commercial space travel intergalactically the four format ships were met by the Mayor of Astraline City and his council along with other planetary dignitaries and a local news crew to give the citizens the update about this technical advancement. Caught off guard Adagio searched his head for words to communicate in the moment because he was not at all ready for the pomp and circumstance of local socio politics but he didn't want to ruin the opportunity. Smiling, he said to the friendly crowd, "Thank you for coming out to meet us today as we deliver three of the first commercial format ships to initiate faster than light travel for your planet. The scientific community on my planet Jazzo is partnering with the scientific community on Astral Keep to advance our reach to other planets and galaxies through time saving travel. Again, thank you for your presence here today." He heard the news reporter say, "That was planet Jazzo's Duke of Northling and COO of Zynoplee Corporation commenting about the format ships that were just flown in this morning." Adagio beckoned the Jazzo head Astronautics scientist to join him in front of the friendly greeters so that he could slip away to get to the twins' estate. Beabop saw the move and had a nearby technician help her get her several travel cases loaded onto the shuttle waiting to take them into the city. After successfully escaping the welcoming party Adagio and Beabop boarded the hover shuttle and were sped away to the Astraline City suburbs to Lilitine and Luling's large estate. When the hover shuttle rounded the driveway in front of the house, its three residents were waiting "all smiles" to greet them. Jazzalin ran to Beabop and gave her a big hug while exclaiming, "Bea, it's so good to see again and we have the whole summer!" The twins on the other hand ran to Adagio and curtsied before saying in unison, "Good day to you Your Grace, it's such a pleasure to have you in our home again. Don't bother about your travel case the service droid will take to your room. There's a light lunch ready in the kitchen if you like." Knowing his affect on the female gender he responded in his most patient and kind manner, "It's good to be back on Astral Keep and I so appreciate you both allowing me to be a guest in your home for the week. I would like to have some lunch. The food on the ship was boring. How's everything with you Jazzalin?" She suddenly realized her rudeness and that she should make a big effort to act normal around Adagio when she answered, "Adagio, I'm fine and forgive my rudeness. I just got caught up in seeing Bea again. Thanks for getting her and yourself here safely. Let's get inside already." The five went down the hallway to the large bright kitchen and set down at the table that was laden with any number of grilled proteins and vegetables, colorful casseroles, sauces, salads, fresh baked bread and summer fruit tarts and a large pitcher of chilled purple tea with citrus. Adagio let out a whistle at such a midday feast as he went to the kitchen sink to wash his hands followed by the others. When they all sat down eating was the priority and they consumed a lot but fortunately the kitchen droid had prepared more than enough for a crowd. Between a bite of salad Jazzalin said to Beabop, "Bea, the twins and I are going to sing as a trio at the summer festival a "Trillia" of Light Songs. We are so excited. The Astraline City Council asked the twins to sing and to include any musical accompaniment they wanted, so I 'm an accompaniment. It's going to be in the Muni Stadium and a very big deal." "You should have the music digitized and sent throughout the Symphonea planetary system. Skyes Music would be happy to handle it for you if that's something you'd consider", Adagio injected. "Well, we never thought of it as a business venture but if you think we should consider it then we would rely on your expertise Your Grace", the twins said in unison. Beabop rolled her eyes at the fawning sycophants the twins were whenever they spoke to Adagio. Whispering to Jazzalin she asked, "I thought they were crushing on those two tech's from your birthday party last year?" Suppressing a giggle Jazzalin whispered back. "Yes, they are having a long distance romance with the techs Metre and Mezzur but I think Adagio is their special first crush. It's amusing to watch how sincere they are about him." After lunch Adagio excused himself due to travel lag he wanted to shower and get some rest. The twins went to their study library to sign into the planetary datafiles and follow their favorites social events and celebrities. Jazzalin volunteered to help Beabop unpack in the room she would be occupying for her summer vacation on Astral Keep. Beabop's room was different shades of green with pale purple accents in the drapes and carpet. It was totally unlike her bright pink, electric purple and intense chartreuse room at Granny's, but it would be quizit for a summer vacation. Opening her travel case Beabop presented Jazzalin with five new outfits her mother had her pick out from the Shop Along Teen Hub. They were exactly what fashion icons were wearing and were interchangeable for casual or evening wear. Jazzalin was so overwhelmed that she immediately called her mother, "Mommy, thank you for the outfits you sent me. Beabop got here about three hours ago and we're unpacking her and getting her settled in her room." "You're welcome dear. Jazzalin, I'm actually in the middle of a charity meeting. I'll call you later. Love you!", Queen Octiva said ending the call. Jazzalin was happy that her mother was busy with her own life and not living vicariously through her anymore. After unpacking the girls used the datafile scheduler to plan a tentative itinerary of the summer leaving room for spontaneity. Jazzalin realized that Beabop was drained so maturely she said, "You're tired Bea so get a shower and go to sleep, we'll talk in the morning. It's going to be a quizit summer!" She gave Beabop a big hug and went to her own room. This had been a seamless day no embarrassing slip ups with Adagio and knowing her mother was not dying of loneliness due to her absence. She went to her desk and pulled up her diary in the secure personal files and documented the details of Beabop's arrival and the spirit of anticipation for the summer together. She had dinner in her room and went to bed early. In the morning Jazzalin woke to the pinging of her bedside commu-tran announcing a waiting message from the twins telling her that they were going to the Platform City to visit their parents and later Astroline City for some shopping. They felt the three Jazzoans could use the time alone to catch up on things. Jazzalin used her access to the kitchen droid to have breakfast started and ready in thirty minutes. Grabbing a nearby robe she sprinted to Beabop's room, tapped on the door and while opening it simultaneously saying, "Beabop are you awake?" "Yes, I'm in the bathroom brushing my teeth. What's up besides the sun?", Beabop replied. "I just input the request for breakfast for us. The twins usually do it but they are doing a day trip to their parent's house and shopping later. They'll be gone all day. So it's just us Jazzoans today", Jazzalin said. Feeling unsure Jazzalin asked, " Do you think I should wake Adagio?" "Oh he had a big meeting with the Astronautical Committee thing today so he would have left long before anyone woke up. He has access to a military driver he remotely schedules whenever he needs to. Let's get some food, I'm starving!", Beabop said. They fell into the easy familiarity of friends as if they had been in each other's company all year not a reunion of just one day. During breakfast Beabop informed Jazzalin, "Your precious twins may be visiting their parents but they are most likely meeting those tech brothers on their excursion today because they were co-pilots on one of the new format ships." "Well, they deserve a little private time. They've been single for hundreds of years living in the pressure of the Sessilum habitat. Their looks and behavior don't indicate age for they are very young in so many ways. I'm happy that they are attempting to grow up relationally which some feel I should be doing as well", Jazzalin said reflectively. "Speaking of relationships, how's your crush on your tutor Mr.Aubade? Are you sending him love notes over summer vacation?" Jazzalin asked as she sipped her purple tea. "Very funny. No, Mr. Aubade is totally mesmerized by that green haired vixen Levitee Chymes. He spent most of his time sneaking into the atrium talking to her on his wrist-tran calling her "Levee". She's so sure of herself. You know Adagio is one of her admirers." Beabop replied. "I didn't know that, I really hope she gets her man. She is beautiful and she's part Ziggabim which explains her artistic ediginess", Jazzalin said thoughtfully. "Let's put on our new Jazzo swimwear and enjoy the twins' huge pool and watch the digi-music programming", Beabop suggested. "Sounds good to me. The weather's made for it so let's get to it!" Jazzalin agreed. Within minutes the two were suited up in bright swimwear, hats, sunglasses, and carrying straw bags containing skin protection oils, and flavored lip balms. The pool was surrounded by an entertainment centered patio. It's striped yellow and white awning jutted out just inches from the pool deck tiling. There were ten lounge chairs upholstered in the same yellow and white pattern strewn with various solid yellow pillows. A theater size digi screen was mounted on the wall and there was an outdoor kitchen and a preservator chamber full of icy drinks and frozen treats. Always the athletically inclined,

Jazzalin chose her lounger placing her things down and headed to the pools edge and made a graceful dive into its bright blue water. She had not swam for a long time and it felt so good to slice through the water effortlessly. Beabop on the other hand deposited her things one a lounger, took a cold red carbonated drink from the preservator and a bag of chips from the outdoor pantry, found the remote for the digi screen and languidly draped her body onto the lounger, no athletics for her. She was able to find the "Skyes" channel which was amazing as the signal had to travel over fifteen light years from the point of origin, planet Jazzo. Symphonea's Astronautics scientists had seeded the surrounding interstellar space with transmitter satellites to carry their media out to surrounding planets and galaxies. Many of these satellites had been destroyed by the Sessilum encroachment but somehow they must have missed a few. Rifling through the channels and streams she found her favorite music and dance show "Fast Feet" and settled there to watch young Jazzoans execute the latest dance steps accompanied by the latest popular music. After an hour they heard a familiar voice call, "Hey, where is everybody?!" "Adagio, we're outside at the pool, come join us. And how did you get in anyway?", Beabop called back. Coming into view Adagio replied, "The twins have added me to their voice recognition security system access. So unlike you Miss Beabop I have unlimited access. Na, na, na-na-na!!!" Beabop shot back, "Wouldn't they just. You realize you are a visitor here from another planet?" "Yes, I'm aware but I can't help it if I'm a favored guest. I think I'll go put on my swim shorts and join Jazzalin for a swim since some of us are too lazy to exercise", Adagio said while pointing at Beabop. Throwing her unused towel at him which he dodged going back into the house to dress for a swim. Adagio dived into the pool and swam a few laps before challenging Jazzalin to a race. "Race ya!" head flinging the water from his thick hair. In response Jazzalin said, "You're on!" Jazzalin held her own in racing with Adagio across the pool but because of his height he won by inches over her. The three Jazzoans enjoyed themselves throughout the afternoon. Later that afternoon the twins returned in time to see Adagio shirtless and wearing swimwear. The sight of him partially dressed caused them to freeze in their tracks and their eyes to enlarge to take in the sight. As he walked past them in the hallway he smiled as he greeted them, "Afternoon ladies." They pivoted on their toes to gaze at him as he sprinted up the stairway to shower and dress. Jazzalin and Beabop overcome with laughter also ran upstairs to avoid embarrassing the twins or themselves.

For dinner the twins had purchased take-out from a nearby rustic grill restaurant renowned for its grilled poultry, bova ribs and patties served with creative sauces and salads. It seemed that the twins ordered enough for at least twenty people so there would be leftovers. After the large meal they all went into the twins study library to watch the datafiles from Jazzo. The twins signed in immediately to their interstellar access which flashed up Skyes Jazzo Channel onto the large theater sized screen. Before he sat down Adagio said, "I could use an Astral Ale to help me enjoy the show. Can I get one for any of you?" Jazzalin and the twins refused the offer but Beabop accepted, "I'll have one." "Two AA's coming right up", Adagio said as he went into the kitchen. Returning to the library he heard the twins saying, "She's so beautiful and she can sing as well. She's always dressed so stylishly." Handing Beabop an opened bottle of icy ale, he plopped down into a comfortable chair in sight of the large digi screen which had a huge smiling image of Levitee Chymes holding the hand of an equally smiling man beside her. He sipped the ale as he watched and heard her say, "Yes, Reed and I have been friends for a long time and now we want to go to the next level which is obviously marriage." Adagio's vision went blank and he nearly gagged on the sip of ale he'd just taken into his mouth. When he momentarily regained his composure he watched the happy couple on the screen kiss in view of an entire planetary system. Beabop was the only one who was aware of what was happening to her friend but as a friend she did not give him away. He stood up and said, "I have to call the Astronautical Board about something. I have to say goodnight to you ladies." Once inside the safety of his room he remoted the military hovercraft to the twins' estate within the hour. He could not remain in a house full of females when one of their gender and made a wasteland of his heart. He would spend the last three days of his stay on Astral Keep in the barracks with the Jazzoan techs at the Astronautics airfield. He had just spoken to Levitee the day before leaving for Astral Keep and she had given no sign of their relationship being in trouble. There was something more to this than met the eye. What he did not know was on the day his crew set out to deliver the Astral Keep's first three format ships, a large floral arrangement with a digi note attached was sent to Levitee's apartment. The digi note allowed the recipient to either read it themselves or have the note narrate the message. Since she was getting ready to go shopping she opted to have the digi narration, "Good day Miss Levitee Chymes. These flowers are a token in esteem for your talent and individuality. Unfortunately, it is also to advise you that all intimate relations with the Duke of Northling, Adagio Jammon Skyes should cease and desist immediately. The Duke is betrothed to another royal and is for all intents and purposes a married man and would not be able to continue any serious relationship with you. If you insist on continuing your relations with the Duke your career on Jazzo or any other planet in the planetary system will suffer greatly before becoming nonexistent. But if you comply you will benefit immensely both in your career and finances. At the South Regions Peoples Bank a new account has been initiated in your name in the amount of three million credits pending your signature within the next forty eight hours. If your signature is not posted on the account within the quoted forty-eight hour window this offer will be voided and you will have lost on all fronts. Because you are such a wise individual you will act in accordance for yourself and all others concerned. Thank you for listening." Levitee had sat down to hear the narration and was in shock at what was said in the note. But what she did hear clearly was the three million credits waiting for her signature. She finished dressing and took a public hovercraft to the South Regions Peoples Bank and its new accounts desk. The bank representative found the account information and verified her identity. She signed the necessary digi docs and her account was active to use, all seven figures of it. Her life had changed and she was smart enough to take the high road. She took out her commu-tran and called an admirer Reed Aubade to make a date. The Duke was out but Reed Aubade was a good replacement who was not under his father's thumb.

Adagio dressed quickly and packed his travel case and went downstairs to wait for the hovercraft. Beabop, Jazzalin and the twins all came out to the entryway curious to see Adagio ready to leave. He concocted a story that they needed his input on a part of the contract that was not clear from the Astral Keep point of view. He hugged the twins who were almost tearful. He turned to Jazzalin and said, "Princess, sorry I have to rush off tonight but I wish you a happy sixteenth birthday next week although I'll be back on Jazzo." Jazzalin replied, "Sorry your stay was cut short but you know you're always welcome here. Thank you for the pre birthday wish, but there won't be a party this year though. I hope everything goes well with your business issue." She shyly hugged him and said, "Goodbye till next time." "Til next time", he said as he hugged her back. Releasing Jazzalin he turned to Beabop who flung herself into his arms and whispered in his ear, "I know what happened and you should ask your father about Levitee when you're back on Jazzo. Goodbye Daggie." "Goodbye brat. See you back on Jazzo", he said. Just then the hovercraft horn blared in the warm night air. Adagio opened the front door and got into the waiting hovercraft and waved goodbye to the four girls standing in the front doorway. Adagio breathed a sigh of relief and fell back against the hard backseat as his mind replayed the scene of Levitee and her male friend. He would see if he could get clearance to return to Jazzo perhaps a day sooner. The next day Adagio requested an earlier departure for his Jazzo team back to Jazzo. The Astral Keep Astronautical Board verified all of their transactions were all in order so the Jazzo team would be free to return home as soon as their ship was ready. Later that same day Adagio and the seven Jazzo technicians boarded their format ship for the fifteen hour flight trip to Jazzo. During the trip home Adagio had signed into the Skyes channel social stream showing the latest celebrity news. There were ongoing stories highlighting the marriage of Levitee Chymes and Reed Aubade. A giddy reporter relayed, " The newlyweds were seen leaving a South Region Wedding Chapel. It's reported from our sources that they'll be honeymooning in an East Region Coast luxury hotel. Our songbird is finally happily joined with her love, and what a lovely couple they make. We all wish Mr. and Mrs. Reed Aubade the best of everything." Unable to take anymore of the sugary platitudes gushing from the reporter he shutdown the digistream and slumped in his seat and tried to take a nap. He thought that everyone seemed to know something that he didn't but he would confront his father as soon as he got back to Jazzo. Adagio was anxious to get home and as fast as the format ship was able but it seemed to crawl through space. Finally the pilot droid announced their presence in Jazzo's upper atmosphere on approach for landing. As soon as the ship's hatch opened Adagio jumped out and headed straight for his hovercraft, and within minutes he was parking at his father's downtown office building roof access. Using his security key he walked down the one flight of stairs to his fathers top floor office. He had the droid admin assistant notify his father he was there to speak with him. Entering his father's office Adagio was straight to the point, "Dad, what do you know about Levitee Chymes sudden marriage only days after I left for Astral Keep?" Hamilton realized he could not be evasive anymore and revealed, "Adagio, remember two years ago when I had you go to the Zynoplee estate to locate the format ship? Well, when King Tempo suggested you to gain access to Lady Zynoplee's mansion due to your friendship with her granddaughter Beabop, I saw the opportunity to advance our family's social standing by insisting that your involvement would be based on the betrothal of his daughter Princess Jazzalin in marriage to you on her seventeenth birthday. This was at the height of the Sessilum threat and the King did not have a choice and he generated the documents and applied the royal seals which made it very official. I saw you were getting a little too involved with the colorful Miss Chymes and she was advised that she should make other plans relationally. So son, I had your best interest in mind from the beginning of this adventure to the recent issue with Miss Chymes. You do know she was seeing Mr. Aubade at the same time she was dating you?" Adagio was too angry to speak and took a few minutes to review what he'd just heard. No wonder Jazzalin was acting so strange around him. She was practically psychotic, poor thing must have thought he would molest her at any minute. He found his voice and replied to his father, "Levitee was free to date other men but she had stopped seeing the others when she started seeing me. Also this whole thing has practically ruined a young girl's life. You know that Jazzalin stowed away on the format ship that rescued the twin zealots and now lives with them on Astral Keep to avoid your matchmaking scheme. She knows and she's miserable about it and so am I!" "It seems a mess now but once you two are married and get to know each other you'll work things out", his father said in an attempt to lighten the mood. "Dad, I can't talk about this anymore. I just got back from Astral Keep and need to do some things at Zynoplee Corp and from there I'm going to be off grid for a while", Adagio said as he proceeded to leave his father's office without looking back. Hamilton immediately called his wife to enlist her help to smooth out this catastrophe with Adagio.

Adagio determined he would notify Lady Zynoplee that he would be taking a leave of absence for the remainder of the summer and would only be available for an extreme emergency. Leaving his father's office he went directly to his apartment. Going to his bedroom he packed a large travel case and filled it with dress, casual and basic clothing and filled another case with shoes. He then put his commu-tran on automated answering mode advising anyone calling that he was not available and would return calls when available to do so. He loaded his travel cases into his hovercraft to start the one hour trip to the North Region to his Northling Estate. Using his accelerated drive speed he got to his destination in just under the estimated time. Putting down the hover in the front driveway he saw the efficient service droid waiting there. The service droid greeted him, "Good afternoon your grace. Would you like something to drink or food brought to your suite?" "Good afternoon. Yes, I would like a magnum of sparkling red wine and a mixed greens salad topped with chopped grilled poultry, fresh baked bread, and a bowl of frozen citrusberry cream." Following the service droid inside and upstairs of the well appointed interior of the large house, he realized how glad he was about being a royal although reluctantly. Once inside his room he got undressed and took a quick and refreshing shower. He dried off and then wrapped the towel around his waist and just then his commu-tran began to ping and flash the image of his mother. His father had wasted no time in bringing her into the midst of this drama. "Adagio, darling please connect the call. Yes, your father called me", Lady Sylphine demanded. "Mother I just got here at Northling, I'm tired and I don't want to talk right now. I just want to rest and relax. You have the access code to the door so you can come over tomorrow if you want but I just can't do this now", he explained. "At least I still have your favor since your father obviously doesn't. I'll come over tomorrow. I'll freshen up the place and prepare some of your favorite dishes and snacks to stock up your preservator and if you want to talk, we'll talk", she said. "Thanks for understanding mother. So you'll come over tomorrow", he agreed. "I won't hold you darling, I know you must be exhausted. Get your rest and I'll see you tomorrow. Goodbye darling", she chirped victoriously. The call disconnected and he realized that his hyper efficient kitchen droid had prepared his meal and the service droid had set up the table with the chilled wine in an insulator bucket. Adagio drank two glasses of the cold sparkling wine before diving into his salad and taking large bites of bread. Finishing the main course he tasted the frozen citrusberry dessert and savored its cold sweet tartness and remembered how he had loved it as a little boy. All sensory reminiscence aside, he needed to regroup and review the information he'd learned today about his father's interference with his relationship of choice only to find out that he was part of an arranged marriage.

CHAPTER 20

With the early departure of Adagio the twins were melancholy for a while but they soon perked up when it came time to rehearse for the Astraline City Summer Festival. When they heard Beabop's melodious alto voice the asked her to join them in singing the Trillia Light Songs. They had another week to practice and run through with the local orchestra to be sure that there were no blunders on the night of the festival concert. Adagio remembered to send them a Skyes Music new client contract so that their concert would be lucrative for them. The twins decided to call themselves "Twins Tunz" and they felt very professional although they were complete novices. Jazzalin's sixteenth birthday was the first event on the summer social calendar for the four females. Even though Jazzalin had let it be known she did not want a party for her sixteenth birthday the twins still decorated the dining room and had a sizable cake made to celebrate on a lesser scale. One the day of her birthday Jazzalin awoke to the twins and Beabop standing by her bed singing, "Wake up and say this is my sixteenth birthday. Childhood gone away, all grownup to stay! It's my sixteenth birthday!!!" "Written and composed by your very best friend "Beabop", Beabop said smugly. Jazzalin sprang out of bed and hugged them all at once. She ran to her bathroom and brushed her teeth and splashed water on her face and she joined the others downstairs in the kitchen for breakfast. The twins had placed a large pink envelope in front of her place at the table, Jazzalin opened it carefully to reveal a credit voucher for the amount of five thousand credits. She was so surprised as the twins had insisted on paying her five thousand monthly for her services as a consultant but this was such an example of their largesse and their financial innocence. It would be pointless to argue about the amount being exorbitant so she said, "Lilitine and Luling thank you for this gift, In gratitude I'd like to use it to celebrate with a shopping spree at the Astraline City Shopping Hub on me." Beabop interjected, " I have a gift for you too." She placed a small wrapped package in front of Jazzalin who opened it with a gasp, "Bea, it's beautiful!" Beabop had given her the latest pink band wrist commu-tran with maximum planetary range. Jazzalin said sincerely, "I have the very best friends in the universe. Let's get dressed to go shopping!" Within thirty minutes the four females were dressed in their latest summer fashion of bright colors and light frothy fabrics. They accessed their chauffeured hovercraft and they were off to Astraline City. The twins had initially enjoyed their notoriety, always happy to sign an autograph or to have a picture taken with an admiring fan but they had learned that if they want to navigate publicly without the well meaning delays fans can cause they should wear dark glasses and hats. Since Jazzalin was now known as the twins' assistant she had to use the same disguise to avert attention as well. They had agreed they wanted to shop for shoes at the onsite factory store "Slip N2 Shoes" and then lunch at the food court and then the latest summer digi action movie "The Hyrogee Garden Warriors". The twins chose four pairs of summer shoes and a pair of short boots each and were happy with their choices. Beabop chose two pair of strappy pastel summer shoes that she had seen on the fashion stream and had never thought she would ever find them anywhere. Jazzalin had chose three pair of shoes which were everyday shoes for walking and working in the garden. The shoe purchases for all four female was two thousand credits and left a substantial amount remaining of Jazzalin's birthday money for lunch and entertainment. After lunch and the movie they came home to find the dining room lit by fluorescent pink and purple lights, a huge vase of flowers of corresponding colors, center of the table, and the birthday cake and other party fare laid out on the large table. Tears rolled down Jazzalin's cheeks as she said thank you to her three friends near her. She had had enough of her last two birthdays but this one redeemed the two previous ones. They all sat around the table for the traditional candle blowing out and the birthday song. Queen Octiva also called Jazzalin who was able to receive on her new wrist commu-tran. They stayed awake late listening to the best of the planetary musical artists, trying on their new shoes, and discussing the upcoming festival concert. All in all it was a perfect day for them all but Jazzalin never could have had such a day without her friends to help her deal with things that were looming on the horizon and she would still need them in the future.

The following day Lady Sylphine arrived at her son's Northling estate. Using her access code she let herself in. The service droid greeted her, "Good morning Lady Sylphine. How can I help you?" Lady Sylphine answered, "Good morning. Please have the several packages in the storage compartment of my hovercraft brought to the kitchen, and have them put away. There's also a large container of flowers in the backseat of my hover that should be brought to me in the study. Is the Duke awake yet?" "No, the Duke had a late night and is still in bed", the droid replied. "Have the kitchen droid make a large pot of purple tea and a tray of dry toasted bread. Let me know when it's ready and I'll take it to the Duke's room. That's all for now." The service droid's internally communicated to it's kitchen counterpart to make the purple tea and toast as he was going to the silver hovercraft that belonged to Lady Sylphine to bring in packages. In a few minutes the service droid brought the tray to Lady Sylphine and said, "Lady Sylphine the tray you ordered is ready but since it's quite heavy I will take upstairs and hand it off to you at the Duke's door." "Yes, that's fine. Go ahead", Lady Sylphine said as she followed the efficient droid to her son's suite. She softly knocked before saying, "It's mother and nearly midday time to get up." She took the tray for the droid and using her foot pushed the door open. She was thankful that he was wearing his pajama pants so she had impressed him as a child not to sleep like a savage in the nude.

She knew of what she spoke since she was a savage and grew up living in a mostly nude state. Clothes had not come into her life until she was a teenager. She placed the tray on the table and saw an empty magnum of sparkling wine. No wonder he was still asleep at midday. Going over to her son's sprawled sleeping form she shook his muscular shoulder while saying, "Daggie, wakeup, it's mother. Wakeup." With slurred speech Adagio responded' "Go away! Leave me alone. Zit's my howz. Ahhumm!!!" "Daggie, I made a pot of purple tea and toast to help with your hangover. I'm going downstairs now. Come down when you can dear", she said exasperated. It would be another hour before Adagio made his way downstairs, unshaven, with his hair wet and disheveled,.wearing a bathrobe. Lady Sylphine saw him ambling into the kitchen and met him halfway there to place a kiss on his scruffy cheek remarking, "So glad you finally had strength to get up while it's still daytime." "Mother don't start in on me", Adagio growled. The service droid had brought down the tray of purple tea from Adagio's room to reheat. After taking a few sips of purple tea he seemed to brighten and become coherent. Lady Sylphine asked, "Can I make you something to eat?" "No mother. I'll have another cup of purple tea. It seems best right now", he replied somberly. "Well that's what happens when you consume an entire magnum of sparkling wine", she said as she busied herself with chopping vegetables, letting him open the gate to address the real issue. "Mother, dad and the King set this archaic betrothal in place. It's not something anyone does anymore. I would have helped the Planetary Alliance without getting trapped in a secret marriage contract", Adagio said to his mother. "I know they were high handed with their actions but Daggie your father would not have allowed the Planetary Alliance to approach you to elicit your services since you were not military trained and just turned eighteen. But look at the advantages: you already know Jazzalin and you have had multiple occasions to interact with her socially. She's pretty. She's a five octave soprano and she's brave enough to act when she feels she's being manipulated. I feel you have a very good prospect for a wife and from recent views of her on the datafiles from Astral Keep her physique is developing where it should. And you still have an entire year to get to know each other before everything is finalized. You have a few more trips to Astral Keep for business and you can make a point of strengthening your relationship with each other. She's a royal and she's living with the heroes of the Sessilum Threat so she's a worthwhile individual way beyond her years", Lady Sylphine said with motherly wisdom. "Mother, I'm on a leave of absence so I'm not going to Astral Keep anytime soon, and my last encounters with Jazzalin have been strained", Adagio replied. "Nevermind, we can still enjoy your leave of absence. I can have some of your musical friends visit you for pool parties or a weekend house party. You've lost touch with your first love since getting involved with that spaceship business. So take heart dear, you won't waste away while I'm around. I'm making a bevy of pasta casseroles that will freeze well. I'm also baking a huge batch of your favorite sweets. Dear, you must realize you are your father's and my only child and we want the very best for you, and sometimes we get the best in ways that not everyone approves of but we've never been slaves of the approval of others. We love you immensely Daggie", she said, coming over to him at the kitchen table where he was sitting to plant a kiss on his forehead. He hugged around her waist as she was a refuge in the storm he found himself in as well a source of wisdom that he could rely on. "Oh, did I mention I'm taking a small vacation at Northling for a few weeks, give or take. I'll mind my own business and only get involved upon request. It's going to be wonderful", she said cheerfully, returning to the work surface to continue cooking. She thought to herself she was going to be mother-in-law of a royal couple, it was more than she could have ever dreamed and she hadn't been an interfering manipulating mother exposing the flamboyant Miss Chymes, it had been Daggie's father. Her Ziggabim initiative had obviously rubbed off on her husband and she was glad of it.

On Astral Keep the day of the Astraline City Summer Festival arrived and the entire city was buzzing with the relaxed atmosphere of summer. The twins and their accompanying singers were scheduled towards the end of the concert. They were all dressed in shades of pink and orange silk tunics and matching silk slim slacks. Since it was an outdoor event and temperatures were expected to be warm even after sundown they all opted to wear their hair up either in buns or a dangling column to assure no overheating while singing. They waited backstage as the other performers gave their presentations, some instrumentals and vocals of jazz or classical music, others of contemporary dance as well as traditional dance indigenous to Astral Keep, and finally it was their turn. The announcer introduced them, "Now it's my pleasure to introduce the heroes of the Sessilum threat. These brave ladies held the line with the Light Songs directed against the galaxy's heinous foe until the Sextillion Brethren vaporized them. Here are the twin zealots Lilitine and Luling accompanied by Princess Jazzalin and Beabop Zynoplee of Jazzo singing the Trillia Light Songs!" The four friends walked onto the large open stage, the twins in front leading followed by Jazzalin and Beabop. Although they had practiced daily they still had the music sheets just in case any of them needed to refer to it. And they sang. " We sing of the light that has shone through our lives, that has brought us safely through the strife. When the enemy growled and bared its teeth saying we were but useless sheep. To taunt and chill our hearts but the light did not depart. To the light that remained faithful and strong from start to blazing victory and beyond." While they sang a bright aura shown above the stage and rumbled like a massive drum. The twins knew it was the Sextillion Brethren communing with their music just as they had when they were stranded on the Sessilum habitat. The audience gave the quartet a standing ovation at the completion of their presentation so that they had to do an encore. This time they sang a very popular song "Jazzo Fling" which described the fling field anomaly as a popular summertime activity on Jazzo. Lady Sylphine had instructed her secretary to keep an open access to the Astral Keep media datafiles and to alert her for any news regarding Princess Jazzalin. The resourceful maven received the stream of the concert early the next day due to the great distance it originated from. Later that day she shared her datafile stream with Adagio, "Daggie, see Jazzalin is not sitting around in a stupor, she's having fun and looking good doing it. If I were you I'd contact the twins and let them know you saw the concert and segue a brief chat with Jazzalin as well. I mean you've got to start somewhere." "Mother, you are a little slow. I have already signed the twins to a new artists contract with Skyes Music as my exclusive account. So I can call them without any ulterior motive and I can speak to Jazzalin as well", he said confidently. "I will call the girls when I'm ready, mother! Hey, I thought you were in no interference mode", he remarked. "I am but I'm just making sure you don't miss valuable information about your future spouse. I thought she was quite lovely in that silk tunic and slacks. She does have a great style for what looks good on her", Lady Sylphine said. Changing the subject she continued, "Daggie I would really like to meet the twins. They remind me of my native people, the Ziggabim. Are they stoic and serious or are they ethereal and mystical?", she inquired. "No mother they aren't any of those things. The twins are sweet, fun, smart, strong and very spiritual. It's their spirit that kept them alive under pressure from the Sessilum. I'd like you to meet them. My next trip to Astral Keep won't be til mid next year, I'll have you put on the passenger list. Since the twins are genius level linguists you can speak to them in Ziggal your native tongue", Adagio replied. "That's wonderful. I can't wait. This is going to be the best ever trip for me. Just think, fifteen light years away from your father", Lady Sylphine giggled as she went outside to the garden.

The rest of the summer for Jazzalin and Beabop was the best, as they did any and everything they could think of. They went to an Astral Keep beach but the water was too cold for swimming but they enjoyed just being there. They also tried astro pack flying which involved a lightweight astro pack strapped on their backs and having a professional flier tether them to himself and they could fly around without breaching the upper atmosphere. The twins also took them to the Platform City to visit their parents and to have a most delicious meal with them and a walking tour around the beautiful neighborhood. They also made an exhaustive study of the Astraline City Shopping Hub. The twins came to Jazzalin and said, "Beabop is the best person. No wonder you like her so much and we do too". When it was time for Beabop to return to Jazzo there teary eyes all around. Jazzalin reminded Beabop that she only had until her seventeenth birthday to remain on Astral Keep before either she returned to Jazzo or her father sent a military envoy to force her to come back. So either way they would both be on Jazzo soon. They both vowed to stay in touch and to send weekly updates on everything even the dullest minutia. Before boarding the ship Beabop said to the twins, "I didn't think I would like you two but you are so special and lovable. You have to come to Jazzo and stay at my Granny's mansion and let me show you around." Turning to Jazzalin she said, "Adagio just found out about the betrothal so he's been in the dark until a few months ago. You need to stop being weird about him since he's a good guy and he's never been anything but nice to you. He can't help it if he was born four years before you either. There, I've said it and I can leave now." Jazzalin gave Beabop another hug and said, "You're special and lovable too. See you through the data stream. Goodbye for now." Boarding the large streamline commercial format ship she waved goodbye and entered the open door which slid shut. The format ship's engines came online with a high pitched whine which lifted it up before it launched into the upper atmosphere and was out of sight of three tearful friends watching from the boarding hub. Jazzalin thought hard about what Beabop said and determined she would do whatever she could to build a relational bridge that would allow easy transit from her to Adagio and from him to her. She had a whole year to work on it.

Adagio was happy his mother, as annoying as she could be, was at Northling. Her artistic style was evident with flower arrangements everywhere. And her no nonsense housekeeping was present with window shades open to let in light all day, and no dust on any surface. There were aromas of things cooking in the kitchen. Her presence had put the kitchen droid in its charger station for days since she was cooking breakfast, lunch and dinner. All this attention gave him freedom to be casual in a way he hadn't been since his school days. He started to swim a few laps every morning and even gardening both in the formal garden and in his greenhouse. He felt relaxed enough to let his mother invite his old music industry friends for a house party which turned out really well since it was in the daytime and she orchestrated everything so that the attendees knew that as soon as the sun was waning they should be on their way. Adagio determined he would set up an office in the study related to his music business at Northling and that way he would be able to keep an eye on the twins' "Twins Tunz" music and give them some tips for any future projects. He might even persuade Jazzalin to do an album since she obviously had a beautiful trained voice. He would get back to his first love, music since he had not chosen the space travel business but was drafted into it. Yes, for the remainder of the year he would stay at Northling and get his life back on track.

Jazzalin and the twins were happy to see that the Trillia Light Song music was well received throughout Astral Keep and the Symphonea planetary system generating them considerable income. The twins were especially glad they had listened to Adagio and let him apply his business acumen to their advantage. Even Jazzalin would benefit in a small percentage of their profit so in gratitude she sent him a commu-tran message to his apartment in South Region Jazzo, "Adagio the twins wanted me to let you know how grateful they are for your assistance in using your music business know how to their advantage and mine too. We look forward to your next visit to Astro Keep. Thank you for everything, goodbye." When Adagio finally checked his commu-tran messages he was surprised at the friendliness he heard in Jazzalin's voice and it put him at ease that somehow they might develop beyond the strained circumstances caused by a secret royal betrothal. He looked forward to his next trip to Astral Keep.

The idyll life Adagio had been enjoying at his Northling Estate for over six months came to a halt in the third month of the new year when he received notice by commu-tran message and digi-note informing him per his contract he was obligated to return to Astral Keep to review and evaluate the status of the Zynoplee Corp's interests regarding the commercial format ship industry. He hadn't forgotten his obligation because he had cloistered himself at Northling, caught up in the ease of life there, his mother's cooking and the company of friends. He knew that Lady Zynoplee would not settle for less than she was paying him a large salary for. He made preparations to close the beautiful house his mother had designed it to be and would return to his South Region apartment to get ready for the Astral Keep flight. Only he, the head Astronautics scientist, and two technicians would make the trip. The night before he was to depart for Astral Keep he received a commu-tran call in his message cue from Jazzalin. "Adagio, it's me, Jazzalin. Hope I'm not disturbing you but I wanted to run an idea by you before you come to Astral Keep. Since we both know that our fathers created a betrothal between us that neither of us had any power to prevent, we can change it so it's completed our way, not by some royal edict. We can announce our engagement when you arrive on Astral Keep and have the local news stream broadcast it to the Symphonea Planetary channels so that it's seen on Jazzo. The engagement will give us an unlimited window of time before a real marriage has to take place. However, for this to work we'll need a ring. Please confirm if you're on board with this idea. I wait for your reply", her message said. Adagio smiled to himself at how astute she was to realize he must have gotten a clue about the betrothal by now. He looked.in his concealed safe where he kept really important documents and other valuables and found the large pink diamond solitaire set in platinum he had intended for Levitee but now it would serve another purpose. He packed the ring in his carryon case since it was significantly expensive and should not be in the baggage compartment of a commercial spaceship. He sent back his confirmation to Jazzalin, "I'm on board with the idea and I have a ring. Will see you soon." Arriving at the Jazzo Astronautical Airfield he and the other three passengers boarded the ship and the pilot android announced their lift off as the ship sliced effortlessly through the air accessing the upper atmosphere then interstellar space.

During the flight he was looking forward to carrying out the engagement scenario and the reaction of his mother when she got the news. Yes, this would make a big difference in the way he related to Jazzalin and she to him. The fifteen hour trip flew by and they were landing at the Astral Keep Astronautical Airfield. He would be five days on Astral Keep this time and not all of that would be work. He and the Astronautical scientist did a walkthrough of the huge commercial format ship factory, from drawings to production and finished product. They would also have the two technicians do test flights with the pilot androids but that could wait until tomorrow. Since they were a small party from Jazzo he had permission for the scientist and two technicians to stay at the twins' estate. The Astronautical Board assigned them a shuttle craft for their use so they were not dependent on the twins or public transportation. They got to the twins' estate late afternoon and the twins, being super intuitive, were waiting in the front entrance of their house smiling as the shuttle hover stopped in the driveway. "Adagio, we're so glad to see you and your associates. The service droid will help with your travel cases. Adagio you will have your regular room and the scientist and technicians will have rooms in the guest house which is at the rear of the property. Jazzalin! We have guests!", they said, progressing to a yell. Jazzalin came out of her bedroom and answered back, "I'm on a call to Beabop. Let me finish and I'll be right there." "No hurry, it's just the regular crowd from Jazzo", Adagio replied. While Adadgio went upstairs the twins led the three males to the rear of the large house across the colorful courtyard to the sizable guesthouse. They advised the scientists and techs "There are five bedrooms with adjoining bathrooms so you can choose the one you want. Once you get refreshed dinner will be served in the kitchen." The brother technicians Metre and Mezzur smiled back at the twins knowing that this would be a good time to get to know the twins better as they had four days to do so. Back in the main house, Jazzalin ran into Adagio as he accessed the second floor landing and greeted him, "Hi Adagio. You got the message I left you and you're a "go" with it?" He was surprised at the change in Jazzalin; in nearly three years she had grown physically to a fuller rounder shape and was no longer the skinny angular sapling she was before. He answered, "Yes. I have a ring and whenever you get your media friends onboard then we can announce our engagement in front of an entire planetary system." "The twins have a friend with the Astroline City datafile current events department. And did you know the twins knew about the betrothal from the time I was a stowaway on the format ship nearly three years ago. They are amazing and they want to help us carry out this reveal of our engagement. After dinner if you're not too tired we can confirm the details and once the newscaster is notified all we have to do is look the part and smile", Jazzalin explained. He smiled at her enthusiasm for the scheme but he was happy she was no longer seeing him as a villain but as a comrade in arms who had been victimized like herself. Dinner was wonderful as the twins in their zeal of generosity had prepared a huge feast with three summer desserts. The four men were up to the challenge and put a sizable dent in the bounteous meal but after second helpings of everything they could only have purple tea to wash it all down, dessert could wait til tomorrow. After dinner the scientist and the technician. returned to the guesthouse to get ready for bed and Jazzalin, Adagio and the twins went into the library to work out the details of the engagement scheme. Jazzalin asked, "Lilitine and Luling when can you tell your newscaster friend that you have a big story for her that she can reveal before anyone else does?" "We can call her now, Daeley always works late. Recently the social stream has dried up. She'll be happy to land this new story. We need to let her know when to come to the estate tomorrow", they said in unison. They agreed late morning, elevenish would be best so they all would be well rested and ready. With that the four friends climbed the stairs to go to bed since they had an exciting day tomorrow and they did not want it to go wrong. The next day Jazzalin got her most princesslike outfit ready and conservative heeled matching shoes. She also opted to wear the pink diamond earrings Adagio gave her on her fifteenth birthday. She inspected her appearance in the mirror and felt she looked the part of a newly engaged princess. The summery pink print dress fit her without being overtly sensual. When she went downstairs only the twins were there and they approached her, "Jazzalin, we're so glad you are not in the dark anymore. You and Adagio will have a brilliant life together so do not despair at all. There's purple tea if you like." Jazzalin replied, "Thank you for the way you did not judge me for being ignorant and clueless. Soon this issue will be common knowledge so I can remain on Astral Keep for a year after my seventeenth birthday." The twins informed her that their newscaster friend Daeley Sohn would arrive with her crew at eleven and they wanted them to do the interview in the side flower garden to give the full romantic effect. When Adagio finally came downstairs it was thirty minutes away from their engagement reveal. His appearance still had its hypnotic effect on the twins even though he was wearing a somewhat casual lightweight jacket and slacks he cut a handsome figure. "Good morning ladies. I'm not too late am I?" All three answered, "No." After he poured a cup of purple tea he turned to Jazzalin and said, "Here's the ring. You may want to put it on now." From his jacket pocket he took out a maroon velvet box and handed it to Jazzalin whose breath was taken away when she opened it to reveal a large pink diamond set in platinum ring. She removed the ring from the box and slid it nervously onto her ring finger and looked up at Adagio to say, "Adagio it's "quizit"! It's a good fit, it's very expensive and I'll be sure to take good care of it. I'd give it back today but I have to be seen wearing it in order for the engagement to be believable. Do you mind that I am somewhat shallow about this?" "No, I understand that you had no plans for marriage at seventeen years old and neither did I at twenty-one but this engagement gives us wiggle room to figure things out without politics and legal actions. I'm glad you like the ring and I see you're wearing the earrings I gave you on your fifteenth birthday." "Yes, my mother reprimanded me not to wear them often because they were expensive but I like them so I wear them a lot", she said unapologetically. A knock at the front entrance and the twins announced, "They're here!" The service droid opened the front door and escorted Daeley Sohn and her voice controlled android crew down the hall, then out the door leading to the side garden where the twins greeted them. "Thank you Daeley for coming. We felt that this story should get exposure as soon as possible and the reporter who releases it would get noticed in the datafile news industry. Princess Jazzalin and the Duke are waiting over there by the cloud tree", the twins said pointing the way. The newscaster walked towards the young couple and directed her droids by their functions, "Camera, sound follow me. Camera on digital mode and follow my line of sight. Sound, wait for my introductory statement to start recording" Once in front of Jazzalin and Adagio Daeley said, "Your highness and your grace I want to thank you for giving me this opportunity to report your story to the Astral Keep public and to the Symphonea Planetary system." "Thank you for being available to report our story", Jazzalin said smiling. "So shall we start. This is Daeley Sohn of Astraline City Social Stream here at the estate of the esteemed hero twin zealots of the Sessilum threat to interview their two friends and guests, Jazzoan Royals who have just gotten engaged here on Astral Keep. It is my honor to be the first to congratulate you both on your engagement, Princess Jazzalin and Duke of Northling Adagio Skyes.", Daeley said with sincerity. "Thank you, Daeley", Jazzalin and Adagio said in unison. "Now when did you two realize it was love and would result in marriage?", the reporter asked. "We've been friends since we were students at the Jazzo First Song Academy and it has grown over the years into something more", Jazzalin said. "Oh, and can we see the ring Princess?", Daeley asked. Jazzalin held out her hand that was adorned with the large pink gemstone which gleamed in the midday sun. Daeley leaned into Jazzalin's hand prompting the camera droid to get a close up of the ring on the hand wearing it and she responded, "Goodness, Princess you may have trouble lifting your hand, it's so big!" Jazzalin giggled at the reporter's true assessment of the ring. In the beautiful flower garden the two Jazzoan royals were very believable as a loving couple. They held hands, looked adoringly into each other's eyes and gave deference to each other when speaking. For fifteen minutes they answered questions about their relationship with as much candor as they dared. And when the newscaster's allotment for the interview was used up she said, "Well there you are, Jazzo's two young royals have announced their engagement today and we are very happy for the pending nuptials of Princess Jazzalin and Duke of Northling Adagio Skyes of planet Jazzo. See you in the datafiles, Daeley Sohn signing off." It had gone well and now they would wait for the parental repercussions.

Lady Sylphine ran into Hamilton Skyes' study screaming, "They did it! They did it! Daggie and Princess Jazzalin got engaged on Astral Keep. They overturned your betrothal to their advantage. I'm sure it was Jazzalin who thought it up. Only a smart woman would see the way to make this situation work out so she could delay an arranged marriage indefinitely. She's going to make Daggie a great wife!" Hamiltion looked up from his work and said, "They may delay the marriage but they will be married." "I'm going to start a design catalog of possible wedding themes. Oh, it's going to be glorious! Me, a mother to a royal couple and a grandmother to their royal babies. I'm so happy I could cry", she said leaning down to kiss her husband's cheek. King Tempo's secretary sent an urgent digi-note detailing the engagement announced on Astral Keep of Princess Jazzalin to Adagio Jammon Skyes Duke of Northling several hours earlier. King Tempo smiled as he read the report because it was Jazzalin at her best overruling the arranged marriage he and Hamilton Skyes had agreed upon. She may look like her mother but she was mentally shrewd like him and he was glad about it. As there were only months until her seventeenth birthday she had initiated this engagement to get her past the betrothal due date for an indefinite time. The king knew that he would hear from Hamiltion Skyes to confirm the legal aspect of the betrothal being in still effect in spite of the engagement. That night in their bedroom the king related to Queen Octiva that Jazzalin and Adagio were engaged and she replied, "Our daughter has been two steps ahead of us about the betrothal from the start. You know Hamiltion Skyes won't release you from the agreement of the betrothal?" "Yes I do. He's already sent me a digi-note confirming the original agreement. He's itching to battle over this but it won't get to that", King Tempo said as he yawned and snuggled into his pillow to sleep.

Beabop and Lady Zynoplee watched the delayed replay of the report of the royal engagement of Jazzalin and Adagio with a sigh of relief since they had known about the betrothal for a long time. "Granny, they finally got this thing under control, at least for them both knowing what their fathers got them into. It was torture to watch them bouncing around like balls in a dark room", Beabop commented. "Well, Bea it was your suggestion to Jazzalin to make a public announced engagement to override the betrothal and it went well. They looked very convincing and the ring was worthy of a royal engagement. I give them until next year and there will be a proper royal wedding. We need to get you a significant other Beabop", Lady Zynoplee said. "I can handle my own love life, thank you very much", Beabop retorted. Lady Zynoplee did not pay any attention to Beabop's flippant reply about her personal life and had already set in motion a series of summer parties at the mansion designed to introduce her pretty and strong willed granddaughter to the eligible single Jazzoan young males. The two replayed the engagement announcement and enjoyed seeing Jazzalin and Adagio looking so complimentary and happy, forecasting a great romance.

By the end of the week that Adagio and his team were scheduled to return to Jazzo, a multitude of congratulatory digi-notes and commu-tran messages had accumulated at the twins' estate. He and Jazzalin seemed to have created a new friendship which previously had been a strained acquaintance. Although they had a long way to go things were much better than before all was revealed. Jazzalin had approached him with another issue about the betrothal which was that she be able to remain on Astral Keep until her eighteenth birthday before returning to Jazzo. He had responded in the affirmative with the stipulation that he would make periodic trips to Astral Keep in the meantime to deter any suspicions about their engagement. Since they found they were in agreement on the time they would be apart before any relational lockdown it made life easier for them both. Jazzalin did accompany Adagio to the Astronautical Airfield to see him off and to solidify their engagement to the public eye, and that entailed a goodbye kiss. She had had her first kiss from Adagio at her fifteenth birthday party which was a brief press of lips but this kiss was much longer and involved being wrapped in his arms, perhaps the way he had kissed Levitee Chymes. She found the effect of this kiss dizzying and caught herself to prevent being immersed in the sensation and pulled away. Lifting her heavy lidded eyes to him she said, "Goodbye Adagio until your return." And he replied, "Goodbye Jazzalin. I wish you a happy seventeenth birthday, and I'll be returning before the end of the year. I'll call you often until then." He seemed unaffected by their kiss as he flashed a radiant smile before boarding the format ship with the other three of his team. Once inside the ship Adagio felt a weight lift off of him as he was very caught up in the goodbye kiss which he would have gladly continued if Jazzalin had not pulled away. For all of her inexperience she was able to remain aloof and not be overwhelmed by the intimacies that lovers are expected to share. He would indeed return to Astral Keep and he would see this marriage through. He knew his mother would be all over him about the engagement and he would have to insist she not come to Northling because he needed to be alone. And once he delivered the statistics from the Astral Keep Astronautical

Format Ship Factory to Zynoplee Corporation, or moreover to Lady Zynoplee he would submit his resignation as he did not want or need to continue in the interstellar travel business. He would woo his bride to be and convince her that she loved him as he realized he loved her. He could not wait to start sending her digi-notes and get replies from her. He would be careful to learn her likes and dislikes and planning his next non-business trip to Astral Keep just to see her.

CHAPTER 21

Two weeks after the engagement reveal Jazzalin celebrated her seventeenth birthday. The twins persuaded her to allow them to rent a "party" hovercraft to take them on an all day trip around the Astral Keep regions returning before nightfall. So on the day of Jazzalin's birthday, the three of them were ready for an early morning pickup by an enormous hovercraft painted in a bright melange of colors that spelled "Party" from front to rear. Their itinerary was first the platform city, next the beaches of the southern region for a swimming and an outdoor meal, third the vast forests, lakes, mountainous regions, and last the great lush farmlands. The trip included all food and drinks and a complimentary birthday cake. Jazzalin had always thought Jazzo was beautiful but the panoramic views of Astral Keep from the huge windows of the hovercraft gave new meaning to the word beauty. Unlike her first visit to the beach with Beabop last summer the ocean was warmer and the purple blue surf was not as rough as it had been on her previous visit. She and the twins thoroughly enjoyed the carefree time they spent playing in the surf and getting covered in the pink sands of the shoreline. Astral Keep was an enormous planet and this day trip would only allow them to see half of it so they were not kept out beyond the allotted time. An hour before they were to return to the twins' estate the flight attendant bought the ornately decorated cake with seventeen candles lit on it. Suddenly there was a storm of streamers, floating globes, and paper snow flurries which set a very festive mood. Jazzalin hugged the twins and thanked them for arranging such a fun way to celebrate her seventeenth birthday. When the party hovercraft delivered them back to the estate Jazzalin received a beautiful digi-book with her name embossed in gold on the cover containing pictures of all the places they had seen, the special fun they had had and especially the cutting of the cake. As soon as they were inside the house Jazzalin's wrist commu-tran pinged to show a call from her mother. Connecting the call she said, "Hi mommy, I just got back from a daytrip with the twins. How are you and father?" "Hi darling, your father and I are just fine. I just wanted to say happy birthday from both of us and congratulations on the engagement. I want you to know how proud I am of you and we're looking forward to your return to Jazzo whenever that may be. Oh, Jazzalin your ring is beautiful", the Queen replied. "Thank you mommy for everything. I discussed the betrothal deadline with Adagio and he's fine with me taking another year on Astral Keep because as a seventeen year old marriage was not on my list of things to do right out of school", she explained. "I know dear. But you have done exceedingly well with the whole thing. You've been brave and wise through all of this, you're my hero!", Queen Octiva said emotionally. "I won't delay you getting settled from your trip. Give my regards to the twins. Tell them how much I can't wait to have them visit Jazzo. Goodbye darling, all my love", said the Queen. "Goodbye mommy, all my love too", Jazzalin replied. It had been a long but enjoyable day and that she was ready to shower and go straight to bed. After the shower her bedside commu-tran pinged and showed "Adagio" was calling in message mode, "Happy birthday Jazzalin. You don't have to connect, I just want to give you a birthday greeting and hope you enjoyed the day. I have shipped a present via the new Astral Keep Format Commercial Spaceline and it should be there shortly. I hope you like it. Goodnight." She thought he's being really nice but a lot needed to be seen in future interactions between them. She wondered about what the present could be that he had chosen for her and was in transit to her. She shook off the query and dressed and ran downstairs as the evening was still young and she and the twins were still celebrating. There was still cake and sparkling wine to be consumed.

Adagio knew she was celebrating her seventeenth birthday quietly with the twins as they were his inside informers on all things Jazzalin. When he had been made a duke he received access to all aspects of the estate which included an old safe which was full of jewels left by the previous duke. When he learned that this cache was his to do with as he pleased, he thought of Jazzalin. He had the jewels appraised and they were amazingly expensive and were designed for the former duke's wife, then passed down to a son who never married. Now it was his good fortune to be engaged to Princess Jazzalin whom he would lavish with these jewels. For her birthday he had sent her a multi-colored gem bracelet set in white gold with a note saying, "I hope you'll wear this the next time I visit Astral Keep. With love, Adagio." He felt confident that he was on a mission and he had ample ammunition to win.

For the remainder of the summer the twins were booked for numerous concerts in Astroline City, and on Platform City. When introduced the announcers would always quip, "It's my pleasure to introduce the group with a very oxymoron name the "Twin Tunz Trio" to sing the Light Song Litany." Neither the twins or Jazzalin minded since they were all about the music and publicity was negligible. Jazzalin shared her excitement with her new singing career with Beabop who was happy that she was not sitting around anxious about returning to Jazzo eventually. Beabop also had news that she had met a fancy Ziggabim musician which meant he spoke clear Jazzoan and he wore clothes. The image she sent of "Mentun Blooz", confirmed that he was tall and very handsome with his lavender complexion and dark purple hair. They had met at the Academy and he had asked her to sing with his band. Jazzalin had laughed at Beabop's assessment of her new boyfriend but she seemed very happy that he was in her life. Beabop always inquired, "How's the ring?" And Jazzalin would reply, "It's still holding on. Only a few more months until all this drama finalizes." "It could be worse, your betrothed could be some muscle head from Audia Prime or some irrhythmic from another galaxy. So you got a rich pretty boy who seems to like you even though you've been spazzing for most of the time he's known you. People are really jealous of you and they feel that you are too snooty, but they don't know you", Beabop explained. "Well I'm allowed to be an individual just like my detractors. Always a joy to talk to you Miss Bea, until next time. Goodbye", Jazzalin said. She realized she was so very fortunate to have Beabop as a friend who did not have any qualms about speaking the truth when necessary but had enough tact to be quiet depending on the situation. She would definitely be the "maid of honor" in the wedding she was destined to experience soon. She intended to squeeze as much enjoyment into her last year on Astral Keep as she could. She looked down at the birthday present Adagio had sent her. It was a hypnotic confection of pink, purple, and green diamonds set in white gold. She had to admit it was beautiful and he was bringing his "I'm rich" game and she did not mind being its recipient. He was due back for the end of the year and asked her to wear the bracelet when he saw her next. Her mother said she was being wooed which caused her to roll her eyes at the idea of such an old fashioned method of courtship. Her mother, as sweet as she was, had no clue that her daughter would have happily remained single until she was thirty with her own jazz group and dating anyone she took a fancy to. And the idea of pregnancy while still in her teens brought on a full blown depression. The twins once found her sitting alone in the library with tears rolling down her cheeks and knowing it must be related to the future marriage they assured her that Adagio would be the best of husbands, which only seemed to make her cry more.

By the end of the year week of celebrations Jazzalin had resigned herself to a modicum of stable behavior that would hide her anxiety and depression. When Adagio arrived at the twins' estate for the holiday week she allowed him to kiss her, she wore the bracelet and smiled at him, hopefully assuring him of her presence in the moment. She would smile when she had to and act engaged but her heart was years in the past before she was used as part of a war tactic. During the eve of the new year Adagio took her hand and led her to the side garden on the estate where they had announced their engagement and looking into her amber eyes he asked, "How long are you going to be quiet before you tell me what's wrong?" "I'm fine, it's just that I'm a little overwhelmed with everything that's pending in about six months time", she said. "Anyway, I'll stay the course and return to Jazzo to a grand and glorious wedding to Jazzo's most eligible bachelor", she said with tears glistening in her eyes. Impulsively Adagio pulled her into his arms and said, "Don't be sad you're not alone in this. We can delay your return another year if you want. " "No, I won't put my father under any more pressure than he already is since he posted the royal seal on the agreement he made with your father", Jazzalin said in a hollow voice. "Jazzalin I've always thought you did not really like me. You were always aloof and sharp, never at ease around me", he remarked. "Well, you are four years older than me and you were always in the company of adoring music business sycophants. Also your taste in females seemed to lean to the older, fast and loose type which wasn't me. We only had Beabop in common and there was no way I was going to have a crush on you, it was unacceptable on so many levels. And when I found out about the betrothal it did me in and I reacted by running away and being standoffish towards you. We were both used in this betrothal but I don't dislike you, I barely know you. There, I said it. I feel better now", she said resolutely. "Good, I'm glad. I don't know a lot about you either, other than you're smart and you are good at finding solutions to situations that confront you. I know my mother likes you and she's a great judge of character", he said. "Oh, she wanted me to give you this. She wanted you to know you can depend on her for any help with your ideas for the wedding", he said, handing her a large bound catalog. Jazzalin took the catalog and began to leaf through it and closed it suddenly and said, "I really like your mother. She has so much style and vitality. Thank her for me and tell her I'll study her ideas and if there's one we agree on I'll let her know." Feeling they had made a major accomplishment in their relationship, Adagio said, "Let's go back inside the twins will wonder where we are." "The twins know exactly where we are. They're creepy that way", Jazzalin remarked. The rest of the new year holiday Adagio made sure to take Jazzalin out to dinner at Astraline City's best restaurants and to always give time to the local data stream media for quick interviews. Jazzalin applied all of her royal behavior skills to project a calm, serene exterior in public to cover her internal turmoil. When it was time for Adagio's return to Jazzo, Jazzalin accompanied him to the spaceport which had become exponentially busier than it was a year ago. The commercial format ships had created a thriving interstellar travel industry that the people of Astral Keep were enjoying. The commercial format ships were limited in traveling only five light years in any direction to neighboring planets and galaxies, any distance exceeding that would require an excessive charge which most were not willing to pay. This travel limitation generated a personal commercial format ship industry which was just getting started on Astral Keep. Soon anyone who had the money and could pass the required piloting and technical tests could own their very own format ship to travel to the farthest reaches of interstellar space.

Jazzalin was getting accustomed to Adagio's touches on her arm and the way he kissed her when greeting or departing, in keeping with their engagement she complied as she realized he was a victim of his father's arrogant bravado as she was of hers. She said, "Goodbye Adagio. I'll see you on Jazzo soon." He replied, "Didn't you know I'm coming to get you in my own format ship. It's being completed now and will be ready in five to six months. Goodbye Jazzalin. We need to create some endearments for each other at some point." Giving her a quick peck on her cheek he boarded the format ship which launched into the upper atmosphere and was gone. Returning to the twins' estate she changed into her gardening gear and went out into the greenhouse and joined the droid "Planter One" and began to work vigorously to clear her head and to use her energy for something other than thinking about her future. By the end of the day she had planted multiple flats of spring seedlings and was sweaty, dirty, and wonderfully tired. She skipped back into the house and up the stairs to her room and ran a bath as a shower would be insufficient. She determined she would live in the energy of light and she wouldn't let herself carry sadness another day.

On Jazzo Adagio told his mother that he'd given her wedding design catalog to Jazzalin and she was receptive and said she would contact her when she found something she liked. Lady Sylphine was ecstatic that her wedding design catalog hadnot been rejected by her future daughter-in-law. Adagio was about to renovate two rooms to create a master suite at his Northling estate and he would eventually call on her to put on the finishing touches, she just had to be patient. She had been patient all her life. As a young girl she was patient when her own tribespeople called her "ugly purple girl" or "skinny purple girl" and then she became the darling of digi-media and Jazzo's fashion runways. She had been patient when she was snubbed by several of Jazzo's royals and social hierarchy and then her son was made a duke and got engaged to the king's only daughter. Patience had always paid dividends for her. She had already begun a proactive campaign to be ready to plan the wedding of her son and the Princess with ease and aplomb. Her keen sense of art and design had helped her design two possible dresses and hats for the mother of the groom which she had sent to her on-call seamstress to produce in floaty lightweight silk prints. She knew this wedding would happen before the end of the year and she was not going to be caught dragging her feet. She had her secretary compose a tactfully worded digi-note to Queen Octiva offering her assistance with any pre-royal wedding tasks. The digi-note requested an in person meeting with the Queen at her convenience to show her some design concepts that might be acceptable and applicable. Again she just had to be patient.

Jazzalin decided she would return to Jazzo a month before her eighteenth birthday so she informed the twins who were saddened that she would be leaving sooner than they had anticipated. A week before Jazzalin was to return to Jazzo the twins called her in the library to speak to her. In unison the twins explained, "Jazzalin since we've known you for nearly four years you have been a friend, a sister, and a welcomed consultant and we wanted to gift you with something that shows how much we appreciate you and how much we love you. So we could not think of any material gift because you are not lacking anything, so we decided that since you are our sister you should have a light guardian just as we have. We reached out to our light guardian and inquired if this was possible and were advised yes it was possible since you have been in our company since the Sessilum defeat and you have educated us so that we can interface and function within the present social constructs. We would have never been able to be on our own without your help in knowing what to do and how to do it. Light Guardian please show yourself." Without hesitation two columns of intensely bright light appeared in the room and announced, "Lilitine and Luling so good to be with you. I am here at your request. With me is the light guardian that has been assigned to your sister Jazzalin." "Thank you Light Guardian. We want our sister to have a guardian because she's going to another planet and getting married there", the twins said. "How wonderful. Her light guardian will start service to Jazzalin now. Jazzalin meet your light guardian Litt JAM", the twins' guardian said. "What an odd name", Jazzalin said. "My name is a composite of my lengthy Sextillion name and the initials of your name "Jazzalin Arpeggia Maximus". You can call me Litt or just guardian. I will travel with you to Jazzo and be there for you and your loved ones", Litt said. "I really don't need a guardian", Jazzalin said. "This gift has already been given and cannot be returned", the twins' guardian said. "I don't want to offend you since this is done out of your esteem for me so, I receive my light guardian "Litt JAM" and thank you Lilitine and Luling for your generosity", Jazzalin replied. "You're welcome. And we've been invited by Lady Zynoplee and Beabop to stay at their mansion on Jazzo indefinitely. We'll close up our estate and we'll be traveling with you to Jazzo, so none of us will miss each other", the twins said happily. "Beabop had mentioned it to me but I was waiting to hear it from you. It's about time you two", Jazzalin said jokingly. "Princess Jazzalin, I'm going to retire to the unseen but I am still present, just as the twins light guardian is always present for them. What a joy it is for me to be in your service. Blessed you are my charge", said Litt JAM as he disappeared from sight as did the twins' light guard. "Goodbye Litt or should I say that I'll see you on your next appearance", said Jazzalin brightly watching her light guardian fade from sight. The rest of the remaining time the three had to get ready to leave for Jazzo was spent packing much wanted items, programming the droid staff on security mode as well as for maintenance of the gardens and greenhouse. Adagio called Jazzalin via commu-tran to confirm her decision for an earlier return to Jazzo, he inquired, "Jazzalin are you sure you want to return to Jazzo before your eighteenth birthday?" Jazzalin answered, "Yes, I'm sure I want to leave earlier. I want to help mother with the wedding preparation. There are dresses to be chosen and fitted, color schemes to be chosen for floral displays, a menu to agree on, and there's a honeymoon to arrange. These are time consuming activities so I don't want to pop in and expect everyone to rush around on my account. I want this to somehow be easy on everyone since I did manage to overcome the pressure of having my future be unlike anything I would have chosen. I don't want to be oppressive to my parents or yours. Did I tell you the twins gave me a light guardian?" "I understand Jazzalin, and no I didn't know you had a light guardian. Fortunately, my format ship has been completed so I can be there by next weekend", Adagio replied. They spoke a while longer on a few more imminent issues and were able to gain insight into the other's heart, but they knew there was some distance to go before they were not second guessing each other.

Adagio arrived on Astral Keep the following weekend and had gotten permission to land in a small launching area at Astraline City's Astronautical Airfield. The twins had their hovercraft there to deliver him to their estate. Jazzalin and the twins greeted Adagio at the door and pulled him into the library. He advised they were scheduled to leave for Jazzo the first day of the week so they would need to have all their travel cases ready to be loaded onboard the format ship the day before. Jazzalin said, "We're all very excited about going to Jazzo. Will there be any media coverage when we land?" "Yes, your father insisted that your return be documented as well as the twins with you. He does not want your return to be a secret, but a joyous event of his daughter's homecoming after being consultant to the zealot twins on Astral Keep. He requested that you be dressed appropriately for digi-media coverage. There won't be any media conference, you'll just leave the ship and immediately get into a waiting royal hovercraft", Adagio explained. "So like my father to put a spin on my return to Jazzo. He's so aboutcontrolling things", Jazzalin said in exasperation. The service droid announced that dinner was ready in the kitchen. As usual the twins had ordered a massive amount of food which was way more than the four of them could consume, there would be leftovers. Due to the fifteen hour travel time Adagio was exhausted and excused himself to get to bed early. Jazzalin and the twins spent the evening verifying that all their loose ends were tied off, like bills and store accounts. Jazzalin especially wanted to make sure her Astraline City bank account would be accessible when she was back on Jazzo and was assured that her funds were available to be transferred or debited from Jazzo. As the twins' paid consultant, Jazzalin had amassed a significant bank balance over her three plus years on Astral Keep. As a royal dependent she had a sizable stipend on Jazzo but she wanted to be able to have ready funds should she have a need of it. And there was the dowry which no one liked to talk about, which the husband could either accept as his own or allow his wife to keep it. She would see which way Adagio responded to the eight digit dowry amount that was attached to her in marriage.

The two days prior to their departure found Jazzalin and the twins deciding on what to wear that was presentable when the digi-reporters posted their images for all of Jazzo to see as well as the entire Symphonea planetary system. This dilemma initiated a reason to go shopping as they did not want to unpack their travel cases to search for an outfit, shopping for a new outfit was easier. Adagio opted to stay behind and relax by the pool and was the Astral Keep media stream. They were chauffeured to the Astroline City Shopping hub and dropped off on the top floor for all things female. Since it was also summertime on

Jazzo they chose dresses and skirt sets in light and airy materials and designer flat shoes in coordinating colors. The twins advised Jazzalin they should also buy warm clothes to wear onboard because space is cold even if you are traveling inside a climate controlled cabin. When Jazzalin and the twins returned to the estate they heard Adagio yell from poolside, "Hey ladies, come here. There's something I want to show you!" The three of them ran outside and found Adagio pointing to the Astroline City data stream on screen showing a detailed report of their shopping trip. The perky reporter spouted, "Today the esteemed twin zealots and their longtime friend and consultant Princess Jazzalin of Jazzo were seen on a shopping spree at the Astroline City Shopping Hub. It seems they were very interested in summer attire as well as casual wear. It's been circulated that Princess Jazzalin will soon be returning to Jazzo to be married to the handsome Duke of Northling, Adagio Skyes. Well, it seems she and her friends will have the right things to wear if their shopping spree is any indication." They all laughed that they were being followed by the media on a trivial trip to the shopping hub. As the time to depart came closer Jazzalin was visibly anxious. Adagio had noticed her tense body language and said, "It's not like you're going to prison. Just take it easy.

Your parents are aware that this is a difficult step for all of us, not just you." "I know it's been a long time since all this began and it's coming to a kind of conclusion and I have to be blunt, I'm not ready for it", Jazzalin replied. "We're all making an effort to get through to a non-cataclysmic finish. I'm on your side and the twins will be with you. You should call Beabop and let her give you a bravery transfer", Adagio said resolutely. "Good idea, I think I will call Beabop. Good talk", Jazzalin said, leaving him in the library to go to her room.

CHAPTER 22

The Astral Keep sky was a pallet of mixed gray clouds on the day of their departure as if the sky was sad to see them leave. Everything seemed to be happening too fast for Jazzalin's liking. Their flight was scheduled for 8:00 morning time for their fifteen hour trip back to Jazzo and at this early hour the parasitic media presence would not be an issue. Since their travel cases had been loaded on the format ship the day before there was no boarding delay when they arrived at the Astronautic Airfield. The huge shiny format ship stood glinting in spite of partly cloudy skies with its hatch open for the four passengers it would carry to their five light year destination. Once inside the ship Jazzalin and the twins noticed that the interior had changed from the original ship that brought them to Astral Keep over three years ago. The cabin was a cool blue color with silver accents. There were ten passenger seats with pull out data stations and a larger upper level with a food pantry and restroom. The twins commented, "Adagio this is so different from the ship you brought us to Astral Keep in. This is so pretty and spacious. Does it belong to you?" "Yes, it was a gift from my former employer Lady Zynoplee", Adagio replied. Just then the pilot droid announced, "Passengers please take your seats and secure your seat belts as lift off is in five minutes." The four took their preferred seats and fastened their seat belts. Jazzalin sat by a window and Adagio took the seat next to her. The twins sat next to each other and immediately deployed the data stations to access the planetary datafiles. The countdown completed and the ship's engines keened lifting it upwards and launching it into the upper atmosphere and within minutes into interstellar space. Jazzalin closed her eyes and prayed that she could get through the next few days without an emotional meltdown.

Adagio intuitively said, "One step at a time Princess. We just made the first of many successful future steps." "Stop reading my mind", Jazzalin retorted. Periodically Adagio would sit next to the pilot droid and confirm flight coordinates. Since starting the format ship industry on both Jazzo and Astral Keep he had learned a lot about astro-mechanics and astrophysics which allowed him to be able to converse with the droid regarding ship functions. The lengthy fifteen hour trip was uneventful except for the last hour when Jazzalin and the twins were changing into their dressy clothes for the media storm once they landed on Jazzo. The droid pilot announced their descent into Jazzo's atmosphere were landing at it's South Region Astronautical Airfield. Once the format ship landed Jazzalin saw from the window a crowd of Jazzo media reporters behind tape barriers and the royal hovercraft waiting closeby. When the hatch opened Adagio stepped out first, followed by Jazzalin and the twins. Jazzalin smiled at the crowd and waved her hand in a friendly greeting to the Jazzoan public. Her father had sent the Royal Guard to escort her to the hovercraft so no one dared get too close if they knew what was good for them. Jazzalin entered the official vehicle followed by the twins and Adagio last. The driver knew that he would be taking the twins to the Zynoplee mansion first since they would be staying there for a while. Jazzalin called Beabop from her wrist commu-tran, "Bea, we're here. We're enroute to your house now to drop off the twins." "Eeeeeeeeeeee!!! I saw the coverage of the landing. That ship is so quizit!! Oh, and Jazz you looked so good when you smiled and waved, all cool and royal. The twins were dressed so pretty in their floral dresses. All of you looked quizit. Granny is so excited to be hosting the twins for as long as they want to stay on Jazzo", Beabop said excitedly. "We're nearly there. Unfortunately, I won't be able to come in as we're being escorted by the Royal Guard and they are all together serious, if you know what I mean", Jazzalin said. "I know but it's making sure the media predators can't ravage you", her best friend said. "They're reporting on the data stream, "the lovely Princess Jazzalin has returned to Jazzo after a long sabbatical as consultant to the hero twin zealots of the Sessilum Threat over three years ago. She is accompanied by her fiance, Duke of Northling Adagio Skyes and the twin zealots Lilitine and Luling. The Princess is being escorted by the Royal Guard and will be traveling to the North Region

Royal Palace to reunite with her father King Tempo and her mother Queen Octiva. The people of Jazzo are looking forward to the Princess's coming marriage in the near future"", Beabop relayed. "I can't wait to see you Bea. You and the twins should come over tomorrow for lunch. Call me first thing so I can have everything ready" Jazzalin said. "You know it. I hear the hovercraft. I'm going to the door as we speak", Beabop said simultaneously opening the large front door. A guardsman opened the door of the hovercraft and assisted the twins getting out of the passenger compartment. The guardsman also took their two travel cases out of the storage bay and bought them into the doorway where a smiling Beabop waited. Jazzalin lowered the passenger window and waved to Beabop, who in turn waved back. The twins greeted Beabop with a hug and followed her into the large house. The hovercraft was on its way again. Adagio said, "You see everything is going smoothly so far and it's going to be that way through the days ahead." He took her hand and kissed it which caused Jazzalin's eyes to widen since she was not ready for any acts of affections. "Adagio, forgive me but I know you mean to be kind but I'm still adjusting to the engagement and I just need some time", Jazzalin explained. "I understand but I'm not retreating on how I feel about you. We have several months to get to know each other better. I intend to make the process as easy as possible", he said, still holding her hand. Jazzalin let herself relax since her fiance was in wooing mode and she had to be somehow compliant. The hovercraft finally reached the North Region and the Royal Palace. Since the palace was gated the media reporters had no access inside the palace grounds but it did not deter them from crowding at the gates to get a glimpse of the princess and her fiance. Some of the reporters used small high resonance aerial digi-transmitters to get pictures of the couple. The hovercraft landed in the front driveway of the palace which was too far for any real images of Jazzalin and Adagio to be obtained by the reporters. The royal press secretary would release approved images of the Princess's reunion with her parents and a close up of her engagement ring which the local media would put their spin on whatever they wanted it to be. As soon as the hovercraft set down in the driveway and the guardsman opened the door for her, Jazzalin ran through the large opened door of the palace entryway into the arms of her parents who were walking towards her. It was a joyous collision of both parents encasing their much older daughter in their embrace. "Oh Jazzalin it's so good to have you home. We've missed you so much", her father said in a deep emotional voice. And Queen Octiva just mumbled, "You're home, you're home. you're home." Jazzalin was speechless between the three way hugs and when she finally spoke she said, "Papa, mommy I'm so glad to be home again. I love you both so much." King Tempo recovered and directed the topic and asked, "Were all of your travel cases in the hovercraft?" "Yes papa they were and the service droids are bringing them in now", Jazzalin replied. "You must be tired and hungry. I had the kitchen staff make some of your favorite lunch salads, sandwiches and summer desserts. I even got that "Lift a Pinky" blue drink you like so much", Queen Octiva said enthusiastically. "Mommy you're the best. I am more hungry than tired, so yes, lead me to the food. Oh, Adagio you know you're included as well", Jazzalin said with a smiling after thought. King Tempo spoke in agreement, "Yes, young man forgive our rudeness. In our joy of Jazzalin's homecoming we completely forgot your massive contribution to her returning safely to us. Thank you Duke of Northling and please join us for lunch." "You're very welcome your majesty and it's been my pleasure to assist with Princess Jazzalin's homecoming and lunch sounds very good right about now", Adagio replied amicably. "This way Duke, the rest of us know the way", Queen said playfully. With their arms still around their daughter they walked into the breakfast room off the enormous kitchen where the counter had been lined with trays and bowls of delicious food to allow for self service. Jazzalin filled her plate with several sandwiches and sizable mounds of grain and greens salads. She had to return to the counter with another plate to get a serving of fruit, cake and cream dessert. Her parents beamed at their daughter as if she were a toddler just learning to eat table food but she was actually eating her meal like a field hand. Adagio knew he was an outsider in this reunion but it was heartwarming to observe the love they had for their only child. After lunch Adagio advised he had to leave for his Northling Estate. With a casual ease he took Jazzalin's hand wearing the huge diamond ring and kissed it and said, "Goodbye Jazzalin. Goodbye your majesties." Turning to his future father in law Adagio asked, "King Tempo, may I have your chauffeur give me a ride to Northling as my hovercraft is at my South Region apartment?" "Of course, I'll walk you out and give them instructions", said King Tempo. Adagio was extremely handsome, polished, and very likable Queen Octiva thought, and if her daughter had to be betrothed to anyone she was glad it was him. Queen Octiva took Jazzalin by the arm and directed to the stairway, "Come with me dear and see the changes we made to your bedroom. It's quizit as you say." Opening the Jazzalin's bedroom door revealed a collage of blues and greens accented by floral pastels. "Mommy, it is "quizit!", Jazzalin said in awe. "We put a planter box on your balcony since we were told you have an entire greenhouse on Astral Keep. I started the planter with pom-pom plants, ruffle cup flowers, and white and yellow petal pops. You can change them to something else if you like, this was just to get things started. Jazzalin, I'm so happy you're back now. I don't think I could have waited until next year for you to return", Queen Octiva said, hugging her daughter again. "I'm glad to be back and I'm not running away again. Mommy, I could use a shower and a nap", Jazzalin said decidedly. "Alright, I'll leave you to get settled in. Dinner's at seven but we can send your's up on a tray, you know how to buzz the kitchen. Love you", Queen Octiva said as she left her daughter's room. What an eventful day this had been for everyone Jazzalin thought and there was much more to come. One step at a time Adagio had said onboard a spaceship traveling faster than light.

Lady Zynoplee came downstairs on the floor lift to meet her two interstellar guests Lilitine and Luling Vizun, the heroes of Sessilum conflict. The great woman was overcome with emotion as she realized they had witnessed her husband Xanaaz's death but had read his thoughts in order to locate the format ship that would be their rescue and allow the Sextillion Brethren to advance and destroy the enemy. She held out her arms to them and hugged them both at once and said, "Thank you for any comfort you were able to give to my husband and son." "It was our pleasure to provide our presence in the midst of the brutal treatment they endured, he saw your face right up to his last breath. We want to thank you for allowing us to stay in your beautiful home, it's bigger than ours in square footage but we have more land", the twins said in bright unison. Lady Zynoplee smiled at their assessment of her house and the childlike attachment they had to each other. She decided to let them determine if they wanted to share a bedroom together or have separate rooms. "My granddaughter will guide you around so you can familiarize yourself with everything. You are very welcome here, my home is your home. And maybe tomorrow I'd like to speak with you about a project I'd like your help with", Lady Zynoplee said. Without hesitation the twins replied, "We would be happy to be guest consultants and mentors for the Jazzo First Song Academies." "Wonderful. I will still need to go over the details with you when you're settled in", Lady Zynoplee said. She forgot that these twins were very special and she was glad she would have this chance to know them personally and musically. Beabop told Lady Zynoplee that the twins were able to read thoughts and she should be careful around them but Lady Zynoplee said, "I'm not a savage and I don't mind them seeing my thoughts. I'm open to being observed by these dear girls. And they are young and I'm sure my mature thoughts are not of interest to them. They were a comfort to my husband and my son, and they are a comfort to me."

When the royal hovercraft approached the Northling Estate Adagio saw his mother's sporty hovercraft parked in the front driveway. He smiled to himself at her awareness of things happening around the city. The king's hovercraft let Adagio out at the entry to his beautiful house with his one travel case. Going inside he was immediately greeted by his mother, "Daggie, I saw the landing this morning. You all looked very calm and sophisticated. I knew you'd be coming here so I rushed over to air the place out. Come here and give your mother a hug", Lady Sylphine said, holding out her arms to her son. Adagio went to his mother and hugged her and said, "Mother you are glorious." "You are so correct and never forget it. I assume you had lunch at the palace with the princess and your future in-laws?", Lady Sylphine said. Adagio replied, "Yes, mother I had lunch at the palace but I could use a snack and some sparkling wine after I have a shower." "And so you shall have your grace. It'll be ready by the time you finish your shower", his mother said enroute to the kitchen. She was caught up in the thoughts of all of the activities of the next several months that would culminate in a resplendent royal wedding and her presence there as mother of the groom, dressed like a queen.

Jazzalin was more tired than she realized and what started as an afternoon nap lasted until the next morning. She was the better for the extensive hours of sleep as she woke up refreshed and ready for the day. Queen Octiva peeked into her room and found her looking out from her balcony onto the formal palace gardens below. "Good Morning Jazzalin", her mother said. "Good morning mommy. I overslept. I guess I was more exhausted from the trip than I thought but I'm restored and I want some breakfast. Let me brush my teeth and I'll meet you in the kitchen", Jazzalin replied. "Sounds good. I'll get breakfast started. How does purple tea and multi grain pancakes with fruit syrup sound?" the Queen inquired while leaving her daughter's room. "Mommy that sounds wonderful, I'm salivating", Jazzalin said. In the kitchen Queen Octiva set down across from her husband who was already having a cup of purple tea. "She was up and enjoying the view from her balcony. She's washing up and brushing her teeth. She'll be down in a bit", said the Queen as she poured herself a cup of tea. "I'm ready for this marriage business to be done. She's grown up a lot and she will not shrink from her duty", said King Tempo. Good morning parents", Jazzalin said walking into the kitchen. After breakfast Jazzalin called Beabop to arrange a time for lunch with her and the twins. "Bea, how are the twins getting along with your Granny?", Jazzalin asked. "Well, they got up before the sun, which is the same time Granny gets up. Granny has a meeting with the chancellor and faculty of the East Region First Song Academy and they went with her. Jazzalin, Granny is loving their weird mind reading thing and they love her for her openness. They may or maynot get back today. I'll let you know. So when are you going to have your bridal shower?" Beabop said. "I don't know, but I think my birthday would be the best time. Two celebrations at once would cut down on multiple massing of royals and socially significant others. Oh, Beabop will you be my maid of honor?" Jazzalin asked. "You know I will but I want to wear something I want to wear, not a pouffy cloud dress. Do we agree on that?", Beabop asked directly. "I agree as long as it's quizit and not "scream cult" revealing. I have to run, mommy is wanting some bonding time and since you're not coming to lunch that's the next thing on my schedule. Bye Bea, call me with an update on the twins", said Jazzalin. "Bye Jazz", said Beabop as she disconnected from the call.

At the East Region First Song Academy Lady Zynoplee introduced the twins to the chancellor and faculty in an assembly in the Lyceum. "I'd like to introduce the twin zealots who held on during the Sessilum threat by their knowledge of the Light Songs which they sang incessantly until the Sextillion Brethren came and they were rescued. Not only did they stand against the enemy but they provided comfort to my husband and son who were captured and tortured by the Sessilum. They have agreed to provide mentoring and consultation to any of our First Song students who either have a need or who want to excel in the Light Songs to benefit themselves and Jazzo. It gives me great pleasure to introduce Lilitine and Luling Vizun our Light Song heroes to East Region First Song Academy." There was a standing ovation as the twins ascended to the stage with bright smiles on their faces. As usual they spoke in unison, "Thank you for allowing us the opportunity to interface with the students of this academy and to share what knowledge we have of the Light Song music with them. We hope to inspire and be inspired in the process. " Again there was thunderous applause as they stepped down from the podium to take their seats. Lady Zynoplee made sure the twins spoke to everyone who mattered from the chancellor, administrative staff and the professors. Invigorated Lady Zynoplee took the twins on a brief walking tour of the campus. Finally she realized she was being overly enthusiastic and she should slow down and take things a little at a time. She apologized to the twins and said they should go to her East Region apartment to stay overnight and they could come back to the Academy tomorrow for the rest of the tour before returning to her home in the South Region. The twins were gracious but they were glad she was sensitive that they were getting tired as she showed them the expansive campus with all its different departments. For her age Lady Zynoplee's stamina was in no way challenged.

It would be another week before Jazzalin got a call from Beabop. Her call to Jazzalin was smothered in apologies because it was not usual for Beabop to miss calling her almost daily. Beabop explained, "Jazz, I'm so sorry it's taken me this long to get back to you but with guests in the house puts me off my regular routine, especially the twins." "You don't have to apologize to me, remember I lived with them for over three years", Jazzalin said. "Let me tell you what happened. When Granny and the twins returned from the East Region it was mid-week and Granny said they should just relax and enjoy some free time by the pool or in the library perusing the datafiles. We had two days of poolside leisure with food catered by "Lift A Pinky", which was quizit. On the weekend the twins called their male friends Metre and Mezzur who showed up at the mansion requesting to see them. The twins told Granny they needed to refresh their wardrobes with new outfits suitable for their consulting position at the East Region First Song Academy. Granny being the trusting soul she is, said of course they could go with their friends since they knew them from Astral Keep. Granny then gave me an obscene amount of money and said I should do some shopping for your bridal shower party but I knew she was using my presence to cover any unforeseen issues. We went to the Shop-Along Center and the twins were buying some really nice professional wear items and I got a glut of fashion acquisitions. Jazzalin, I spent close to five thousand credits and still had more than half the money Granny gave me. I won't need any money from her for a while. I have five designer party outfits and matching heels and boots. Oh, I'm digressing. After we finished shopping we were driving past a "Fling Field Festival", and the twins asked what it was since it was full of people, noise and color. Metre and Mezzur explained to twins about the fling fields being gravitational anomalies that if anyone stands in the no gravity field they would be carried skyward into the upper atmosphere, but as a way of allowing the public safe access to the anomalies there are parks set up with tether stations which anchor the participant to enjoy a "no gravity fling" and safely be reeled down to earth. So the twins got all excited and insisted we go to the Fling Festival. We parked and while Metre and Mezzur were going to pay for our passes for the fling, the twins walked into the no gravity field and started to ascend upwards without being tethered. People including myself were spazzing and screaming as they were nearly out of sight. Then suddenly they begin to descend making loops in the air as if they are being twirled by something. Finally, they landed outside of the no gravity area and everyone was staring at them in shock and awe. I quickly yelled at Metre and Mezzur that we needed to leave as we did not want to be the subject of a media storm, they agreed and they gave away the fling field passes they just bought to some random people waiting in line for the field and we got in the hovercraft and left really fast. The guys treated us to lunch at "Lift A Pinky", but didn't mention anything about the twins' fling field episode. When they dropped us back at Granny's and unloaded all of our shopping goodies, the twins told them they'd call them later. I didn't dare tell Granny anything about the fling field incident and I didn't speak to twins about it either. Jazzalin, the twins are way weird in a good way but weird just the same. Sorry to be so long winded but I have not spoken to you in a while", Beabop said hissing out an exhausted breath. "You know they have a light guardian who is always with them. He was their protector when they were in the Sessilum habitat. They were reckless to go untethered in the fling field but since they're alright I wouldn't let it bother me. You can confront them and tell them that they should be a little more careful about the liberties they enjoy with their invisible protector when others are not able to enjoy the same type of security. Oh, they assigned a light guardian to me for my birthday. I tried to refuse but they said there are no returns allowed on light guardians. My light guardian is "Litt JAM". It's a combo of his name and my initials, sounds like a jazz band's name. Well, you've been initiated into the wonderful world of the twins. Now Bea show me what you bought", Jazzalin replied. "Before I show you my quizit purchases, do you mean they've made you an honorary weirdy?", Beabop asked. "Yes, Beabop. The twins were being kind in assigning the light guardian to me since they knew I might not see them again and it would make them happy to know I had a guardian just like they do", Jazzalin replied. "Have you seen your guardian?" Beabop asked. "Yes, I think so. It was a blinding column of light at first and then it faded from view but assured me that he would always be there. I don't want to talk about that, show me your new party clothes", Jazzalin commanded her friend. The two friends spent the next two hours discussing and critiquing Beabop's new party clothes and confirming that she and the twins would have lunch at the palace at the end of the week.

Queen Octiva and her secretary were somewhat at a loss as to how to arrange the details of Jazzalin's birthday and bridal shower as one event. The Queen actually reached out to Lady Sylphine to provide some insights. The flamboyant socialite and businesswoman was more than happy to lend her expertise in organizing her future daughter-in-law's double celebratory event. She showed up to the royal palace with her event planner, interior designer, clothier, and her caterer. They laid out the plan in the huge palace library. The designer presented a design for the invitations worded "King Tempo and Queen Octiva are requesting your presence on the eighteenth birthday of their daughter Princess Jazzalin pending her marriage to the Duke of Northling on Springsday 15, 5113. This is a formal festive event and requires the appropriate attire and accompanying gifts. Please reply at the commu-tran access number provided to confirm your presence. We look forward to having your presence at this double celebration." Queen Octiva commented, "Yes that is an appropriately worded invitation. Lady Sylphine here is a list of guests that the royal family would like to invite to Jazzalin's double event. Also Lady Sylphine you can invite twenty guests of your choice to this event". Lady Sylphine said, "Thank you, Your majesty. I'll have my team get the invitations generated and sent out today. Also your majesty what color scheme will be used for the invitations and party decorations. I have some suggestions if you have not made a decision." "Lady Sylphine, I think I should bring my daughter into this discussion since this is all about her. Using her wrist commu-tran the Queen entered Jazzalin's access code and heard her answer, "Hi, mommy. I'm helping the ground's droid dead heading in the cutting garden and I've made a quizit bouquet too. Do you need me for something?" "Yes dear, if you could come into the library for a minute we need your opinion on something", the Queen said. "I'll be right there", Jazzalin replied. Within minutes Jazzalin entered the library wearing a disposable paper coverall and boots and greeted her mother, "Mommy I'm here. What do you need my help with?" The Queen explained that she and Lady Sylphine needed her input with some details for her birthday and bridal shower, such as, color scheme, decorations, music, and food. Jazzalin peeled off the coveralls which covered her clean casual wear beneath and said, "Sure mommy, I would love to help. I was wondering when I would be included in prepping the events. Lady Sylphine so nice to have your assistance with everything." "It's my pleasure Princess and since we're a family I feel I should assist to make these events as flawless and fabulous for my future daughter-in-law as possible.", Lady Sylphiine remarked. Jazzalin knew she was being kind but she felt the pre-marriage activities were growing into a huge bubble that would pop and cause immense damage. Smiling at her beautiful future mother-in—law, Jazzalin said, "Thank you Lady Sylphine for your input. Well, my choice for color scheme are all shades of pinks and purples, for decorations the usual is fine, coordinating streamers, floating air globes, and colorful paper rain. For music it should be a mixture of jazz fusion, classical world jazz, and regional ethnic music. I can compile the music and upload it into the datafile." Lady Sylphine replied, "Wonderful Princess. My staff will draw up decoration plans and provide them for your review. Now Princess, have you thought about what you'll be wearing for the event? If not I can have my personal designer show you some sketches or you can create your own ideas in collaboration. Let me know." Jazzalin knew Lady Sylphine was a small planet around which satellites of party planning, designer clothes and shoes, and fashionable living rotated in exact precision which she did not want to get caught in the orbit. Jazzalin determined to be agreeable and to do what it took to get to the finish line of the wedding marathon she was running.

Beabop and the twins arrived at the palace by means of Lady Zynoplees chauffeured hovercraft. Jazzalin was overjoyed to see them since it was over a week since they had returned to Jazzo. Beabop rolled her eyes heavenward and gave a small whistle displaying her anxious experiences of the last week with the fearless undaunted twins and greeted Jazzalin, "Hi Jazz. We're here and I'm ready for lunch. I only had a cup of purple tea for breakfast and I'm starving." When the twins were introduced to King Tempo they did a deep curtsies to him but he responded by taking their hands and pulling them up to their feet, before hugging both of them. He said, "You are forever ensconced in my heart for your bravery in defeating the Sessilum and for providing a safe haven for Jazzalin when she was in distress. I love you both." "We thank you for helping us escape the Sessilum habitat. Without your swift response to our plea for help all would have been lost", the twins said in unison. Jazzalin injected, "That's enough emotional obligations, we have a lunch to enjoy. Father please join us if you like." The King gave his daughter a sharp glance and broke into a big smile as she lead her guests to the airy atrium where lunch would be served. Lunch was abundant with multiple entrees of grilled poultry, succulent seafood, and lean bova steaks, salads of all kinds, numerous baked casseroles, fresh baked breads and an entire table of colorful, fruit filled, cream covered and frozen desserts. The King spoke a blessing over the food and began to help himself to the bountiful fare that lay before him.

For several minutes no one spoke as they all were involved in eating with full enjoyment. "Jazzalin, this is so good it reminds us of the times you made dinner for us on Astral Keep. Everything is so yummy!", the twins said. "I didn't cook anything, I only chose the menu and the ingredients and the efficient kitchen staff did the rest. So glad it meets your approval", Jazzalin said between chewing. The King having eaten his fill said, "Ladies I'm going to excuse myself from your delightful company and retire to my royal duties. It's been a pleasure Lilitine and Luling to finally meet you and break bread with you. I'm sure I'll be seeing you more in the near future. Enjoy your stay on Jazzo." "Thank you Your Majesty. Jazzalin your father is so good and strong, your fiance reminds us of him. You are so fortunate in Adagio", the twins said. "You guys are so man crazy. How's things going with Metre and Mezzur since you've come to Jazzo?", Jazzalin asked. "They took us shopping and to a fling field last week. It was so wonderful. We have to call them to set up another date. Our male friends are fine but they have a lot of growing up to do. So Jazzalin when is your date for your wedding?", the twins blatantly inquired. "I don't know yet but it should be by the end of summer. I want you two as bridesmaids so you'll know when I know", Jazzalin answered. The four friends spent the rest of the day enjoying mutual camaraderie and singing some of the light songs they had sung at the festivals on Astral Keep. Jazzalin asked them to review the bridal shower plans Lady Sylphine had drawn up with her event planner. Beabop gave a very thorough evaluation from a present Jazzo feminine point of view and was surprised that a woman much older than she or Jazzalin knew how to compose a spot on party design. She gave the party plan her youthful yes. Whereas, the twins just looked at the plans and said, "It's so pretty and she's going to use "Lift A Pinky" for the food. Good plan." Noticing the time Beabop said, "Granny wants us back before midnight so we need to leave if we're going to make that window. Jazz, I'll call you or you call me. You know how we stay in touch. Come on twins, we have to go now." The twins said, "Goodbye Jazzalin. Please tell your parents goodbye for us and we'll see you at the bridal shower and your wedding of course." Jazzalin had them wait briefly while she had a service droid bring out a sizable box of snacks and desserts to take with them. "Goodbye, you three and tell Lady Zynoplee hell-o for me. Thank you for coming.

See you at my bridal shower in two weeks. Make sure you bring Lady Zynoplee ", Jazzalin said waving to them from the palace entrance. The three got into their hovercraft and waved back at Jazzalin before the vehicle sped skyward taking them back to the South Region and Lady Zynoplee's mansion.

CHAPTER 23

T he week of Jazzalin's bridal shower Adagio made a date with her. He came to the palace and he first spoke to King Tempo and Queen Octiva as he had not seen them for over a year. "Good evening your majesties. I'm here to Jazzalin out to dinner. She said she has not been outside the palace since returning to Jazzo", Adagio said. "Good evening Adagio. Yes, Jazzalin has been busy with the planning of her birthday and bridal shower so she's been quite busy", Queen Octiva answered. "Where are you two going for dinner?", King Tempo inquired. "I was able to get reservations for us at "The Ascent", the five star restaurant on the Jazzo space platform. I took my mother a few weeks ago and she loved it so I felt I'd take the Princess there since it was so highly rated and mother liked it too", Adagio explained. Jazzalin said, "Here I am", coming downstairs as Adagio's eyes lit up at her appearance. Her thick purple hair was brushed shiny and sweeping above her shoulders, and the pink diamond earrings he'd given her were sparkling in her ears. She was wearing a multi pastel dress of a lightweight fabric that seemed to float around her with a life of its own. Her parents smiled at the sight of their daughter who had grown up so much over the almost four years into a dazzling beauty. Turning to her parents Adagio said, "I'll have her back in a reasonable hour your majesties." "Goodnight Papa and mommy", Jazzalin said as Adagio took her by the arm and escorted her through the palace's front entrance and held the door of his sporty blue hovercraft for her. The King and Queen watched as the sleek vehicle climbed into the night sky and was soon out of sight. King Tempo remarked, "I'm sure Adagio knows that the royal guards will have them under surveillance the entire time they are out." "And I'm sure Jazzalin knows it too but I'm sure they'll both ignore them", Queen Octiva said with a giggle. Adagio had set his hovercraft's music selection on jazz fusion, planet ethnic and light songs which he knew were a few types of music Jazzalin liked. "You can change the music if you want to listen to something else", he said. "This is fine. I don't know this group. Are they a new group on your Skyes label?", Jazzalin inquired. "Yes, it's Beabop's latest heartthrob "Mentun Blooz's" trio and some background singing is Beabop. They are really smooth and fresh sounding", Adagio said proudly. "They are good. Beaboop never said anything about going professional. Well, she doesn't have to tell me everything", Jazzalin remarked. "We're here", Adagio said as he maneuvered the hover into the parking area below the brightly lit restaurant. After parking the hovercraft they walked to the floor lift that would take them to the restaurant's entry. Adagio whispered to Jazzalin, "There may be a small media storm when we get to the "Ascent". I'm just warning you so you won't be overwhelmed." Smiling back at him Jazzalin said, "And you should watch your step so you don't trip over the royal guardsmen who are joining us on this date." They both laughed at the reality of being in the public eye and having to deal with unwanted attention of one kind or another. Adagio had reserved a window table that looked out onto starry space. They ordered with the help of a service droid from the eclectic and creative menu and the food was surprisingly good. And to their amazement the media stalkers did not disturb their dinner and the guardsmen were very discreet as if they knew this was a special outing for the young couple and that they should keep their distance. After finishing the sumptuous meal Adagio offered to show Jazzalin his Northling Estate which he obtained as part of his investiture. Adagio guided his hovercraft over a forested area and farmlands which surrounded a large central house, several smaller buildings, and greenhouses. Jazzalin gasped, "Adagio, is all this yours?" "Yes, and in a few months it will be yours too. We have time to look inside, if you like", Adagio replied. "I'd love to", Jazzalin replied. He landed the hovercraft in front of the large house which was lit by huge round globes fixed on stone columns. At the front door of the house Adagio entered his access code and an audible "click" could be heard and the security system said, "Good evening your grace. The door is open for your access." Pushing the door he stepped aside to allow Jazzalin to enter first. She gasped again and said, "Adagio this is quizit. Who did the decor, was it your mother?" "Yes, mother helped me with the decor and interior design", he said. He let her explore the first floor but the second floor was off limits due to construction. She was pleased with the colors, the furnishings, accents and everything. If this was going to be her future home she was fine with it. Adagio directed her to the adjoining canopied courtyard and pool area which was beautiful even at night. "There's a large garden a little farther back but it's better looking in sunlight. I think we should leave now to get you back in time", he said. "Oh I wouldn't worry about that", Jazzalin said. "Jazzalin, I want your parents to know that I'm a man of my word. I said I'd get you home by midnight and that's what I'm going to do", he said with finality. "Well thank you for the tour. Tell your mother she's a true artist", Jazzalin said truthfully. Adagio replied, "I will", as he activated the security system to the house and then he and Jazzalin got in his hovercraft enroute to the palace. The hovercraft easily transversed the distance from his estate back to the palace. When they landed in the driveway of the palace, Jazzalin said, "Adagio, this was an enjoyable date. It was quizit", she said as she brushed a kiss on his cheek. He then turned his head at an angle that allowed him to kiss her full on the mouth. It was a sweet kiss but nonetheless passionate. When he raised his head he saw her eyes were still closed, but momentarily flutter opened to reveal the dilated pupils of her amber colored eyes. "That's happening a lot when I see you. I'd better get inside before the royal guard arrests you", she said jokingly. "Yes, kissing you is destined to happen a lot. Let me get the door for you", he said, coming around to open her door and help her out of the hover. Looking at his wrist chronometer and smiling as he said, "See we have fifteen minutes to spare. Goodnight Jazzalin, and have a great party and bridal shower." "I thought you were going to come with your mother?", she asked. "No, I have a meeting with my board of directors for Skyes Music on that day but I might stop by after we're done", he replied. "Well goodnight and try to stop by for the party", Jazzalin said as he walked back to his hovercraft and waved to her before lifting off and speeding away into the night. She thought to herself that she liked him and his kissing was addictive. She wondered if had kissed Levitee Chymes the way he kissed her. She shook her thoughts clear as she entered the palace to find her father walking towards her in his robe carrying a glass of juice and a plate of cookies. "Father, were you waiting on me to get back?" she asked him. "No you were not what I was looking for. I was thirsty and hungry so I came downstairs to satisfy my late night cravings", her father said. "Well I had a lovely dinner and I'm going to get ready for bed. Goodnight father, love you", she said as she ascended the stairway. "Goodnight bundle, love you too", King Tempo said. Her father took his snack into his study and accessed his datafile and saw the local media did not disappoint. Even though they had not pounced on Jazzalin and Adagio they had reported, "The lovely Princess Jazzalin and her handsome fiance the Duke of Northling Adago Skyes were seen having an intimate dinner at the posh space platform restaurant "The Ascent". The attractive couple seemed to quietly enjoy each other's company pending their imminent marriage. They are very well matched since both are royals and have connections with the heroic twin zealots from the Sessilum conflict and both have spent extensive time on Astral Keep. We are looking forward to covering their brilliant wedding in the near future." The king had condemned himself for not standing up to Hamilton Skyes over three years ago to refuse the betrothal demand for the involvement of his son in the Sessilum conflict but seeing them together now he knew it was providence that circumstances were playing out so smoothly. He threw off the regret that had weighed him down while Jazzalin was on Astral Keep. She was a bit headstrong and wild but Adagio would not restrict her uninhibited nature since he was cut from the same cloth, and as the media reporter had described them as well matched. He thought he should watch his diet since he had to fit into his formal suit to walk Jazzalin down the aisle in two months' time so he opted not to eat anymore of the tasty cookies that were still on the plate in front of him. He thanked the Creator for the path Jazzalin's life was taking which would have been very different and precarious if left to her own devices. The parental meddling of two fathers was showing to be a good thing after all.

Beabop and the twins arrived the day before Jazzalin's birthday and bridal shower for a sleepover and because they did not want to be rushed. Lady Zynoplee said she would attend but she would come on the day of the event since she did not want to sleep in someone else's house when she had her own. The four friends spent the day prepping hair, skin and fingernails with the help of the Queen's hair and makeup team. After deciding what outfits and accessories they wanted to wear, they did not sleep much since they were caught up in a reverie of memories of various experiences in their individual and collective lives. They laughed, teased, and sang together way into the night until the Queen demanded they go to bed so they wouldn't be exhausted the next day. Heeding the queen's reprimand they went to their respective rooms like naughty children. As predicted the four friends had to be wakened in the morning to avoid oversleeping. To help them get their eyes open the Queen had the service droid bring them each a large cup of hot purple tea, which did the trick. Since the girls had wisely laid out their clothes for the party the day before they just had to shower, apply makeup and dress. Jazzalin had chosen and outfit she purchased on Astral Keep, it was a multi-layered pastel, just above the knee skirt and a floral embroidered organdy top worn over a silk purple camisole. She chose pointy satin purple heels with a large decorative bow at the toe. Her mother suggested she wear her hair up and so she pinned her thick purple hair up and fixed a fresh pink flower at the top. She would also wear a small jeweled crown above full cut bangs. Beabop chose a bright orange and pink tunic worn over muti-colored legging and a pair of orange and pink jeweled short boots. She opted to straighten her curly red mane and used a gem studded black velvet ribbon as a band to accent her straightened hair with full cut bangs. The twins chose blue green abstract print party dresses, strappy green pumps, and their shoulder length purple hair adorned with halos of orange and yellow summer flowers. The four got an inspection by the Queen's makeup artist and maid both who confirmed they were all very pretty and would be admired by the many guests at the party.

Jazzalin's double party was scheduled from two in the afternoon until eight in the evening which would give all their guests time to sate their party appetites in fellowship, food and fun. Lady Sylphines event planner staff as well as the palace staff had worked through the night to get the large ballroom decorated and coordinated for the combo birthday/ bridal shower. There were hundreds of pink, purple, green, blue, and yellow floating globes with ribbons dangling from them and colorful streamers hung down from a network of string attached to the very high ceiling. There were also large vases of summer flowers strategically placed around the room as well as garlands of the same flowers fixed to the serving tables and around the small stage for the live musicians. It was estimated that two hundred fifty guests were expected to attend the party and the ballroom could accommodate that number plus a few more. The "Lift A Pinky" staff had arrived before sunrise to start setting up the food. They had prepared thousands of finger foods prepared multiple ways either baked, fried, fresh and chilled. There were creative snacks of salty, tart, sweet, crispy, chewy, and hot flavors strategically placed around the perimeter of the ballroom. There were two drink stations where drums of fruit juices, cases of sparkling wines as well as carbonated drinks would be available for guests. And there was a wonderland of colorful and enticing desserts both large and small at a dedicated table labeled "SWEETS". And finally there were the cakes. The Queen had insisted that there be two cakes of equal size and creative design specific to each celebration and the pastry chef at "Lift A Pinky" had succeeded in doing just that. Jazzalin's birthday cake was a thirty-six inch diameter three tiers of pink cake with a fruit and whipped cream filling and covered with a rich pink sugar frosting with "Happy 18th Birthday Jazzalin" inscribed in silver icing and eighteen pink candles encircling the rim of the cake. The bridal shower cake was the same size and tiers as the birthday cake but it was a rich dairy cake with a blue whipped cream filling and covered in blue sugar frosting with "Blue Skyes for the Bride and her Groom" inscribed in pink and purple icing encircled by a sugar flower bridal bouquet. Each cake had its own table and guests were expected to have portions from each cake. Also there was a gift depository manned by the Queen's secretary who handed out thank you notes to the generous guests who chose to give the Princess a gift. All was in readiness for the royal festivities focused on Princess Jazzalin and her right of passage into womanhood. When the palace security team verified the invited guests had all arrived the Queen's secretary notified the live band to take the stage, and the serving staff to man their stations in the ballroom. Jazzalin, Beabop, and the twins were alerted to make their way downstairs to the ballroom to start the party. As they descended the stairway the palace herald announced, "Your attention please. To all guests gathered here today it is in celebration of the 18th birthday and imminent marriage of Princess Jazzalin Arpeggia

Maximus of Jazzo, daughter of their majesties King Tempo and Queen Octiva." Every eye in the ballroom was on her and she had never been so shy in her life. She remembered to smile and nod in recognition of many royals she knew from childhood and friends from her Academy days. Once she was fully in the center of the large room with the King and Queen beaming as they stood on either side of her she said in her best voice, "Thank you for coming today and please enjoy yourselves. Let the festivities begin!" Suddenly the Mentun Blooz's small jazz band started to play an airy energetic fusion full of clipped keyboard notes and dreamy inserts of the harp and flute and lively beat of the electric drum. The party had officially begun. Service droids carrying large trays of Lift A Pinky treats navigated the large room offering guests to indulge and they were all too willing to do so. Jazzalin walked to her father and took his hand to initiate a partner dance with him. King Tempo was a very good dancer he had taught Jazzalin all the formal dances acceptable among the royal community. She on the other hand had attempted to teach him the current dance trends but he had flatly refused saying, "I will not disgrace myself jerking and twitching to that incoherent offensive noise." The King leaned down and whispered,"Bundle this is the best ever. My heart is full of joy that you came back to us." He then took her hand and twirled her and glided with the music around the floor as others joined them. The twins found themselves surrounded by guests who were asking questions about the Sessilum habitat. Jazzalin saw them becoming anxious and said, "Papa, I need to go rescue the twins." "Yes, I see. I'll dance you over there to handle the bullies and I'll take your mother for a spin around the floor", King Tempo said. King Tempo delivered Jazzalin in front of the twins and she said, "Thank you papa for a wonderful dance." Turning to the twins she said, "Lilitine, Luling please come with me." To the aggressive inquisitive guests Jazzalin said, "You'll excuse us, I need to speak with the twins. Please enjoy yourselves." The trio departed enroute to where Lady Sylphine and Lady Zynoplee were standing like two beautiful exotic birds in their designer party dresses. Dressed in a radiant yellow and purple silk sheath and her pink hair swept up in a curly mass accented with sparkling amethyst pins, was Lady Sylphine smiling as they approached her. Holding the twins hands Jazzalin said, "Good afternoon Lady Sylphine and Lady Zynoplee so glad you were able to come today. Lady Sylphine here are the twins you so wanted to meet." "Happy birthday and bridal shower Princess Jazzalin. I would not have missed this for the world and I'm so glad to meet you twins", Lady Sylphine said, holding her hands out to the twins. Taking their hands in her own she said, "My son has told me so much about you, how you were so brave to help find the format ship and how you gave him his own room in your home on Astral Keep. I want to give you an open invitation to stay at my home whenever your schedule permits." "Lady Sylphine your son is much like you, kind and beautiful. Thank you for your invitation and we will make room in our schedule to visit your home", the twins said. Lady Zynoplee said between sips of a glass of wine, "They are currently my guests and when they do visit Lady Sylphine, it will be just that a "visit" as my home is their home on Jazzo." The five females all giggled at the tug of hospitality between two of Jazzo's wealthiest households for the twins to take full advantage of them. The Queen's secretary approached the group and in a low volume spoke to Jazzalin, "Excuse me Princess, but there's a personal call for you in the Queen's office. It's the Duke of Northling." Excusing herself from the friendly group and a very noisy party atmosphere at this time she followed the secretary and went to her mother's office. Sitting behind the Queen's desk she connected to the call, "Adagio, is there a problem?" "No, I wanted to tell you that there was no real board meeting but a surprise groom's shower. They started out pretending it was a meeting and then my father announced that it was a gathering in honor of his son who would soon be marrying, then sparkling wine showed up and every kind of party snack and there's a comical cake shaped like the format ship. Metre and Mezzur showed up and the rest of the Astronautical science team too. I'll send you the pictures on datafile", he said playfully. "I'm glad they gave you your own party because you couldn't come to mine. We're having the best time. Papa danced with me, your mother and Lady Zynoplee are fighting over whose house the twins will visit, and Mentun Blooz's quartet is quizit. Lift A Pinky's food is heavenly as usual and I have two cakes", Jazzalin said. "Well, that's as it should be, since it is your birthday and it was smart to add on the bridal shower otherwise two celebrations on two different dates would be exhausting. Well, they're calling me back to festivities. Enjoy your double purpose party! I love you goodbye," he said and disconnected before she could respond. She thought that she should do a callback since he didn't wait for her to say goodbye. Although she had accepted the betrothal intellectually she had not entered into the emotional expressions that are foundational to people who are betrothed. She was not ready for the "I love you's" of being betrothed, but it seemed Adagio had done a deep dive. She would not confront the issue yet since she wanted to enjoy the party, and her guests did not deserve a birthday/bridal shower hostess raining on their fun. From the time Beabop had entered the ballroom she had found a spot in front of the small stage in order to be close to her current boyfriend Mentun Blooz. The handsome musician was very aware of her presence and directed his gaze to her during each of their selections. When someone would ask her to dance she would refuse. Jazzalin was happy for Bea since she had never had a real boyfriend when she was at the Academy and she deserved to be happy. When their quartet's set was over and the datafile music downloads started to play Beabop made a straight line to Mentun. He obviously reciprocated her affections, pulling her on the dance floor in a Ziggabim fashion that communicated intimacy and possession. Lady Zynoplee had left the event a while ago so she was not available to contest the way the couple were dancing in public. The twins were standing by the palace entry speaking to a guardsman to allow Metre and Mezzur into the party when they arrived. They were just in time because the gate guard had refused them entry but he got the signal from his superior to let them through. The twins grabbed their friends and led them into the ballroom to dance. Everyone was in the best of spirits and enjoying a beautifully implemented event, even her mother and father were having fun. Jazzalin felt that her doubled up event was executed really well and that she could only hope that the wedding and reception would proceed as well.

After the last guests had departed for home Jazzalin heard a Adagio's voice in the palace entry. "Jazzalin, my grooms party ended thirty minutes ago so I thought I'd stop by to see how you were faring. It seems I'm a little late", he said. "Yes, the party was from two in the afternoon until eight in the evening. That's six hours of concentrated partying with two huge cakes to consume. There's some left, would you like a piece?", she inquired. "No, but I will take some of the Lift A

Pinky treats I see on the service table", he said. "Help yourself. I was just about to go upstairs but I'm glad you're here. I have a question for you. When you called me this afternoon you ended the call with "I love you". Are you trying the phrase out on me because I'm not in that frame of emotion yet and I don't mean to be remote it's just that I'm not ready to say it back to you. There, I said it!", she said triumphantly. Choosing his words carefully Adagio replied, "Jazzalin I know you still feel like your trapped and believe me I feel a little trapped too but I really can say "I love you" without deceiving myself. I genuinely care for you and I want to be with you." His explanation left her dazed but it was lucid and succinct. She felt embarrassed for being so childish but she responded, "All I ask is the time and space to attain to that level of emotional commitment. You've always been kind to me and I can appreciate that so that's my point of relational origin with you." "I appreciate your honesty. I think I started loving you back when you shot me down at my birthday party all those years ago. You were just a little girl but you stood up to me in your full royal sovereignty and left my party without looking back. You've always been honest with me so that's my point of relational origin with you", he replied. She offered her hand for a handshake which he took and pulled her into an embrace and whispered, "Lovers don't shake hands Jazzalin, and we are lovers." She allowed herself to relax in the warmth of the embrace and to stay focused on being as amiable as possible. She stayed with him in the disheveled ballroom while he enjoyed a plate of finger foods and sugary goodies. Finally a service droid inquired, "Princess Jazzalin should we leave the cleanup until morning?" "No. Adagio, bring your plate, we can go into the kitchen", she said. "Alright, but bring a bottle of the sparkling wine and two glasses, I want to toast you on your birthday", he said. "Will do", Jazzalin replied. The two stayed in the kitchen for another hour talking and finishing the entire bottle of wine before they both determined they needed to get some sleep. She admonished him to drive safely and he advised her that his hovercraft was equipped with auto drive navigation. He kissed her at the door of the palace before getting into his sporty vehicle for his Northling Estate.

Somehow she hoped they would make their arranged marriage work, but if it didn't she had amassed enough currency between her personal accounts on Jazzo and Astral Keep to allow her to go back to live on Astral Keep.

In the weeks ahead Queen Octiva went into overdrive with the preparation for her daughter's wedding. Daily she would send a datafile with wedding dress designs for Jazzalin to review to approve. Jazzalin was not impressed with traditional wedding dresses that her mother was prone to. She sent her mother a note after ten rejections of designs that would make her look like a mountain with a head on it or a puffy cloud person. Jazzalin couldn't get her mother's dress maker to see that fashion and style had changed in the year 5113. Jazzalin remembered the portfolio that Lady Sylphine had sent her on Astral Keep where she found several designs that Lady Sylphines design team had drawn up which were cutting edge and quizit. Jazzalin with monumental tact and discretion spoke to her mother, "Mommy I'm going to call Lady Sylphine and speak to her about the designs she sent me for a dress. The designs she provided are more in tune with what I would feel comfortable wearing. Please don't take this as a negative, it's just that your dressmaker is working from an outdated module that doesn't work anymore, at least for me it doesn't." Queen Octiva did not take offense and encouraged Jazzalin saying, "Sweetheart I appreciate your honesty. I would not want you to wear something that would make you unhappy. You have a very good eye for what looks good on you and I have every confidence in whatever you choose. There's nothing traditional about this wedding and your father and I don't expect it to be." When Jazzalin called Lady Sylphine who was exponentially excited and invited Jazzalin to meet with her and her designers at the Ethers mansion to go over the drawings and to make a decision for the bridal gown. Lady Sylphine thought her head would explode since she never thought that Jazzalin would prefer her designs over her mother's dressmaker's. She was not only the mother of the groom but the dress designer for the bride. After hours of going over the designs with Lady Sylphine's team Jazzalin chose a silk loose fitting sheath with an embroidered organdy floor length overlay and a short veil around a wreath of small white flowers for her head. It was simple but elegant and not stuffy and heavy like a traditional gown would be. The dress would be cut and sewn within a week plenty of time to make any necessary alterations.

As the day of the wedding grew closer Jazzalin became aware that as a royal the bride would come with a dowry. She was dying to ask Adagio as she had to know where his head was at regarding her dowry. On one of numerous dates with him she casually asked, "Are you satisfied with my dowry?" "Your father gave me the dowry voucher and I have already signed it over to you. We can go to your local bank and transfer it to your account anytime you like. To put you at ease, I don't need your money. I have a billionaire father, my own lucrative streams of income, and stocks and bonds that provide exponential dividends. On my own I'm wealthier than your father", Adagio said in an even tone of voice. "You think I'm petty. Well, I'm not, I just wanted to be sure my father didn't hold back on you", Jazzalin replied bashfully. "No, I don't think you're petty. I think you're stressed out about the wedding and all that it entails but you are holding up well from what I can see", Adagio said, smiling back at her. Tossing a bread crumb at him, Jazzalin laughed as he successfully dodged it and tossed one back at her. It was a good thing they were having lunch in the garden at his Northling Estate or observing eyes may have been critical of the young couple as being undignified and improperly behaved for royals. Neither Jazzalin or Adagio could have cared less about what people thought. After her date with Adagio she called Beabop to let her know she had asked the dowry question, "Bea, I asked Adagio about the dowry and he shot me down. He explained that he's richer than papa and that he's signing the dowry over to me." "Well now you know he's not after your money. Now you're really a wealthy woman Jazz. With the money you made as the twins consultant for over three years and the dowry you should have a tidy sum stored up", Beabop remarked. "Yes, and I intend to make sure it's ready to access should it become necessary to use it", Jazzalin said profoundly. In her heart of hearts she hoped that she would only have to use it for material purchases, not for a ticket on a format ship destined for Astral Keep.

The palace chapel had a maximum capacity of five hundred so to make sure there would be ample room for everyone only four hundred fifty invitations were sent out. These invitations were to close family and friends so no one who was not in these categories would be admitted. A week before the wedding the datafiles society notices were announcing the wedding of the year of Princess Jazzalin to Adagio

Skyes Duke of Northling. There was a buzz of anticipation around the entire planet. There were live datafile discussions regarding what dress the Princess would wear or what her maid of honor and bridesmaids would wear. There were also contests with prizes for guessing what would be the prominent color scheme of the wedding reception, how many tiers the cake would have, and which mother would wear the largest hat, the bride's or the groom's. Jazzalin had had a fitting for the gown and it had fit just right, accentuating her lithe developed figure without being ostentatious. Lady Sylphine's stylist suggested that she wear her hair up to give a more polished feminine effect. Jazzalin took everything in stride as she was determined not to have a mental collapse before, during, or after the wedding. She found that talking to Beabop daily helped keep her perspective, because she could depend on her to be open and straightforward with her. "Bea, it's only a few days until I'm a married woman, and I'm not at all ready for that. I mean Adagio is really great but if this hadn't happened I would most likely be vacationing in the West Region with a group of my best friends. My Jazzoan "girl on her own years" are gone", she said sadly. "Jazzalin, that might be true but you've been on a type of vacation since you ran away to Astral Keep. You've been working with two of the most famous people in the galaxy and getting paid more than someone with a consulting degree. You've had experiences many people would envy, so you should be more objective, all things considered. I know you wished something other than marriage at eighteen but you are getting the best of both worlds: a wealthy handsome husband, a huge dowry deposited to your bank account, to live at Northling Estate, and still have friends over fifteen lightyears away to visit when you want to", Beabop said in a no nonsense way. "Well, I've been shot down by my best friend and maid of honor. Thank you for your sympathetic ear", Jazzalin replied. "You know I'm right, but I'm always there for you in a pinch. Haven't I always been?", Beabop responded. "You're my dearest friend and I'm so glad you're in my life. Now, have you decided on what you're wearing to the wedding?", Jazzalin asked, changing the subject. "Yes, I'm wearing a polished silk pink and green backless dress with a matching shawl. My hair will be straight with a large silk pink flower pinned on the side", she described. "Sounds quizit. I'll be wearing white you know", was Jazzalin's reply. "Stop being a smart ass.

And where are you two going on your honeymoon?", Beabop snapped back. "The twins suggested a water planet close to Astral Keep that has floating cities called Acquannis. On the datafile it shows there are ten floating cities and they circumnavigate the planet every fourteen days, and you choose the city based on the climate you want to experience. I spoke to Adagio about it and he said it was alright but he wants to stay on Jazzo for a month and then we can make reservations for a beach house in one of the floating cities. We'll see", Jazzalin explained. "Sounds like it's going to be fun, just make sure you do your research on the accommodations and make contact with the responsible parties so you don't get disappointed. Five and half lightyears is a long way to make a turn around trip on a fluke", Beabop said soundly. "I'll keep that in mind. Have to go now. Oh remember you and the twins are staying over the night before the wedding", Jazzalin reminded. "Yes, bride to be, I remember. Talk to you later. Bye!", Beabop chirped, ending the call.

CHAPTER 24

T he weather on the day of Jazzalin and Adagio's wedding was picture perfect temperate with voluminous puffy clouds set in blue skies as if blessing the coming celebration. The wedding was to take place in the palace chapel at one o'clock to allow time for out of region guests to arrive in time. The palace was active very early on the wedding daty to get the bride and her party prepped. Lady Sylphine loaned her stylist out to help Jazzalin with hair and makeup as well as anything else she might need. Beabop and the twins also received the attention of the stylist to make sure they were presentable compliments to the bride. The guests began to arrive around midday and were seated according to friends and family areas of the chapel. The King had allow only on media agency to attend under strict conditions that they be discreet and unseen. A royal guardsman was assigned to the media team to make sure they stayed within the guidelines. As the guests arrived the chapel became an array of colorful eclectically formal dressed royalty and Jazzoan elites. Adagio, Hamilton Skyes, and Lady Sylphine Skyes were seated on the front row right side of the flowered bower where he and Jazzalin would stand for the ceremony. Across from the groom's family were the reserved seats for King Tempo and Queen Octiva. When the Queen, wearing a pale purple dress and matching hat was seated and all the invited guests had arrived a trio of musicians consisting of a harpist, flute and keyboard began to play. Lilitine and Luling were first down the aisle dressed in pastel blue dresses and wearing blue flowered garlands in their hair and carrying blue floral bouquets. Next came maid of honor Beabop in her beautiful pink and green dress which was "quizitly" elegant and carrying a matching bouquet of flowers. Seated in the second row on the brides side Lady Zynoplee was teary to see her radical granddaughter in such an exalted procession. Finally, down the blue carpeted aisle came King Tempo in all his regalia with his radiant daughter on his arm. Jazzalin was the picture of loveliness and the dress she'd chosen was designed and fitted to perfection, holding a pastel floral bouquet, she was the archetypal bride every woman fantasizes she'll be. All eyes were focused on her as she walked next to her handsome father to the front of the chapel where her groom waited. Adagio was blatantly handsome, and today he represented the kind of man every woman would dream of marrying. He wore a tailored gray formal suit and striped silver and purple necktie, and a perfect pink flower in his lapel. His green gold eyes smiled as he watched Jazzalin advance to the front of the chapel with King Tempo. His mother was near hysteric with the entirety of everything and that she had played an integral part in getting the bride ready to marry her beloved "Daggie". Sensing his wife's heightened emotions Hamilton Skyes whispered to her, "Sylphie, take it easy we have the whole day to get through my love." Turning to him Lady Sylphine smiled before kissing her husband full on the mouth. Because of Hamilton's business savvy her son was a duke and was marrying the king's daughter. She envisioned the chapel as a zero gravity fling field and she was floating above it all in this dream come true for the savage skinny purple Ziggabim girl. King Tempo and Jazzalin stopped just before the bower to allow Adagio to come to stand next to her as her father placed her hand in his. King Tempo kissed Jazzalin's cheek before going to sit next to Queen Octiva. Jazzalin and Adagio then stepped into the bower in front of the presiding priest. The priest lead them in their ring ceremony and vows, pronounced a blessing over them, and finally said, "I now pronounce you man and wife. You may kiss the bride. I now present to you Mr. and Mrs. Adagio Skyes, their royal highnesses, the Duke of Northling and Princess Jazzalin, Duchess of Northling." The newlywed's kiss was just long enough to show there was definite chemistry between them. After the kiss they turned to face their family and guests with bright smiles and walked down the aisle to the applause of all in attendance. In the anteroom of the chapel the young couple was barraged by family and friends with hugs, kisses, and exponential well wishes. Taking her position seriously, Beabop was able to wedge herself between the congenial crowd and lead the couple down the hallway to the palace area dedicated for the reception.

Following the wedding the guests were directed to the gardens where tables were set up beneath colorful tents to accommodate them all. The food had been catered by "Lift A Pinky" from their standard wedding menu which allowed guests to choose from three main courses, soups and salads, and multiple trays of small desserts for each table. The bride and groom with their families were seated on a platform area decorated with artistic swags of flowers and a separate table for a huge seven layered cake topped with sugar sculpted figurines of the bride and groom. Following the wedding the guests were directed to the palace gardens where tables were set up beneath colorful tents to accommodate them all. Holding hands and smiling, Jazzalin and Adagio greeted their guests and family as they streamed into the garden for the reception. The food was catered by "Lift A Pinky" from their reconfigured wedding menu which allowed guests to choose from three main courses, soups and salads, and multiple trays of small desserts for each table. The bride and groom with their families were seated on a canopied platform area decorated with artistic swags of flowers and a separate table for the huge wedding cake. As the sparkling wine was being served Hamilton Skyes using the small sound amplifier called for everyone's attention, "May I have your attention please, I would like to make a toast to the bride and groom. As father of the groom there were times I felt this event would never happen but providence was with us and saw fit that these two wonderful young people found their way to each other. May they live together in an atmosphere of love and understanding eternally and produce many grandchildren to my wife's delight. To the bride and groom!" All of the wedding guests followed suit holding their wine glasses aloft before taking a sip. Jazzalin's cheeks tinged pink with embarrassment at Hamilton's reference to grandchildren. Only King Tempo knew exactly what Hamilton Skyes had alluded to in his toast and smiled that his meaning was unknown by many of the guests. King Tempo stood next and made a toast, "I also want to toast the newlyweds and to their future together; may it be filled with light, discovery, and beautiful progeny to thrill and delight us all. To my daughter Princess Jazzalin, the bride and her husband Adagio, Duke of Northling. To the bride and groom!" "To the bride and groom!!!", the wedding guests said enmasse.

A spacious dance floor had been set up in the courtyard adjacent to the garden with the palace musicians playing upbeat and celebratory music as well as jazz fusion. Following the toasts the palace herald announced, "Presenting Mr. and Mrs. Adagio Skyes in their first dance as husband and wife." Adagio led Jazzalin onto to floor and whispered, "We've danced before without accident this should be a piece of cake, Duchess." She nodded in affirmation and followed him effortlessly around the dance floor. They were graceful, both tall and physically matched as they moved in unison and rhythm on the floor. Adagio whirled Jazzalin around for the last strains of the tune ending by smoothly dipping her over his arm. The onlooking guests gave them a thunderous applause and joined them on the floor for the next lively set of music the band had begun to play. Jazzalin noticed the twins were having a wonderful time dancing with their male friends Metre and Mezzur, as was Beabop who was intently gazing into Mentun Blooz eyes while swaying to the music. Even the elegant Lady Zynoplee was taking a turn around the floor with her date, the newly appointed chancellor for the East Region First Song Academy. King Tempo and Queen Octiva were elegant as they navigated the dance floor and not to be outdone, Hamilton Skyes and Lady Slyphine showed themselves to be skilled dancers as they traversed the dance floor. Finally it was time for the "cake cutting" of a seven layer confection covered in pastels of pink, purple, blue, green, pale orange, bright yellow, and cream frostings. The newlyweds held the knife together and made a ceremonial cut into the bottom layer of the cake and removed a good sized piece. Jazzalin turned to Adagio and said, "Open." Obediently Adagio opened his mouth to receive the offered cake and began to chew as his eyes brightened to indicate "that was yummy". The top layer of the cake would be boxed for the newlyweds to take with them and the palace servers began to expertly cut the cake and distribute to the waiting guests. The matrimonial reverie went on for several hours until the king's secretary notified the couple that the royal hovercraft was ready to take them to Northling. Jazzalin and Adagio climbed the stairs to a small balcony facing the garden while the herald announced, "Will all the ladies come forward for the bride's tossing of the bouquet." In no time there was a crowd of well dressed females standing a few yards away for the balcony jockeying for the best spot to catch the bouquet. Jazzalin was intent that Beabop would catch the bouquet and she made sure the trajectory was in her direction. Having always been athletic Jazzalin fired the dainty floral arrangement at Beabop and her boyfriend Mentun turned her by the shoulders and pushed her arms up to successfully catch it. Everyone applauded the snap catch by Beabop, who held up the bouquet in triumph. Jazzalin blew a kiss at her best friend before she and Adagio disappeared to go to the royal hovercraft waiting to take them to the Northling Estate. The hovercraft had been decorated with fluffy paper flowers and streamers as well as a sign attached to its storage compartment that said "Just Married". Wedding guests crowded to the front of the palace to bid the handsome couple congratulations on their marriage and all the best for their future together. King Tempo said to Queen Octiva as they stood watching the couple's departure, "Our baby bird has fledged and is flying away." The Queen emotionally replied, "And what beautiful wings she has." The gaudily decorated royal vehicle climbed into the air bearing its passengers to their waiting new home together.

Normally the trip to Northling took an hour, but since the royal hovercraft had clearance to exceed standard speed limits they arrived in half the time. From the hovercraft the newlyweds saw the main house was lit up with a banner that read "Welcome home to Duke Adagio and Duchess Jazzalin". Jazzalin remarked, "So is my princess title to be subordinate to your title, I'm only Duchess Jazzalin now?" Adagio rolled his eyes skyward and replied, "Jazzalin no one is trying to diminish your royal status at all, least of all me. My mother had the sign made and she didn't know to put Princess before "Duchess" in proper royal recognition. "Just checking", she curtly replied. The hovercraft landed on the front driveway of the enormous house and the android driver opened the passenger door to allow the couple to exit. Suddenly a delivery hovercraft with a transport trailer in tow landed a few feet from the royal vehicle and it's driver approached the newlyweds advising, "King Tempo requested this trailer of wedding gifts be delivered to his daughter and her new husband at this address." "I'm Princess Jazzalin, King Tempo's daughter", Jazzalin volunteered. "I need your signature on the delivery verification", the driver replied offering the digitab to Jazzalin. Taking the digitab Jazzalin used the attached stylus to sign off on the delivery of a trailer full of wedding gifts. Jazzalin smiled to herself and whispered, "Thank you papa for your attention to details and putting family first." Adagio directed the hover driver to leave the trailer on the vacant area in the rear of the house and returned to his original intent of carrying his new bride over the threshold of their home. Grabbing Jazzalin's hand Adagio led her to the door of the main house and using voice recognition to open the door he swung his surprised bride into his arms and walked into the entryway of the large house Once inside the brightly lit entryway the handsome groom allowed his wife's feet to touch the floor. It was obvious Lady Sylphine had been at work as the entire hallway was filled with receptacles of bright cut flowers. Jazzzalin smiled, commenting, "Adagio, your mother's taste is quizit. This is beautiful times infinity." Walking down the hall Jazzalin marveled at the extravagant floral decorations mingled with twinkle lights. Still wearing her wedding gown she resembled an ethereal sprite exploring her domain. Adagio's heart keened with emotion watching his lovely bride roam from room to room with her large amber eyes shining with joy. He blessed his mother for being so intuitive to capture Jazzalin's imagination. Catching up to Jazzalin he took her hand and followed her out to the rear courtyard which had also been a recipient of Lady Sylphine's artist's touch. In the air overhead there was a soft instrumental playing and a nearby bucket of iced sparkling wine. The couple enjoyed a glass of wine toasting each other and with a knowing look they stepped into each other's arms to follow the dreamy rhythm issuing from the sound system. After a while Adagio realized they were just standing still in spite of the music playing and he said, "Princess it's been a long day, let's get some sleep." With a sigh and lifting her head from his shoulder she muttered, "Ummm, yes it has been a really long day and I'm totally drained." Fatigue overriding any hesitation she might have felt otherwise allowed her to take her new husband's outstretched hand to walk upstairs to the master suite.

Adagio had had two smaller rooms joined to form the massive suite while he waited for Jazzalin to return to Jazzo. He initially tried doing the redesign without asking his mother for help but once the construction was finished he was at a loss about colors, furnishings, textures, art and flow. But once he had gotten Lady Sylphine on the project within weeks the large space took on personality with neutral colors and gradient shades of green, highlighted with bright and muted purple furnishings, and carefully placed accessories and plants. Lady Sylphine's genius for decor and design turned the suite into an opulent and refreshing haven. Jazzalin did a sharp intake of breath when Adagio led her into the space for the first time. They walked to the suite's lengthy balcony overlooking the fragrant garden below. Adagio put his arm around his bride's waist and they just stood there absorbing the ambience of their lover's environ. He eventually helped Jazzalin with the back zipper of her wedding dress. She was shy about the whole undressing necessity but she knew it was unavoidable. She opted to use the enormous walk-in closet as her dressing room. She found a large set of storage drawers. Opening the top drawer she found several delicate diaphanous gowns and matching jackets. She chose the most concealing one and modestly finished dressing in the closet away from Adagio's line of sight. When she came back into the bedroom Adagio had changed into a complementary shiny pair of men's pajamas. His physique was larger than she remembered when he had visited her on Astral Keep and before that on Jazzo. It was not a gangly boyish body but a chiseled grown man's body. She knew her own body had matured from the skinny gamine it was three years ago. She had been proud of how she looked in her wedding dress, and she knew she was considered shapely. Looking up, Adagio saw Jazzalin advancing toward him wearing a floating shimmery lavender gown which sculpted her body like molten metal. She was beautiful with a faint smile playing on her mouth. He knew she was putting her best foot forward but at any moment she would run scared to a safe corner trembling like a small animal. He had activated the sound system in the suite to play softly to ease any tension she might be feeling. She asked in a bright voice, "Are there any news updates on the wedding on the data stream?" "I haven't activated the datafile. I'll do that right now", Adagio replied. The large wall mounted datafile screen came alive with vivid images of them and a menu of every related topic about their nuptials. Relaxing Jazzalin sat down next to Adagio on the small couch facing the screen, Choosing "general wedding information" it showed the couple saying their vows, the couple's kiss, the newlywed's first dance, the cake cutting, and the newlyweds" departure to their home at Northling. Pulling her legs underneath her on the couch she watched the commentary about what designers the royal guests were wearing, what Skye Music celebrities

were invited and who with their dates were, and even a complete review of the food that was composed and served by the "Lift A Pinky" culinary experts. She lifted her hand to cover her yawning mouth and Adagio, noticing, said, "Princess you're sleepy and so am I. Let's get some rest." "I'm glad to be married to you", she said drowsily. At her last word he caught her chin in his hand and guided her mouth to his. This was a lover's kiss, tentative, lingering, exploring, and knowing. When the kiss ended Jazzalin said, "Mother said intimacies between newlyweds can be awkward and stressful if the couple doesn't know each other." "I think we know each other well enough to proceed, Mrs. Skyes, Duchess of Northling, Princess Jazzalin, but you needn't worry about any physical actions towards you by me tonight. I'm pretty much drained from all the day's activity", Adagio said undaunted. Getting up from the little couch he offered his hand to his sleepy wife. Jazzalin took his hand and was led to the large bed that had been turned down and perfumed and adorned with lily petals. Without any formality Jazzalin crawled into the inviting luxuriant mattress to a pillow she claimed as her territory and lowered her heavy head and was instantly asleep. Adagio smiled and slid into the bed next to the peaceful Jazzalin who was rhythmically breathing fast asleep. He couldn't resist placing a kiss on her cheek. It had been a long journey to get to this point and he was not going to risk ruining it all by being impatient.

Jazzalin awoke to find herself nude and laying beside her an equally naked Adagio. She vaguely remembered waking up suddenly making a startled crying which caused Adagio to wake as well. "What's wrong Jazzalin?", he asked concerned. She looked at his sleepy visage and was impressed at how handsome he was in his disheveled state. She leaned towards him and started to unbutton his pajama top and laid her cheek against his muscular chest. In response he found the hem of her gown and lifted over her head and tossed it aside. She set across from him smiling at him which gave him the permission he needed to consummate their marriage. She got up and found her gown and found the commu-tran in the adjoining bathroom and input Beabop's number. Beabop answered groggily, "Beabop here." "Bea, it's me. I had to let you know I went through with it. I'm a full fledge married woman! Emphasis on woman. I'm calling you from the bathroom so as not to disturb Adagio. I just had to let you know", Jazzalin said excitedly. "Jazzalin, so you had sex with your husband, how original", Beabop said unimpressed. "Well, I just wanted to share this with my best friend since all of this satisfactory ending to a scrambled drama involved you from the beginning. Aren't you happy for me?", Jazzalin inquired. "Jazzalin, I'm ecstatic for you but I was asleep so forgive me for not screaming your praises for becoming the next pregnant female on Jazzo", Beabop replied between yawns. "Oh no! A week before the wedding mommy took me to her female specialist and got me a prescription of "no pregnancy the first year" meds, so I'm not getting pregnant until I want to", Jazzalin said assuredly. "So did you act all prudish and demur?", Beabop asked. "Well we were tired from the wedding and then we drank an entire bottle of sparkling wine so I think that we were kind of drunk. We fell asleep and I woke up startled because I realized that I was in bed with a man and then Adagio woke thinking I was spazzing about something. He looked so cute all sleepy and half awake so I started to unbutton his shirt and then he pulled my gown over my head. We stared at each other for a while before exploring each other and going full throttle intimate. The start was kind of unpleasant but after we got past that it was really nice. I think we had two episodes of marital bedded bliss. I think Adagio has some experience in the area of sex. Yes, he definitely has experience", Jazzalin explained. Beabop laughed, "Do you remember all those sparsely clad girls hovering around Adagio at his parties and the ones he was seen with on the datafiles, all of them had been interviewed and chosen based on them being interactionally safe so if they did have sex with him there would not be any little ones as a result. So you're right your husband had plenty of experience in the area of sex." "Well your boyfriend doesn't seem to be a novice in the sex area either!", Jazzalin shot back. "You are so right. Mentun is very astute sexually and I'm happy to say so am I", Beabop said smugly. "So you're on the pregnancy prevention meds as well?", Jazzalin asked. "Yes, Jazzalin I am. Granny confronted me the minute she saw Mentun and took me to her specialist. I have an open end prescription at her druggist", Beabop replied. "I should have known. You two seemed a little too close not to be doing something physical", Jazzalin said knowingly. "Jazzalin! Jazzalin!", Adagio yelled from the bedroom. "Oh, Beabop Adagio is calling me. He probably thinks I've run away again. I'm in the bathroom Adagio! I have to go now. Thanks for listening. I'll call again when I get another chance. Bye now", Jazzalin said to her friend. "Bye Mrs. Princess Duchess", Beabop replied with a giggle. As Jazzalin ran back into the bedroom she said, "Don't worry husband I haven't run away." "I thought you may have thought you'd made a mistake and gone back to your parents. I'm so glad you are still here" Adagio said, much relieved. "I'm not going anywhere unless you're going too", she said, pouncing onto the big bed to kiss him. They began another blissful wedded episode which they would do repeatedly.

EPILOG

It would be another three years before the twins Lilitine and Luling decided to marry their Jazzoan sweethearts Metre and Mezzur Bynary. It would be a double wedding held at the Zynoplee mansion in the company of their friends the Duke and Duchess of Northling who were pregnant with their first child, Lady Zynoplee, Beabop and her fiance Mentun Blooz. The twins' parents from Astral Keep also attended wearing environ suits because Jazzo's atmosphere was too heavy for them to breathe. Not to leave anyone out, the twins invited their entire East Region First Song Academy class. It was a wonderful love festival, even their light guardian was present hovering over the brides with radiance.

A very pregnant Jazzalin and her husband Adagio beamed, being encapsulated in their own happy place. They were Jazzo's favorite royals due to deliver their first child in a few weeks. Lady Sylphine was also in attendance not so much for the wedding but to keep an eye on Jazzalin. She was determined that there would be no hiccups with the birth of her first grandchild. The elegant socialite had completed a birthing class just in case she had to deliver the child. She sat next to Jazzalin smiling at her like a colorful maternal bird. Both Jazzalin and Adagio were long-suffering knowing her actions were anchored in love. Their child would be extravagantly spoiled by Granny Sylphine.

During the after wedding activities a huge cloud formed over the Zynoplee Estate and a rumble of singing voices. The Sextillion Brethren had come to bless the twins nuptials. The wedding guests became still as they listened to the celestial harmony coming from above:

"We are here to sing and bring you joy,

Let our light stream with crystal beams to your planet's heart That we vanquished the foe with a fatal blow

Who sought to blot you out,

But light prevailed and darkness failed to all our great delight We are the Sextillion Brethren, all bright and true

We are the Sextillion Brethren always watching over you! Bright and true watching over you.

With the last verse of their harmonic song a shower of crystal particles rained down on the company of wedding guests dispersing great peace and clarity to all present. Jazzalin's unborn child began to jump around in her womb as the starfall rain penetrated the liquid environ the infant floated in. Lady Sylphine saw the strained look come over Jazzalin's face and she immediately slipped her hand under her daughter-in-law's elbow to help her stand and walk to an exit. A worried Adagio joined his wife and mother scooping his wife up and carrying her to a nearby guest room. His mother took command but Adagio notified their doctor about the baby's imminent birth and that she should hurry. Within minutes after Adagio had called Dr. Nova, Lady Sylphine had successfully delivered her granddaughter "Chantelle Voxxia Skyes" into the world. The baby girl weighed seven and a half pounds and her grandmother's Ziggabim genes had prevailed to adorn her round head with pink hair and amethyst eyes. Lady Sylphine wrapped the infant in her silk shawl and kissed her forehead before giving her to her waiting mother. Jazzalin was overwhelmed with joy as tears rolled down her cheeks seeing her tiny wiggly daughter as she whispered, "Isn't she quizit!" Adagio was speechless and happy to see his daughter safely delivered. He leaned down to get a better look at his daughter, stretching out a trembling finger to touch her cheek. Intuitively the infant wrapped her tiny fingers around her father's finger. Lost in love for his tiny daughter, tears ran down the new father's face. Dr. Nova arrived accompanied by the local hover ambulance to transport mother and baby to the South Region Health Center for physical evaluation and documentation of the birth. Adagio refused to leave his wife's side and rode in the ambulance with her and their baby. Lady Sylphine jumped into her custom hovercraft and followed the ambulance to the South Region Health Center. Mother and baby were determined to be in excellent health and would be released in the morning.

Adagio had filled Jazzalin's room with fresh flowers and pastel floating globes. He and his mother sat by her side as she and the baby slept. Suddenly Chantelle began to cry in a tiny baby wail. Suddenly a nurse appeared with a bottle of infant formula and handed it to Adagio to hold and then lifted his daughter and placed her into his arms saying, "She's hungry. Feed her", and left the room. Adagio softly pressed the bottle's dispenser tip to the baby's small red mouth and instinctively she knew what to do. "That's my smart girl", her father whispered. He was overwhelmed at her tiny weight in his arms. Her eyes remained closed as she enjoyed her first meal outside the womb. Jazzalin woke to see Adagio feeding their baby and giggled and remarked, "She's already got you waiting on her." "And I always will be," Adagio replied. Lady Sylphine took a turn feeding the little girl who seemed ravenous for someone so small. When it was time to be discharged there was a noisy shuffling of feet in the hallway which turned out to be the rest of the grandparents; King Tempo, Queen Octiva, and Hamilton Skyes who came crowding into the room. Looking up from her granddaughter Lady Sylphine smiled joyfully and said, "Hamilton isn't our granddaughter darling!" "She's our granddaughter too!", King Tempo said sternly. A health center administrator appeared at the door making a respectful bow to King Tempo advising that their large hovercraft was blocking their main landing area. The administrator also officially declared Jazzalin and the baby Chantelle were medically sound enough to be discharged from the health center. Two royal guardsmen came into the room and began to lift Jazzalin onto a floater gurney. Adagio immediately stood up and said, "I'll carry my wife, thank you." The two guardsmen stepped aside as Adagio carefully lifted and carried his wife leaving the healthcare room, followed by Lady Sylphine possessively carrying her granddaughter. The three remaining grand- parents followed close on the heels of their loved ones to travel home. Adagio deposited Jazzalin in a passenger seat of the royal hovercraft. Lady Sylphine begrudgingly handed the baby to her mother, then she and her husband hopped into her sporty hovercraft to follow the larger vehicle heading to the North Region and to the Northling Estate. Arriving at Northling the new parents with their daughter entered their home going directly to the nursery prepared by Granny Sylphine. The nursery was a confection of soft pastel pinks, oranges, greens and blues painted murals of flowers and winged chubby etherflits keeping watch over their tiny mistress's domain. The baby's crib was made of woven reeds shaped like an open lavender lily with a dangling mobile of etherflits holding flowers. The room was lit by a blown glass ceiling light of flowers. The sleeping infant was gently placed in her bed while downstairs her grandparents opened bottles of sparkling wine to toast her birth. Unknown to the celebrating family was the presence of a battalion of Sextillion Brethren hovering over the domicile of their new charge asleep in her crib.

One night Jazzalin went into the nursery to find a light guardian in full radiance next to Chantelle's crib. In a female's voice the guardian said, "Don't be afraid Duchess, I am Nfinni 737377 assigned as Lady Chantelle's light guardian. We visit her often to infuse her with light data which she will use in her future. Even in her infancy she is a delight to know." Composing herself, Jazzalin asked, "Can we schedule appointed times for your visits to see the baby?" Without hesitation the guardian replied, "No, because our relationship with Lady Chantelle exceeds all others. If you should forbid our interaction with her, it would be overridden by the Creator's authority. Her tiny form has been anointed with starfall now moving and interfacing with her. Look, she smiles in her sleep as she communes with the Creator in the forever. What a beauty she is now and continuing into her future." Jazzalin leaned over the edge of the crib to see her chubby daughter with a sweet smile on her lips. The light guardian continued, "She will be a bright energetic child but not always obedient. Her singing vocal range will exceed yours by an octave, and she will choose her grandmother Sylphine's people as her favorites here on Jazzo. We are building her a planet which she will occupy with her future husband from a nearby planetary system. Theirs will be a great love. The Sextillion Brethren's gracious surveillance will continue now and into her future for she is greatly loved." Jazzalin returned to her bedroom where Adagio was sleeping. Getting into their large bed, her attempt not to wake her husband failed as he inquired, "Everything alright with the baby?" In her brightest tone Jazzalin replied between yawns, "Yes, I was just talking with her light guardian. The Sextillion Brethren are building her a planet and she's already betrothed to someone from another planetary system. Oh, and she will favor your mother's Ziggabim people. Lady Chantelle is just fine. Goodnight love, see you in the morning." Yes, her daughter, based on good authority, would challenge parental authority and social convention and push the limits of Jazzo's royal protocols. So much to look forward to in the future, but in the meantime she would enjoy peaceful sleep in the here and now. With a delayed reaction to Jazzalin's reply, Adagio sat up straight in their bed and looked over at his wife who had closed her eyes and was fast asleep.